CODE OF RAINBOW

Soaring Flame and the Dragon-transcending Magimal

(Book I)

WEIQI WANG

Editor: Bonnie Karrin

There could be more than one type of philosophy to explain the world

One of them is called science

Another one is spelt M-A-G-I-C

Weiqi Wang

All names and plots in this book are made up.

CONTENTS

Weiqi Wang

PURPLE, GREY, YELLOW, BLUE?

Filton worked in a small rural village as a carpenter and a tree-feller. Although he worked very hard, he wasn't a rich man and lived a tough life. What made life even tougher was that he had a baby boy to feed. But Filton never complained. Even though the boy wasn't his son, he still loved him so much.

The boy's name was Soarame.

Little Soarame had a cute, chubby face and a pair of big twinkling eyes. Filton believed that the boy had been born very curious – he kept stretching out his little hands towards the air, waving and grabbing at it. Then, after he learnt to speak, he repeatedly used just two words – "here" and "there." This amused Filton for a while but then started to worry him, because it's obviously a pretty odd behaviour for a toddler.

The worry kind of went away when Soarame started to learn more words; then his favourite words became colours, specifically, "red". After Filton taught him more words on colours, the boy started to shout out different colours one after another.

'Purple, grey, yellow, blue!' On this particular day, the now five-year-old Soarame was once again running around the house and counting colours.

'What happened to white?' Filton asked, working on shaping a bedpost.

'It's not white, it's grey!' Soarame stopped running. 'You just told me yesterday, remember?'

'Of course, grey is different from white.' Filton smiled at Soarame but he sighed inside – if this boy didn't have a problem with his young brain, then he's doing a good imitation of it. 'What about red, then? I remember it's your favourite colour before.'

'It's not red, it's purple!' Soarame clapped his hands. 'You taught me that long ago!'

'Oh sure, sure.' Filton stroked Soarame's little head. At first the boy used to shout 'Red, white, yellow, green', but now three words out of four had been replaced. Thinking of that, Filton had a sudden idea. 'So, it's not green, it's blue?'

'Yes!' Soarame was running and jumping around. 'Blue, blue!'

'Okay, it's blue.' Filton wasn't sure what he could do. *Wait, what about yellow, then? Maybe it's not yellow, it's orange?* Thinking of this, Filton asked the boy.

'No, it's yellow.' Soarame stopped and looked at Filton, seemingly surprised. 'I thought you were smart?'

'Well…' Filton almost choked up. 'Maybe not as smart as you are.'

'It is yellow, right?' Soarame pointed at something. 'Orange is different.'

Puzzled, Filton couldn't help asking. 'What yellow? Where?'

'Here. See?' Soarame was still pointing at something. It's hard to tell if the "something" was nearby or far away.

'See what?' Filton looked in the direction Soarame was pointing. *Come on, there's nothing there*!

'The yellow dot!' Soarame claimed. 'Between the blue one and the purple one!'

'What yellow dot?' Filton was confused. 'Blue where? Purple where?'

'What's wrong with you?' Soarame became impatient. 'They are right here! Oh, the yellow dot flies away now.'

'What are you talking about?' Filton became worried this time. It seemed that Soarame was seeing something colourful and was therefore trying to describe it – or maybe them.

'Your eyes are bad!' Soarame seemed very unhappy. 'There are so many of them!'

'Oh, I see!' Filton decided to play along. 'So, you were running because you were chasing them?'

'Yes, but they keep flying away.' Soarame seemed frustrated. 'I can't catch them.'

'Okay, let me try.' Filton was determined to figure out exactly what's happening. He asked the boy to point at one of the

2

mysterious "coloured dots", and he tried to snatch it out of the air –

'No, it just flies away, see?' It seemed that Filton's first attempt had failed.

'You aren't aiming right!' The second attempt seemed to be worse.

'What are you doing? You missed it completely!' The third attempt, again, no luck.

'I'm done with you!' Soarame finally ran out of patience, and rushed out of the house to play.

'Be careful! Don't come back too late!' Filton was sweating after his intense bout of elusive dot-chasing. He watched the boy run out, deep in thought. *Maybe I should take him to a doctor.* Filton had always wanted to do that, but seeing a doctor was expensive, so he had always hesitated to do it.

The village had always been a safe place, and Filton was happy to let Soarame go out of the house by himself. But the trouble was that the villagers didn't seem very nice to little Soarame.

'Look, it's the troublemaker again.' As Soarame ran down the village, a baker and his customers talked.

Although their voices were low, Soarame was sensitive enough to catch it. He stared at them, not happy. He had been experiencing unwelcoming situations like this since forever, and he had sort of guessed out the reason: he could see something that no one else could – a large number of coloured dots. The dots were everywhere around him, so he didn't understand why nobody could see them. Soarame had always wondered what exactly these dots were, but since no one else could see them, he couldn't get an answer.

The unpleasant experiences agitated little Soarame enough that he ran towards the small hill out of the village. He had never been there before, because Filton told him there were wild animals and dangerous traps. But Filton's words were not always convincing – for example, he claimed he could see the colourful dots yet he obviously couldn't.

So, little Soarame decided to go wild. He really liked the beautiful and quiet forest with no annoying gossip. And there's no wild animal either, at least not yet.

'I just knew you were bluffing again!' Little Soarame humphed and walked deeper into the forest. He kept running and jumping after the colourful dots – they were everywhere. Until, suddenly –

'Ahh!' Soarame felt his legs get bundled together by something, and before he knew it, he's rotated over and dragged upwards.

'A trap!' Seeing a thick hemp rope strapped around his legs, Soarame's heart sank and he started to cry. It seemed that Filton wasn't always bluffing; his claim could be true.

No matter how hysterically the poor little boy cried, no one was coming to help him – he's too far from the village to be heard. Instinct for survival forced the boy to make a desperate attempt, and he took his thin legs out of the rope.

The next moment, his little body fell.

At the same time, a blast of wind came from nowhere and supported the little boy. The wind seemed to blow from Soarame's body towards the ground, so that it slowed his fall and he landed with a light thump. He checked himself over and realized he's barely even bruised from his fall.

'What?' A dumbfounded Soarame climbed up and stared at his hands. He vaguely recalled what happened in the last moment – a blast of grey dots surged at him and attached themselves to his hands and feet. As he reflexively waved them off while falling, the odd wind emerged and saved him.

'That's awesome!' Little Soarame had always felt that the grey dots seemed to like him, but nothing like this had ever happened before. He kept staring at his hands, but the grey dots had gone away and became untouchable again.

'Soarame, what's the matter?' Filton opened the door, and saw his boy with dishevelled hair and a dirty face. 'God, what did you do? Where have you been?'

'Just walking around.' Soarame brushed the dirt from his body.

'Nonsense! You got flowers and leaves on your butt!' Filton checked him up and down. 'These are from the hill!'

'Help! Someone help!'

Right then, a scream came from somewhere in the village. Filton looked out and saw several people running and screaming –

'Boar! Run!'

'What a weird day!' Filton frowned and relented in his interrogation of Soarame. 'How could a boar be here in the village?' As a tree-feller, Filton had encountered lots of wild animals like boars, but they only showed up in the wild forest and never came close to a village. Filton was wondering if those people had mistaken something else for a boar, until he went outside and saw the beast with his own eyes.

'Holy crap!' Filton dashed back into the house and fetched an axe, then closed the door before rushing back out. 'Soarame, stay inside!'

'Everyone! Come and help!!'

The street was in total chaos. As Filton had seen, it's a ferocious beast, although he wasn't certain if it's a boar – he had never seen one as big as an elephant before. The beast was about ten feet tall, with a giant head and nose just like boar's, and a pair of boar-like tusks over three feet long. Its eyes were red and its body was covered by some kind of black fur, long and thick. The beast was on a rampage, tearing around, ripping buildings up. If it had been aiming at people, some would have been killed.

'Filton, thank god you're here!' Everyone was happy to see Filton come to help. 'You are experienced at this, so tell us what to do!'

'I would if it's just a boar!' Filton yelled. 'But I don't think it is! Unless its mother accidentally over-fed it!'

Wooaaal! The beast roared, and stood on its hind legs like a bear.

'That's not a boar! Something's wrong!' someone yelled.

'What, then?' another shouted back.

'Defend yourselves! We can't let it destroy our village!' Filton shouted. 'We don't know what it is, so don't attack, just stick together!'

Wooaaal! The beast pounced on a lone man, knocking him away like a stray leaf. Filton joined the other men in attacking the beast, hacking and slashing at it with all kinds of weapons. However, the unknown beast seemed to have a really thick layer of skin; it's very difficult for Filton to hurt it even with his tree-felling axe.

'We can't beat it!' People started to fall back. 'What now?'

'We can't admit defeat! This monster is knocking down our houses!' Filton yelled anxiously. 'If we let it go through the village, we'll all be homeless!' Filton was right; especially as his house was the nearest one and Soarame was inside.

'But we can't... Arghhh!' A man tried to argue with Filton, but the beast threw him up into the air.

'Darn it!' Filton cleaved hard at the beast's neck with the axe once again. This the axe cut through its tough skin, but it got stuck in its muscle. The beast was enraged by the sharp pain; it swung its neck and tossed Filton away like a roll of paper. Filton landed right on the steps of his own house. His forehead smashed against the wooden handrail, stunning him and making him bleed furiously.

'Filton! Watch out!' The villagers were dumbfounded to see this. They wanted to help, but no one dared to charge at the beast anymore. The enraged beast swang its neck to throw the axe off, then turned towards Filton, charging at him.

'NO!!'

Right then, the door of the house opened, and a little figure jumped out. 'STOP!'

'NO! Get away!' People screamed at Soarame, but it's too late.

Just when everyone was expecting the beast to crush the poor boy, something weird happened – it abruptly changed its trajectory and knocked into the house, barely avoiding both Soarame and Filton. The big weight and tough body of the beast knocked the house left and right, but fortunately it didn't collapse.

Filton came to sense at the noise, and he's terrified to realise what had happened. 'Soarame, are you out of your mind?' There's chaos around the house; some men were motioning to take Filton and Soarame away from the beast, but all they managed to do was shaking and hesitating as the big creature turned back from the house.

'GO AWAY!' The little boy was howling at the big boar-like beast, ignoring Filton. Everyone panicked; the beast must be ready to strike again.

However, the beast's reaction puzzled everyone. It pulled back from the little boy, hesitating, seeming to sense a threat somehow. Instead of attacking, it's staring at him, but didn't move closer.

'GO! AWAY!! YELLOW!!' Soarame howled as loudly as he could. Although the boy tried his best, his voice was still neither scary nor commanding. In fact, it wasn't even that loud. However, the next second, the beast turned around and ran away. The villagers looked on, dumbfounded, jaws hanging like they were about to drop off.

'What the heck?' Filton struggled to his feet on shaky legs. His knees were knocking like his legs were trying to clap. 'Soarame, didn't I ask you to stay inside!'

'Hey, Filton, he saved your life!' Everyone came over. They sized Soarame up and down with wide, frightened eyes. 'Boy, what did you do?'

'I told it to leave!' Soarame answered, rubbing his sore throat.

'Of course.' The neighbours were amused, despite their remaining fear. 'What exactly did you say? Go away, yellow?'

'Yes! It's yellow and I think it's afraid of purple!' Soarame claimed. A few minutes ago, when Filton was in danger, the colourful dots suddenly started to gather around him again; this time the purple ones. Although Soarame didn't know what they could do, he's filled up with courage and had decided to strike at the scary beast.

'The beast is yellow?' People were not sure if they should agree with that – the beast was black. As for purple... there's nothing purple at all.

'Never mind, just leave it.' Filton waved towards the crowd. 'Let's take care of the wounded first, then the collapsed houses.'

'Right! You don't really think a five-year-old scared the beast off, do you?' Another man agreed. 'There must be something else, like it suddenly missed its papa.'

People chuckled and walked away to help. Meanwhile, Soarame was looking at his own little hands, flipping them up and down – a cluster of purple dots were leaving his hands, back to his surroundings to start swirling again. Only then, Soarame suddenly felt a wave of fear; he had no idea why he suddenly toughened up and challenged the beast. But he had a strange feeling that it's due to the purple dots – they brought him the courage and power, so that he felt fearless and scared away the beast.

The rumour about what had happened started to spread. However, most people talked proudly about how they fought bravely against the beast, and finally defeated it. Of course, Filton and Soarame were in the story; but, as the story went, the beast ran away because it feared the crowd of brave villagers. Soarame, on the other hand, was a poor kid living in an illusion.

****

One day, Filton was watching Soarame again – chasing some invisible colourful stuff. Right then, there's a knock on the door.

'Greetings!' An old man was standing outside, wearing dishevelled clothes.

'Hello, can I help you?' Filton assumed the man was a beggar.

'Yes, I need some help, but it's hard to explain...' The old man said, embarrassment visible on his face.

'Not a problem at all.' Filton smiled. 'I will get some bread and water for you right now, but, I'm sorry, I don't have any coin to spare.'

'That's nice of ... wait, what?' The old man seemed puzzled.

'Sorry, I know this house looks big, but I'm really not rich at all.' Filton sighed and was about to turn around.

'Hold on...' A look of realisation crossed the old man's face. 'I would just like to rent a spare room from you. I'm new to this village.'

'Pardon?' Filton was surprised. This old man was indeed a new face, but he did not look to be able to afford a room. After chatting a bit, Filton was convinced that this man was no threat. 'My name is Filton. Please come in.'

'Scankeen. Pleasure to meet you.' The old man seemed like a gentleman with a decent education. Scankeen took a quick look at the only vacant room, and he decided to stay. 'This should be enough for a year, but if not let me know.'

'Err... sure... hmm...' Filton was bewildered when the old man put a bag of silver coins into his hand. 'Scankeen, you don't need to pay this much in advance.'

With that, Filton couldn't help sizing Scankeen up – tall and thin in shape, white beard to his waist, wrinkles all over his face, and a cloak matted with clay. Filton was amazed that this person actually possessed so much fortune. He staggered because of distraction, and hurriedly propped his body against the door plank, causing a series of noises somewhere.

'Watch out!' Scankeen suddenly raised his voice – a wooden beam was falling off the roof. This was most likely a delayed effect from the beast's attack last time, and Filton's impact on the structure made it happen.

Filton caught a glimpse in his peripheral vision. Arms protecting his head, Filton was surprised to feel nothing but his cold sweat. The beam should have fallen right onto his head, but...

'What's this?' Filton raised his head, and saw the beam floating on top of him quietly. A few feet away, Scankeen was pointing at it with his index finger.

'What. Is. Going. On?' Filton was stunned.

'Grey?!'

The next moment, Soarame's joyful shout aroused Filton. Before he reacted, the boy had already dashed to them. 'You are full of grey!'

'Shh!' Filton stopped Soarame. Scankeen's mysterious performance had already overworked his brain and he didn't want any more trouble. 'Go ride your wooden horse, boy.'

'No, it's dull!' Soarame protested. 'I wanna play with grey!'

'Not now. I'll be your horse later, but you be quiet now!' Filton commanded. Riding a horse had been Soarame's favourite game; of course, sometimes his horse was Filton. Ever since Filton had let Soarame ride him for the first time, Soarame would ask from time to time, giving Filton real headaches.

'Hold on.' Scankeen cut in. He looked interested. 'What do you mean by "grey", boy?'

'The grey dots!' Soarame exclaimed. 'On your finger!'

'What!' Scankeen looked surprised. 'So, you are talking about these small grey dots that keep swirling around my finger?'

'Yes! And on the wood!' Soarame pointed at the floating wood beam. 'See? Filton, your eyes are bad! He can see them!'

'What's going on?' Filton was confused. He looked at Scankeen. 'You are kidding him, right?'

'No, he's not!' Soarame yelled before Scankeen had a chance to speak. 'He can see them!'

'Well, let me make sure we are indeed talking about the same thing.' Scankeen seemed really excited for some reason, his breath becoming rapid. With a slight wave of his finger, the wood beam landed in a corner of the house. 'Where are the grey ones now?'

'Oh my god!' Soarame's eyes suddenly widened. 'They moved to your left foot! How did you do that?'

'Oh my god.' Scankeen's eyes widened too. 'You really can see them!'

'Oh my god...' Filton's eyes widened even more. 'What's going on?'

'What else can you see?' Scankeen asked urgently, completely ignoring Filton. 'Any other colours?'

'Purple, grey, yellow, blue!' Soarame was proving his colour naming skills to be quite proficient. 'Can you put purple in your hand?'

'Sorry, dear, I can't.' Scankeen said quickly. 'One more time, tell me where they are now?'

'On Filton's legs!' Soarame clapped his hands excitedly. 'How did you do that?'

'What. Is. Going. On?!' Filton screamed. 'You are all kidding me, right?'

'I'm kidding no one.' Scankeen finally realised that he'd been rudely ignoring Filton. 'Your boy is special – he can see *magic elements*!'

'What?' Filton wasn't sure if he'd heard right. 'Magic?'

'Yes, the colourful dots have a name – magic elements.' Scankeen nodded seriously. 'In other words, your boy has magic gifts and could grow up to be a wizard!'

MAGIC ELEMENTS

'The dots are magic elements?' Filton looked at Scankeen with an odd expression on his face. 'You're sure they are not stars in his eyes?'

'Err… if those stars have different colours, they probably have a different name.' Scankeen was amused. 'Like rainbow-stars or something.' With that, Scankeen handed a small piece of metal to Filton. It's of a fairly plain design in an ancient style. On the surface two words were carved –

'Sunrise Alliance?' Filton read them out loud; this name rang a bell. 'What's that? Why does it sound so familiar?'

'So, you have heard of this name before? Good.' Scankeen smiled. 'Maybe from books? Try to recall it.'

'The Sunrise Alliance! The wizards' alliance!' Filton smacked his own head. 'It's real?' Filton had read stories about the alliance of wizards when he's little, but he had thought that they were just stories in books – Filton doubted if anyone in the village actually believed in its existence.

'As real as this wand.' Scankeen took out a stick and let it go. The stick didn't drop but floated there, prompting Soarame to scream again. 'Grey! Grey is on the stick now!'

'Yes. The grey dots are elements for Wind magic.' Scankeen stroked Soarame's head and looked at Filton. 'Now do you believe us? Your son can see magic elements – lucky that we met each other!'

'See? I told you! The colourful dots!' Soarame made faces at Filton and then looked at Scankeen. 'But he's not my dad, he's my uncle!'

'Okay, excuse me. But I just want you to know that there are quite many wizards in the world.' Scankeen was amused by both Soarame and Filton's faces. 'This village is very small and rural. If you lived in one of the big cities, especially the capital, you'll see wizards once in a while.'

'Oh my... so the tale of the Great Spanflow Libral is real, too?' Filton dragged his eyes away from the floating stick to look at Scankeen, and his mind was still immersed in his memories of the stories that he'd read. Most of the stories involved a familiar name – Spanflow Libral, the guardian of mankind. 'He really led the Sunrise Alliance and saved mankind?'

'It's not a tale, it's history.' Scankeen nodded solemnly. 'Without the Great Libral, we wouldn't be talking here today, in peace.'

'Your Honour, I'm so sorry.' Filton hurried to change the way he addressed Scankeen. 'I should really dig out those books and read them again.' If all this was real, then civilians needed to address a wizard as "your Honour" – as the books said. Filton was embarrassed when he recalled the first moment he met Scankeen – *Dear lord, did I just treat a wizard as a beggar?*

'It's fine, it all happened thousands of years ago and you are not the only one to think it's just a tale.' Scankeen seemed to understand Filton's worry. 'And most importantly, your nephew is going to be a wizard – if you allow me to be his master and teach him magic!'

'Is this real? This pumpkin head will become a wizard?' In the backyard of the house, Filton was watching Scankeen and Soarame playing games together. At that moment, Soarame was raised aloft in Scankeen's arms, and he grabbed Scankeen's beard and played with it. The beard pulling actually hurt, but Scankeen was still laughing with pleasure; it's Filton who became worried.

'Soarame, enough!' commanded Filton. Soarame stopped immediately.

'Don't scare him. This is my beard, not yours!' Scankeen was laughing; he had already started spoiling the boy. 'You like my beard? Just go ahead, no problem!'

'No, I'm okay,' exclaimed Soarame. 'I want to play something else!'

'And what's that?' Scankeen asked.

Soarame's answer almost made Filton fall over. 'I want you to be my horse!'

'Oh no...' Filton was struck by his horse headache again. Just when he tried to stop Soarame, Scankeen spoke up. 'Soarame, do you want to ride a real horse?'

'Yes!' Soarame became excited. 'But they are too big for me!'

'Well, here's a small one, just for you!' Scankeen waved his hand, pointing at the middle of the backyard. With a whinny, a mini-horse – just the right size for Soarame – appeared, jumping and running around him.

'Woooww!' Soarame screamed in joy. He couldn't believe what he's seeing. 'A real horse? Why is it so small?'

'Because it's for you, my boy.' Scankeen was happy with his work. 'However, he can only be here for a few minutes, so why don't you hurry up!'

'Yeeesss!' Soarame had never been so excited. He jumped onto the horse's back. 'Go, go, go!'

Standing aside, Filton wasn't sure how many times he had been shocked today. It's his first time seeing a real magic creature. Soon enough, the little horse disappeared. Soarame anxiously turned to Scankeen. 'Where did he go?'

'He went home.' Scankeen smiled. 'He's a boy, just like you, so he had to go home.'

'Oh... when can I see him again?' Soarame asked. 'And what's his name?'

'It's Richie, and you can see him once a month.' Scankeen smiled. 'It's me who summoned him for you, but Richie's family doesn't want him to play with an old man like myself. So, if you can summon him yourself, that will help.'

'How do I summon him?' Soarame asked, hurriedly.

'Once you learn magic, you can summon him.' Scankeen lowered his head, eye to eye with Soarame. 'But it's a difficult thing to do, so you will have to work hard.'

'I will!' Soarame exclaimed. 'Teach me now!'

'I certainly will.' Scankeen was happy about Soarame's reaction. 'Before you can summon Richie, you need to be able to summon grey – they are related.' With that, Scankeen turned his hand and a large piece of carpet appeared in it. He recited some incomprehensible incantation aloud, then tossed the cloth into the air. What happened next made Soarame shout again – the carpet was floating in the air, stretched wide.

'Grey is under the carpet!' screamed Soarame, excited.

'Yes, that's why it's called a magic carpet.' Scankeen picked up Soarame and sat on the carpet. With a wave of his hand, the carpet began flying up and down in the air. Soarame had never experienced anything like this; he squealed with pleasure. Scankeen was satisfied by the boy's reaction. 'See? When you can control grey like this, I'll teach you how to summon Richie!'

It took quite some effort to get the over-excited boy to go to bed. After that, Filton finally had a chance to sort out his questions with Scankeen over tea.

'So… grey is wind?' Filton asked, amazement in his eyes.

'Magic elements for Wind magic appear grey in colour.' Scankeen rephrased it. 'That's the technical way to put it.'

'I see…' Filton nodded. 'But what exactly are magic elements anyway?'

'The short answer is, they are the source and resource of magic.' Scankeen lifted the teapot and poured a stream of tea into his cup. 'Think about it this way: let's say this tea stream is a magic spell, then each water drop within it is a magic element. In this case, the water drops are Water magic elements and the spell is a Water magic spell.'

'I see!' Filton was enlightened. 'So, they are the magic itself?'

'Pretty much so. Same story here: Wind elements formed Wind magic and flew the carpet, as you just saw.' Scankeen was happy to see himself understood. 'Wizards can perform magic because they can sense and summon magic elements, which ordinary people cannot do. Without the elements, there is no sense of magic in the first place.'

'That's amazing. It makes me feel that I'm spelling Water magic now.' Filton poured himself some tea. 'What about purple, yellow and blue, then?'

'Each colour represents a different type of magic element; in formal terms, a different *lineage*.' Scankeen picked up his cup and tasted the tea. 'Let me check tomorrow on Soarame first, before I answer you.'

'Okay. So only wizards are able to see magic elements?' Filton followed up. 'Such as Soarame and your Honour?'

'Yes and no. It's not that simple.' Scankeen was stroking his beard. 'I never said I can *see* them; I can only *sense* them, and that's because I've practised magic all my life. However, Soarame can literally *see* them with his naked eyes, and without even learning magic – that is something substantially different.'

'Although magic elements do exist in the world, they are not supposed to be *seen* – not even by wizards. Usually, wizards can *sense* them only with great concentration; they need to be calm and close their eyes, eliminating any distraction brought by vision. Only through this can they sense the colourful dots of the magic elements that are all around.' Scankeen patiently explained the basics. 'Soarame, on the other hand, can see magic elements with his eyes open. As far as I know, very few can do that; and they don't include me.'

'So it is.' Filton nodded. 'It's really lucky for Soarame then.'

'Well, it's hard to say.' Scankeen said deeply. 'It's not always lucky to possess something too good or too rare. There is envy and greed – if you know what I mean.'

'Pardon?' Filton became anxious. 'You mean people will envy Soarame and do bad things to him? But everyone here already knows that Soarame sees colourful dots!'

'Well, fortunately, nobody in your village understands what that's about. They don't even believe in the existence of magic.' Scankeen tried to comfort him. 'It should have been an inconvenience, but in this case, it's actually in our favour.'

'I see!' Filton seemed relieved.

'So I plan to stay here to protect Soarame, till he grows up,' Scankeen carried on. 'The first thing to do is to give Soarame a magic test tomorrow and see what exactly he can see.'

'Thank you so much!' Filton was so grateful for this. Soarame's colour naming had been confusing him for years.

'It's a pleasure.' Scankeen pondered a bit and said, 'And I'm even thinking about making a fake name for myself.'

'Hmm… Would that be necessary?' Filton was puzzled.

'What if I tell you that I've been hunting many evil wizards and they hate me? They don't know I'm here, so we don't need to worry right now. But I don't want Soarame to be implicated when he grows up, if he accidentally mentions my name.' Scankeen crossed his hands. 'Soarame doesn't seem to have heard my name, so it's not too late to fake one.'

'Dear lord! I see.' Filton was alarmed. 'But what fake name do you have in mind?'

'How about Stunfolk?' Scankeen pondered a bit and suggested, 'A variant from the Great Spanflow Libral's first name, you know.'

'Err...' Filton indeed became a stunned folk. Thinking it over quickly, Filton tried to be polite. 'It's not bad, but would it be better to make it Swanfolk?'

'You mean more poetic?' Scankeen muttered. 'How about Swanflew then?'

'Swanflew? Sure, that's... that's good.' Filton wasn't sure if the new name was poetic, but at least it's better than Stunfolk. 'I can tell that you greatly admire the Great Libral. I've heard about his story, but you must have known much more.'

'Yes, he's a great, great man. He won us our freedom, founded the Sunrise Alliance, and did many other things just as profound.' Scankeen nodded, full of respect. 'And I didn't just hear about his story. I was there to witness a part of it.'

'Pardon? You met His Honour in person?' Filton asked, astonished.

'Oh yes, but back then I was just a young man.' Scankeen smiled. 'About your age.'

It had been quite a while since the last time Filton had been told something like that; it felt kind of odd to a fifty-year-old. Scankeen realised this and added, 'You may not believe this, but I was born in 3425 CC.'

When was 3425 CC? Filton calculated in his mind. *It's now 3896 CC, so Scankeen was nearly five hundred years old? Is it a joke?*

'I know it sounds unusual.' Scankeen was expecting this reaction from Filton. 'Wizards can live much longer by soaking up the energy of the environment and being nourished by the magic elements. The greater a wizard's magic power is, the longer his lifespan will be. Now you can imagine how many bad guys I've gone after in the last five hundred years. So, remember, my name is Swanflew from now on.'

'Swanflew? Okay...' Filton's eyebrow arched. 'How about this:

let's make it Mr Swanflew, and no one knows your first name. What do you think?'

With that, Mr Swanflew came into being and stepped into Soarame's life. Thanks to him, Soarame's colour naming problem was finally solved, and everything looked like it's going to work out perfectly. Luckily, Scankeen didn't know Soarame's first impression of his poetic name selection –

Swine flu? What's that?

'Morning, Mr Swanflew.' The next morning, Filton brought Soarame to Scankeen for the magic test.

'Come on in!' Scankeen was waiting in his bedroom. 'I'll take you to a fun place, ready?'

'Dear lord, what's this?' Filton and Soarame were both dumbfounded to see themselves appear in a completely new world. One second ago they'd seen Scankeen holding a crystal-like gem, and the next second they somehow came to this new world, and they were standing in a big yard. Filton could see an ancient castle farther away, and, strangely, there's some vague screeching coming from it.

'What's that?' Filton was alerted.

'Don't worry, this place is very safe and no one will get hurt here. We are inside a *palatorium* – a magic space within the gem you just saw. From now on, I'll teach Soarame magic here.' Scankeen smiled at Soarame. 'Boy, you can call me "master" from now on. Do you like this place?'

'Yes, master!' Soarame couldn't wait. 'Is Richie here too?'

'He's not right now, but he can be here when the time comes.' Scankeen winked at Soarame. 'Remember our agreement?'

'Yes!' Soarame exclaimed. 'I want to learn magic right now!'

'Hmmm…' Scankeen was happy. 'Good, but can you tell me what magic is?'

'Magic is to summon Richie!' Soarame came up with this, eyes twinkling.

'Well… yes and no. Richie is a magic-gifted animal, which is usually shortened to *magimal*. But magic is not just for summoning a magimal.' Scankeen stroked his beard, amused. 'However, you do need to be a wizard in order to summon magimals like Richie.'

'Master, I don't understand!' Soarame grabbed Scankeen's robe and tugged it. 'Can I summon Richie after I learn magic, or not?'

'Soarame, remember the magic carpet?' Filton cut in. 'If you can fly, why do you want to ride a horse?'

'Richie is not just a horse!' Soarame protested. 'He's my friend!'

'Well said. Wizards and magimals ought to be friends.' Scankeen praised the boy. 'But magimals like Richie only make friends with wizards, so you need to learn magic properly first. In particular, you need to develop enough *mind power*.'

'Mind power?' Soarame asked. 'What's that?'

'Well, good question.' Scankeen started his lecture. 'In order to understand mind power, you'll need to first understand magic elements...'

It didn't take Soarame long to accept the knowledge of magic elements. Scankeen was happy to see a fresh mind absorbing new ideas much faster than grown-ups.

'The basic idea behind performing magic is to use your mind to summon magic elements, bringing them under your control.' Scankeen continued his tuition. 'Remember how your landed from the trap safely, that day?'

'A gale saved me!' Soarame's eyes brightened. 'It's Wind!'

'Exactly. Your fear helped you summon Wind elements and make the gale happen.' Scankeen nodded. 'So, you can see, as a wizard you have a special power to control magic elements. This power is called *mind power*. It's one of the most important things to a wizard.'

'Mind power is consumed as the magic is being performed – like how, when a pot of water boils, it becomes steam and disappears.' Seeing Soarame immersed in the lesson, Scankeen was pleased. 'Now try to recall, after you landed, how did you feel?'

'I felt tired.' Soarame answered aloud. 'Because I lost mind power?'

'You didn't lose it; you used it. It will come back after you have a good rest.' Scankeen ruffled Soarame's hair. 'Usually, a wizard's mind power is large, so instead of a pot of water, it's actually an ocean, called the *mind ocean*; and the water in the mind ocean is mind power itself. The mind ocean is the core part of a wizard's mind – it's not material, but does reside inside the brain in a special form, which is too hard for you to understand right now…'

'Yes, I don't understand!'

'It's okay. You will later.' Scankeen laughed. 'When you learn how to cast spells, you become a *Novice* wizard. A wizard's rank is according to his magic power: from a *Novice*, to an *Adept*, then to an *Expert* wizard, and finally a *Master*.' Scankeen noticed that Soarame looked bored with the knowledge, so he decided to take a break. 'How about we play a game?'

'Put your hand on this crystal ball and concentrate. Imagine you are in danger, and ask all the magic elements you can see to help you.' With that, Scankeen flipped his hand and there appeared a crystal ball. 'Try to feel your mind power, and with it drive the magic elements into the crystal ball.'

Soarame took the crystal ball and did it as Scankeen instructed. Soon enough, the crystal ball began to light up, with different colours shining outward.

Good! Although prepared to see this, Scankeen was still excited – the multi-coloured crystal ball was solid proof that Soarame could perform more than one lineage of magic. The crystal ball was specially made to show the existence of the magic elements to everyone, wizard or not. Even for senior wizards like Scankeen, it's easier to test and observe magic elements using this method.

'Oh my! These are magic elements?' Filton marvelled at seeing the different colours. 'They are beautiful!'

'Yes, the world is beautiful thanks to them.' Scankeen had believed that Soarame was most gifted in Wind, so the dominant colour should be grey. However, it turned out to be – purple!

Soarame was certainly doing a great job; the purple dots became more and more dense. Checking again, Scankeen noticed other colourful dots too, but they were fewer than the purple ones and therefore not as remarkable. But still, he could see a good amount of grey dots, a reasonable number of blue dots, and a small number of yellow and white dots.

'No wonder Soarame was calling them everywhere.' Filton's eyes were wide. 'I see the grey Wind elements, but what about the rest?'

'Purple for Lightning, blue for Water. These two are plentiful so Soarame will be able to practise them.' Scankeen measured carefully. 'Yellow for Earth and white for Lightness, but as you see those are few, which means Soarame will not be as good at them as the first three.'

'So, there are five types of magic elements in total?' Filton asked.

'There are seven. Fire and Darkness don't show up, but that's normal because no one is supposed to have gifts in all seven lineages.' Scankeen paused, as if he's thinking about something. 'The abnormal thing is that he is most gifted in Lightning... that's strange.'

'What's wrong with that?' Filton asked.

'Nothing, but Lightning elements are the most unbridled ones.' Scankeen turned to Soarame. 'Boy, did you ever use purple in the forest? I hope not, because it will cause a fire if it hit the trees!'

'No, purple only came to me for the boar.' Soarame answered. 'Then the boar ran away!'

'What boar?' Scankeen looked puzzled.

'Oh dear, that's what it was?' Filton was startled. 'Your Lightning scared off that beast?'

'Yes! And it's yellow!' Soarame exclaimed. 'Now I know it's Earth magic!'

'What!' Scankeen looked anxious. 'Soarame, did you say you saw a boar with Earth elements?'

'I suppose that's what he meant.' Filton quickly told the story.

Scankeen became nervous this time. 'That's a wild magimal! You were lucky to both survive!'

'Magimal?' Both Filton and Soarame were surprised. 'That monster was a magimal too?'

'A magimal is an animal with magic gifts. It could be smaller than Richie, or larger than that boar-like beast.' Scankeen looked serious. 'Plus, it can be either a friendly one that you can rely on, or an aggressive one that you have to fight against. Most magimals are wild ones, which means that they don't like humans, won't be tamed easily, and follow nothing but the law of the jungle. That boar would be a wild, aggressive magimal with Earth magic gifts, so it must possess a very tough body.'

'Correct!' Filton recalled that his axe couldn't even cut into its neck.

'Again, you were really lucky.' Scankeen said. 'For one thing, that magimal seemed to not aim at people; it's just misbehaving itself for some reason. Second, the danger made Soarame summon Lightning elements and scare it off. Again, that's instinctive – Wind for landing from the tree, Lightning for deadly enemies, because Lightning spells are deadly too – the boar could tell that, so it fled!'

'So, it's really him...' Filton gazed at Soarame. 'This boy saved me and everyone?'

'Looks like it.' Scankeen noticed a flattered Soarame. 'But, boy, don't you try it ever again; instinct does not always work!'

'So, that's why this village looks wrecked?' Scankeen then turned to Filton. 'Including the beam that nearly fell on you yesterday?'

'Yes and thanks for saving me! Apparently I'm not a good house builder.' Filton mocked himself. 'I'm only good at making small carpentry decorations.'

'Which is why I liked the decorations on your house, and why I chose to come to you... hmm.' Scankeen stroked his long beard. 'What a coincidence! Fate had guided me here? Was it really Fate?'

'Thank god for this!' Filton praised it with great joy.

'Indeed. Praise Libral for this.' Scankeen also praised it. 'By the way, wizards say "Praise Libral" because the Great Libral offered us the world to live in. Soarame, you need to learn this too, since you are going to be a wizard soon.'

'Okay. Praise Libral!' Soarame nodded and tried out the new phrase. 'Master, can we go and find another boar?'

'No. Don't you even think about it!' Scankeen rebuked him. 'From now on, you need to learn magic well before anything else. When you become an Expert wizard, you will have your Expert trials, there you can encounter as many boars as you want.' Scankeen then realised that Soarame was still trying something with the crystal ball in his hand. 'Enough, Soarame, you got them.'

'They don't listen to me!' Soarame looked anxious. 'The red and black dots don't listen to me, but I can see them!'

'It's okay. You can practise Lightning, Wind, and Water magic. That's enough to summon Richie!' Scankeen stopped Soarame, then turned to Filton. 'Just out of curiosity, where are Soarame's parents? He said you were his uncle?'

'Yes, his parents are not here.' Filton hesitated a bit. 'Why?'

'Nothing. It's just that the Lightning gift is rare, but Soarame is best at it.' Scankeen sized up the boy. 'If possible, I'd like to talk to his parents, to see if there's anything special about them.'

'Filton, where's Dad and Mom?' Soarame also asked. He had been wondering about his parents, but his uncle never talked about it. Every time Soarame asked, Filton would distract him with a funny story or a toy.

'Well, it's complicated.' Filton sighed. With the eager look from Soarame and suspicious look from Scankeen, Filton finally decided to tell the story.

WIND MAGIC

'Go, hurry!' Five years ago, a team of tree-fellers were running out of the forest. 'It's going to rain, don't stay under trees!'

Suddenly, luminous lightning split the sky and the whole cloudy atmosphere glowed purple. Soon enough, a huge rumble of thunder burst out.

'How strong the lightning is!' Everyone looked up. The man in the lead yelled. 'Run faster! I don't want to get hit and die here!'

Boom! After another fierce bolt of lightning, the deafening booms came one after another, terrifying the tree-fellers. The clouded sky was dim, with only the bright lightning flashes providing any sort of contrast, vanishing almost instantly after illuminating the sky. The peals of thunder roared, one after another, growing fiercer and fiercer. Any of the lightning bolts could have randomly hit a tree and snuffed out all the lives around it.

Suddenly, one man in the middle of the group stopped running, causing people behind to bump into him.

'What are you doing?'

'Filton, move! Now!'

'There's something there!' Filton pointed towards somewhere not far away from them. 'It's a cotton bag!'

'So?' A friend of his, George, wasn't impressed at all. 'Do you prefer your life or a cotton bag? There may not be anything in it!'

They all tried to drag Filton away, but Filton persisted. 'Listen, what's that?'

'It sounds like crying?" The group waited for a second, trying to distinguish the vague noise from the howl of the wind. 'Is something crying in the bag?'

Filton rushed to the cotton bag and was shocked when he picked it up. 'It's a baby! For god's sake! Let's take it before the rain really hits!'

'A baby?' They were dumbfounded for a second, but then the thunder brought them to their senses. 'Hurry up guys! Get it and get out here!'

A huge noise from somewhere nearby sounded. 'Dear lord, what's that!' screamed another tree-feller named James. Everyone saw the huge lightning bolt crash into the mountain Cloud Soaring Peak – a mile away from them, but clearly visible. Something on top of the peak had been struck and flames rose up, creating a brush of crimson between the dim sky and the earth.

CLAP!

As always, the peal of thunder came after the flash vanished, but this time there's something else coming with it –

'Ahhhh ——'

It's a distant voice, overwhelmed by the loud thunderclaps.

'Hey, did you hear *that*?' Filton asked.

'Who didn't hear that?' answered the others. They had no chance to continue the conversation, because, out of nowhere, the earth was beginning to shake.

'Oh my… an earthquake!'

Immediately, the group was in chaos. Everyone tried to keep his balance at the same time as they tried to escape from the forest. They kept stumbling along their way off of the hill and back to their village; it's even harder for Filton because he's holding the baby tightly to keep it safe. They barely made it back before the downpour soaked them. Screaming could be heard here and there from inside the village, and smashing noises as the earthquake shook houses to their foundations. Fortunately, the shaking and tumbling didn't last too long and everything returned to normal after a while.

'It's a boy! Looks like a new-born!' Filton took the crying baby out of the cotton bag. The crew of tree-fellers had gathered at Filton's place for shelter, because it's the closest and he had a relatively big house – it included his carpentry workshop.

'That's odd,' George frowned. 'He does look like a new-born.'

'What happened to his parents?' voiced another guy, a question everyone was wondering.

'Look, there's something embroidered on the bag.' Filton stretched a corner of the cotton bag, where there's a word in emerald green. 'Jadeking – what's that?'

'It should be a family name,' James commented. 'Some families write their names on things like that.'

'Do you recognize it, then?' Filton asked. 'Which family is that?'

'Gee, how could I know?' James shrugged his shoulders. 'Never heard of it before.'

'Suppose it's indeed a family name, it's not from our village,' said George. 'I know most people here but I've never heard of a Jadeking.'

'Great, so we have an unnamed baby, and a soaring flame out there.' Filton frowned. 'What shall we do now?'

'Maybe send him to an orphanage?' Another tree-feller suggested. 'I heard there's one a dozen miles away…'

'No, that's cruel for a baby!' Filton disagreed.

'What do you want then?' Obviously, none of Filton's friends wanted to spare their meager earnings on an unknown baby. 'Don't count on us to take care of him!'

'Fine, I'll take him.' Filton was of a very different style; he's actually very happy about this. He once had a wife and a son of his own, but they were all gone and Filton didn't want to recall that history. Since then, he had been all by himself in this workshop, not sure what to do with the rest of his life. So the baby seemed to have turned up at the right time.

'Great, hope you can survive that.' His friends hurried to leave, as if they were worried that Filton would change his decision. 'Good luck.'

'Well, help me find the Jadekings,' Filton requested. 'If it's really a family name.'

The crew agreed and left. The search for the Jadeking family wasn't successful, at least not around the village where they lived. Nonetheless, Filton still decided to give the baby the family name of Jadeking. And that's how a baby boy, named Soaring Flame "Soarame" Jadeking, was raised in a small village in the Arkwald Empire, on the Thundeross Continent.

With all of the rumours surrounding the adopted boy, the

menacing thunder and mysterious voice were all but forgotten – until five years later, when Scankeen brought it up.

'Mom and Dad...' Soarame muttered, tears welling up in his big eyes. Now he finally learnt that he's actually an orphan.

'I'm sorry Soarame, but one day we will find them.' Filton sighed. 'Now you know why your family name is Jadeking.'

'Sorry, I shouldn't have asked about this.' Scankeen regretted the pain his inquiry had caused the young child. 'I'll help you find your parents, Soarame.'

Soarame nodded, sobbing. He didn't really cry out loud like a child usually did – he's sobbing but quietly. Soarame had been influenced by Filton's toughness towards hardships in life, so the little boy was more resilient than people would normally expect.

Jadeking... Never heard of it. Scankeen was thinking hard but couldn't find a clue in his memory. Sighing in his heart, he looked down into Soarame's eyes. 'Sweetheart, I'm sure you'll find your Mom and Dad, especially after you become a wizard.'

'Yes! I'll fly on a magic carpet; it's fast!' Soarame wiped away the tears.

'Mr Swanflew, Soarame could see red and black dots, although he couldn't summon them?' Filton wanted to switch topics to distract Soarame. 'So, can he practise Fire and Darkness magic or not?'

'No, he can only practise three lineages properly: Lightning, Wind and Water. As I mentioned, the rest are not strong enough.' Scankeen shook his head. 'But three is already a great gift. If he has gifts in all seven, that would be worrying.'

'Why?' Filton didn't understand. 'He doesn't have to learn all of them.'

'And I'm not able to teach all of them. I can only teach him Wind.' Scankeen smiled with a sigh. 'But the point is, no one is supposed to have gifts in all of the seven lineages – except dragons!'

'I beg your pardon?' Filton almost choked. In contrast, Soarame was pretty calm – it's his first time hearing of dragons, and he didn't know what that's about.

'Yes, dragons. You heard me.' Scankeen looked serious. 'When wizards talk about all the seven lineages at the same time, "dragons" is always the first word that comes to their minds.'

Filton tried hard to stay calm. 'Don't dragons only exist in the legends?'

'No, dragons do exist. It's just that it has been so long since one was seen, people tend to forget that's all true history.' Scankeen shook his head. 'Speaking of this, have you found your old books yet? What did they say?'

'Yes!' Filton took out a book with an old and dusty cover. As he flipped its pages, he read some keywords out aloud. 'The *Great Libral*... the *Grand Migration*... dragons! Here they are... but it's history after all, so you mean dragons *did* exist, right?'

'No, they *do* exist.' Scankeen cracked a bitter smile. 'They never vanished, ever!'

'What?' Filton became nervous. 'Dragons still exist? The tale of the Holiness Continent is real?'

'It is not a tale, Filton. It has never been.' Scankeen lowered his voice. 'As I said, it is history – the Great Spanflow Libral, the Grand Migration... They are all real history. And dragons – they are the remaining part of the history!'

'Let me... read it more carefully then...' While Soarame was confused, Filton was astonished. He decided to leave the palatorium in order not to be a distraction and read the books more carefully.

'Are you ready to learn magic, Soarame?' Seeing Filton off, Scankeen asked.

'Yes, master!' Soarame claimed. 'Are you going to teach me how to fly?'

'I'll do that later.' Scankeen chuckled. 'You need to learn how to make a leaf fly before you can fly yourself.'

'I know how.' Soarame crouched and blew at a leaf on the ground, so the leaf flew.

'Well... not bad.' Scankeen was amused. 'But can you make it fly without blowing at it?'

'Yes, I can.' Soarame crouched again and waved his hand fast, and the leaf flew again.

'Hmm... smart boy.' Scankeen didn't know what else to say. He stretched his index finger and pointed at the leaf. 'How about this?'

The next second, the leaf started to spin and rise, then dance around in the air as if it were alive. Scankeen made it perform different tricks and circle around Soarame, making him cheer.

'So, would you like to learn this?' Scankeen let the leaf fall into Soarame's palm. 'When you are skilled with this, then you can try the magic carpet.'

'Yes yes yes!' Soarame was jumping with excitement. 'Teach me now, please!'

'I'm certainly going to.' Scankeen patted Soarame's head gently. 'But magic can be dangerous, so I need you to promise me that you won't hurt people with it.'

'I won't!' Soarame couldn't wait. 'A leaf doesn't hurt!'

'Oh, boy, Wind magic can do so much more than just making a leaf fly.' Scankeen could always manage to pull out a crystal ball from somewhere; another duly appeared.

'Master, where did you hide it?' Soarame wouldn't let go this time – the crystal ball was just too big to be hidden in his robe.

'It's called a *space-ring*. I put the crystal ball in there.' Scankeen showed Soarame a ring on his finger. 'It looks like a normal ring but there's a room inside it, just like this palatorium but usually smaller.'

'Wow, can we get in there?' Soarame wondered.

'No, it's different from a palatorium. A space-ring can only store items, so people cannot get in,' Scankeen said shortly, as he didn't want Soarame to get distracted. 'Okay, now let's see what Wind magic can do.'

With that, the crystal ball suddenly began to shine, casting a large, dynamic hologram to its surroundings. The scene showed the inside of a forest, with trees, rocks, rivers and more; everything looked vivid, as if it's all real. Beside a big tree, a man was wearing a robe that looked similar to Scankeen's. He's facing the other way with his back to Soarame, so the boy couldn't see his face.

'Wow.' Soarame's eyes were wide open. The hologram was large enough that the forest illusion surrounded Soarame, and he could hear the birds singing, the noise from insects, and some small animals somewhere. Just when Soarame was about to ask something, there came a loud, bass roar from the deep forest. Soarame couldn't tell what that's about, but it sounded scary enough to make him grab Scankeen's robe.

The roar sounded like it came from some predatory beast, and it became louder as if the beast were approaching fast. Soarame stepped back to Scankeen's legs and looked up to Scankeen's face, expecting his master to say something, but Scankeen was silent.

The next second, something swooped out from the cover of the big trees, jumping on the man in the robe. It's a big, fierce and fast figure, looking like a humongous bear of some sort, but covered with scales all over its body.

While Soarame screamed in a panic, the strange man was calm; he took a step sideways and dodged the creature. The bear-like beast seemed surprised that its strike didn't land; it stood up on its hind legs and started beating its chest like an ape. At the same time, the man turned around to face the beast, so Soarame could see his face a little – he's a handsome young man with a pair of sharp eyes. Although the beast stood up three times as tall as the man, he didn't look afraid at all. Looking at the beast, the young man stretched out his index finger and crooked it.

The beast seemed to understand what that gesture meant, and burst into anger at the sight of it. It roared like a thunderclap, and a blast of flame burst out from its big mouth.

What's that? Soarame's mind was blown, because he knew that bears or apes couldn't do that.

The young man looked serious this time, and he jumped up to dodge the flames. While Soarame expected him to come down again in a second, instead he floated in the air.

'Wind magic!' Soarame couldn't help yelling. 'He's a wizard!'

'Indeed. Keep watching, boy.' Scankeen patted Soarame's head to ease his nerves. 'Actually, let's go over there to get a better look.'

'No, it's dangerous!' Soarame dragged Scankeen's robe hard backwards, making Scankeen chuckle.

'It's okay, boy. It's not real, it's just an illusion.' Scankeen grabbed Soarame's hand. 'Trust me. I'll protect you if anything happens.'

Although Soarame didn't really want to believe that, out of curiosity he walked slowly with his master, holding the hem of Scankeen's robe tightly in his small hand. This amused Scankeen; he picked Soarame up in his arms and moved towards the young wizard. Soarame put his arms around Scankeen's neck and peeked at the battle.

Seeing this, Scankeen waved to the crystal ball and the entire scene stopped immediately – no more movement of any sort, and no more noise came out of it; even the young wizard's robe stopped fluttering. 'See that? They can't hurt us at all.'

'Wow…' Soarame looked back and forth between the crystal ball and the scene, bewilderment in his big eyes. 'So, is that man… you?'

'No, it's someone else. Just focus on the battle for now, Soarame.' Scankeen smiled. 'This is a magimal that can spell Fire. This young man is a Wind wizard, and they are going to fight.' With that, he waved his hand again and the scene proceeded. Right then, the young wizard started to talk.

'Bend over to me and be my mount, and I'll spare you pain.'

'What's that?' Soarame lowered his voice. 'Why is he talking to a magimal?'

'He wanted this magimal to be his mount – his horse, just like you and Richie.' Scankeen teased Soarame by scratching the tip of his nose. 'See how different magimals can be? Richie is small and super friendly, but this one is huge and tends to burn people, just like dragons. Speaking of which, dragons are a special kind of magimal too; just like humans are a special kind of animal.'

'Wow…' Soarame nodded while looking up and down. 'And this magimal can understand him? Dragons can understand us, too?'

'Dragons can, but this one probably can't.' Scankeen was amused by the question, but this one actually made a point. 'That young man just likes to show off.'

Scankeen paused the scene again and walked right underneath the wizard, so that Soarame could look up in the air and see a black magic wand in his right hand. When they passed the standing magimal, Soarame felt overwhelmed as if he could barely breathe – its body was as big as a small house. Underneath the open mouth of the unnamed magimal, Soarame could clearly see its sharp teeth and the dark-red cavity of its mouth. Each of its scales was bigger than Scankeen's hand, shining cold and threatening.

Scankeen went back to the wizard after stopping beside the magimal for a few seconds for Soarame to observe it. 'Now we'll see what happens next – ready?'

With another wave from Scankeen, the wizard's robe started to flutter again and the magimal came back to life. It seemed to sense a strong threat from the floating man, and it hesitated before launching another attack. In that few-second ceasefire, the young wizard floated in the air at the same height as the head of a thirty-feet-tall magimal, eye to eye. They stared at each other, at a stalemate.

The stalemate didn't last long; the magimal moved first. It stamped hard on the ground and bounced up, throwing itself at the target, firebolts spitting out one after another. The wizard sneered at this and swiftly dodged all the bolts, at the same time waving his wand –

With a buzzing noise, something seemed to emerge in the air, distorting the light. The next second, it shot at the magimal, cutting into its body.

The magimal roared in pain – a bleeding incision appeared on its shoulder as the scales there were cut through. The magimal had tried to dodge the invisible attack, but the mysterious weapon was just too fast. The wizard seemed to be satisfied by his performance; a curve lifted the corner of his mouth, as if he were smiling. Soarame was so focused on watching that he didn't notice Scankeen heaving a sigh on seeing the wizard's smile.

The pain enraged the magimal. Its eyes blazed red, muscles expanding and claws stretching longer. After an earth-shaking roar, it swooped at the wizard like a flash. The attack was so fast and so sudden, that it had already reached to the wizard before Soarame screamed out. The wizard seemed to be frightened too, as if he didn't expect such a huge body to move at such a fast speed. However, he's still quick enough to summon something invisible in front of him that hindered the magimal's mobility. As a result, although the attack landed, it only grazed the wizard's left arm, tearing off his sleeve.

After getting injured, the wizard looked angry and became much more serious. He flew higher in the sky and took full advantage of his mobility to dodge the magimal's attacks. He launched numerous invisible attacks, hitting the magimal all over. The few attacks which the magimal managed to dodge were so powerful as to cut down big trees and even split rocks down the middle. Feeling the pain of his numerous bloodied wounds, the magimal finally started to flee.

'Okay, enough.' With a sigh, Scankeen waved the scene away. Everything disappeared all of a sudden, leaving only the crystal ball on the table.

'Master, wait!' Soarame protested. 'What happened next? Did he get the magimal as his horse?'

'No.' Scankeen shook his head. 'But it's not because he couldn't. He didn't want it anymore.'

'Why not?' Soarame kept at him. 'What happened, then?'

Scankeen pondered and decided to only answer the first question. 'Because he's spoiled. And because of that, he grew up to be a bad person. You don't want to be a bad person, do you?'

'No, no I don't,' he answered without hesitation, although he's confused.

'Good.' Scankeen seemed less happy than before the scene was cast, but he took a deep breath and smiled at the boy. 'What do you think about Wind magic now?'

'It's awesome!' Soarame cheered up, hands clapping. 'How did he hurt the magimal?'

'It's called *windblade*, a powerful spell in Wind magic.' Scankeen knew Soarame would ask this. 'Now you know why I asked you not to hurt people after you learn Wind magic.'

'I see! And I won't!' Soarame was eager. 'Teach me now, please!'

'I am teaching you already, but we need to take it step by step.' Scankeen was happy to see his efforts working. 'First of all, you need to learn the basics about Wind magic – the flow of the air.'

With that, Scankeen flipped his hand and a leaf appeared on the table. 'Remember the dancing leaf? Only after you learn this can we move on to the next level, and then bit by bit to the magic carpet and windblade.'

Soarame nodded, although he seemed disappointed. But his attention was soon attracted by a shining thing in Scankeen's hand – a wand looking similar to the young wizard's, only golden in colour.

'Watch carefully, this time I will do it slowly.' Scankeen moved the wand, drawing in the air, at the same time chanting something. What came right after was a soft puff of wind, which blew the leaf off the table. 'Did you see that?'

'Wow.' Soarame looked at the flying leaf with his eyes wide

open. He could see a breeze of grey magic elements accumulate and fly towards the leaf, lifting it up and pushing it off the table.

'What I chanted is called an incantation. For each spell there is an incantation to learn. This one is the simplest one in Wind magic, called *wind summoner*, and it's your homework today.' Scankeen looked at Soarame. 'I won't teach you more spells until you master this one.'

'Yes, master!' Soarame was excited. 'What did you do with the wand waving?'

'Nice catch. That's for drawing the wind summoner *hexagram* – you need that for the spell too.' With a flip of his wrist, a small magic wand appeared in his hand. 'This wand is yours from now on. Now, chant the incantation after me…'

Soarame took the wand, full of joy, and started to learn seriously.

He tended to fail a lot at the start, but he kept trying without much complaining, which was a rare thing in Scankeen's experience. Scankeen was very pleased to see this boy so devoted already; it seemed that the Wind magic in the hologram had carved deep into this young heart.

And so, every day in the palatorium of Scankeen, Soarame would swing his wand, pointing to the leaves on the ground, and chant some incomprehensible incantation over and over again…

IT IS TIME

Seven years passed and Soarame was now twelve. He had grown to be a vigorous young man standing five feet tall, with brown-blackish hair and light tan skin. Thanks to the magic practice, Soarame's eyes looked brighter than others of his age, and the expression in them was filled with determination. Scankeen always taught Soarame that, as a wizard, his backbone should be as straight as his nose bridge. Whenever Scankeen praised Soarame for something, the boy would crack a bright smile, his white teeth visible.

'Master, master!' This day, in the palatorium, Soarame shouted with excitement. 'Master, check this out!'

Hearing that, Scankeen smiled. 'You can do it? Already?'

Soarame didn't reply but waved his wand and recited an incantation. Instantly, a gust of wind blew and made the trees in the garden swing to and fro, causing the leaves to drop one after another. Then, he drew a circle with the wand so that the direction of the wind changed immediately, spiralling on the spot. The falling leaves were drawn into the cyclone and continued spiralling into the air. Soarame harnessed his mind power and strengthened the cyclone, causing chairs and a round table to be drawn into it, swirling together alongside the cloud of leaves.

Soarame wasn't done yet. In total concentration, he slowly drew two triangles, one pointing upwards and the other downwards, with his wand and cast a few dots in the air, mumbling a more complicated incantation.

Scankeen saw the whole thing. Piecing the two triangles together manifested the foundation for all magic and magic arrays

– the *magic hexagram*. When the hexagram was decorated with various marks and corresponding incantations, different magic spells could be performed.

As Soarame pointed his wand at the swirling airborne table, a transparent crescent shot out from the tip of his wand. The crescent was about ten inches long and caused turbulence due to its super speed, making its outline vaguely visible to the naked eye. The crescent went straight to the table and left a deep score. Soarame repeated this three times more and stopped after emitting the fourth crescent, which knocked the wooden table out of the cyclone and down to the ground, one leg broken.

'Not bad.' Scankeen nodded, smiling. 'You've mastered the windblade and could do it four times in succession. Well done.'

'Master, that's not what I want you to see.'

'What's it then?'

'The table!' Soarame's eyes gleamed mischievously as he ran to the table. He then gathered power in his right leg, and gave it a hard kick.

With a *pang,* the table broke neatly down the middle. Scankeen was puzzled – fighting skills? Soarame had learnt fighting skills behind his back? Seeing the table in two neat halves, Scankeen realised something in the next second. 'You... you can control the windblade so precisely?'

'Heh-heh!' sniggered an elated Soarame.

Scankeen stared at the table. The two halves were the same size and the cut was as neat as though cut by a knife, but there were three connection nodes. What this showed was that the directions of the four windblades Soarame shot were so well controlled that they were aligned in a perfect line, end to end, across the table – a single windblade wasn't long enough to cut the table in half, but four of them together could do it. The process sounded easy, but the table was swirling inside the cyclone; to align four windblades in a perfectly straight line was truly difficult.

'If you try your best, can you chop this table into two halves directly with the four windblades, without kicking it?' Scankeen raised his head, realising that Soarame was even better than he thought.

'No, but I will soon!' Soarame was a little frustrated to admit this. 'Or I could shoot four more windblades right on top of the previous four!'

Scankeen suddenly realised the key question. 'How many windblades can you cast in one go?'

'I've tried twenty,' answered Soarame. 'I didn't try more than that.'

Hearing Soarame, Scankeen was shocked into silence. Generally speaking, spelling windblades was impossible for a twelve-year-old, because it's the hardest spell in the Novice level. That is to say, with the capacity to spell twenty windblades, Soarame was probably no longer a Novice wizard. Besides, the *cyclone summoner*, which ranked just under the windblade spell, was already a challenging spell, but Soarame's cyclone was strong enough to draw a 300-pound table into the air.

'Twenty? That's enough for today, then. Have a rest and fill your mind ocean through meditation.' After pondering for a while, Scankeen made a decision. 'Tomorrow I'd like to see how many windblades you can cast in one go, using your best effort.'

'Wait, master. Did you forget something?' Soarame's eyes suddenly started to twinkle.

'Oh yes… you want to try it again?' Scankeen knew what's going on. 'You are too big to ride Richie now, my boy. What are you going to do, even if you can summon him?'

'It doesn't matter. I just want to try it.' Soarame was persistent. In the past few years, Scankeen had told Soarame that Richie was a special kind of magimal that couldn't really be *summoned* by anyone – Scankeen could call him up only because Richie lived in his palatorium. However, Richie wasn't anyone's magimal – that is to say, Richie had never been *bonded* with anyone and therefore had never had a master.

When a wizard said *summon*, he meant call up his *bond* magimal. *Bonding* was a magical process that connected a wizard and a magimal, after which the magimal recognized the wizard as its master. This had never happened to Richie though, because for some unknown reason, even Scankeen wasn't able to bond with the mini-horse, which had left him very bewildered ever since.

'Okay, there you go.' Scankeen waved his hand and the gate of the castle opened. The next second, Richie ran out from it towards Soarame. The boy and the little horse ran together and cuddled; both were happy to see each other again. Seeing this, Scankeen cracked a smile and walked towards the castle, leaving the two youths to have fun together.

'Richie, why are you not growing?' Soarame asked the little horse, although he isn't expecting an answer. 'Master says you are special, so it takes longer for you to grow up, is that it?'

Richie merely nibbled Soarame's hair with his lips.

'But that's okay. Master also says once you grow up you'll be very powerful.' Seeing Richie respond with his naïve whinny, Soarame stroked his long neck. 'The problem is, because you are special, I still can't bond with you. Shall we try one more time today?'

Richie responded with a whinny again, encouraging Soarame to try. Soarame grabbed his magic wand and drew a Hexagram towards the ground, which kept expanding in size and gathered the boy and the horse inside it. The hexagram then started to shine as if something was going to happen, but seconds later it broke into bright spots and scattered away – it had failed.

'I knew it.' Soarame sighed. 'What's wrong? Master says you can't bond with anyone so far, but why?'

Richie just blew air out his nose in reply.

'How about it, Soarame?' After a while, Scankeen came back out from the castle. 'Are you sure you don't want to bond with another one instead?'

'No, you said a wizard should only bond with his favourite magimal, because once the bond is formed they are responsible for each other forever.' Soarame answered right away. 'Richie is my favourite, so I'll keep trying!'

'My boy, you are not upset with me for this?' Scankeen sighed and asked the question that he had always wanted to ask. He had been using a possible bond with Richie as a white lie to stimulate Soarame.

'Richie is free, right? As long as he's not bonded to anyone, I don't blame you at all.' Soarame looked at Scankeen. 'One day I'll get him to bond with me, sooner or later!'

'Well said, my boy. You will, one day.' Scankeen was relieved to see Soarame's determination, yet he still needed to warn him. 'However, in the meantime, if you see another magimal that you really like, you should still bond with it. It doesn't hurt as long as you don't overdo it, and you can always come back for Richie later…'

'Why didn't you bond with another one, then?' Soarame suddenly interrupted Scankeen. 'Volsta was badly injured and still cannot work with you, but you still have him as your only magimal.'

'That's different, my boy. I've spent all my life with Volsta, and he has saved my life many times. He's been my best friend all along.' Scankeen sighed over Soarame's question. Having spent all these years with Soarame, Scankeen had told him that the vague roar from the castle was his magimal, Volsta, a really powerful creature that had been badly injured in a battle years ago, before he came to meet Soarame.

'I'm sorry, master. I hope Volsta will recover soon.' Seeing Scankeen sad, Soarame wanted to make him feel better. 'When I see another magimal I like I will bond with it, but not yet.'

'It's fine, and Volsta will be fine too.' Scankeen smiled. 'You are right; you shouldn't rush for magimals. However, bear in mind that friendly magimals are rare and they are usually less powerful. The powerful ones are mostly wild ones that need to be tamed – and it's very hard to tame one.'

'Is it harder than bonding with Richie?' Soarame didn't really buy that.

'Don't play smart, boy.' Scankeen stroked his beard. 'You need to subdue and capture a wild magimal first before you tame it. And it's likely to be a powerful beast with magic spells – just like the one you saw in your first lesson years ago – so, think about it! That's why powerful magimals are always rare, even if you offer to pay a high price.'

'Price?' Soarame was surprised. 'They can actually be purchased?'

'Yes, just like buying pets, but far more expensive.' Scankeen sighed. 'As you may have realised now, wizards can be really powerful and they do different things – good or bad things. The magimal business is a grey zone in that sense – on one side we do need to battle magimals to protect our people, on the other we overdo it and become greedy…'

'How about Volsta? How did you meet him?' Soarame suddenly asked, but the next second he realised it might not be the best question. 'May I ask?'

'Don't worry, he isn't purchased from anyone, but we did battle against each other to become friends.' Scankeen looked towards the castle as his mind sank into old memories. 'That's a long time ago, when I was taking my Expert wizard trial in the *Fallen Forest* – that's Volsta's home.'

'The Fallen Forest? One of the most famous magimal colonies?' Soarame's eyes brightened. 'So you two fought because Volsta thought you broke into his home?'

'Yes and no. Volsta's clan attacked our civilians around that area, so I was summoned to the battle as an Expert wizard.' Scankeen ruffled Soarame's hair. 'I was extremely lucky to get Volsta in the end. He's top-ranked but young back then, so he's easier to tame and bond with. If Volsta was of his current age and power, he would have been impossible to tame.'

'So how did he get injured then, if he's so powerful? And after so many years, he's still not healed?' Soarame finally asked the questions that had been stuck in his mind for a long time. 'And why do you not allow me to meet him? I still don't know what Volsta looks like!'

'Because there are powerful wizards who are capable of hurting him. He's badly injured and it's a scary scene. I don't want you to see the bloody, bony wounds on him. Also, because he still needs some time to fully recover, I don't want him to be distracted.' Scankeen hesitated for a bit but made up his mind. 'Soarame, you are growing up, so maybe I should tell you a little more now.'

'Yes please!' Soarame was so excited to see his master finally offer an explanation after so many years.

'As you know, there are bad wizards out there, and I tried to arrest one of them years ago. Unfortunately, it didn't go well and Volsta almost died in the fight, so we had to withdraw.' Scankeen crouched and held Soarame's shoulders. 'See how dangerous the magic world can be?'

'I'm sorry.' Soarame felt bad. 'Please tell Volsta I wish him all the best.'

'I just did, and he asked me to give you this.' Scankeen handed over a large feather. 'This is a feather from his body, and he wants you to have it as a little gift.'

'Wow! Thank you!' Soarame took the feather, amazement in his eyes. The feather was larger than his palm and all black, with a metallic lustre; Soarame couldn't help picturing what Volsta looked like and imagining the battle. 'What did that bad guy do anyway, to deserve being arrested?'

'He stole the most valuable treasure from the druids.' Scankeen tried to simplify the story. 'So we need to get it back for them, otherwise the druids will see all humans as enemies.'

'Druids?' Soarame's eyes widened; he had heard something about druids during the past few years. 'The human-animal people?'

'Yes, they can transform themselves into animals, which is an amazing magical ability.' Scankeen held up a ringed finger of his. 'However, that didn't stop their property from being stolen – the bad guy had a space-ring. You see the point?'

'I see,' Soarame nodded. He remembered that a space-ring had storage space in it, and that it could only store inanimate items. The thief must have put the item into the space-ring, which was much easier than carrying it. The good thing was that space-rings were very rare, even among top-ranked wizards, so people normally wouldn't have to worry about thefts involving space-rings.

'Okay, that's too much for you to know. For now, just keep practising magic and improving.' Scankeen urged. 'Bear in mind, my boy: a wizard's world can be dangerous – much more dangerous than for civilians! Yes, we have magical powers; but that's also why we have responsibilities and duties accordingly.'

'I see, master!' Soarame clenched his fists. 'I'll work hard and become stronger!'

'Very well. Now go take a break, and tomorrow we'll test you and see how strong you are already!'

The rest of the day should have gone quickly, but Soarame felt that it's too slow.

'Okay, let's start.' The next morning, Scankeen pointed to a stone pillar in the palatorium. 'Your target is that pillar. Let's see how many windblades you can spell.'

Soarame nodded excitedly, quickly drawing a magic hexagram and reciting the corresponding incantation. A crescent of wind shot rapidly at the stone pillar, leaving a slight score on it. Repeating the spell, the windblades shot into the stone pillar one after another, the noise of their incisions buzzing up and down. As it went, Scankeen's eyes became wider and wider –

'Fifteen, sixteen, seventeen, eighteen…'

'…thirty-three, thirty-four…'

Soarame was soaked with sweat by the thirty-six, and had started to lose his balance when he reached thirty-nine. Finally, Scankeen stopped him as he tried to generate the fortieth windblade.

Scankeen rushed to Soarame, covered his forehead with his hand and let his enormous mind power gently seep into Soarame's mind ocean until it's full again. Soarame looked up at Scankeen. 'Thank you, master!'

'Soarame, how many times have I told you that it's a NO-NO for a wizard to try too hard when practising magic? It will harm your soul if you force the magic when your mind ocean is drained!' Scankeen looked very upset. 'Look at you, what were you thinking!'

Chastised by his master, Soarame lowered his head.

'NEVER do this again, unless it's a matter of life or death!' said Scankeen seriously. 'You hear me?'

Seeing Soarame nodding obediently, Scankeen finally cracked a small smile. 'Soarame, I must say you surprised me. With thirty-nine windblades, your mind power has been proven to be far above the Novice level! Congratulations for being a well-qualified Adept wizard!'

Hearing that, Soarame beamed with joy. Letting Soarame cheer up for a while, Scankeen spoke again. 'My boy, now that you are an Adept, it's time to move on to the next step.'

'Yes!' Soarame was excited. He hoped that meant that Scankeen was going to teach him flying spell, which he had always been eager to learn.

'You should go to school,' said Scankeen, unexpectedly. 'It's time now.'

'Go to school? For what?' Soarame puzzled. Although he knew from Scankeen that there were magic schools out there, he wasn't crazy about the idea.

'To study magic, of course.' Scankeen smiled at Soarame.

'Why?' Soarame was confused. 'Master, aren't you teaching me magic right now?'

'Yes, I am, but I am only teaching you Wind magic.' Scankeen smoothed out his long beard. 'Don't you remember you have gifts in Water and Lightning as well? A magic institute can help you learn those too.'

'But why now?' asked Soarame. 'Why didn't you mention this before?'

Scankeen was prepared for the question. 'That's because you were little and new to magic. When you have multiple lineages, it's better to focus on one lineage until you reach Adept. Now that you have gotten this far, it's time to change.'

'So I'm going to learn three lineages at the same time?' Soarame muttered. 'That's a lot.'

'Yes it is, so here is my demand.' Scankeen patted Soarame's shoulder. 'I want you to only study Water in school at first, until you become an Expert wizard in Water. Lightning is hard to practise and you can easily hurt yourself if you don't manipulate it well, so let's leave Lightning for later.'

'Okay... but why not Wind, then?' Soarame asked. 'I still haven't learnt the flying spell!'

'You can learn it on your own, but I want you to keep that as your secret and let no one else know about it. Don't take Wind classes from school, but instead learn from this.' Scankeen handed over a book to Soarame. 'The Flying spell and beyond are all in there. It's enough for you to learn.'

'But why?' Taking the book from Scankeen, Soarame raised his head. 'Why can't people know about my Wind magic?'

'As I said, the wizards' world can be dangerous, and I want you to be always prepared.' Scankeen looked at Soarame with tenderness and affection. 'Remember Volsta? He's almost killed because the enemy knew him well and set up a delicate trap against him.' Scankeen sighed. 'His strengths and weaknesses were all well studied, so he's still resting in the castle right now trying to heal. So, promise me...'

'Thank you, Mr Swanflew, I get it.' Soarame was smart enough to understand Scankeen's worry. 'I will keep the secret, I promise!'

'Good, remember that!' Hearing Soarame call him "Mr Swanflew" instead of "master," Scankeen knew this boy was serious enough to make a promise as a young man to another man. But on the other hand, Scankeen was also feeling bad that he couldn't risk telling Soarame his real name. 'More importantly, about your special sight – I want you to keep that as your top secret!'

'I will.' Soarame had been warned by his master about this for many times in the past. 'Master, are you sure no one else can see magic elements? I'm the only one?'

'Actually, there are a few more in the world, but only a few.' Scankeen sighed. 'And I suspect that Volsta was injured by one of them.'

'What!' Soarame screamed. 'Who was it?'

'If you want to know, keep your promises well and level up to an Expert wizard in school.' Scankeen looked at Soarame. 'Can you do that?'

'Yes, master!' Although Soarame's mind was full of questions, he had learnt from previous experiences that if his master wasn't willing to tell him something, there's no way that he could make him do so. 'So, I still can't go looking for my parents?'

'After you become an Expert, then you can!' Scankeen knew Soarame wouldn't let go of this, although the boy had kept it buried inside him. 'But the world is huge, so don't expect this to be done in any easy way, even after you become an Expert. If I were you, I'd leave it aside for now and keep improving at school.'

'Fine. But where is the school?'

'It's in the Cylone City, thousands of miles from here.' Scankeen was relieved to see Soarame accept this arrangement. 'I will send you there soon and you will do a fine job. Now you can go and talk to Filton and get prepared; if he's okay with it, we should arrange the travel soon.'

'What about Richie?' Soarame was anxious. 'I won't be able to see him once I go to school, will I?'

'No, but when you graduate, you two will re-unite.' Scankeen nodded. 'I'm sorry… I know it's hard for you, but trust me, you'll appreciate it later. So take your time to hang out with him these last few days. Once we start on the trip I will stop using this palatorium, so you won't be able to come in here and see him anymore.'

Soarame was very upset that he's going to have to leave Richie. However, over the past few years, Soarame had understood that although his master was kind and nice, once he decided on something, there's no way to make him change his mind. So all that Soarame could do was to treasure every single minute that he could spend with Richie before they set out.

'Seven peaceful years have been very satisfying... Thank you, Soarame.' Watching Soarame walk away, Scankeen sighed to himself. The real reasons behind this sudden decision were much more than he had said – Scankeen had never planned to stay here for this long in the first place. If he hadn't met Soarame through coincidence, he would have left a few years ago.

Now Scankeen really had to leave, because he had received a classified request from the Sunrise Alliance, one that he had been expecting for a while. Scankeen had been worried that Soarame had hardly any social experience so far, so on the bright side, it's also a good opportunity for the boy to make friends with other young wizards.

Filton was surprised to hear the sudden change of plans, but he respected Scankeen's judgment, especially after witnessing Soarame's capability as a wizard. Therefore, although Filton was still a little concerned about the boy being all alone out there, he started to pack for the journey.

The school Scankeen chose for Soarame was named the Institute of Libral. It's located in the central part of the Arkwald Empire, far from their village in the northeast. Founded by the Great Libral thousands of years ago, the Institute of Libral had always been one of the best magic institutes in the world.

A few days later, the trio started on their way. Thanks to Scankeen, they had a magic carriage to travel in. The carriage didn't come with horses, but powered itself by using energy stored in a crystal cube, thus it didn't need to stop. This was very convenient for the trio, and they could take advantage of the time that they saved for sight-seeing and other activities. It's a fun trip, and the three had a good time.

Soarame and Filton realised soon enough that people along their way did recognize wizards, and they were really respectful to Scankeen. Almost every time they arrived at a new place, people greeted Scankeen as "your Honour". Filton was finally convinced that his village was too closed off from the outer world. He had been thinking about travelling the world, and now he felt even more determined to do so.

A month of travelling passed quicker than the trio thought, and they arrived in the Cylone City in good shape. Unfortunately, their arrival also meant that Scankeen finally had to leave.

'Mr Swanflew, why not come with us to the school first?' Filton was so grateful to this sweet senior wizard, who had spent years teaching Soarame without asking for anything in return.

'Let's leave the school part for Soarame to explore on his own. Trust me, it's fun to do that.' Scankeen took out a black pendant and gave it to Soarame. 'My dear boy, keep my token with you at all times, it will keep you safe.'

Soarame was attracted to the black pendant, not only because of Scankeen's words, but also because he sensed the intense magic pulse being emitted from the inconspicuous object. Strangely, the pulse seemed to radiate green light to Soarame's special eyes – a colour not included in the seven colours of the magic elements. 'Master, why is the colour in this pendant green?'

'So, you can see that too.' Scankeen nodded. 'The green is not one of the seven magic elements, but a special energy – the Energy of Life.'

'What's that?' Soarame wondered. 'You never mentioned this before.'

'There's a lot more that I never mentioned before, and you won't stop being amazed as you keep learning about the world of magic.' Scankeen smiled. 'This pendant is an Epic *magigear*, which binds only to its owner upon contact with a drop of his or her blood – you should try it.'

'Epic?' Soarame checked the pendant carefully, eyes wide in amazement. Soarame knew that a magigear referred to any item that had magic functions, such as a wand. He also knew that, unlike an ordinary magigear, which could be used by whoever wore it, a magigear classified as "Epic" could only be used by its owner – the one who claimed the magigear with his blood. Unless the owner died, others wouldn't be able to use his Epic magigear even if they fetched it.

Following Scankeen's instructions, Soarame scratched his finger and let a small drop of blood drip onto the pendant. The blood drop was then absorbed by it like a sponge, which amazed the boy.

'Wear it as a necklace and keep it with you at all times.' Scankeen hung the magigear round Soarame's neck. 'Remember, NEVER take it off. It's for your safety, ok?'

'Master, when are you coming back to us?' Soarame would have asked for more details about the Epic token, but at this moment he's in no mood for that.

'Well, we'll meet again sooner than you think.' Scankeen blinked at the boy. 'Or else, once you can practise Wind, Water, and Lightning magic all to the Expert level, you'll see me then – in the Headquarters of Sunrise Alliance.'

That meant a long time – Soarame was smart enough to realise it; tears welled up in his eyes. 'Master, take care!'

'You too, my boy. And don't forget your promises!' Scankeen put his forehead onto Soarame's. 'Your special eyes and the Wind magic!'

Filton and Soarame watched Scankeen as he disappeared after turning behind a building. Soarame suddenly rushed towards the building and looked behind it, yet there's no one there. Filton chased after Soarame, only to see the boy tearing up.

****

The next morning, Filton and Soarame began walking towards the Institute of Libral, passing through the Cylone City. This city was very well known to the world because of the Institute of Libral; it attracted crowds of tourists from all over the world. So, people here spoke different languages and dialects, making it hard to communicate with them sometimes. At the moment, Filton and Soarame were trying to ask for directions.

'Institute of Libral? That road there.'

'It's just over there, in the hill.'

'Yeah, just keep walking – into the hill and out the two towers.'

Obviously, not everyone was proficient in the language of the Arkwald Empire. Soarame and Filton had to ignore the grammar issues and try to understand the instructions. Finally, the two got to their destination – the foot of two giant towers, as someone had said. Soarame and Filton were shocked by the size of the giant towers, each with a foundation bigger than Filton's house. In front of the towers there's a big area, where a team of warriors were on patrol duties.

The two checked the towers up and down. There didn't seem to be a door to enter the tower, but between them was a giant cave that's cut into the hill, covered by hazy smog.

The two looked at each other. 'What's this?'

'It's the entrance to the institute, called the Libral Gate.' Lots of people were gathering by the towers, and one of the strangers offered this information.

'The entrance?' Soarame was confused. 'You mean the towers?'

'No, I mean the cave. The towers are not really towers; at least they are not treated as towers here.' The stranger smiled. 'They are the gate of the institute; or you could see them as big doorjambs, although there's no door.'

'So, they are more like a symbol of the institute?' Filton marvelled. 'And the institute's campus is... in the hill? Really?'

'We thought they meant *on* the hill when we were told it's *in* the hill.' The two saw the surprise in each other's eyes. They walked towards the Libral Gate, but were stopped by a guard. The guard looked to be in his forties, tall and robust, with grey hair and short beard. 'Gentlemen, only students or staff of the institute can pass this point. No family members, please.'

'Sir, this boy is new to school, so I'm here to help with the registration.' Filton urged. 'Can you please...'

'I'm sorry, but this has been the rule for centuries. No exceptions, please kindly understand,' the guard said resolutely.

Filton pondered for a while, then pulled Soarame back and give him a bag. 'Soarame, everything you need is in here. The money is not that much, but it should be enough if you manage it well.'

Soarame nodded, taking the bag and walking to the guard. 'Sir, Can I come out after registration?'

'Tomorrow is the last day of the registration. So you can come out, but must come back in by the end of tomorrow,' the guard answered. 'After that, the institute will be sealed by magic and you can only get out on weekends.'

'Sealed by magic?' Filton was amazed – no wonder the institute didn't need a door.

The two were interrupted from their musings by a commanding voice from not far away. 'Please step back!'

Filton looked around and saw another group of people stopped by the guards, but these people seemed unwilling to obey.

'Excuse me? It's still a thousand feet to the gate!' A bulky, bald-headed man was staring down the guards. 'We came from thousands of miles away! Do we not deserve a closer look?'

Behind him was a group of people, magnificently dressed, escorting a young man with a pale face, adulation glowing on their faces. On the other hand, the young man looked quite displeased.

'I'm sorry but that's the rule here, so please step back,' said the guard who had stopped Filton. Soarame overheard someone refer to him as Sachastain.

'Okay, I can step back,' the bald man said, pointing at the young man. 'But that is a prince of Astandos. You'd better let him pass.'

Hearing that, the entire crowd started whispering in surprise – a prince, from the Astandos Empire!

Everyone knew that the Astandos Empire was one of the most powerful countries in the world, located on Snowhill Continent – which was far to the south. The prince, named Deltaley, was travelling the world and had now arrived at the Institute of Libral, wanting to make this stop worthwhile by visiting the campus. However, he found his whole entourage stopped by the guards, far away even from the towers. This was definitely not something that pleased him, so he sent his follower to have a word, hoping for the same privileges that he always gained elsewhere.

However, the guards seemed not to care about his royal status. The young prince knew that this was the Institute of Libral, so he had to bear with it…or so it seemed. He still signalled to his followers to figure out a way to bypass the rule.

At the same time, Soarame was instructed to proceed. Just then, a voice came from behind. 'Hey, excuse me!' It's again the bald man from Astandos. 'Boy, where are you going?'

'Excuse me?' Filton stepped forward immediately. 'He's my boy, speak to me if you have questions.'

'Your boy goes to school here? How impressive!' The bald man turned from angry to smooth in the blink of an eye. 'How long has he been studying here?'

'It's his first day, so if you don't mind, we want him to register now.' Filton wasn't interested in this conversation.

'Of course. So your boy is not a student yet?' The bald man nodded to Filton and looked at Sachastain. 'You heard that, right? This kid is not a student yet, but he can enter?' Obviously, the conversation with Filton was just for paving the way for the prince.

'You heard him. He's registering as a new student.' Sachastain peered at the bald man. 'If your prince wants to register as a student too, he can also enter.'

'Sure he is,' the bald man said. 'Can he proceed now?'

'You do know that one has to have magic gifts to qualify as a new student, right?' Sachastain became impatient at this spontaneous lie. 'Tell your prince to perform magic, then he can pass.'

'What?' The bald man was upset. 'Why did you not ask that kid to do some magic too?'

Sachastain had little patience for talking to the irritating bald man, so he turned to address Soarame. 'Hey my little friend, you can perform some magic, right?'

'Sure, but I only know Water magic.' Soarame stepped back from the gate. 'Is that ok, sir?'

'Call me Sachastain. I heard your name is Soarame, right?' Sachastain shook Soarame's hand. 'Water magic is great. Please do something.'

Soarame took out his wand and began to cast an easy spell that Scankeen had specifically asked him to learn from a Water book. Soon enough, a flow of water appeared out of nowhere and Soarame controlled the water to flow around his body. Cheering and applause arose from the crowd, as the shining look of the water flow and Soarame's proficient control amazed everyone. The guards were also quite surprised, as they had seen many wizards and knew that controlling water flow like this wasn't a trivial feat for a prospective student.

'Well done!' Sachastain gave a thumbs-up to Soarame and turned around to face the bald man. 'Your turn.'

'Alright, alright.' Deltaley finally spoke to Sachastain for himself. 'You want to see magic? Here it is.' Deltaley began to mutter some kind of incantation, then waved his hand and shot a firebolt towards the sky. 'Satisfied?'

Seeing that, everyone was surprised – it seemed that Deltaley was really a wizard!

The guards felt it so absurd. The crowd was also whispering. But with the evidence of Deltaley's magical skill, Sachastain had to let him pass.

'That bracelet...' Soarame exclaimed as Deltaley passed by, sounding amazed. 'Is that a...'

'Silence!' Deltaley suddenly looked nervous. He interrupted Soarame and walked faster towards the gate.

'Sir, please stop!' Sachastain suddenly realised something and shouted to Deltaley. Deltaley didn't want to listen, but the next second he found himself surrounded by the guards.

'What do you want?' Deltaley was very upset. He's so close to getting what he wanted yet was stopped because of the interference of an unknown boy.

'Sir, I just have one last demand.' Sachastain was the captain of the guards, so he's the one to speak up. 'Let me take a look at your bracelet.'

'How dare you!' Deltaley stared at Sachastain. 'That's a royal symbol of Astandos! You think anyone can just ask for a look?' At the same time, the Astandos crew started shouting and complaining.

'No, I have no intention of offending your royal symbol, so you don't have to show it. But you don't have to approach to the gate either.' Sachastain stared into Deltaley's eyes. 'So here's my final offer – leave immediately, or let me examine your bracelet to make sure it's not a magigear that can spell firebolts.'

Hearing Sachastain's words, everyone was enlightened – was it the bracelet that had spelled the firebolt? If so, the prince was cheating!

The Astandos crew went quiet. If the suspicions were proven to be true, it would reflect badly on Astandos as a country. Deltaley certainly knew this too; therefore, although he looked really angry, he's actually sweating. The bracelet was indeed the source of the firebolt, but he just couldn't understand how a boy could spot it.

At the same time, Sachastain was sweating, too. He wasn't

really confident about Soarame's claim and, if he failed in this gamble, he would have big troubles. But applying his forty years of experience to examine the reaction of the young prince, he believed that he had made the right call.

'To visit a campus, in exchange for insulting the royal dignity?' Deltaley was his haughty royal self again. 'I say never!' With that, Deltaley stared at Soarame and stepped away from the gate, walking back to his entourage and leaving right away.

Deltaley's reaction convinced Sachastain that Soarame was right, and he's amazed – as far as he knew, there's no way to ascertain that. Sachastain shouldn't be blamed, because no one would have ever expected Soarame to be able to see the movement of the magic elements.

'Thank you, Soarame.' Seeing the Astandos entourage leave, Sachastain saluted Soarame. 'You protected the dignity of the institute. We owe you one!'

'No, I just...' Soarame was astonished to see all the guards saluting him. 'I didn't do anything?'

'Whatever you say, sir. You may proceed to your registration. Good luck!' Sachastain smiled at Soarame. 'With your talent, I'm sure you can easily pass the entry test and become a student.'

'The entry test?' Soarame asked, puzzled. 'What's that?'

THE INSTITUTE OF LIBRAL

'You didn't know that?' Sachastain was confused. 'You came to check in but you didn't know there's an entry test?'

'No?' Soarame looked over to Filton. 'Did Mr Swanflew say mention that?'

'I don't think so.' Filton shook his head. 'But I think that's because he's very confident in you.'

'Swine flu? What?' Sachastain was puzzled. 'Anyway, the Institute of Libral does not automatically accept just any wizard to study here. The school is picky about admission, so there's an entry test.'

'I see, so the registration will take longer than we expected.' Filton nodded. 'Soarame, why don't you go ahead, I'll be waiting here.'

Soarame trotted towards the gate. As he entered the cave, Soarame felt a pulse of dizziness, causing his vision to be completely clouded for a few seconds. After that, he found himself inside a tunnel, facing an exit. Soarame looked back, yet saw nothing behind him except for complete darkness – it felt like a large space, but the darkness made it impossible to see to confirm.

Puzzled and amazed, Soarame decided to move forward. Once he stepped outside, he finally saw the campus –

It's a whole new world.

The exit had deposited Soarame on a small cliff, with a packed-dirt road leading downwards to a forest. Soarame opened his eyes wide, seeing no boundaries to this forest and the campus. Blinking his eyes a few times, Soarame speculated that this must be some kind of space expansion magic – the hill inside which the school was located was definitely not this big.

But when Soarame looked up, he found something that he couldn't understand. Inside of a cave, how could there be a sky, clouds, and even a sun? However large the space was expanded to be, how could the sun come in here?

Thinking to this, Soarame couldn't help marvelling at this magic world, and admiring those great wizards who had created all this. His melancholy thoughts about leaving his master and Filton were soon replaced by determination.

After Soarame walked away from the exit, a figure appeared in the shadows behind him. It's none other than Scankeen. Scankeen wasn't only capable of Wind magic; he also practiced Darkness. But he didn't want to talk about it, for longstanding reasons.

'Good.' Seeing the change in Soarame's countenance, Scankeen was relieved. Scankeen hadn't really left the city after parting from Soarame, but instead he had gone to the campus first to meet a friend there – the current Principal, Gazbell Raymend.

Soarame walked along the winding and forking forest road, trying to find the right direction. Strangely, the road seemed to be changing all the time, so Soarame found himself back at a point he had passed before.

'It's a maze? Really?' Soarame muttered out loud.

'What are you looking for, boy?' A voice came from nowhere and scared Soarame.

'Hi, err...' Soarame was trying to find a proper way to reply. 'Sir, I'm a new student reporting in.'

'Are you? Let me see... Alright, you look fine,' the voice replied after seeming to evaluate Soarame from an unknown perspective. 'Okay, this way, then.' Following the voice, a tree grew out from the soil beside the road, with a sign showing the directions.

'Wow.' Soarame had expected to see some unusual things here, but still he's amazed. He approached the tree and touched it; it felt completely normal. It's a real tree, one that had grown in front of his eyes from nothingness to full maturity.

'Admission Centre – Entry Test.' Soarame read out the sign. 'That's exactly what I want! Thank you, sir!'

'You are welcome, and good luck with the test,' the voice replied. The next second, the tree was still there, but the sign on it vanished.

'Wait, the sign just disappeared?' Soarame couldn't help asking.

'Yes. It's a maze, so we only allow students and staff in,' the voice replied.

'So what happens if someone sneaks in?' Soarame was thinking about Deltaley.

'That wouldn't be nice, would it?' The voice sounded a little surprised. 'If that happens one day, I don't mind keeping the sneaker here forever.'

'Wow...' Soarame was surprised. 'So you are the guide of the school? Without your guidance no one can get in?'

'I'm the security of the school. So yes, no one gets in if I say no,' the voice explained. 'My name is Chelonad. You can call my name any time if you need help.'

'Thank you Chelonad, my name is Soarame.' Soarame was happy. 'Are you around? How can I see you?'

'You won't see me, Soarame.' Chelonad sounded like an old man. 'If you do see me one day, that means something really bad has happened.'

'Okay...' Soarame wasn't sure what Chelonad meant exactly, but he continued towards the admission centre, imagining all kinds of possibilities as to what Chelonad might look like. The road finally brought Soarame out of the forest to reveal a big wooden house – the admission centre. Strangely, the house has no door.

'Chelonad?' Soarame asked the air. 'Can you hear me?'

'No need to call Chelonad. Come on in.' Soarame was expecting Chelonad's voice, but another sounded instead. The next second, a swirl emerged in the wall of the house – it's a magic archway cutting straight through the wood.

Soarame walked into it with eyes wide open. He entered a big hall through the tunnel, where a handsome man in a green cloak waited quietly. The man had beautiful, long blond hair and charming crystal-blue eyes, which inspired people to like him instantly when they saw him. There's one special thing that attracted Soarame's attention – the ears of this man looked longer than a normal person's. Even his long hair couldn't cover the pointed upper tips of his ears.

'Hello, my little friend, my name is Aertiuno. It's nice to meet you.' Aertiuno looked kind and gentle. 'May I ask what your name is and how old you are?'

'Soarame Jadeking. I'm twelve,' Soarame answered right away, but only after he finished did he realise that he wasn't in control of his response. It felt to Soarame that it's Aertiuno who made him speak and tell the truth, rather than Soarame himself wanting to speak!

That's a really weird feeling. Soarame was a little nervous because he began to doubt this man in front of him. Could he manipulate people's thoughts?

Thanks to Scankeen, Soarame had heard about this rare kind of ability; yet the first person he met in the school turned out to be capable of it.

'Very well, thank you Soarame.' Aertiuno nodded. 'So, which lineage are you gifted in?'

'I...' This time Soarame was prepared, and he noticed a captivating pulse that's hard to describe, which was trying to make him talk and tell the truth. Trying hard to suppress it, Soarame took back control of his own mind. 'I am gifted in Lightning and Water, but I'm new.'

'Oh?' Aertiuno was surprised to see that Soarame was able to conquer his *persuasive whisper*, a unique type of mind-control ability. He evaluated Soarame carefully up and down. 'That's it?'

'I can sense a bit of Earth and Lightness, but not as much,' Soarame answered. He had promised Scankeen to keep his skill in Wind secret, so he would.

'OK, we will see that together right now.' Aertiuno pointed at a crystal ball beside him. 'Inject all the magic elements that you can summon into this crystal ball, as much as you can.'

A magical gift test? Soarame was relieved, as he had lots of experience at this. However, the difficult part would be trying to exclude the Wind elements while summoning other lineages. But for Soarame, that's still doable. Soon enough, the crystal ball was full of purple and blue dots, mixed with a small portion of yellow and white ones.

'Very good, you passed.' Aertiuno seemed impressed. 'You are very talented in Lightning, with a "superior" level of gift, followed by Water with a "capable" level... Hmm, that's very lucky for you.'

'Lucky?' Soarame wondered.

'Well, you may not know this, but some magic lineages, such as Lightning and Fire, are hard for a beginner to practise,' Aertiuno said. 'But if one has another lineage to practise before them, that will make it much easier and safer. Therefore, I strongly recommend that you start with Water magic only.'

Soarame nodded, as he recalled Scankeen had told him the same thing before.

'You'll start from Grade 1 in the Water department.' Aertiuno paused and asked, 'You do know how to improve to Grade 2, don't you? If you think you'll automatically get into Grade 2 after a year, you are wrong.'

'To be able to cast a Grade-2 Water spell?' Soarame guessed.

'Yes, but in order to do that, you need to satisfy two conditions,' said Aertiuno. '<u>One, to learn the incantation and magic hexagram. Two, to possess enough mind power to cast the spell.</u> Remember: the more gifted you are in a lineage, the less mind power you need to consume for a spell. So, you will feel a little difficult to grade up in Water, but don't give up.'

'I see...' Soarame realised that Aertiuno was trying to encourage him, because his Water gift was a mere "capable". This meant that he would have to consume much more mind power compared to someone with a "superior" or "high" gift, to spell Water magic.

'Take this Libral Emblem; this is your identifier as a student.' Aertiuno gave Soarame a small device. 'Now that you've got a department, the next step is to apply for a college.'

'A college?'

'Yes, the college is independent from the department and your magic gifts. Consider it a place for making friends and having fun.' Aertiuno usually wouldn't talk this much, but he found Soarame special due to his immunity against his persuasive whisper. 'When you get out, just ask Chelonad for directions.'

Soarame followed the instructions, pulling his new Libral Emblem over his head, and left the house. He looked around but didn't see anyone, so he tried to talk to a tree in front of him. 'Chelonad, can you hear me?'

'Yes, of course.' Chelonad's voice sounded. 'Why are you facing a tree?'

'Err... Where should I be facing?' Soarame asked back.

'Never mind.' Chelonad sounded amused. 'How can I help you, Soarame?'

'Do you remember my name because we just talked, or do you remember everyone's name here?' Soarame decided to ask this first.

'I remember names. They are easy.'

'Wow... I wish I could do that.' Soarame was amazed. 'I always find names so hard to remember, and I was told there are thousands of students in the institute, is that right?'

'3,891 students and 68 teachers. Is this what you called me for?'

'No, I need to apply for a college,' Soarame said. 'Can you show me where to go?'

'I can, but isn't there a sign just behind you?' Chelonad answered.

Soarame looked back and saw a sign of "College Application". 'Oops, I'm sorry. Aertiuno told me to ask you for help, so...'

'I knew it!' Chelonad laughed. 'That guy is so bad at directions that he has to lock himself inside the house. And he assumes other people to be as silly as himself.'

'Really?' Soarame was surprised. 'He looks pretty smart.'

'Smart at anything but directions,' answered Chelonad. 'Let me tell you a funny story that you're not gonna believe...'

'Soarame, stop talking to that chatterbox and go mind your own business!' Aertiuno's voice passed through the house. 'Don't you have a college application to worry about?'

Soarame giggled and ran down the road. Soon enough, he arrived at the college application centre. Unlike the test centre, there were quite a few boys and girls of Soarame's age here, queuing, each holding a piece of parchment – they were all new students applying for colleges. There were also several older students maintaining order; some of them were explaining things to the younger ones.

Soarame was so excited to see others his age, and was wondering how to say "hello" as he approached the crowd. Just then, there came a soft and delightful sounding voice. 'Hi there, are you here for a college application?'

Soarame turned around and saw a teenage girl walking towards him. She had ocean blue shoulder-length hair and was dressed in an elegant light blue robe. As she got closer, Soarame could see that the girl's limpid blue eyes shone like crystals, her long and elegant eyebrows portraying a feeling of softness and amiability to Soarame. The girl looked at Soarame with a sweet smile. 'I'm Dileys, may I help you?'

'Hi... I'm... Err... Soarame... nice to meet you.' Soarame had never been afraid of strangers, but he didn't know why he's suddenly shy about talking to this pretty girl. Well, he didn't realise how few girls he had ever talked to. 'Yes, umm... I was told... told that I need to... to find a college.'

After Soarame's fumbling replies, Dileys thought the boy might have language problems, so she spoke more slowly to help him understand. 'Sure, here's a list with colleges to choose from. You can pick three in the order of your preference.' She then gave Soarame a piece of parchment, together with a big warm smile. 'Take your time, and feel free to ask me questions.'

'Thank you!' Soarame noticed that the nice girl had suddenly slowed down her speech, although he didn't know why. 'But I... I actually don't know... which college to apply for.'

'You don't?' Dileys was surprised. 'Your parents didn't give you suggestions?'

'Well...' Soarame wasn't sure how to put this. 'It's a long story.' Soarame wasn't sure why his master hadn't told him about all this – maybe because this was another test for him?

'Okay, don't panic. I'm here to help. Let me see your emblem,' Dileys said. 'Water department? Plus Lightning, but not activated yet... So you have gifts in Lightning, but are only allowed to learn Water for now?'

'Yes, is that... okay?' Soarame sensed a change in Dileys' reaction.

'Ah, of course, it's good! I'm a Water department student too!' Dileys looked very happy. 'It's just that most students in Water are girls; there are almost no boys. But no worries, you are most welcome to join!'

Soarame was just about to ask why when he heard a harsh voice. 'A boy in Water? Ha-ha... Let me have a look!'

Soarame raised his head to find a tall boy walking towards him, looking at him with contempt. At the same time, everyone looked over, curious about what's going on. Dileys stepped in front of Soarame and yelled at the boy. 'Casavin, mind your own business!'

The boy had small puffy eyes, a wide pug nose, and a few whelks on his cheek. He didn't really care what Dileys said and walked over to Soarame, laughing. 'My name is Casavin, what's yours? You know what... it doesn't matter. I'll just call you Water Boy!' Before Soarame could answer, Casavin waved his hand, 'You're probably the only boy in Water this year.'

Grabbing Soarame's emblem, Casavin sneered. 'Water with a "capable" gift? You do know that's the minimum requirement of this school, right?' In here, "capable" actually means "common"...'

'Go away Casavin, no one needs you here!' Dileys grabbed Soarame's emblem back. Giving it back to Soarame, Dileys said gently, 'Soarame, ignore him and keep this emblem with you, okay? It's your identifier in school, so don't let anyone take it.'

Soarame nodded while Casavin laughed at his side. 'Ha-ha...a Water boy, who wants his emblem anyway?'

'Shut up!' Dileys was upset. 'Casavin, you are jealous because you can't practise Water. I'm sorry you don't have the gift!'

'Whoops, you are sorry? I'm not,' Casavin giggled. 'I don't blame you for protecting him – he's probably Water's only hope, with his "capable" gift!'

Soarame was by no means happy, but he sensed something tricky. He kept his temper and asked as everyone was giggling, 'Casavin, what's wrong with Water? Are you saying Water is weak?'

Strangely enough, after Soarame's question, everyone went silent.

Soarame didn't realise that his question was a solid one. In people's ordinary opinions, water could put out fire and that's just the way it is. However, in the magic world, it's actually the opposite. When water meets fire, it's true that fire may vanish, but water doesn't cause as much immediate damage as fire, and that counts for a lot during magic battles. Think about it – when two fight, one gets burnt while the other one only gets wet, who wins?

Therefore, Water magic could only compete with Fire at a higher level – when it upgrades to Ice magic and counters Fire with its freezing capacity. That said, in the institute, where most students were at a lower level, not many had the power to do that.

As Soarame asked his question, many of the new students started whispering –

'I heard that Water is the weakest magic for attacking, and works best at nourishing and healing, so only girls like it.'

'That's right, how could Water compete with the others? Especially Fire, it's far more powerful!'

'Lightness is even better! It's the best at mind attacks and also great at healing!'

'No way, Wind is the best! Do you know how much damage windblades can do? Plus, it has the Flying spell!'

'Nah-nah, Darkness is the best! With a *shadowcape* spell one can be invisible. How can you attack someone invisible?'

Hearing the discussions around him, Soarame began to realise what's going on. No wonder he might be the only Water boy this year – boys usually wouldn't choose the Water lineage as their major.

'Actually, it's not that bad to go to Water,' Casavin carried on. 'There are so many pretty girls there – maybe I do wish I could go!'

Seeing Dileys becoming angrier and angrier, Casavin knew it's his moment to leave.

Dileys looked at Soarame and sighed. 'Soarame, don't listen to them – especially Casavin. He's always rude; from now on, just keep away from him.'

Soarame didn't agree. 'Why? Why would I hide from him?'

'It's...' Dileys forced a smile. 'That guy doesn't have manners...'

'You can't beat him, silly. So if you don't hide, what else can you do?' A sniggering voice sounded from behind them. Soarame turned around to find a chubby boy giggling.

'Is there nothing else, other than fighting or hiding?' Soarame frowned. The new arrival had several moles around his humourless lips. Yellow-blond hair framed his round face, his skin the colour of coffee with a reddish undertone.

'Ha, interesting... what do you suggest instead, crying?' As the plump boy continued his teasing, the giggling around them became even louder.

Dileys frowned and pulled Soarame away from the laughing crowd. 'Soarame, ignore all of them. Although fights are forbidden in the institute, there are still bullies. If someone picks on you, just tell me and I'll take care of it.'

Soarame was about to say something, but he didn't. If his master hadn't specifically told him not to reveal his secrets, he'd have pulled out his wand already. Dileys certainly noticed that the boy didn't look happy, and she quickly changed the topic. 'Soarame, time to talk about your college application.'

Hearing this, Soarame was roused from the distraction and looked down at the parchment. A number of colleges were listed, each name followed by a brief description. New students were supposed to make their choices with the help of their family before they came to the institute, but since Soarame was an exception, he had to ask some naïve questions. 'Dileys, why do these names read like people?'

'Because those are people's names,' Dileys patiently explained. 'The Institute of Libral is named after the Great Libral, and the colleges are named after the first names of the founders. For example, "Joseph College" was founded by the Master Joseph Carloon.'

'Then is this "Spanflow College" named after the Great Spanflow Libral?' asked Soarame.

'Exactly. Spanflow College was founded by the Great Spanflow Libral.' Dileys nodded. 'It is the most prestigious college and has the best facilities, but it only accepts the best students too.'

'Then I'll go for Spanflow College!' Soarame said immediately.

Just when Dileys was about to speak, there came a familiar voice. 'What? You? Spanflow College?'

Soarame turned around and stared at the same chubby boy – getting used to such challenges had been always difficult. Seeing Soarame taking an unconscious step towards the boy, Dileys hastened forward to hold Soarame back. 'Just ignore him! But you do need to think it over – Spanflow College is the best. Most students there have "superior" gifts, "capable" is rare there... don't risk it!'

On her other side, the chubby boy yelled. 'How dare you stare at me? Water Boy!'

'Oh, I thought I just did? And my name is Soarame!' Soarame had never been one to provoke but he had always been responsive. 'What about yours? The Mouth?'

The chubby boy was irritated by the Water boy firing back at him. How could a Water fire anything? This was simply unheard of. 'Wow, you actually have a backbone! You remember my name: Kraigen! I'll deal with you later.'

'Kraigen? Good name!' Soarame laughed suddenly. 'So you cry, and "cry again"?'

Hearing Soarame, everyone laughed. Even Dileys couldn't help chuckling.

Kraigen's face reddened with anger. He rushed towards Soarame to charge at him, but was pulled back swiftly by an older student.

'Enough!' exclaimed a sonorous voice from a distance, and the whole crowd quieted down. Soarame raised his head to find a tall and sharp-featured male student walking towards them. The student looked dignified and imposing, especially with his dark brushy eyebrows and bright eyes. The sharp line of his jaw smoothed into his cheekbones, accentuating his firm mouth with its slight downturn at the corners. He seemed to be revered by the other older students, including Dileys. They were all standing rigidly upright. 'Rodka!'

Rodka nodded and walked up to Soarame and Kraigen. 'All freshers listen up, especially you two! This is the Institute of Libral, not some street corner. Fights are strictly forbidden! You'll be excused today because you are new here, but if this happens again you'll be suspended – and after that, you'll be expelled! Do you understand?'

'Yes!' Everyone answered together, including a pale-faced Kraigen.

'I'm going to mark your name down, though.' Rodka turned towards Soarame. 'What's your name?'

'Soarame,' answered Soarame. 'He started it!'

'I know. But that doesn't mean making fun of others' names is right.' Before Soarame could argue, Rodka turned to Kraigen. 'You were laughing at Soarame for majoring in Water, correct?'

Seeing Kraigen's awkward countenance, Rodka looked around at everyone. 'This is another lesson to you all – in this school, no fighting is the first rule. The second rule is no discrimination of any kind: race, gender, age, magic power, magic gifts, lineage of magic, or one's original country, anything at all! We have zero tolerance against discrimination, and you'd better keep it in mind at all times!'

'But Rodka...' Kraigen complained. 'Casavin was the first one to mock Water... you just missed him!'

'What? It's Casavin?' Rodka glanced at Dileys. Seeing her nod, he frowned. 'I'll go and get him right away.'

With that, Rodka turned and left under everyone's gaze, especially the new students.

'Who's that Rodka?' Soarame couldn't help asking Dileys.

'He is the captain of the Campus Discipline Watch, so he's very famous here. He's also a Grade-5 tri-lineage wizard of Wind, Fire, and Lightness – a genius!' Dileys blushed as she spoke. 'Compared to him, Casavin is nothing more than a joker!'

'Agreed!' Soarame nodded. 'So you are familiar with him?'

'Well, I do know him pretty well, but he doesn't really know me.' Dileys sighed. 'Oh, he is in Spanflow College, by the way. If you can get in there you could see him a lot.'

'Then Spanflow College it is!' Soarame was excited to hear this. 'Okay, I'm going to queue then!'

'Ah! You really want to take the risk?' Dileys tried to persuade Soarame to think it over, but couldn't defeat his determination. And if Soarame could really get into Spanflow, she would have more chances to see Rodka through him as well. 'Fine, but you can pick three colleges in order, so you should at least choose two more for backup.'

'Okay, but which two?' Soarame looked at Dileys. 'Dileys, which college are you in?'

'Bosstin College,' answered Dileys.

'Then Bosstin is my second choice!' Soarame marked a number two before "Bosstin College" with his pen.

'Wait!' Dileys watched Soarame, speechless. 'Soarame, don't you want to think it over? Bosstin College is a very ordinary college, far from Spanflow. You are jumping from one extreme right to another.'

'I already thought about it. If I can't be in Spanflow, I want to be in the same college with you.' Soarame believed this reason to be good enough. 'Which college is Casavin in?'

'Ah... that pest is in Halston College.' Dileys answered after a pause. 'Wait, you aren't thinking...'

'Then Halston is my third!'

Soarame's words almost struck Dileys down. 'You can't be serious, Soarame!' Dileys was anxious. 'It's okay to go for Rodka or me, but why Casavin?'

'If I can't be with friends and be happy, then I want to be with challengers to make me tough!' Soarame's words were surprising to Dileys.

Seeing Soarame's eyes glow with innocence, Dileys couldn't believe those were his words. In fact, they were not – the boy was actually reciting Scankeen's words once in the past. Dileys thought it over and over, but it seemed she could only come up with one reason to contradict Soarame. 'But Halston College ranks far higher than Bosstin College. If you truly want to apply, you should make it your second choice.'

The second Dileys said it, she almost wanted to bite her tongue. *What the heck was I thinking?*

Just as she's about to correct her words, Soarame declared. 'No need. I decided to punish it because of Casavin!'

Dileys had to chuckle. As Soarame happily went off to the queue, Dileys couldn't help wondering how the school would react to his application form. Soarame's style had rarely been put into practise before – everyone here exhausted themselves fighting for a better chance, but Soarame just threw dice.

Soarame handed in his application and came scampering back. Dileys wanted to show Soarame around the campus, but it's getting dark here. Soarame knew that Filton was still waiting and it's a long walk back to the Libral Gate. Therefore, they said goodbye and agreed to meet each other again two days later.

Stepping out of the campus from the same cave he had entered through, Soarame saw Filton waiting for him. At the same time, he also noticed something odd: inside the campus the sun was about to set, but here it wasn't quite there yet.

'Congratulations!' Filton was certainly pleased to know that Soarame passed the test; so were Sachastain and the guards. The tourists also saw Soarame walking out of the cave, so they gathered to cheer aloud for the boy too.

'Well done, Soarame!' While the visitors cheered and applauded Soarame, Sachastain got close and looked at Soarame's emblem. 'You have a superior gift in Lightning? Wow!'

'Yes, but I can't practise it right now.'

'Oh, take your time on it. That's a minor issue.' Sachastain sized Soarame up. 'The Lightning gift is rare. Be patient and use your gift well!'

'Thank you, I will. Sachastain, will you visit me some time?'

'Of course! I promise you that I will visit your dorm some time after you settle down.'

The three talked a bit and Soarame left with Filton. Watching Soarame's back, Sachastain was seriously thinking about something –

Maybe, this boy is the one I'm looking for?

THE CAMPUS AND CITIES

The next morning, Filton and Soarame were walking along the streets of Cylone City, eyes large in wonder. Most of the buildings were built of brick and stone, though a few even boasted metal supports allowing them to reach higher than any building in their small village. Even the shorter buildings seemed grander, with intricate carvings decorating lintels and edges, carvings that even the finest stonemason in their village would pause to admire the craftsmanship. The market streets the pair wandered down were filled with brightly coloured awnings and the sounds of merchants hawking their wares to the bargaining passers-by.

It's very busy everywhere, with a variety of street shows and activities going on, and people from every corner of the world dressed in more styles than Filton and Soarame ever thought possible gathering and participating. Greetings, laughter and loud conversations surrounded them. Witnessing all this, Filton had to sigh deeply for how tedious his life in the village had been. But all that would be in his past; once Soarame settled down in the school, Filton would travel to different places and enrich his experiences.

Soarame and Filton enjoyed themselves watching the antics of the performers with their fire torches flying through the air and the crowds gawking and turning their heads to follow the torches arch ever higher. Music of all kinds floated through the air, competing to be heard, and Filton pulled Soarame away from a snake charmer as his snake lifted out of his basket to look at him in the eyes.

Now Soarame was watching a street artist painting with ink in his own special way – unlike other painters, he simply poured ink onto the canvas and blew on it to make the ink flow, generating different shapes and patterns. Soarame was fascinated by his skills

– a vivid plum-blossom tree emerged on the canvas as if by magic.

'Hey, how are you guys?' A tall man came along and greeted Filton. 'We are having a game here, want to join us?'

'What game?' asked Filton. 'As long as you're not going to put a giant snake on my boy.' Filton was leaving the next day and Soarame was feeling sad; Filton thought that a game might cheer him up a bit.

'Ha-ha, no. It's a fun game and pretty easy, all you need to do is pour the beer into the bottle. The player with the most beer in a bottle wins the game and gets a gold coin. If you can fill the bottle more than half full, you get an extra prize!' The performer was holding a bowl of beer and a narrow-necked bottle. 'Only twenty silver coins to play, it's very cheap.'

'Well, that…' Realizing that it required payment, Filton went silent. Twenty silver coins wasn't a small amount to him, especially as he had to save money for the trip back.

'It's okay Filton. I don't want to play anyway.' Soarame saw Filton's hesitation and clearly knew why.

'If you can't afford twenty silver coins, why are you here?' the performer rolled his eyes. 'You do know this is Cylone City, not your country yard, don't you?'

Soarame had been ready to leave until hearing this. Seeing Filton's embarrassed face, Soarame was enraged. 'So what's the extra prize? If I can fill half of the bottle, what do I get?'

'Ten gold coins!' The performer looked at Soarame, sneering. 'Why not give it a try? It's worth a month of your papa's work.'

'Let's do it.' Filton was mad too. He paid the fee and got a bowl and a bottle for Soarame. 'As long as he can fill the bottle up, right?'

'Oh, if you fill it up, I'll give you twenty gold coins! But you only have one minute.' The performer laughed and checked the other players. 'Everyone ready? Three, two, one, go!'

With that, all started to pour beer from their bowls into the narrow bottlenecks. The bowls were wide and flat, and the bottlenecks were so narrow that the game was rather difficult. Plus, the bowl could only hold as much as the bottle, so filling the bottle up was a mission impossible. As a result, everyone ended up spilling most of the beer. Soarame had realised the trick straightaway, and he knew that the same thing would happen to him if he were not a wizard, especially a Water wizard. However –

'Oh dear, look at that boy!' The audience started to notice Soarame soon enough, because he hadn't spilt a drop.

'What?' The performer was stunned to watch Soarame easily pouring the beer into the narrow bottle opening. 'No way!' Seeing Soarame's bottle was already full, the performer almost cried. However, a deal was a deal, so he had to hand over twenty gold coins with a fake smile. Many people in the crowd had witnessed what had happened from the beginning of the encounter. They had felt sorry for Filton and Soarame being insulted until now – there's the chance for them to cheer for the boy's fabulous play and force the performer to live up to his words.

'Well done, Soarame!' Walking down the street happily, the two enjoyed looking at the different shops and restaurants. They approached a building and found it to be a magigear store. They were curious and entered it, and soon find out that even the cheapest wand cost more than they could afford. Interestingly, there's a dog-like magimal in the store and Soarame went to inquire about it, only to realise that it cost a hundred times more than the wand.

'Well, I thought we could use the prize to buy you a magigear,' Filton sighed as they walked out of the store. 'Looks like we can only get lunch instead.'

So the two of them entered a restaurant and enjoyed their last meal together. Filton wanted to leave the city in the afternoon, so that he could get a cheaper dinner and a hotel outside the expensive city.

Soarame knew Filton must be feeling really sorry about his meagre coin purse, so he's determined to make money somehow during his school life here. The two talked a lot during lunch before they went back to the Libral Gate. After repeatedly urging Soarame to take care of himself, Filton finally saw Soarame disappear into the cave again, holding back his tears. This time it's official – Soarame would start his school life and Filton would start his new life of travelling, all alone.

'Chelonad, can you hear me?' Soarame walked out of the tunnel after passing through the Libral Gate. 'I want to go to my dorm.'

'You should have done that yesterday,' Chelonad's voice

sounded soon enough. 'I know it's hard to leave your family for the first time, but don't worry, you will feel great here.'

'Thank you. We had fun today in the city.' Soarame briefly told the story about the twenty gold coins.

'Why didn't you just tell him you are a wizard?' Chelonad sounded amused. 'He'd have apologised quickly enough.'

'Well, Filton does need the money for his trip back.' Soarame chuckled. 'By the way, are there any jobs on campus?'

'For you?' Chelonad sounded surprised. 'You want to get paid?'

'Yes, can I?' Soarame was anxious to know the answer.

'That's interesting. Your master didn't...' Chelonad suddenly stumbled over his words. 'You must didn't... know that a wizard can always find money.'

'How?' Soarame didn't notice Chelonad's stuttering. His eyes brightened up. 'I want to start now!'

'Well, the school only allows you to work on the weekends. You can find out details later. Okay, your dorm is here.'

'Here?' Soarame found himself in a small, very empty grassy clearing. 'What do you mean?'

Soarame's question was answered right away – a small house with brown walls rose from the ground and emerged in front of him.

'Wow, Chelonad, you are not only good at growing trees!' Soarame marvelled.

'Of course. I'm good at a lot of things,' said Chelonad, his voice full of pride. 'This is just your bedroom unit. It will relocate after your college is determined.'

'Relocate? How? Where?' Soarame wondered.

'I won't know that until you are officially assigned to a college. Then this unit will fly somewhere and merge with several other units to make a full dorm house there.'

'Wait, did you say *fly* there?'

'Yes, and you can enjoy the flight within the unit. This is deliberately designed for freshers here. You can also invite up to four guests to fly with you, if you know anyone here,' Chelonad added. 'Okay, I will talk to you later.'

'Thanks, Chelonad!' Soarame went over to the unit and opened the door. It's a small but neat en-suite bedroom, completely furnished with everything. There's a magic symbol on the wall, so he touched it and the room lit up. Soarame then put his hands on the wall, trying to figure out what material it's – it definitely wasn't wood, metal or rock. Soarame was amazed to find the wall felt warm and almost soft, as if it's alive.

This place is just amazing! Soarame praised deeply. Hours ago he's excited about twenty gold coins, and now the boy started to realise how silly that was.

This night, Soarame had a dream – himself flying in the sky, enjoying the magnificent views of Cylone City and the countryside beyond the city walls. There, he saw a line of carriages with the royal symbols of Astandos.

Deltaley? Soarame was surprised to see this face again. The prince of Astandos was getting into one of the carriages. Soarame landed beside Deltaley but found that no one could see him, as if he's transparent; so he followed Deltaley into the other carriage out of curiosity.

'Filton?' Soarame was surprised to see that Filton was sitting there, eating the same meal as their last lunch together. 'Why are you here?'

Filton didn't respond, probably because he couldn't see Soarame either. So Soarame turned around to check on Deltaley, but found he had disappeared. Soarame got out of the carriage, but suddenly found himself surrounded by Astandos warriors, fully armed, with spears pointing at him. Deltaley walked up from behind the warriors, sneering at Soarame.

'What's all this and why? You can see me now?' Soarame was anxious and tried to talk to Deltaley, but Deltaley only responded with a hand wave – the warriors pounced forward and attacked Soarame with their sharp spears.

'Ahh!' Soarame woke up, soaked in cold sweat. 'Praise Libral, what the heck was that!'

Getting up from his bed, Soarame washed his face and laughed at himself. He must have been too tired and had a weird dream. Seeing the sun already high in the morning sky, Soarame tidied himself up, ate the light breakfast and went to the admissions building – the results of college application would come out today.

The admissions building became crowded with new students jostling to see the results. Soarame and Dileys made efforts to get close to the callboard.

'Soarame, look!' Dileys said. Soarame followed Dileys, only to find that it wasn't his name she's pointing at –

'Kraigen, major in Wind and Fire, minor in Darkness, Halston College,' he read aloud from the board.

'Remember that chubby boy?' Dileys said in surprise. 'He's actually not bad! This means that his gifts in Wind and Fire are both good. He's not that good at Darkness, but he still can give it a try.'

Dileys knew that there were lots of basics Soarame didn't know, so she carried on. 'In our school, the grade of a student is based on the magic power he reaches, regardless of his age. For example, the age of a Grade 3 usually varies from ten to fourteen, but it's not surprising when someone is younger or older than that. Also, someone could be Grade 4 in one lineage and Grade 2 in another at the same time.' She continued, 'A student of any major can graduate as long as he reaches Grade 6, and must graduate if he reaches Expert level, which maps to Grade 7 – but we don't have that grade here.'

Soarame listened and nodded. Each grade matched to each level, simple. His master had told him about four tiers for wizards: *Novice*, *Adept*, *Expert* and *Master*. Accordingly, Levels 1 to 3 were different sub-levels within Novice; 4 to 6 were for Adept; 7 to 9 were Expert; and finally, Level 10 meant Master. Soarame knew that his master wanted him to become an Expert before graduation, not just a Level/Grade 6. 'How many years are we supposed to stay here?'

'It really depends. Most graduate in a few years, when they are about twenty years old. But I heard that a crazy genius girl graduated as young as sixteen in the past, although I have no idea how she managed that.' Dileys marvelled. 'But most people spend much longer than that, because Grade 4 and 5 usually take two years each.'

Hearing this, Soarame had to ask, 'How old is Rodka, then?'

'Ah... Rodka is an absolute star here!' On hearing the name "Rodka", Dileys' eyes suddenly shone. 'Grade 5 in Wind, Fire and Lightness, but only sixteen! What a genius... do you know how hard that is?'

'Grade 5 in three lineages? Wow.' Soarame couldn't help his

feelings of admiration – he didn't think he would be able to do that.

'Told you he's the star of Libral!' Dileys looked very proud, as if she's the great one herself. Seeing her face even become pink, Soarame chuckled and realised something.

'What are you looking at?' Noticing Soarame's reaction, Dileys hurriedly changed the topic. 'We haven't found your name yet, Soarame, hurry up!' The two again started searching for Soarame's name.

'I've found it!' said Dileys after a while. 'Your college is... What? Why?'

****

'Your name is Soarame Jadeking?'

In a meeting room, a skinny old wizard in a leather chair raised his head, scrutinising Soarame. Lined up on either side of him behind the long table were five other wizards, gazing at Soarame too. Soarame recognised one of them, Aertiuno, who had given him the entry test the other day.

'Yes, I'm Soarame.' Soarame was a little nervous; he had no idea what's happening.

'Soarame,' said the old wizard expressionlessly. 'You are a new student, with a mere "capable" gift in Water, and you choose not to learn Lightning for now. Why do you think Spanflow College should admit you?'

'Err...' Soarame pondered for a while but didn't really know how to answer. 'Sir, why am I the only one here? Everyone else has their colleges announced.'

'Because they all picked their college in a reasonable way, unlike you.' The old wizard was still expressionless, the wrinkles in his face giving nothing away. 'You can call me Dean Romboton. I'm the Dean of Spanflow College.' Dean Romboton indicated the wizard on his left with his hand; he's a red-faced, pot-bellied man, quite different from Dean Romboton. 'This is Dean Akex, the Vice Dean of Spanflow College. You've already met Aertiuno,' he continued as Aertiuno nodded at Soarame from

Vice Dean Akex's other side.

Motioning towards the other three wizards, he introduced them as the Deans of the other Colleges Soarame had applied to. The medium-height wizard standing on Dean Romboton's right and wearing a voluminous deep purple robe which contrasted with his vibrant green hair was Dean Harries of Bosstin College. On the far right with his close-cropped salt-and-pepper hair and long black goatee was Dean O'heven of Halston College. Between them was a tall, almost lanky aged wizard with long, thick white hair, but Dean Romboton did not introduce him.

'Soarame, in case you didn't know, students who apply for our college are all highly gifted in at least two lineages. I see you have a superior gift in Lightning, but that's just one lineage and it's deactivated for now,' Dean Akex took over from Dean Romboton. 'With only a capable gift in Water, it's likely that you will be the weakest student in maybe the entire institute – assuming that you work hard enough. And you should know that, in the magic world, power counts for a lot.'

Soarame listened in silence. When his master first started teaching him magic, he had once told him that the rule of gift assessment had been in dispute for decades. This was especially the case when it came to school admission scenarios. Normally, a student should not be judged on his gifts; but this was a magic institute, cultivating wizards to protect the world, so it judged students' potential not only for the greater good of the world, but also for the safety of its students – if one wasn't gifted enough to learn a certain spell but went for it anyway, it could result in serious injury.

Therefore, after accidents had happened multiple times in the past, the institute enforced this seemingly cruel gift-assessment policy. On top of that, the colleges competed with each other in all kinds of events in order to achieve their rankings in the institute, and they all wanted their students to be as strong as possible at all times.

As a consequence, Soarame, the Mr weakest, had to face this tough situation this day. Recalling Dileys' bewilderment upon seeing his name on the callboard with "college to be confirmed" appended, Soarame crossed his fingers nervously.

'Soarame, are you with us?' Dean Romboton's voice broke into

Soarame's thoughts. 'Why were you so daring as to choose Spanflow?'

'Err... I can perform Lightning later?' Soarame wasn't sure what else to say; he really wished his master hadn't asked him to keep the Wind gift secret. 'And I really adore the Great Libral, so I chose his college.'

'Well, this puts you at risk now. If you can't impress us today, you might be denied by all three colleges, and we are not sure where to put you if that happens.' Dean Romboton looked at Soarame. 'How about this? I offer you another chance to redo your college application. Think carefully now and tell me your new first choice.'

Soarame pondered but wasn't willing to change his mind. 'Spanflow College is my first choice.'

'Are you sure?' Dean Romboton arched an eyebrow. 'You won't have another chance.'

'Yes sir.' Soarame took a deep breath and recalled Scankeen's education over the past few years. 'I must give it a try, otherwise I'll regret it!'

Hearing Soarame's words, the unnamed old wizard showed a hint of smile on his face. Soarame didn't know it, but this wizard was actually the most senior member of the committee – the Principal of the institute, Gazbell Raymend, the one whom Scankeen had visited before he left. Hearing Soarame's words, Gazbell knew that this boy had passed the first test. Dean Romboton and Vice Dean Akex glanced at each other, and both found a hint of approval in each other's eyes – they were also pleased to hear what the boy had said. The school seemed to be cruel to students by judging them by their gifts, but at the same time it could test their confidence, attitude and belief, too.

'Nice job, Soarame,' Dean O'heven chipped in before anything. 'You adore the Great Libral so much that you decided to put Bosstin College before Halston College? Do you know how hard we work to get a better ranking for our college?'

Soarame puzzled briefly before he realised what's going on – there's some rivalry between the two Colleges.

'Dean O'heven's question makes sense. Why did you put Bosstin before Halston? It's a sharp contrast to the rankings,' Dean Romboton asked.

Soarame pondered for a bit but finally decided to tell them the true reason. 'Because I think Halston may not welcome Water students as much as Bosstin.'

'Nonsense!' Dean O'heven was astonished to hear that. 'Who told you that? In our school, we treat students of any lineage equally.'

'Mr Dean, a student from your college laughed at me for majoring in Water,' Soarame had to speak up for himself. 'But I can't tell you who... I don't wanna bad-mouth people behind their backs.'

'Not possible!' Dean O'heven was struck to hear Soarame's accusation, and he glanced at Gazbell. 'Halston does not have this kind of student; you must be mistaken.' Immediately after he had spoken, Dean O'heven already regretted challenging Soarame. A matter such as Soarame described could be as bad as people wanted it to be, or as trivial. Therefore, in front of the Principal, this had to be properly handled.

Gazbell looked completely impassive, but he's amused inside. He's the one who had made this interview happen, because he wanted to observe Soarame in person. Of course, he hadn't told anyone about the boy, so that they would feel free to ask tough questions. In that way, Gazbell would have a chance to see Scankeen's student's reaction under pressure, and see if he really had a strong enough heart to become a great wizard later on. However, he hadn't expected that Soarame would be able to turn the pressure back on them, and he didn't want this topic to get out of hand. 'Dean O'heven, you should clarify this matter soon, but for now let's move on.'

'Certainly. I'll go do it immediately.' Dean O'heven was thankful that Gazbell let him walk away. He left the meeting room, with one last glance at Soarame.

Once he had closed the door, Dean O'heven looked thunderous. He knew that Soarame wasn't lying; all senior wizards were very sensitive to people's mind waves, which resonated when one was performing magic, thinking hard, getting emotional or nervous – such as when telling a lie. Dean O'heven guessed who Soarame was describing – one of his favourite students, named Casavin, fit that style. He had been turning a blind eye out of fondness for the boy, and it had been so far so good. However, mistakes had happened; therefore, actions had to be taken.

Back in the meeting room, the rest of the committee was at a loss for what to say next. Gazbell had to suppress his amusement and asked the purple-clad wizard beside him. 'Dean Harries, the Deans of Spanflow and Halston have both asked their questions, what about you?'

'Mr Principal, I have no question to ask; but I would like to thank Mr Jadeking for considering Bosstin College,' Dean Harries answered with a big smile. 'Also, I have learnt that Mr Jadeking does have a special gift that may satisfy Spanflow College – Aertiuno, would you like to talk about your persuasive whisper?'

DUEL PACT

'Cheers!' In the restaurant, a vivacious blonde girl in suspender pants and a pale pink shirt lifted her glass of fruit juice. Beside her, Soarame and the three other girls gathered around the table. Once Soarame had told Dileys about his interview, she had gathered her three best friends and fellow students in the Water department. They were all about the same age, but the girls had started school earlier than Soarame. Hearing that Soarame was admitted into Spanflow by successfully passing his unique interview, they were so madly excited that they kidnapped him and rushed him out to celebrate their new Water-mate at Aquamarine Sky, a popular restaurant on campus.

The girl leading the toast was Catheray. While she's Soarame's senior at the institute, she didn't look older at all. She had big twinkling golden eyes and her short hair fell just below her ears. Although Soarame had only just met her, he's already convinced that she's lively and playful.

'Great job, Soarame! We are really proud to have you on board!' Another girl, Jemario, elbowed Soarame gently. She's wearing a long lavender dress which matched her long hair. Her clear and bright pupils, framed by long, thick eyelashes, shone above her graceful cheek bones and full lips, giving her a charming look of mystery and exoticism. Soarame was also curious about her dress; it boasted elegantly-stitched silver patterns which shimmered and seemed to move whenever she moved.

'Yes, Soarame, welcome to the Water family!' Another girl, Vivarin, exclaimed warmly. She's wearing a fitted dark brown leather suit, her dusky silver-coloured hair brushing her shoulders where it escaped from her high ponytail. When people first saw her, they often thought she's a sword-fighter rather than a wizard.

The twittering and chirping from the girls attracted the attention of male students in the restaurant. The boys squinted towards the table now and then; but finding that the focus of the girls was actually a boy, they were all puzzled, and some started to look sour.

'Okay everyone, time to let Soarame tell us about his amazing experience of striding into Spanflow College as a pure Water!' called out Jemario as she stood up.

'Yeah!' Applause picked up in volume all around them; all the girls craned their necks, waiting for Soarame to tell his story.

'Jemario, it's…' Soarame felt so shy. Jemario had exaggerated, which made it hard for him to carry on.

'Pure Water?' a voice from another table sounded. 'Meaning single-majored in Water? How could someone like that get into Spanflow?'

The girls looked over and saw a few boys from a table nearby standing up. One of them, with red hair, stomped towards them and spoke to Soarame. 'Hey, pure Water, is that true? You only practise Water magic?'

Hearing the contemptuous voice, Jemario shot to her feet and rebuked the boy. 'Who are you? Watch your manners!' As a Water student, Jemario was fed up with contempt of all sorts, and so were all her friends. 'He's pure Water and so are all of us, so what?'

'No, nothing… that's cool.' The male student was stunned by Jemario's beauty and hurriedly replied, 'My name is Robert, Grade 4 in Fire, Joseph College. What's your name?'

Robert was looking at Jemario, but Jemario had already dismissed him and turned to whisper with Catheray, not heeding his words at all. Robert was embarrassed, and he chose to stare at Soarame for that.

'What's your problem?' Seeing that, Dileys stood up in front of Soarame, gazing at Robert. 'Why are you staring at him?' Vivarin also came to Dileys' side, staring at Robert with hands akimbo, signalling *I'll teach you a lesson if you don't behave.*

The Water girls had been known to be super protective of each other. Because Water magic before Expert level is commonly acknowledged to be not as powerful, the Water students naturally grouped together to help each other. Now that Soarame had become a member of the Water family, they were showing him the tradition.

Just as the situation came to a head, everyone heard the creaking door of Aquamarine Sky. In walked another male student, tall and thin with a recognisable pug nose. Seeing who it was, Dileys instantly had a headache. *Oh no, not him again... at this moment!*

The person who had stepped in was none other than Casavin, followed by his friends.

Casavin had the reputation and nature of a troublemaker; stirring things up was his favourite hobby. Seeing the conflict between a crowd of girls and boys, Casavin was instantly alert. Although neither side welcomed him, Casavin quickly chose to take the girls' side so as to impress them. Standing beside Dileys, Casavin turned to Robert and thundered, 'Who the heck are you? Stay away from my friends!'

'Stay away yourself!' A friend of Robert stepped forward to Casavin. 'You don't remember me, Casavin? We are both in Grade 4, Fire.'

'Saja? Of course I remember you,' Casavin sneered. 'The "brave" boy who ran away from me last time.'

'Who ran away?' Saja yelled. 'You had five others with you, last time! If you ever dare for a one-on-one, I'm ready.' Obviously, these two had had problems before and it's still not settled.

'Saja, don't!' Robert stepped forward and blocked Saja. 'As far as I know, his Earth magic is Grade 5.'

'It's okay. I won't use Earth for our one-on-one.' Casavin shrugged his shoulders and glared at Robert. 'You heard him, he dared me, so I must take the challenge!'

'Okay, then! Let's go sign a duel pact!' Saja was happy. 'Fire vs. Fire, deal?'

'Of course!' Casavin confirmed without hesitation, and turned to the crowd in the restaurant. 'You guys all witnessed this; we'll move on to the arena! Everyone is invited to watch!'

Soarame and the girls looked at each other, not sure what to say – once Casavin showed up, the centre of the trouble naturally moved to focus on him. The dinner plans were therefore aborted. Casavin took the lead out of Aquamarine Sky, and everyone followed out of curiosity, including Soarame and his new friends.

Weiqi Wang

The Institute of Libral forbade spontaneous fights between students, but allowed formal duels on a teacher's authorization. Any student could issue a duel challenge to another in an equal or higher grade – but not lower – then they were free to compete in an arena under a teacher's watch.

This day, everyone was going to see a live duel. Fire vs. Fire, this one was going to be worth watching because both sides were good at attacking. As the crowd headed for the arena, more and more students came from all directions and joined them. Seeing that the crowd had grown to hundreds upon arrival at the arena, both Casavin and Saja were quite satisfied; they couldn't wait to show off their powers in front of the crowd.

Stepping up to the closed gate, Casavin put his hand on a magic symbol beside it. The symbol lit up and passed his voice through to the teacher on duty inside. 'This is Casavin and Saja. We are here for a duel. Please let us in!'

Shortly after, the gate to the arena opened and a gorgeous female teacher came out. 'Welcome, all of you. You can call me Sandoray.' For a teacher she looked quite young, in her late 20's at most. Her black hair cascaded off her shoulders like a waterfall, matching up gracefully with her fighting-leather clad long limbs. 'Casavin and Saja, step forward, please.'

After checking the Libral Emblems of the two students, Sandoray looked at Saja. 'You are challenging a Grade 5 as a Grade 4? That's impressive.'

'What?' Saja was puzzled. 'We are both in Grade 4.'

'No, Casavin is in Grade 5.' Sandoray lifted Casavin's emblem. 'As is clearly shown here.'

'What?' Robert and Saja became anxious. 'Casavin, when did you level up to Grade 5? And you didn't tell us?'

'Well, you didn't ask.' Casavin shrugged his shoulders and sneered. Casavin's friends had to hold back their laughter; they were the only group of people who knew that Casavin had just upgraded in Fire. That's actually the reason why they had gone to Aquamarine Sky, to celebrate.

'Cheat!' Robert thundered.

'Watch your mouth, boy!' Casavin was upset. 'I didn't ask for the duel, he did!'

'This isn't fair. He tricked you!' Robert wanted to drag Saja

80

away. 'Screw this! Let's go.'

'Wow, look at these cowards.' Casavin burst into laughter. 'What happened to the "dare a one-on-one"? You dared me, remember? Now you want to run away again, just like last time?'

'Shut up, cheat!' Saja was caught off guard. He couldn't just walk away when so many were watching and whispering. 'Shame on you! Tricks are all you're capable of!'

'Enough, both of you. You are wizards, not shrews!' Sandoray shook her head on hearing all this. 'If you still have the guts for the duel, walk into the arena and sign the magic pact. If either is afraid, admit it and off you go.'

'Saja, don't go in there!' Robert tried to stop his friend, but Saja didn't really have much choice – Casavin's gang spared no effort in their mocking and sneering, and the whole crowd was watching – so he agreed to proceed.

Sandoray pulled out a piece of parchment and used her wand to point at it. The next second, her statement for the duel appeared on the parchment in words, as if she had written everything on it by hand. Casavin and Saja both pointed their wands at the pact; their signatures appeared below the statement, meaning they agreed to carry out the duel.

A magic pact was an oath from a wizard to the *God of Fate*, written in mind power; whoever signed it must fulfil the agreement in it. It's a serious thing for a wizard to sign a magic pact because there's no way to break it – the violator would sacrifice his soul and thus die, or become a soul-slave of the beneficiary party in the pact, if there's one.

In this case, there's no beneficiary party between Casavin and Saja because the pact was just to promise that they would have a match on this day; it didn't matter who was the winner. However, if either side refused to have the match or decided to postpone it, the immediate cost would be his life. Hence, because of the seriousness of a magic pact, when wizards made promises or pledges to each other, they always signed a pact so the deal became absolutely trustworthy.

'Why are you doing this? You heard us, Casavin set a trap for Saja!' Seeing that Sandoray was watching this happen without emotion, Robert was anxious. 'Why did you allow this to happen?'

'Because you boys are supposed to be righteous wizards, not

cowards that only dare to bully the weak.' Sandoray stared at Robert, expressionless. 'It's degrading to your position as a wizard if you look for troubles in the beginning, but quit later out of fear.'

'They are just kids, Sandoray. Kids make mistakes, and you should give them a break,' interjected another teacher named Thomas, who had heard all the commotion. He stood more than seven feet tall, with a square face and short golden hair. 'Improving in your Water magic has also given you a frozen heart. I'm a bit worried about you now.'

'I did offer that boy a chance to quit if he admitted his cowardice, but he's so peacockish to actually sign the pact. That's not merely a mistake, that's a big blunder,' Sandoray answered coldly. 'These kids need to learn that unless they are completely sure about something, *do not ever* sign a magic pact. Once a pact is signed, they are bound to it and have to fulfil it no matter what; even if it's unfair or has traps in the first place.'

'But Saja may get hurt.' Thomas frowned. 'And we are here for the purpose of protecting the students.'

'I'm protecting him from getting killed in the future by letting him get hurt a bit now,' Sandoray answered. 'Since when did you become such a pacifist?'

Thomas went quiet. He had to agree that Sandoray was actually right about this.

'Boy, you'd better try your best.' Meanwhile, Casavin was already on the stage inside the arena. 'Don't make it too easy for me.'

'Show me what you've got.' Saja stepped forward, knowing that there's no way back. The crowd was cheering for both sides, although few people believed Saja could win.

'Why don't you take the first move, as usual?' Casavin said. It's an unwritten rule that the side with the lower grade would have the attacking privilege, as a courtesy.

Saja didn't speak, but held his magic wand in his hand and started an incantation of Fire magic. He then waved his wand and a simple firebolt shot rapidly towards Casavin.

As a Fire wizard, Casavin could certainly tell that the incantation was a firebolt; he didn't even use magic to defend himself, but just moved his body sideways to dodge it. Seeing Casavin's obvious contempt, Saja felt insulted and began another incantation. Casavin recognized that Saja was summoning a much more powerful spell this time, so he became serious and started an incantation of his own.

The incantation didn't take long. Saja dashed forward to Casavin when he's about to finish the incantation, and cast a blast of flame rolling towards his rival. It's a *flamerush*, a spell ranked as Grade 4 in the institute. Casavin had to back off while chanting too, and a large ring of fire appeared around him right before the flamerush got him. The *firering* and *flamerush* collided with each other and vanished – they were of equal power.

Seeing that Casavin and Saja had a tied round, the crowd cheered aloud. Shortly after, Saja finished the preparation of his next attack, casting a number of firebolts in succession at Casavin. Casavin had not finished his incantation yet because it's more complicated, so he had to dodge erratically left and right. However, Saja's firebolt wave was more intense than Casavin had anticipated and his incantation was almost cut off while he's dodging.

Seeing how Casavin was suffering in the fight, the audience were amazed at Saja's performance and began to applaud. At the same time, Saja's next incantation was already underway as Casavin finally finished a Grade-5 spell – *double firering*. One firering emerged around Saja, encircling him around the middle, while the other one surrounded Casavin as protection. Having finished this, Casavin sniggered. 'Not bad, boy. But now you are trapped; once I tighten up the firering you are done! So yield now!'

Although encircled by the firering, Saja didn't seem to care about Casavin's warning. He speedily finished his fourth incantation and swung his wand – flamerush again, but more powerful than the last time. The flamerush pounced towards its target in the air and broke into Casavin's defensive firering. Casavin instantly used the defensive firering to intercept the invading flame, only to find that his ring vanished after a second but the flamerush was still coming at him, although weakened. Casavin was caught off guard and had to roll over on the floor to dodge it. But he didn't make it; his left arm got burned and black smoke billowed upward.

'Ahh!' Casavin couldn't hold back his cry of pain. A Grade-4 spell was no joke; it could certainly hurt, even kill if taken full on.

'Great job, Saja!' Robert led the cheering and part of the crowd joined in, while the other part was screaming at Casavin. Casavin was enraged by the sharp pain. Seeing that Saja was still preparing for his next spell, Casavin tightened up the firering surrounding Saja. Seeing that the flames would soon swallow Saja up, the crowd began screaming again.

Just as the raging flames overwhelmed Saja, there's a sizzling sound followed by a large cloud of vapour. The firering then vanished – it seemed like a Water spell!

'*Water-shield*? No way!' Everyone was surprised, including Casavin; but he quickly realised what had happened. 'It must be his magigear!' Just as Casavin was about to cast another spell, a new firering appeared around him.

'I'm sorry, Casavin, the magic pact didn't forbid the use of magigears.' Saja stepped out of the vapour, completely uninjured. 'Yes, I relied on my *Nymph's Guard*, but I beat you, after all.' Everyone suddenly noticed that Saja was wearing a silver necklace of some sort – the magigear that had cast the water-shield.

'Nymph's Guard! That's the name of the necklace?' In the crowd, Dileys' eyes were shining. The necklace looked beautiful, and it's an actual magigear that could cast spells. Soarame was also pretty taken by the necklace and whispered with his friends about it.

'Humph, I was wondering when you became a glorious Water!' Casavin mocked. 'But of course, it's only a trick after all.'

'Water beats Fire in this case, so I don't see your point.' Saja was tired, but couldn't help feeling cheerful because he's winning. 'Plus, you started the tricks – remember our grade difference?'

'Water beats Fire?' Casavin laughed. 'Give it a hundred years, newbie! I'll show you what real Fire magic is like!' With that, Casavin stamped his foot and suddenly a circle of flame emerged and extinguished the firering Saja had put around him.

This time it's Saja who was surprised. 'What's that?'

'Something you don't know, obviously.' Casavin wasn't happy and started his next incantation right away. 'Thanks for making me mad!'

Saja clenched his teeth and prepared for a final strike. In the meantime, the crowd was amazed by the appearance of Casavin's boots; even Thomas was staring at them and assessing them with Sandoray.

'You are right; the boots do look like *Trampling of Feriathan*,' Sandoray said to Thomas. 'But imitations of low quality.'

'Which is still surprising, don't you think?' Thomas sighed. 'These kids are just Grade 4 and 5, yet already they have magigears like that.'

'They are spoiled and don't even understand the rareness of magigears,' Sandoray scoffed, not impressed. 'Magigears are to save lives at the last minute, yet they use them in a show. What a shame!'

'It's the age of peace nowadays, my lady.' Thomas didn't quite agree with Sandoray. 'What you said was right once, but it's a heritage from the Great Libral's age.'

While the crowd was whispering, like Sandoray and Thomas, Casavin was trying very hard to chant the incantation; drops of sweat began to emerge on his forehead. Saja was also struggling; his face turned paler and paler, as he's exhausting all that he had.

'What's Casavin chanting this time?' Many began to wonder in the crowd, but no one seemed to know. On the contrary, everyone could tell that Saja was chanting the same incantation once again – it's another flamerush.

'Does Saja only know flamerush?' Jemario whispered to Soarame. 'He's been doing that all along. Casavin will win then.'

'No, it's hard to tell yet.' Soarame whispered back. With his eyes wide open, Soarame saw plenty of Fire elements aggregating rapidly around both Casavin's and Saja's wands. The power was pretty much equal, so it's really hard to predict the result of this ferocious battle.

Saja finally finished his last attack, his body shaking out of exhaustion. Knowing that Casavin would spare no efforts, Saja dared not waste time and swung his wand right away –

A huge flame roared out, searing and rushing at Casavin. This time it's far more than an ordinary flamerush; it's almost twice the normal size – a super flamerush. This final strike exhausted all of Saja's remaining power. Seeing the huge flame make its way over to Casavin, the crowd gave a collective cry – if it caught Casavin, it could burn him to ash. Sandoray looked serious too; she's ready to cut in and stop this dual.

'Eat it, *firefairy*!' roared Casavin at the last second. The Fire elements that Casavin had summoned rapidly aggregated in front of him and formed into a human figure – Casavin had finished his final spell too.

'A baby *firefairy*?' Sandoray was already on the stage to rescue Casavin, but stopped upon seeing this. 'Not every Grade-5 can summon a fairy, even a baby one... Casavin is actually not bad.'

Wooo — The baby fairy stood up, a weird roaring sound coming from its mouth. As the roar went on, the super flamerush rapidly weakened and finally was sucked into the fairy's mouth.

'What!' Saja's eyes widened; he couldn't believe what had just happened. The upgraded flamerush was his masterstroke, how could the baby-sized fairy swallow it just like that?

Surprisingly, by absorbing Saja's flamerush, the baby fairy grew bigger. Witnessing the sudden change in the situation and Casavin's obvious victory, the crowd gave their warmest applause. Saja's only option for the challenge was to yield, but Casavin wasn't pleased at all. He looked first at Saja, then at his fairy, and didn't know whether he should feel proud of his masterwork, or upset that the match had been much harder than he expected.

Soarame and the girls were also excited to see the entire battle. Soarame was actually thinking about something: the power of the magic elements summoned by Casavin and Saja were pretty much equal, but why did Casavin beat Saja so badly?

'Congratulations, Casavin.' Sandoray stepped into the arena and raised the magic pact parchment. The parchment suddenly started burning and completely vanished from sight, meaning the pact was fulfilled and both parties were released from it. After thunderous cheering for the winner, the crowd stepped forward and circled the firefairy for a closer look.

'Casavin, the competition is over, so how will you deal with your fairy?' Sandoray asked. 'You are not allowed to take it out of the arena.'

'I actually have a plan.' Hearing Sandoray's question, Casavin raised his head. 'I'd like to challenge you with the help of the fairy, ma'am!'

Hearing Casavin, the students were dumbfounded.

'What?'

'Really?'

Challenging a teacher? What a whimsical idea. It might not be the first time that a Libral student had ever challenged a teacher, but it's definitely a rare thing to see. The crowd stepped back from the stage and looked at Casavin and Sandoray. Soon enough, whispers sounded everywhere –

'I got it, Sandoray is a Water wizard!'

'Oh! No wonder Casavin dares! Plus, he already has the firefairy ready!'

'And thanks to Saja, the fairy actually became stronger than what he can manage to summon!'

Casavin heard the comments from the crowd and sneered. The crowd was right; this was exactly why he wanted to gamble. Now, the question was whether Sandoray was willing to take this unfair match; because once she did, Casavin could just let the fairy immediately charge at her – in that case, the match sort of became Sandoray vs Casavin plus Saja. Plus, Sandoray wouldn't even have a chance to prepare her spell.

Everyone soon figured out Casavin's plan and they were waiting for Sandoray's answer – she seemed to be pondering and looked worried. Seeing this, the students were convinced that she felt threatened by the fairy and wasn't confident about this challenge. The atmosphere therefore became embarrassing. The arena grew quiet, no one talked; only some faint breathing could be heard, and the sound of the burning flames on the firefairy.

'Casavin, you were exhausted in the last challenge, so it's an unfair challenge for you. Besides, the fairy is too weak; I wouldn't rely on it if I were you,' Sandoray said after a few seconds. 'Are you sure you want to challenge me?'

'What?' The crowd began whispering again. 'She actually said that? Unfair to Casavin?'

'Ma'am, feel free to destroy it if you think it's too weak,' Casavin raised his eyebrow. 'Now that it has been summoned, it's a shame not to make full use of it.'

Hearing that, Sandoray nodded. 'Fair enough. Go ahead once you are ready, then.'

'Okay... then can I attack now?' Seeing Sandoray standing there completely unprepared, not even taking a spell-casting stance, Casavin was feeling insulted and ready to show the lady some colours.

'Yes, go ahead or you won't have a chance later.' Sandoray didn't sound as if she cared at all.

'Okay, watch out then!' Casavin waved his wand and the firefairy charged at Sandoray. Sandoray simply raised her index finger and made a swinging motion with it, without chanting an incantation or even holding a magic wand.

In the next second, a bunch of long, thick ice arrows came out of nowhere, piercing the air and dashing towards the fairy with a *whoosh*.

'Ahh!' Casavin was knocked over before he had a chance to react; he didn't even know what had happened. Part of the crowd, however, was lucky enough to catch the sparkling view – the ice arrows pierced through the body of the firefairy in a blink and smashed into Casavin. In the next blink, Casavin was lying on the floor and Sandoray was just standing there; she didn't bother to look at her rival.

The whole crowd fell into complete silence, their mouths wide open. After lying on the floor moaning for a few seconds, Casavin tried hard to beat the killing pain all over his body; he felt that he might have some broken bones. After pulling his upper body off the ground, Casavin was astonished – his firefairy had shrunk to a quarter of its original size. The only explanation was that the ice arrows had extinguished most of it during the momentary contact.

'What was that!' Soarame would never have believed it had he not witnessed the whole thing with his own eyes. But then he recalled what his master had said before:

'Among different lineages of magic, there's no such thing as "stronger lineage" or "weaker lineage"; it's all up to wizards' power.'

'Different lineages have pros and cons, and they may counter one another in some cases, but no one is more powerful than another.'

'For those that naturally counter each other, such as Water vs Fire or Lightness vs Darkness, the one with greater power wins!'

'Casavin, you are blindly confident in Fire.' Sandoray was inscrutable, as always. 'I've seen lots of students like yourself; you didn't get the big picture. There has never been such a thing as a stronger or weaker lineage. Water magic is less powerful for attacking purposes only for Novices and Adepts, but not for an

Expert.'

Everyone was silent, witnessing the scary power of this beautiful yet cold lady. If not for having seen it with their own eyes, no one would believe this.

'As a student, being able to summon a fairy is impressive,' Sandoray continued. 'But in front of any teacher in the Institute of Libral, it's just too weak.' With that, Sandoray waved her hand; a blast of freezing air poured out from her palm and covered the little fairy. After a fierce sizzling, the fairy simply vanished.

After that, for the first time Sandoray chanted some incantations and a warm spray of mist covered Casavin. Casavin felt a gentle and refreshing wave flow down his body, after which all the burns and bruises started to heal.

Coming back to his senses, Casavin slowly got up and made sure he'd recovered. He had to admit that he's completely defeated. 'Ma'am, how could you summon that many ice arrows in a blink? Is it your magigear?'

'As a Grade 5, haven't you heard about *insta-cast*?' Sandoray asked in reply. Performing magic instantaneously, aka insta-cast, was one of the criteria for becoming an Expert wizard. Scankeen had told Soarame before that a magic hexagram, an incantation, together with a magic wand, were all supplementary means to strengthen magic power. Once one's power grew strong enough, the magic hexagram and incantation wouldn't be necessary. That's why senior wizards didn't need drawings or incantations when performing junior magic, just like what Sandoray had done.

'As a teacher in Water, I especially want to tell Water students about this. I know many students doubt the power of Water magic, but that's only because they haven't gotten to see the real world beyond the campus.' Sandoray looked around, verifying that everyone was paying attention. 'A Master of Water can summon thousands of ice arrows with a single hand wave! That spell is well accepted to be one of the scariest spells, called *purgatory storm*!'

The Water students burst out cheering loudly. The doubts in his heart against Water magic were gone. Although Soarame had known most of this from his master, he still couldn't help feeling proud. From this point on, Soarame couldn't wait to learn Water magic.

As the cheers faded away, the students spread out, leaving the arena and talking about what had happened along the way. The Water students, however, didn't leave but instead chose to have a party. They had seldom been as excited as they were on this day.

Soarame joined them as one of the proud Waters, but he wanted to use the restroom first. Just when he turned around to leave, he found his arm grabbed by someone from behind.

'Hey you, where are you going?' The voice was clear and sweet, with a hint of mischief. Upon hearing it, Soarame knew exactly who it was. Turning back, he found Jemario tugging his arm and smiling. Jemario's slender fingers slid along Soarame's arm, making him feel good for no reason he could understand. Soarame meant to say something, but found his mind sliding away at her touch; he just stood there and stared at Jemario with his mouth half-open.

Unconsciously, Soarame observed Jemario in detail: glossy lavender hair fell in waves around her exquisite cheeks, limpid eyes shining through her long lashes. Under the golden afterglow of the evening, Jemario's lavender dress shimmered as it clung delicately to her slender, fairy-like body. Everything about her seemed so perfect, causing Soarame to lose his mind, unable to do anything but keep staring in silence.

Under Soarame's stare, Jemario felt a little shy. 'Emm...'

Soarame suddenly came to his senses at that, his cheeks flushing. 'Sorry Jemario, that... err... that wasn't on purpose.'

'It's okay, don't worry.' Jemario was amused to see Soarame's reaction.

'I need to use the restroom... I'll be back in a minute,' Soarame said uncomfortably. He noticed a few girls were sniggering at him, so he hurried off towards the arena's exit.

'Hey, the restroom is the other way!' Jemario called out after Soarame, but he's already gone.

'How awkward!' Soarame ran aimlessly for a while and finally stopped, still unsure of the best thing to do.

Should I just leave like this? Should I go back? If I go back to Jemario, what should I say? Soarame pondered but didn't know what to do. While Soarame was immersed in his inner turmoil, he felt his sleeve grasped by a hand again.

'Hey you, where are you going?'

What? Really? Soarame couldn't help breathing heavily. *Jemario actually followed me here?*

However, the second that Soarame turned around, his heart sank. He's so disturbed that he had not even realised the voice was a boy's.

'What are you looking at?' The male student wasn't happy with Soarame's response – actually, his lack of a response. Soarame pulled himself together and looked up at the boy, who was nearly a head taller than him. 'Robert?'

Ever since earlier at Aquamarine Sky, Robert had been paying attention to Soarame – till the duel challenge was done and the Water party had started.

'Yes, Water Boy. It's me,' Robert sneered. 'Where are the girls? They ditched you?'

Soarame wasn't too stupid to figure out what's going. He tried to walk past Robert and ignore him, but Robert leaned over and nudged Soarame's chest with his shoulder.

'How dare you!' Soarame was offended. 'What do you want?'

'You don't turn your back on me, Water,' Robert challenged him, grabbing Soarame's shoulder.

'I just did. What can you do?' Soarame felt his temper flare. Ever since he'd started learning magic back at home, his master had banned him from using magic against people. Soarame had been bothered about that, especially when his hometown villagers insulted him at times. Robert's challenge felt like those old days, and Soarame would not tolerate it anymore.

'What can I do?' Robert sneered. He pulled out his magic wand. 'I want to make friends just like Casavin did! Do you dare to duel, Water?'

Before Soarame could say anything, a silvery voice rang through the air. 'Soarame! There you are! What are you doing here?'

'Vivarin?' Soarame was surprised to see that Vivarin was leading a bunch of girls towards him. 'What are you doing here?'

'Well, anything other than going to the restroom, apparently,' Vivarin teased Soarame, taking a glance at Robert. 'Is there a problem here?'

Robert was embarrassed, but before he figured out what to do, Soarame answered, 'No, we were just talking. I will be back in a minute.'

'No, it doesn't work that way.' Vivarin blocked Soarame. 'Someone just said he'd be back in a minute, but now it seems he's ditched his friends and is keeping them waiting.'

'Err... sorry!' Soarame scratched his head. 'Okay, then. Let's go.' Soarame stared at Robert and walked towards Vivarin.

'Really, Water Boy?' Robert was very unhappy to see Soarame walk away like this. 'I thought you were ready to duel, but you're going to let the girls call the shots for you?'

'Are you serious?' Before Soarame reacted, Vivarin cut him off. 'As a Grade 4, you challenge a fresher for a duel? Why don't you go after Casavin? Your friend just got his butt kicked, thanks to you!'

'Shut up, this is none of your business!' Robert was upset for Vivarin poking right at his sensitive spot – he's indeed the instigator of everything that had happened today.

'Don't you talk to my friend like that,' Soarame said coldly as he stared at Robert. 'You saw Casavin lose badly, and you still have problems with Water?'

'Oh wait, I never said I had a problem with Water.' Robert was clever enough not to break the rules of the school. 'Now that Water is so great, why don't we have a duel?'

FOR THE FRESHERS

'You got it.' Soarame glared at Robert. 'We will have a duel when I reach Grade 4 in Water.' Although Soarame had promised to keep his Wind magic secret, he so wanted to teach this Robert a lesson.

'Soarame, that's nonsense!' Vivarin exclaimed. Although Vivarin had witnessed Casavin's loss, she did not think Water could beat Fire at a low level.

'Ha ha, nice try.' Robert laughed. 'By then it will be long after I have graduated!'

'No, you won't.' Soarame was confident that he could reach Grade 4 in Water soon, because his mind ocean was already at Grade 4, enabling him to cast Grade-4 Water spells once he learnt them. It's the same reason why Casavin had achieved Grade 5 in Fire quicker than people expected – his mind ocean was Grade 5 thanks to his practice in Earth, so all he needed to do was to familiarise himself with Fire spells.

'Oh, really?' Robert sneered. 'If you are sure about it, why don't we sign a magic pact?'

'No! Don't you dare sign one, Soarame!' Vivarin was anxious and burst out in anger. 'Go away, Robert! I'll report you to the school for this!'

'I won't sign any pact with you because you don't deserve it.' Soarame squinted at Robert. 'But you have my word – you and me, we will have a duel upon either your graduation or my Grade 4, whichever comes first.'

'You got it!' Robert was excited to hear this. He didn't expect Soarame to keep his part of the bargain, but this boy was actually stupid enough to do so.

'Soarame, what the heck is wrong with you!' On the way back to the arena, Vivarin complained. 'I know you are confident and you made it into Spanflow, but Water simply is not a match for Fire at Grade 4!'

'Relax. I can handle it.' Soarame smiled reassuringly at her but didn't explain.

After getting back to the party, the first thing Vivarin did was spread the news to every one of her friends – including Jemario, Dileys, and Catheray. The Water students were all worried and kept trying to think of a solution; the mood of the party was dampened because of this. Soarame felt sorry for being a party-pooper, but at the same time he's very touched that his Water mates actually cared about him like this.

Welcome to the Water family! As Soarame recalled the scene at Aquamarine Sky, he thought that this did feel like a family. The boy had to admit that he's starting to feel that he belonged here, and he couldn't wait for the next couple of days – he would enjoy the special flight of his bedroom tomorrow!

****

The next morning, Soarame opened the door and saw the four Water girls from the restaurant yesterday. 'Soarame, thanks for inviting us!'

'You're welcome.' Soarame let the girls in. It's the dorm-flight day; each fresher was allowed to have a maximum of four guests enjoy the flight with him, so Soarame had invited Dileys, Jemario, Vivarin and Catheray.

'Chelonad, we are ready, please take us away!'

'Hmm... Soarame, you make friends quickly.' Chelonad's voice sounded. 'Okay, enjoy your flight!'

'Yeah!' As the crew cheered, the unit began to shake a little then floated up steadily. Everyone inside the unit could feel that they were rising and saw from the window that the ground was falling away from them below.

The five of them walked to the windows, watching the trees becoming smaller and smaller, and enjoying the mild breeze coming from outside. The unit's square and had two windows, one each in adjacent walls.

'Why are the two window walls next to each other?' Soarame wouldn't have paid attention to this if not for the wind blowing in. 'Wouldn't it be better if they face each other?'

'You'll see the reason very soon,' said Dileys mysteriously.

'Anyway, this is incredible!' Soarame marvelled, standing by the window. The girls agreed, thinking Soarame was talking about the beautiful scene outside. They didn't really understand Soarame's true meaning – in Soarame's special vision, the unit suddenly started glowing green when the flight started. Soarame had thought that if there's any colour coming out of the wall it would have been grey – meaning Wind; yet his eyes were telling him otherwise.

Energy of Life? Soarame was astonished as he recalled his master's words on the trip mere days ago. *And the room itself is actually a magigear?*

Because Soarame had promised his master that he would keep his special eyes top secret, he couldn't share this discovery with his friends. *But this is unbelievable!* No matter how much Soarame was dying to shout about his discovery, he had to keep his observation to himself. Vivarin noticed Soarame's wide eyes and flushed face; she chuckled and told Soarame to relax. But Soarame ignored her; he put both of his hands on the wall next to the window he stood at, trying to secretly feel the Energy of Life within it.

A magigear? The entire room? Soarame seemed to be looking outwards and enjoying the view, but he's actually concentrating on the feeling from the wall. *Whoever made this happen must be a genius! Is it Chelonad?*

No one could answer Soarame, and, unfortunately, he couldn't ask anyone, Chelonad included. The magic world was truly miraculous though, and Soarame couldn't be more eager to grade up and become capable of exploring the truth behind it.

'Soarame, what are you staring at for this long?' Vivarin patted Soarame's shoulder and startled him out of his thoughts. 'Wow, you are really immersed! What are you thinking?'

'He must be peeking at some pretty girl down there,' Catheray teased. 'Tell us which one?'

'No, no way.' Soarame blushed, and glanced at Jemario unconsciously. This brief action didn't escape the girls' attention; they all looked at Jemario, winking and chuckling.

Jemario blushed too as a consequence. She's shy enough to change the subject right away. 'Look, that's the lake! My favourite part of campus!'

'And that's the Water department!' Dileys pointed at a giant building that looked like an enormous blue crystal cluster, surrounded by a group of other buildings that looked like smaller crystals. As the unit flew by them, the halo shining from the "crystals" dazed Soarame and made him wow; he already started imagining the scene of himself having classes there.

As the unit flew, it passed all of the seven departments. The Fire department building looked like a sheet of orange flames spreading over its territory; the buildings in the Wind department were all a cool, metallic grey in colour and streamlined in appearance, in sharp contrast to the bulk and dense feeling of the Earth department's squat buildings of mud brick. Buildings in the Lightness department were made of unidentifiable materials that changed their colours when observed from different angles; the Darkness department was just the opposite – the imposing buildings were all black, and the friends couldn't find the doors and windows in them. The last one they passed was the Lightning department, the only department that had just one building – it's a skyscraper, tall and thin with its glassy facade. Vivarin commented how she had always wanted to climb to the top of it – it must be a marvellous view of the entire campus.

It's about the lunch time, and Soarame noticed that the unit's approaching an area that looked very different to the department sections. 'What's that?'

'It's the town zone.' Catheray said. 'The morning tour only covered the students' zone, which is restricted to wizards only. There's a town on campus too, and it's very different – most people there are not wizards; it's almost like another Cylone City! You will be amazed.'

'How big is this campus after all?' Soarame couldn't help asking.

'It's big enough for you to have more fun than you can handle. In fact, we seldom go out to Cylone because we don't need to,'

Jemario claimed excitedly. 'The students' zone has all kinds of clubs to join; they hold a lot of events and activities. The town has so much going on too; lots of students get jobs there for practise.'

'Jobs?' Soarame's eyes brightened. 'I want to find a job too, to make some money.'

'Already? You just got here!' Dileys was surprised. 'What kind of job are you looking for?'

'I don't know, but I want to have a look and choose.' Soarame scratched his head.

'Okay, we are going to land in the town zone for lunch anyway, so let's go and find out. I suggest picking some work where you can practise magic at work.' Dileys took out a booklet from her bag – it's a list of regular job openings. 'I got myself a gardening job, because I can practise with Water while I'm doing it.'

'That's cool. But don't all jobs require magic here?'

'No, most jobs here are ordinary, as most people in town are not wizards.' Dileys explained some of the basics as she's paging through the booklet. 'Let's see... chop firewood? Carry timber? No, the age limit is older and it's probably better for Wind students... Library work? Mail delivery? These are fine, but are not relevant to Water magic... How about washing dishes or mopping floors? These could suit you.'

'No thanks... I've done that at home. Are there any fun jobs?' Soarame was a bit disappointed to see that most of the interesting jobs were for older students.

'Fun jobs?' The girls went further through the booklet with Soarame for a little while until he poked his finger at a listing.

'How about this?' Soarame appointed at a job listed as "Ice engraving – helper. Minimum age: 12. Minimum school grade: 1." According to the description, this job was to help the engraver artist prepare ice cubes, cut roughcasts, sand the work and so on, so that it could be exhibited to the public when it's ready. This looked very interesting to Soarame, as he had always appreciated the few arts in his village – especially because he had been living with Filton, a carpenter.

After the unit landed by the edge of the town zone, they got to the engraver's studio following the instructions in the booklet. The studio wasn't a giant building; in size it's similar to Filton's, but well decorated with intricate stone carvings of strange beasts and plants lining every window and accentuating the support pillars.

Soarame was excited. 'I can't believe we actually have an art studio here!'

'I know, right? The campus is big and has a lot of different things,' Vivarin agreed. 'This is just the edge of the town. There's a lot more to see further inside the town. You'll be impressed when we get there.'

'How can I help you?' A middle-aged man with brown mustachios came up to greet the friends soon after they walked into the studio building. Dileys introduced Soarame as a new student looking for a job. The man, Dafinol, was impressed by Soarame's eagerness and happily showed them around his workshop as the three of them talked and got to know each other.

Dafinol explained how he had conceived this studio and all the tools he used inside of it. The sculptor was very easy-going and showed the two to his exhibition room, so that Soarame could see if he liked his place. The room was freezing, and they saw lines of ice sculptures ranging from barely formed blocks of ice to intricately detailed on the tables there.

'You can touch them if you want,' Dafinol suggested. 'They won't melt as long as you don't hold them for too long.'

Soarame put his hands gently on a sculpture of a dragon. He recognized this one at first glance, and he's impressed by the mighty-looking of it. Upon physical contact through his bare hands, Soarame could feel the extremely slow but steady movement of Water elements within the sculpture, as if they were trying to talk to Soarame and convince him that they were alive. Soarame suddenly had a feeling that if he's able to guide them, they were ready to follow his will.

'You like dragons?' Dafinol seemed proud of this work, which he called "Dragon Roar". He's glad to see Soarame so entranced by it.

'Ahh, yes of course.' Soarame woke up from his thoughts. 'It's so vivid and alive – did you ever see a live dragon before?'

'I wish,' Dafinol sighed. 'But I've only seen pictures.'

'They are dangerous,' said Jemario, as every wizard was told. 'You are not afraid to see a real one?'

'No, if I could get to see a real one, I'd happily do anything in exchange.' There's fanaticism in Dafinol's eyes. 'I live for carving and would die for carving. That's what I do with my life. If I could see a real dragon and make a sculpture of it, I would never regret it no matter what.'

As they enjoyed their conversations, Dafinol confirmed his willingness to take on Soarame as his helper, so he would work in the engraving studio on the weekends. As for the salary, Dafinol was generous enough to offer ten gold coins a day, which was more than Soarame had expected – very soon, he would be able to send money to Filton!

'This job is fun, right?' Everyone was happy that Soarame had got what he wanted. 'And there are a lot more going on here. The campus is as much fun as Cylone City.'

'Oh right, it does look like Cylone City – is this a bank?' Soarame asked as they walked past a big beige stone building decorated with red diamonds. 'I have some coins in my dorm to deposit.'

'No, it's an office of the Cylone Auction Hall. People can deposit their works here so that they don't have to go out to Cylone for the auction every time,' Dileys explained. 'Dafinol must be familiar with it; I bet his sculptures are popular there.'

'How much does a sculpture usually fetch?'

'That I don't know, but it won't be cheap.' Catheray suddenly thought of something. 'Soarame, if you can carve your own work, you'll make a lot more money.'

'Oh yes! Why didn't I think of that?' Soarame was enlightened. 'I'll ask Dafinol if he's willing to teach me.'

The friends enjoyed their lunch together in the town, and went back to Soarame's unit to continue their flight. Though it's smaller and less busy than Cylone City, it still captivated Soarame with numerous restaurants boasting dishes from every corner of the Arkwald Empire and every profession needed for a self-sufficient town. Soarame enjoyed the tour and found all kinds of interesting things to see and try. Upon Jemario's insistence, Soarame even had got his hair cut and now looked even cuter, with his hair tamed to fall just above his eyes.

The unit flew for another couple of hours after the friends left the town zone, and it began to descent. Dileys looked at Soarame. 'We are about to land! How do you like it?'

'It's amazing,' Soarame said somewhat distractedly, looking at the wall once again.

'There's more amazing things ahead!' Jemario cut in. 'See that house there? I bet that's where we're landing.'

'Oh yes, it seems everyone is waiting for us,' Vivarin said. There's a group of students surrounding a house not too far away; it's the lower part of a complete house, with its first floor a square shape but the roof wide open. Soarame could see the furniture and shared living areas from the air. Beside the house were three units that looked similar to Soarame's; the doors on the units were open, so the group must have come from those units.

'Look, he's here, finally!' Just then, a loud voice sounded from somewhere among the students. Although there's still quite a distance to go, Soarame could hear the voice clearly. The next second, a chubby boy with golden hair walked out from the crowd, followed by two others.

'Hey man!' The boy shouted really loudly as Soarame's unit floated closer. 'Come out here already!'

Soarame's unit landed beside the house to the applause and cheering from the crowd. Soarame felt suddenly shy, but he had to go out in front because he's the focus right then. 'My name is Soarame, nice to meet you all!'

'Soarame, it's good to meet you! My name is Kardiac, your roommate.' The chubby boy immediately came up and shook Soarame's hands with a warm, two-handed grip. Then he looked past Soarame and puzzled for a second. 'Oh dear… all girls, really? You are the man!' he exclaimed, releasing Soarame's hands to clap him on the back.

'Err…' Soarame wasn't sure how to respond, and everyone chuckled. Kardiac was round all over, but judging from the speed with which he came out of the group, he's quite nimble and light on his feet. His golden hair shone in the sun, the freckles on his face making him look both amiable and funny.

A boy with square features came up from behind Kardiac. 'My name is Halgon, nice to meet you all.' He had a square-shaped face with bright eyes, dark bushy eyebrows matching his close-cropped black hair, and a healthy glow to his tanned skin, looking quite masculine and rough compared to Soarame's light skin and delicate appearance.

The last roommate was a handsome yet almost fragile-looking boy in fashionable silk clothes, his demeanour gentle and quiet. His sapphire blue hair fell around matching sapphire eyes in a delicate face. He extended a hand to Soarame, his movements almost shy. 'Omifo.'

After everyone else had introduced themselves, the students spent time getting to know each other, especially the four roommates. The school was considerate enough to have prepared food and drink on the main floor of the dorm house to encourage the students' social life from the very beginning of their time at school. Four freshers meant sixteen guests, which made a good size and a lively atmosphere for a house-warming party.

'Soarame, if you are from the Corrugon Peninsula, it must be easy for you to come here,' Omifo said, drinking some orange juice. 'You are almost a local.'

'Not exactly, I spent a month on the way!' Soarame couldn't help sighing, as he's reminded that Filton must be still on his way back.

'Only a month and you are complaining?' Halgon shook his head. 'Do you know how long it took me to get here? Five months!'

'Are you serious?' Soarame was surprised. 'Halgon, where're you from?'

'Moniton Empire, Knighton Continent,' Halgon said. 'Between Knighton and Thundeross, there's the Azure Ocean – it took much time to cross it.'

'Halgon, five months is not too bad, given that distance. I live nearer, but took longer than that because I had to bypass several magimal colonies along the way!' said Kardiac. 'I was just a kid when I started travelling!'

'You still are,' Catheray cut in as she came over. 'Oops, I just overheard you, sorry.'

'Well, apologies accepted, as long as you tell me how old you are.' Kardiac blinked at Catheray. 'I'm a kid? I'm thirteen! I bet you are younger.'

'You wish, I'm not telling you my age,' Catheray chuckled. In fact, Catheray had just turned thirteen, but she came to school early and was already a Grade 3. Among Dileys' best friends, their ages ranged from Jemario at twelve to Vivarin at fourteen. The only one in Grade 4 was Dileys, who was also fourteen. Similarly, Soarame's roommates were all about the same age.

'Guys, shall we call Chelonad now? The house is still not assembled yet,' suggested Vivarin, running over.

'OK, guys, you ready for the new house?' Chelonad's voice sounded soon enough. 'You can go into the house or the units and watch from inside, if you want.'

Everyone picked their preferred spot and got ready to witness the due assembly. Soarame and his roommates ran back into their units, and most of the guests went into the ground floor of the house. The boys picked their favourite corners for their units, and Chelonad flew the units up again and allocated them accordingly over the first floor; the units then became the bedrooms. Soarame finally understood why the windows in his unit were in adjacent walls – these two walls became the exterior walls of the building, so that the other two became interior walls.

Soarame opened his bedroom door and found himself next door to Kardiac and opposite Halgon – on the other side of a gap. Looking downwards, Soarame saw their guests spread out on the ground floor looking up at them.

'Now what?' asked Soarame. 'How do we get down there?'

Right after he voiced his question, Soarame's bedroom started shaking slightly and green light – that only he could see – glowed out of the walls. The floor then began to stretch out and connected to Halgon's stretching floor, and filling up the gap in between. The boys then walked out of their bedrooms and into the corridor; Soarame carefully jumped and stamped on the floor, to confirm that it's strong enough to hold them. At the same time, they saw the ceiling of the house forming too – the bedroom roofs stretched out and attached themselves together to form the ceiling of the entire house, blocking out the sunlight which had lit the open space just moments before. Soarame touched the magic symbol on the wall, which lit the ceiling up and the house became bright again.

'This is awesome!' Kardiac marvelled. 'We actually built the upper floor just like that!'

The next second, Soarame's and Kardiac's bedrooms shook and split from each other, a gap emerging in between them; the edge of the corridor by the gap began to extend downwards, forming a staircase leading down to the ground floor. The boys went down the staircase and saw their friends waiting in the living room, all cheering. 'Welcome to Libral!'

'Wow!' The four fresher boys were excited. 'So the house can actually change shapes?'

'Not only that. Your bedrooms can move around once a year, if you want to swap positions later,' another student explained. 'And if any of you grade up, you can choose to upgrade the style of the house. For example, you can choose to add a fireplace in the living room wall – that's a popular option.'

'You can change the exterior, too,' Jemario followed up. 'Remember the dorms we saw during the flight? They all look different because most of them have been upgraded.'

'We can even change the dorm to be round?' Omifo asked. 'I saw some round ones during the flight.'

'Yes you can, but you don't want to,' another student chuckled. 'My friends did that, and they regret it, because a round shape doesn't really work that well for rooms. And changing shapes is a major upgrade, so they cannot change it back until they all grade up one more time.'

'That's sad.' Vivarin was amused. 'Also, if you win prizes from the school, that sometimes gives you extra upgrade opportunities.'

The house-warming party went on for the rest of the day, and the guests didn't leave until late evening. After that, Soarame could finally do something that he hadn't had a chance to do during the day. Putting his hands on the wall, Soarame tried to focus and feel the Energy of Life rippling inside the wall. *There are so many dorm houses on campus – does that mean Chelonad is the owner of all of them? That kind of makes sense, because he's the security guy...*

Soarame tried to communicate with the energy over and over again in different ways, but all of his attempts failed. Feeling frustrated, Soarame finally had to give up.

It's ok. I'm living here from now on, so no rush. Soarame comforted himself and pressed the magic symbol beside the bed. The ceiling light switched off and Soarame took a deep breath, falling almost instantly asleep.

The next day, Soarame woke up to find it's already noon. He finished lunch quickly with his roommates, and the boys went to

Spanflow Hall. There were already quite a few students there, both old and new, in smart suits, standing around and chatting. Soarame's crew didn't know anyone here yet, but the older students were all warm-hearted and out-going; they came up to talk to the freshers to help them feel comfortable. Soon enough, Soarame got to know quite a few new faces and made some friends.

Just then, a student came by and delivered a message. 'Soarame, someone is waiting for you outside. He said his name is Casavin. He's from another college, so he can't come in here.'

'You are popular!' Omifo patted Soarame's shoulder. 'The school year hasn't really started yet, but you already have so many friends from other colleges?'

'Yeah! Especially yesterday, all those pretty girls!' Kardiac winked at Soarame.

'No, this one is a troublemaker, not a friend.' Soarame wondered why Casavin had come for him, but he still stood up and walked towards the door.

'Wait. A troublemaker?' Kardiac stood up too. 'We will go together, then.'

'No, don't worry, I'll be back in a minute.' Soarame was happy about Kardiac's sense of their brotherhood.

'Are you sure?' asked Halgon. 'We will go check it out if you don't come back soon.'

'Alright, thanks!' Soarame felt reassured by his friends' words and walked towards the door confidently.

'Soarame, I'm here to apologise! I'm sorry, okay?' The second Soarame stepped out of the dining hall, Casavin's words surged into his ears out of nowhere. Before Soarame could even see him clearly, Casavin had already turned and was walking away, leaving a puzzled Soarame rooted to the spot.

'Dean O'heven sent him to apologise,' A mature voice said from behind him. 'Soarame, I must say you surprised me.'

'Rodka?' Soarame turned around and was surprised to see Rodka standing there.

'Remember the other day at the college application?' Rodka waved his hand vaguely in Casavin's direction. 'I went after Casavin, but it's hard to get an apology from him, even for me. But you just made it happen.'

'I did?' Soarame puzzled. 'How?'

'By what you did the other day in the interview,' Rodka smiled. 'You've been keeping yourself busy, huh? I heard you even accepted the challenge from Robert.'

'How do you know all this?' Soarame was surprised.

'People talk,' Rodka winked at Soarame. 'The school year hasn't started yet but you're already famous.'

'No way...' Soarame wasn't sure if this was a good thing. 'How do you know about the interview, anyway? Plus, I didn't mention Casavin's name back there.'

'I know, our Dean told me. And locating Casavin is not hard for Dean O'heven.' Rodka patted Soarame's shoulder. 'Oops, the event is starting, let's go.'

'You are familiar with the Deans?' Soarame was surprised but didn't have time to ask, because in the hall Dean Romboton was already stepping onto the stage to host the event.

'Everyone, attention please.' The Dean's loud baritone sounded from the stage, causing everyone to quiet down. 'Tonight is the welcoming night for the new students. Let's start this with our warmest applause for them!'

'As is tradition, it is my duty and pleasure to introduce the history of Spanflow College, as a core part of the Institute of Libral, to the new students.' Hearing the cheering and applause that erupted, Dean Romboton carried on. 'Our college was founded by the Great Libral three thousand years ago, as the oldest college in our institute.'

'Every year, we gather everyone in our college for this ceremony, to review the long-passed history.' Seeing many new students impressed at the number three thousand, the dean wasn't sure if he should be feeling proud or worried – most students seemed to have forgotten about their history lessons, or they hadn't cared about it. 'If you are not familiar with the past, today you've come to the right place. Today, we will witness it all together – the history full of darkness but also glory!'

'Witness?' Soarame was paying enough attention to have captured this unusual word.

'For the older students, you've seen this part before, because we have been doing this every year, and we will keep doing it in the future – why?' Dean Romboton paused deliberately for effect.

'Because we are wizards! We carry great responsibilities since the day we came into existence! We must remember firmly where we are from, and how we came to be here!' The dean was becoming effusive. 'We must memorize this till the last day we may live: We are the glory of mankind! We are the future of the world! We are the guardians of the peace of the entire human world!'

Cheering, whistles, and applause peaked, one wave after another, and the Dean seemed satisfied. 'Now, let's use our own eyes to see what exactly happened three thousand years ago, before the era of mankind started!'

As he finished speaking, everybody suddenly felt their body become light, and as a group they all rose into the air. With a wave of cheering and screaming, they floated higher and higher, until they were near the ceiling of the hall.

'I'm flying!' many new students shouted joyfully, but their voices were not a match for Kardiac's.

'Soarame, look at me already!' Kardiac laughed as he turned a somersault in the air.

'Yes, I know,' Soarame said, amused. He's also surprised to find himself flying effortlessly, but since he had experiences like this with Scankeen, he didn't feel inclined to over-react. Soarame looked around and realized most of the older students were reacting much like himself. As for his roommates, Omifo was just as excited as other new students, although less so than Kardiac. Halgon seemed to be more like the older students, with little excitement showing on his face.

Just then, the light suddenly went off, plunging the entire hall into darkness. Next, a dim light came out from somewhere, together with a large burst of fog. Soarame realized that he's floating in the fog together with everyone else though he could barely see them, and that they couldn't see anything else of their surroundings.

'As wizards, the first thing you need to know is: there are six continents in the world. Their names are Thundeross, Snowhill, Knighton, Rainbow, Holiness, and Allsouls.' As Dean Romboton spoke, the fog below them dispersed, revealing six discs of different shapes. Soarame was smart enough to recognize that the discs were holograms, just like what his master used to teach him ever since his first Wind lesson. The discs looked to Soarame as if they were very far under them, and he's floating above them in the fog.

'Now, you are looking at the six continents. Thundeross, Snowhill, Knighton and Rainbow Continents are dominated by mankind, and they basically constitute the entire human world.' As Dean Romboton continued, four discs lit up and flew towards the students one by one in a curving path. As they flew by, they expanded rapidly along the way. When they reached Soarame, they had become enormous and borderless, as if they were going to become real continents.

'Since three thousand years ago, human empires and kingdoms, both big and small, have been founded on different continents – some became powerful and enormous, some suffered from all kinds of problems. Most big empires were peaceful and prosperous, but some small kingdoms in chaotic areas could disappear or appear overnight.'

Soarame gasped as the discs expanded to be overwhelming. Dean Romboton went on. 'Our school is located within a very powerful empire, named Arkwald Empire…'

Soarame nodded silently while listening. Although he had heard similar stories from his master, Scankeen hadn't used such a vivid display to show him all that. At the moment, Soarame's eyes were locked on the stylised discs representing Thundeross Continent, which had floated above the other discs to come to a rest right under the students. On it, countless small humps were forming – they represented cities and towns, the civilization of mankind.

'For those of you who live on Thundeross, feel free to ask your Libral Emblem to highlight your hometown on the hologram.' As the dean spoke, the disc for Thundeross took on the appearance of an actual landmass, and stopped underneath the gathered floating students. Many new students hurriedly took out their emblems and different spots on the landmass started to glow, with the students' names overlaying their hometowns. Soarame found his name at an unimpressive location at a corner of Corrugon Peninsula. He noticed that there were no models representing cities anywhere near his village. Yet, further away, cities and towns of different scales appeared in clusters large and small.

'This outline is the national boundary line of Arkwald Empire.' the dean continued, and a red line appeared on the landmass, encircling about one third of the entire Thundeross Continent. Soarame counted and realized that not many students were from Arkwald; most students from Thundeross Continent lived in other countries.

The Thundeross landmass kept expanding, causing the students to feel as though it's going to push them into the ceiling. Soon enough, their entire field of vision was occupied by Arkwald Empire, and the landmass stretched as far as they could see. Soarame could see all kinds of different geography within the territory of Arkwald, as detailed as if he were floating above it high in the sky.

A big city in the northern part of Arkwald shone red. The model of this city was clearly more complex than others, indicating its prosperity and significance. 'The shining red city is the Headquarters of Sunrise Alliance, which is right next to the Capital of Arkwald Empire. The green city is where we are right now. So you can see how far your hometown is from these two places.' At the same time, a green city in the middle of the country also shone – the Cylone City. Soarame now clearly saw that his hometown was far from both, in a rural area.

After leaving some time for everyone to watch and marvel, the Thundeross landmass began to shrink in size, and its edge appeared once again in people's vision as it reverted to its disc form. Soarame quickly looked to the Arkwald capital, only to see that it had become a dot. He tried to look for his hometown again, but how could he still see it when even the capital was so small?

'Such a big continent…' Soarame marvelled, thinking that the world was so very big, yet his parents were nowhere to be found; he started to feel bad, and his attention wandered from the ceremony. By the time he came back from his disturbed thoughts, the dean had finished introducing the other three continents. The four continents then flew away from the students to join the other two. Altogether, they formed a flat, disc-filled version of the current world map.

'Why does the map only show the four human continents?' Omifo couldn't help muttering. 'What are on the other two?'

THE UNIQUE WIZARD

'Good question. On the other two continents, there's a forgotten history!' Dean Romboton answered, surprising Omifo that he had clearly heard him. 'The key point of this ceremony is to show you that part of history, so pay attention and watch it carefully now!'

With that, the models representing human civilizations on the continents began to shrink rapidly. Seconds later, all of those models were gone, leaving only primeval forests, mountains and prairies, as if the time was flowing backwards to ancient times.

'What's that?' Someone suddenly called out – on every continent, there emerged a number of model animals of a similar appearance. They looked like different coloured lizards, but each of them possessed a large pair of wings on its back.

'These are...' Omifo's eyes widened as he recalled that he'd seen them before. 'Dragons?'

'Count them – how many different colours are there?' Dean Romboton's words verified Omifo's guess. Soarame was staring at the model dragons like everyone else, and nodded silently – over the years his master had told him that, before the human world was established, it's the dragon clans that had dominated all the six continents. But this was the first time that Soarame saw it in such a vivid way; the model dragons spreading all over the place looked stunning to him.

'Red, yellow, blue, grey, purple, white, black – seven colours!' someone yelled loudly. 'The same as with the magic element colours!'

'Exactly. The clan of dragons have seven sub-groups, each with guaranteed born-gifts of the corresponding magic lineage as their primary lineage,' Dean Romboton's voice echoed in the fog. 'That doesn't mean a dragon only has gifts in their primary lineage though. Most dragons have gifts in more than one lineage, and the strongest ones could have all seven – those are called *top-tier dragons*. So far, top-tier dragons are the only creatures that we know of to have gifts in all seven lineages!'

All the new students looked shocked; they hadn't heard all this much. 'Top-tier dragons... how strong!' someone gasped.

'They were more than strong. They were scary, and horrible – not only the top-tier ones, but any dragon. Dragons used to be the rulers of the six continents, enslaving all other species, including mankind.' Dean Romboton said deeply. 'They didn't only have great magic gifts, but also possessed incredibly tough bodies – bodies that were tougher than most weapons. So, in the times of savagery and fighting, dragons ruled the world. They enslaved not only mankind, but also orcs, elves, druids and all kinds of magimal species...'

'What!' Someone muffled a shout of surprise. 'Orcs? Elves?'

'See them for yourselves.' As Dean Romboton waved his hands, more models of different colours and shapes appeared among the dragons. At the same time, the Thundeross Continent landmass flew up towards the students again, and it expanded even more drastically this time. As it got closer and larger, Soarame felt as if he's falling onto the landmass. Fortunately, the hologram didn't crash into them; instead, the landmass enlarged, it became a vivid land with clear scenery. Right then, the students were all floating in the sky above a mountainous area, exclaiming loudly as they marvelled.

'Now, we are going to visit an orc tribe – remember there's a model orc on the plate?' Listening to the dean, Soarame recalled that, as the plate was enlarged, they had been indeed heading towards a green model of a human-like shape – it must be an orc. Right then, the model became a cluster of tents by the mountain, with some sort of symbolic patterns on them.

'That's their totem,' Dean Romboton explained, referring to the patterns on the tents. Everyone was staring at the orcs, muffling their shocked reactions one after another. As the dean brought the students in closer as they were "flying" by, the orcs could be clearly seen – their skin was mostly green, their muscles a lot more significant than humans and they had scary fangs in their mouths.

By the edge of the tribe, a team of orc warriors were besieging an elephant-sized animal. An orc warrior missed his strike, so his mace hit a stone and smashed it into pebbles.

As the students were frightened by the strong orc warrior, the dean's voice rang out again. 'This is an ordinary orc tribe. Orcs are naturally-born warriors because of their muscular bodies, but they are less capable of using magic. That said, there were still some orc wizards too, and most of them were Earth wizards...'

Dean Romboton didn't spend long on the orc tribe. He soon flew the students away from it, heading towards the forest atop the mountain next to the tribe, flying through all kinds of large and tall trees. From time to time, Soarame caught the flash of a scene of different animals through the tree leaves, many of which appeared dangerous and powerful at a glimpse – they must be wild magimals of some kind. Soon enough, they arrived at the central part of the mountain, and Soarame was sensitive enough to notice the abnormal quietness of this place, as a sharp contrast to the previous busy magimal areas of the forest.

'Why is there nothing here?' someone asked.

'Because this area belongs to a powerful creature. He's the lord of the mountain and he banned everyone from getting close, because he's sleeping,' said Dean Romboton. 'He's right there, just on top of that peak.' At that, everyone looked towards the highest part of the mountain looming above them.

'Sleeping?' someone else couldn't help asking. 'He's sleeping over there; why does he need to vacate such a large place here?'

'That's why we don't like him – he's brutal and arbitrary.' Dean Romboton sighed. He sped up their flight again, towards the peak this time. Soon enough, as they rose above the peak, Soarame's sight locked on a gigantic body that's being revealed bit by bit –

A dark red body, ten times bigger than the biggest orc warrior, was lying on its stomach. To Soarame, it looked exactly the same as Dafinol's dragon sculpture, the big wings on its back vibrating along with its regular breaths. The creature's exhalations were powerful enough to shake the nearest trees back and forth, the noise echoing around, and a wave of panic rushed through every new student.

'A dragon!' Kardiac screamed, along with many others.

'It's a common red dragon, not even close to one of the top-tiers.

But he's still the most powerful being within this vast area.' Dean Romboton said. 'Not only the countless magimals in the forest down there's ruled by him, the orc tribe was also. We just saw the orcs hunting the elephant – they were trying to use it to pay their tribute to the dragon, in exchange for not being eaten after it wakes up.'

'So, it just eats and sleeps, sleeps and eats?' Omifo was relieved to see the dragon didn't wake up. 'If it wakes up to find no food, it eats orcs?'

'That's why I told you dragons were bloody and savage,' Dean Romboton's baritone voice echoed in the space. 'They ruled the entire world this way. They didn't only eat orcs; they ate everything, including humans.'

'What we are looking at now happened about five thousand years ago. Back then there's no such a thing as a human world, let alone the Cylone Calendar. Mankind was the one of the weakest species, because we were born small in size and fragile.' As the dean's deep voice continued, the students flew away from the dragon nest, heading somewhere new. Soon enough, on a flatland, Soarame saw a human tribe. Unexpectedly, there's nothing alike a town or a village, but a tribe that looked even more raw than the orcs'. Unlike the orcs though, people here looked skinny and weak, dusty and frustrated.

'Due to the weak nature of the human body, we were on the bottom level of the food chain. Magimals fed on humans all the time; people were living under fear. The reason they survived at all was that humans were one of the few species that's capable of mining, and dragons adore shining stuff, such as gold and diamonds.' Dean Romboton's voice became heavy. 'So, most human tribes were located beside mineral sources, and most humans were working in the mineral caverns day and night, until they died. Right now, we are looking at the minority human population here – they are farming and herding, which was really lucky for them.'

'This dark era lasted for god-knows-how-long, until one day,' Dean Romboton paused for effect. 'One day, we discovered a way to practise magic.'

With that announcement, the students rapidly rose and left the plains far below. The continent became smaller and smaller, till the scenery disappeared and the entire land became a stylised disc again. This time, the animal models on the disc had changed and human models showed up at different places – not only the Thundeross Continent, but also every other continent.

'It took a few centuries between the first humans learning magic to the thriving of wizards and humanity as a whole.' While the human models multiplied, Thundeross flew away from them, and the disc representing Holiness Continent came by. 'Till three thousand years ago, when mankind started a major revolutionary war against dragons.'

As the Holiness Continent finished expanding like the previous ones had, everybody was struck to find themselves falling to the middle a ferocious battlefield – tens of thousands of human wizards, in similar gowns to Dean Romboton's, were battling countless dragons. The war was savage and brutal; every second there's someone burnt up by the flames spat by dragons. Meanwhile, dragons were also bombarded to ashes by human's spells.

'The leader of mankind was named Spanflow Libral, as you have all heard. He led mankind to defeat dragons eventually, and forced them to yield with a permanent Magic Pact of Peace.' Dean Romboton didn't want the students to see too much more of the brutal scene given how scared they already sounded; so they soon started to rise and leave the battlefield. 'Since then, the savage era in history ended. Spanflow Libral was therefore referred to as *the Great Libral*, and he founded the Sunrise Alliance and our school.'

Hearing this, Soarame suddenly recalled that he saw a middle-aged man in the centre of the battlefield, followed by many wizards, but he's too far away and Soarame couldn't see his face well.

Meanwhile, everyone had risen high in the sky over the Holiness Continent. This time, they saw thousands of dragons, of different colours, coming towards them from different directions. Looking farther out, Soarame realised that the dragons were coming from the other five continents. Looking downwards again, he saw countless ships leaving the land under them at the same time.

'As a part of the Magic Pact of Peace, the entire dragon clan was forced to migrate to the Holiness Continent, while humans on this continent left it for the other ones. This migration of dragons was named *the Grand Migration*. It's the start of a new era in the entire world and the start of the human world as well.' Dean Romboton's voice became passionate and excited. 'To celebrate it, the Great Libral started the Cylone Calendar (CC) on the day that the Grand Migration was accomplished. The calendar was called Cylone because he wanted it to be named in honour of his master, Albert Cylone.'

The Dean had stopped talking. Everyone was silently immersed in what they had seen, until the Holiness Continent shrunk to be a disc again.

'So... the Holiness Continent still exists today?' Omifo asked. 'As dragons' privilege? Why have I never seen it on maps?'

'Of course it still exists. But it's not dragons' privilege; it's more the dragons' cage. Dragons are not allowed to leave that continent. Humans are allowed to visit, but no one wanted to – dragons wouldn't forget their humiliating defeat, and would by no means welcome humans in their cage,' Dean Romboton said. 'You got the point, right? That's why it's been excluded from most maps – it's there in the old days but, sadly, it had caused many curious people to lose their lives.'

'What about the sixth continent, then?' Soarame cut in. He's surprised to notice that one of the discs had gone missing, so they only numbered five now. 'Where's Allsouls?'

'Nice catch,' Dean Romboton smiled. 'According to the documentation, the Allsouls Continent broke due to the destruction of the war, and its pieces sank into the sea. The details about this were untraceable, but the point is that we won – we beat the dragons and became the rulers of the world, for the most part.'

'On our lands there have always been other species living too, such as orcs, druids, elves, dwarfs, and of course, magimals. Thanks to the peace since the Grand Migration, some of their individuals have grown to be really powerful nowadays,' the dean carried on. 'Hence, the Sunrise Alliance, founded by the Great Libral during the revolutionary war, has been keeping the peace between us and them.'

As he spoke, the four continent discs started to exhibit the previous development of civilizations process again – different models of human cities and towns began to show up, and so on.

The only difference was that, this time models of magimals and other species were also shown on the discs.

'We are very different from dragons. We don't want to enslave other species, but try to keep the peace with them, including wild magimals,' The dean paused a bit. 'However, over the course of thousands of years, we became convinced that most magimals don't care about peace. They kept invading us, and we kept fighting them. So your job is to keep all this in mind, and grow up to be helpful to the human world.' The dean's voice took on a tone of imparting great responsibility. 'Protect our people from the wild magimals, but don't invade their world. If we become too invasive into their world, we'll end up just like dragons one day. Do you understand?'

'Yes!' The students answered in union, completely taken by all they had just seen and learnt.

'Good!'

As the holograms gradually disappeared, the students slowly landed, still immersing in this special event. Dean Romboton appeared from the dissolving fog. 'By the way, there's a competitive game derived from the history of the grand wars between mankind and dragons, named *Dragon&Empires*. It's a derivation of the history you've seen, and the game tests players' abilities by engaging in real battles, so you should all practice it. As for the details, you can find out from the game club later.'

'Dragon&Empires?' Soarame was interested. He memorized this game and decided to check it out later.

The four roommates gathered again after the event finished. Getting to know the students in Spanflow College, Soarame was impressed again and again that everyone was highly talented, including all of his roommates. Kardiac had high gifts in both Fire and Wind; Omifo mainly practised Lightness with a superior gift, but could also practise Earth; Halgon was similar to Kardiac, with high gifts in Earth and Darkness. With all that said, they were just normal students in Spanflow College compared to everyone else. The top talents, such as Rodka, were even more gifted. Soarame was now strongly convinced that Spanflow College was the most powerful one in the school; his own magic gifts didn't really stand out compared to others here.

From that day on, Soarame settled down and became a formal student of the school. The Water department didn't let the freshers idle; a couple of days later, Soarame was walking towards his classroom. The boy was quite excited, as this day he's going to have his first Water class.

'Chelonad, please guide me to the Water department.'

'The tour for freshers was held just days ago and you have already forgotten the way?' Chelonad's voice answered right away. 'No wonder Aertiuno likes you.'

'Thanks... wait, what?'

'Aertiuno, remember? He's as good as you are at getting himself lost.'

'Oh, there's no way I can compare to him.'

'Then why was he supporting you in the interview?'

'You know about the interview too? The Principal said it's a private one, but everyone seems to know about it.'

'Hold on – I'm not everyone, boy. I know because I'm Chelonad.'

'Rodka knew about it too, so I guess it's because he's Rodka?'

'Bah, that kid is the Deans' favourite student, so he's an exception.'

'Well, are there any more exceptions?'

'No, there are not. You don't believe me, humph?'

Hearing Chelonad's tone, Soarame was picturing the expression on his face and sniggering to himself. For a second, Soarame really wanted to provoke Chelonad so that he perhaps would show himself, but he decided to try that later. After all, he needed to get to class and he definitely did not want to be late.

'Of course I do. Chelonad, please show me the directions,' Soarame urged.

'Tell you what, there's no secrets from me on this campus.' Chelonad wasn't done yet. 'Everything is under my surveillance, so I'm not an "everyone"!'

'Sure, of course not, and I'm sorry, Chelonad!' Soarame was getting a little anxious. 'I believe you! Please show me the way so that I won't be late for my very first class!'

'I already highlighted the route in your emblem, take a look at it.' Chelonad took pity on Soarame, just this once. 'Other than the maze by the entrance of the school, the rest of campus is on a map in your emblem. If that's still not enough, call me and I'll put signs along the route for you, just like last time.'

Soarame took out his emblem and checked it out. The emblem was a well-designed magic device that could deliver messages from the school to the students. One side of the emblem showed the student's name and all kinds of basic information, while on the other side it delivered private messages to the owner; the campus map could be shown there too. If one wanted, (s)he could even cast a holographic screen into the air with holograms and sound to share with others.

Moreover, by injecting mind power into it, one could establish a mind communication channel to another person's emblem, allowing them to talk at a distance. However, the consumption of mind power for remote communication, as well as any other function, wasn't negligible and a student usually couldn't afford a long conversation thereby. Therefore, the messaging system was always more popular; one could send text messages to another just by injecting a small amount of mind power, hands-free.

Soarame had already established channels with Dileys and her friends, but he had not used it so far because he wanted to act like a real fresher. So, Mr Fresher found the classroom that he's supposed to be in and was amazed by the scene in it –

It's truly all girls, as they had said.

The young girls were talking and laughing before Soarame arrived. Then, when Soarame came in, everyone went quiet abruptly and stared at him. This made Soarame feel shy; in fact, he's sweating. His original plan was just to sneak in and find a seat, but after being stared at by everyone, he froze by the door, not sure what to do next.

'Hi there, are you Soarame?' asked a girl with light brown hair and eyes sitting by the door.

'Hi... Yes, I am. Sorry, you are?' Soarame scratched his head self-consciously.

'Elizabeth. Nice to meet you!' The skinny girl stood up and shook Soarame's hand.

Another girl came to Soarame and introduced herself. 'Hey, I'm Beatrice, nice to meet you, Soarame!'

'I'm Angel, nice to finally meet you!' said a short, chubby girl.

'Hey, I'm Adele!' said another one.

Soarame was flattered to be receiving such special treatment. In just a few minutes he had probably shaken hands with more girls than he ever had in the past twelve years, which made him quite nervous. The girls had heard that there's one, and only one, boy in their class this year, and they were curious about him.

The girls whispered back and forth for quite a while, asking Soarame lots of questions and keeping him very busy, and very flushed. They finally had to quiet down because the teacher came in. Everyone found their seats and composed themselves, looking at the teacher. She's small and willowy, with wavy hair falling to just above her shoulders.

'Hello sweethearts! Look at you all, so beautiful!' The teacher's first words came out very naturally, causing all the girls to start chuckling and look at Soarame. Soarame realised what's going on and flushed even more, but there's nothing he could do about it.

'Oh, you're Soarame, aren't you?' The teacher said as she noticed the only boy sitting in the middle of the classroom.

'Yes Ma'am, greetings to you!' Soarame stood up hurriedly.

'How lovely.' The teacher was happy. 'My name is Nicole, sit down please, cutie!' Watching Soarame sit down with a "cutie" blush, everyone sniggered.

'We are all family, relax, Soarame!' Nicole sensed Soarame's shyness, holding back her amusement. 'Okay, let's start our first class – Water, mother of lives!'

'Water gives rise to all lives; therefore Water magic is best-known for its nourishing and healing nature. Every time there's a battle, there would be lots of Water wizards, taking charge of healing the wounded,' Nicole launched directly into her lecture. 'Besides that, Water magic is also good for defence and attack, so it's the most balanced lineage.'

'Water magic is especially known for its *Area of Effect* spells – or AOE spells – for example, a high-level Water wizard could spell *moistening dewdrop* and heal hundreds of people at the same time.' Nicole paced elegantly back and forth across the stage, her wave-patterned dress swishing around her legs. 'When battling, the spell *frozen world* could freeze a large number of enemies, and flip the situation of a battle, even a war. That said, those are high-level spells and we need to start from the basics…'

This was the very first class for the freshers and everyone was excited, including Soarame. However, after a while, the boy figured out that Nicole was only going to talk about beginner's Water magic stuff because this was indeed a class for real freshers. Therefore, Soarame lost interest sooner than he thought he would – he had been an Adept wizard thanks to his education from Scankeen. Nicole's class was good for true Novice wizards, but useless for Soarame.

Halfway through the class, Nicole threw a question to the crowd. 'What are the practical advantages of performing Novice-level water magic? Let's hear as many as you can think of.'

'I know one,' A pretty girl with curly auburn hair raised her hand. 'Water magic keeps my skin clean and soft; I really like it!'

'Good!'

While Soarame almost burst out laughing, he's surprised to find that Nicole actually agreed and was happy. 'Not only does it keep your skin in good condition, but also it can make you look prettier and prettier if you keep practising it!' As she spoke, she waved her hands at the students, spraying a cloud that spread the across the classroom.

'Wow!' The cloud landed on everyone's faces and the girls clapped and cheered; they were in favour of Water's skin benefits. Soarame looked around and found that everyone was actually serious about it, so he could do nothing other than try to blend in with the others.

The beauty and skin topic continued for a little longer than Soarame expected. Just when he's getting impatient, Nicole caught him off guard. 'Soarame, would you be willing to share something with us?'

'Err...' Soarame raised his head and stuttered. 'Yeah... I mean... sure. I agree that water is good for the skin ...'

'Oh come on Soarame, you are the only boy in this class, surprise us with something different!' Nicole interrupted Soarame and teased him with a friendly smile.

'Ahh...' Soarame scratched his head at this request – *Really? I was trying to fit in your style!* 'Then... performing water magic can save time to get water when you are thirsty... how about that?'

A girl couldn't help laughing, followed by many more.

'Nah, that is boring.' Obviously, not everyone agreed with Soarame.

'My sister says boys are always boring...' Some girls began to chatter amongst themselves.

'Hold on, everybody. Soarame has a point.' Nicole fought back her laughter. 'But can you give us something with a bigger scope?'

'A bigger scope?' Soarame wanted to say *I can think of nothing bigger than the scope of beauty*, but he dared not. So, instead he said, 'Water magic is useful in many areas. Let's say you want to go skating, but it's summer, then all that you need to do is freeze the lake in front of you.'

'That's a good thought,' Nicole nodded. 'Yet you have to have enough power to do that.'

'How about snow?' Another girl followed up. 'Summon a snowflake when you feel unhappy, or want to enjoy the romance!'

'That's also a good point, yet both of you are talking about a higher level of Water magic – controlling temperature. At Novice level we are not there yet.' Nicole waved her hands again, and this time a cluster of snowflakes appeared and floated everywhere. Seeing this caused another round of excited cheers, she smiled and turned to Soarame again. 'For now, can we talk a bit more about water itself, before we level up?'

'Hmm...' Soarame had to really think about it because he did have problems thinking of useful Novice-level Water spells. 'I think the healing nature of water comes from the fact that the body contains a large amount of water.'

'Excellent point!' Nicole was a little surprised. 'Please keep going!'

'Therefore, Water magic can both heal the body and do massive damage to the body.' Soarame organized his thoughts bit by bit. 'It's all up to the wizard's will. For example, if an evil wizard chooses to drain water from people's bodies...'

'Okay, that's a very incisive thought.' Nicole cut Soarame off before he scared the girls by finishing his horrible hypothesis. 'However, the water in one's body is controlled by the person himself, which is a huge difference from water in free form. Therefore, your thought wasn't practical, at least not at a level under Master. So everyone, please don't be scared.'

Nicole was trying to calm down the girls, some of whom already had pale faces thanks to Soarame's words. 'No one has ever done that, by the way. Plus, it would be much easier to perform a normal attacking spell, such as *icearrow*, which does remarkable damage.'

Finishing in a rush, Nicole breathed a sigh of relief. She hadn't expected Soarame to go this far and was surprised by the abnormal idea. Although a bit scared herself, she's fascinated by Soarame's talented insight on magic. She wanted Soarame to keep going, but on less scary topics for Novices. 'Well Soarame, I'm curious about how you feel as the only boy in the class. Does it feel good, as you have a very different way of thinking from us?'

'Sure, it feels great.' Soarame answered with a naughty grimace in his heart. *What else do you expect? "No, I wish I wasn't here?"*

'Great, we also feel good having you here.' Nicole smiled. The girls were all watching Soarame with curiosity. 'What do you think is the reason that we have so many more girls than boys in our department?'

'Because most boys don't know how to appreciate Water magic,' answered Soarame. Obviously this answer was favourable, as more girls nodded their agreement.

'Again, some more details please.' Nicole was glad and pushed the topic.

'Many people tend to think that Water magic is less strong in attack than other magic lineages, such as Fire, but they don't realise that this is actually wrong,' Soarame spoke up, confident now. 'High-level Water magic is second to none in attack, plus its nature makes it the most comprehensive magic.'

'Yes it is! Water magic is famous for its balance in all purposes, you got it right!' Nicole was excited. 'Then why do you think most boys still choose to go for other lineages when they have Water gift? You are not the only one who knows the merits of high-level Water magic.'

'Because of peace.' Soarame again gave an unexpected answer.

'Peace?' Nicole was confused.

'We are living in an era of peace. Even wizards don't really have to fight that much, so they are not under pressure.' Out of nowhere, Soarame felt as though something were swarming in his body. He stood up unconsciously, looking around, and said, 'They care more about looking cool than the actual purposes of magic. They think Fire magic looks powerful and sounds ferocious, so they go for it. Water magic has even been unfairly labelled as "girly" since god-knows-when, and boys try to prove they are manly.' As Soarame spoke, everyone else sat in silence, listening intently to him. 'If we were at war, this problem wouldn't have happened because the war would tell us the truth! People are too spoiled nowadays.'

Silence.

Everyone was stunned by Soarame's insight. Soarame, on the other hand, was really excited to finally get a topic that fitted him well. His response was actually thanks to Scankeen's lessons, as old man had told the boy many stories of wars from his hundreds of years of experience.

Seeing the attentive yet confused eyes of the girls surrounding him, Soarame stopped talking. He looked at Nicole, waiting for her to react.

'Err... hmm...' Nicole took some time to recover from the shock. 'Interesting point, now let's talk about something else...'

'...What?'

THE MAN OF THE DAY

Why do I look like an alien here? After class, Soarame was walking out of the building, feeling disappointed. Obviously, Nicole was of a very different style from Sandoray; she didn't want to talk about negative things in front of her young students. Therefore, every time Soarame tried to make a real point, she redirected the lesson.

'Soarame!' Just as Soarame was complaining to himself, a graceful-sounding voice came from behind him.

'Hi, how are you guys?' Soarame turned back and greeted the group of girls walking towards him.

'We're well, but we are girls, not guys.' A pretty girl with straw-blond hair and glittering hazel eyes teased him. 'I know we met already, but we haven't really talked. So, my name again is Julia, in case you forgot.'

'I remember you, Julia.' Soarame managed a white lie; there's no way that he could remember dozens of names at once. 'Hope I didn't bother you during class.'

'No, not at all!' Julia smiled. 'In fact, we came to say hello because we liked your talk!'

'Really?' Soarame suddenly felt much better.

'Yeah!' another girl wearing loose-fitting trousers and a jumper followed up. 'We find it inspiring, and we are all interested!'

'Really?' Soarame couldn't help feeling excited.

'Really! We enjoyed listening to your ideas and hope you can tell us more later,' Julia claimed, the girls all nodding in agreement with her.

'Really?' Soarame was too happy to realise that he's repeating himself, and he's not good at talking to girls in the first place.

The girls started chuckling at his parroting. Julia approached Soarame. 'Hey, can we friend each other on our Libral Emblems?'

'Huh?' Soarame was puzzled, but soon he realised what Julia meant. 'Oh, you mean open a chat channel?'

'Yeah, exactly,' Julia said, looking shy. 'May I?'

'Oh sure, sure, sure!' Soarame handed his emblem to Julia. 'It's just that I can't really use it to talk.'

'I know, I can't either.' Julia took Soarame's emblem and injected her mind power. The back of the emblem flashed for a second and a name emerged on the back – Julia Swift. The next second, an image of Julia's face was emitted by the emblem. A voice sounded. 'Confirm friendship?'

'Yes,' Soarame answered. He did the same thing to Julia's emblem and Julia also saw his face and name appear – Soarame Jadeking.

Like that, Soarame soon made a lot of friends. One week passed quickly and the first weekend arrived. Soarame was excited because he could finally go to Dafinol for ice carving for the first time.

'Hey buddy, there you are!' Dafinol was waiting for Soarame by the door. 'Ready to have some fun today?'

'Can't wait!' Soarame cheered.

'Alright, we are going to start with basics.' Dafinol led Soarame to a table; there were a number of different engraving tools on it. 'The first step for you is to know these tools.'

There were a variety of tools such as tongs, chisels, jigs, forks and more, and each of them had different subtypes, with different shapes for different purposes. Dafinol briefly went through those basics and gave Soarame a quick demonstration on how to use them on an ice cube. The engraving took time; by the end of the day Dafinol had only managed to finish the rough shaping. So Soarame came back the next day and got to see Dafinol finish this work, which he had shaped into a seated dog – in Dafinol's words, this one was just for teaching purposes.

'How much can it sell for at an auction?' Soarame was curious. In his eyes, the "rush work for teaching purposes" looked pretty good.

'I don't sell scraps like this.' Dafinol shook his head. 'My reputation is built on my more detailed and elegant works. Selling stuff like this would make me look like a joker.'

'But I think it looks great!' Soarame looked up at Dafinol, surprised. 'What's wrong with selling it?'

'A real artist destroys dissatisfying work; a dealer sells it. I'm the former,' Dafinol informed Soarame. 'To settle your curiosity though, it can be worth up to five hundred gold coins, because of my name.'

'Seriously!' Soarame was stunned. 'And you want to destroy it?'

'Yes.' Dafinol tossed the work into the trash bin. This made Soarame swallow – *Five hundred gold coins! Praise Libral!*

'Don't be surprised. My name is worth a lot more than that.' Dafinol was amused to see Soarame's expression. 'My elegant work sells for at least a hundred ruby coins per piece, and the reason is what you just saw.'

That's ten thousand gold coins, and that's an "at least"? Soarame was struck. He took a deep breath and tried to make himself calm down. Thinking for a while, Soarame had to agree that Dafinol had done the right thing to protect his reputation. But still, he's crying inside for those five hundred gold coins – everything that Filton had given him was less than that, so Dafinol had just thrown away the equivalent of Soarame's total assets.

Soarame went back to his dorm that evening as if he's sleepwalking. His mind was entirely occupied by two numbers: five hundred and ten thousand. It felt absurd to Soarame that Dafinol actually made that much, yet he didn't seem interested in money – his studio was pretty small, his clothes were very simple, and he didn't even have a helper until Soarame showed up. Dafinol seemed to read Soarame's thoughts, and he had told Soarame something that left the boy unsure whether to laugh or to cry – 'a great wizard makes tons more! No wizard ever worries about money.'

Well, at least I'm a unique wizard, then. Soarame mocked himself. The good news was that the future was bright, so Soarame had to re-order his mind and focus on his studies. After all, the most important thing to a wizard is his power, and Soarame especially wanted to improve as fast as he could for his missing parents and his journeying master.

****

Mixed with joy and annoyance, Soarame's school life got underway for a few months, and he worked hard in his Water classes. Nicole still tried to cut him off, from time to time, once he began to discuss things a little too provocative in her opinion – *Boys are headaches, I just knew it!* But she still had to appreciate Soarame's odd yet interesting thoughts now and then.

After class Soarame would go back to his bedroom to practise Wind magic secretly, or to hang out with his friends – Soarame had made quite a few friends, but his best friends were still his roommates, plus the four girls who had joined him for the dorm flight.

Most weekends, Soarame helped Dafinol with his ice carving, at the same time learning the skills. Soon enough, Soarame noticed a very "bad" habit of Dafinol's – this man threw away things all the time. Most of Dafinol's work ended up in trash bins and melted; Soarame was upset to watch a few thousand gold coins becoming water, until he finally couldn't stand it any longer –

'Dafinol, isn't there a better way to deal with this?' Soarame stopped Dafinol from throwing away another work – it's named "Horseman", and showed a knight riding a horse. It's so nicely done that it reminded Soarame of his dream years ago – himself on Richie when they both grew up. In Soarame's opinion, this work was already elegant enough, but Dafinol was still about to toss it.

'Soarame, if you really want it, you can have this one.' Dafinol put down the sculpture, 'You can choose to sell it, keep it, or maybe work on it – you mentioned you do want to make your own work one day, right?'

Soarame took over the work in joy, but the next second he sighed – he certainly would prefer to sell it and get the money, but he couldn't. Selling "Horseman" meant jeopardizing Dafinol's reputation and destroying his trust, so finally, Soarame decided to leave the work at the studio – he couldn't keep the icework from melting in the dorm.

I need to learn faster! Soarame had to push himself. *I can't sell Dafinol's work, but I can sell my own work if I can make something nice. But carving is so hard...* Soarame looked at the corner of his table, where his own unfinished work was sitting. He couldn't think of a name for it, because even he couldn't tell exactly what it was.

Carving demanded hands that were strong enough, in addition to all the other skills, but as a boy Soarame just couldn't handle that. He had been trying to use Water magic to carve, but it's way too hard to control the frozen Water inside an ice cube – he wasn't powerful enough yet.

I can't make the Water elements move in an ice form. I need to try another way. This day, after coming back to the dorm, Soarame sat down and really spent some time thinking. *I have to do it step by step, by controlling them in liquid form first... yes, that's it!*

Soarame jumped up and rushed to the living room – he finally had an idea. Soarame recalled that during his visit with Filton in the Cylone City, there had been a street artist painting by blowing ink on a canvas. Now Soarame was going to do the same thing, only instead of blowing, he would use magic.

It's the same as pouring beer into the bottle that day! How could I have taken so long to realise it? Soarame berated himself while he poured some writing ink onto a piece of paper. However, the paper was too absorbent to keep the ink on the surface, so it got sucked in right away and formed a big splodge; when Soarame tried to move the ink around using his mind power, it's already too late. Soarame therefore had to buy a canvas from a campus store. This time it worked much better, and Soarame could direct the ink on the canvas to make some patterns, yet it's still far from being artwork – or maybe too much of artwork for people to understand.

That's ok, at least it can work! Soarame was encouraged by his progress; all he needed to do was to keep trying. So Soarame spent the rest of the day painting by magic, until his roommates came back.

'Soar, what are you doing?' Kardiac came over to see and soon worked it out. 'Praise Libral, you are trying to paint with Water magic? That's a genius idea!'

'Thanks, I call it *mind-painting*, but it's so hard.' Soarame was tired. Kardiac wanted to try it himself, but he couldn't perform

Water, nor could Omifo and Halgon, so they could only offer some suggestions.

The news spread very fast. Soarame's classmates came to visit days later, marvelling at Soarame's efforts. The girls were all Water wizards, so they also tried it but found that it's incredibly hard. Dileys' crew also came, and they had a really hard time trying to work it out too, even as Grade-3 and -4 students. Finally, they all gave up, except Soarame, the unique wizard who needed money.

Soarame wasn't surprised to see even Dileys fail. After all, his mind power was actually at the Adept level, higher than most of his friends. But he's new to Water magic, so before mastering Water spells at a higher level, he had to stay a Grade 1. To be frank, his best shot at Water magic so far was still to manipulate water for painting, or, perhaps, summon a glass of water to drink – as he suggested in his first Water class.

'Soarame, you must be insane!' Realising Soarame was actually aiming to make an ice sculpture with mind power, Vivarin was perturbed. 'How did you get this idea?'

'Well, it's a good way to practise Water magic at the same time as making art,' Soarame shrugged his shoulders. 'I can't do it Dafinol's way anyway.'

'Soarame, if you really like painting, my uncle is a good painter,' said Jemario suddenly. 'I have learnt something from him, so maybe I could be of help.'

'Really!' Soarame was overjoyed. 'Sure, please teach me!'

'Hmm?' Catheray watched Jemario in a suspicious way. 'You never offered this to anyone else, not even at the painting club that you joined. Why do I smell something odd here... ahh!'

She's cut off because Jemario poked her in the armpit. The two girls then started romping, and Kardiac came close to Soarame's ear. 'Man, that looks good for you!'

'What's that?' Soarame was confused. 'What looks good?'

'The mind-painting plan!' Catheray overheard Kardiac and cut in. She hurriedly jumped over and knocked him on the forehead. 'What are you thinking?'

'Ouch!' Kardiac covered his forehead and yelped in pain. 'How dare you...'

'Oh I just dared.' Catheray drew closer to him, chuckling. 'So what?'

'I... I want a duel!' Kardiac forced himself to say that.

'What? A powerful Fire wizard wants a duel?' Before Catheray could respond, Vivarin cut in, faking a threatening face. 'I'll take your challenge! I so can't wait!'

'Never mind... I'm just joking...' Kardiac gave up right away. Seeing everybody chuckling, Kardiac dragged Omifo into the conversation. 'Man, I remember you are about to grade up; help me out here!'

'I'm not a match for Vivarin.' Omifo smiled gently. 'Don't forget she's older than us.'

'Excuse me?' Vivarin stared at Omifo. 'Are you saying I'm old?'

'No, no!' Omifo hurriedly waved his hands. 'I'm just telling the truth...'

'What?' She moved towards him aggressively, with one arm akimbo, the other pressing on Omifo's shoulder. 'Say that one more time?'

'I'm sorry!' Omifo put his hands up in surrender. 'Kardy, I'm done.'

Kardiac couldn't blame him, so he turned around to seek out Halgon. But Halgon had already disappeared upstairs, calling down behind him, 'I've got a bad belly, sorry!'

'No!' Seeing Catheray coming towards him aggressively, just like what Vivarin had done to Omifo, Kardiac's whine echoed in the dorm.

'Soar, mind-carving could be more difficult than you think. I'm in Grade 4 and I can cast the freezing-related spells, but that's just for freezing water into ice; the shape of the ice is random,' Dileys said to Soarame as she watched her friends playing with the boys. 'So I think you are making a wise decision to go with mind-painting first. Now that Jem can help you, it's a great opportunity. Do take advantage of it!'

'I will.' Soarame looked at Jemario, only to find that she's looking left and right, just not back at him. So he asked, 'Jemario, what are you thinking?'

'Ahh... Nothing.' Jemario finally had to look at Soarame. For some reason, she looked nervous and her face became pink. When their eyes met, Soarame couldn't take his attention away –

Jemario's violet eyes were filled with something special that he wasn't sure about; but they were so beautiful, like deep and serene spring pools with something arcane hidden within. He felt that his mind was taken into the pools and locked up there; he kept watching her, and the others read his expression as one of being stunned.

Jemario was reminded of the last time Soarame watched her like this – in the arena. She hurriedly tried to distract him. 'Emm... we should be going, let's keep in touch via the emblem!'

The four girls left together. Catheray turned back by the door. 'Soar, be confident and don't give up! If you like something, push yourself forward for it!'

'Sure.' Soarame didn't notice Catheray's special eye signal to him; he thought she's talking about the painting and carving. And he still hadn't gotten over Jemario's gaze a few seconds ago – *What a pair of eyes... how beautiful!*

'Congrats, man! It really looked good for you!' Kardiac came close to Soarame before the latter came back to his senses. The chubby boy talked in a tone as if he's very experienced. 'As I recall, that situation has happened to me many times before. But as I've put on some weight and am getting older, it's your turn now... Go for it, and feel free to ask me for advice if you need it.'

'Sure, sure,' Soarame responded distractedly.

'And tell me what they think about me too!' Kardiac hurriedly added. 'To be honest, I think Catheray likes me... don't you think? Hey, hey, man, are you listening?...'

Like that, Soarame continued his school life with his friends – each of a different style. He kept practising hard on his mind-painting every single day, and became a little better each day. The story of Soarame's mind-painting skills spread wide on campus and amazed a lot of students – although they were unwilling to admit it, none of them could do it.

With Soarame's friends gathering to watch him mind-paint regularly now, the venue of his mind-painting practice had changed from his dorm to a self-study room in the Water Department. The friends were soon used to gathering there and watching Soarame paint, Jemario being his coach and everyone else hanging around for company. They had become very familiar because of that; the most typical example was Kardiac and Catheray, both of whom were playful and lively.

As a contrast, Omifo didn't show up nearly as often; he seemed to prefer staying alone for his own activities. Except for when he's forced by Vivarin to attend the gathering from time to time – the girl seemed to enjoy "bullying" him from that day on – he probably would have been absent all the time. And the friends seemed to enjoy watching Vivarin bully Omifo; their complicit chuckles made Omifo quite helpless.

On the downside though, having spent most of his time on Water magic, Soarame was bitterly convinced that his "capable" gift was indeed merely "capable" – in sharp contrast to his Wind spells, which he found much easier to learn and master, he made little improvement in Water spells. All his roommates had managed to grade up, but only Soarame had a hard time learning Grade-2 Water spells, regardless of how well he could control Water elements for mind-painting.

In sharp contrast, Julia had been pretty much lying around and having fun all day, yet with a superior gift she had levelled up to Grade 2 already. Interestingly, the talented girl had seldom kept in touch with Soarame since then.

Soarame wasn't sure how he felt about that, but fortunately he still had his roommates and Dileys' crew. Thanks to their continuous encouragement, Soarame kept trying and his efforts finally started paying off. One great day, as one of the last few new students who were still in Grade 1, Soarame passed the skills test and graded up.

Although it wasn't even close to a glorious achievement, it's still good news. Soarame updated his friends via the emblem, and they agreed to gather for a celebration at their place – the self-study room where Soarame practised mind-painting.

So, Soarame came to the room early all by himself, waiting for everyone else to join him. During the wait, he took out a piece of canvas and spread it before him, ready to warm up his hands by mind-painting. Well, it's to warm up his mind, actually.

However, after he had finished painting a plum tree, no one had come to join him yet. This was a bit odd because the sun was setting and it's almost dinner time. Just as Soarame was becoming suspicious, a voice passed through the door. 'Soarame? Are you in?'

Soarame raised his head and saw a vivacious figure coming into the room. 'Jemario, there you are!'

Soarame couldn't count how many times he had been impressed by Jemario's beauty, especially when she looked at him a certain way. But as a naïve and rough boy from countryside, Soarame really didn't know what's the best way to deal with his feelings. And because there's always a group of his friends hanging out in the same room as them, he had never been alone with Jemario, thus never had to focus on this question. But this time...

'Congratulations for your grading up,' Jemario smiled at him. For some reason, she seemed a little nervous; the way she looked at Soarame was different from usual.

'Thanks... thank you.' Soarame looked at her in the eyes. He again felt his heart beating fast. This time, there's only the two of them, nobody else; so the boy finally had to face the long-pending question of how to deal with his unusual feelings, as well as their symptoms – such as his pounding heart and quickened breath.

'Let's start practising then.' Jemario glided past Soarame, lowering her head and not looking at him. This made Soarame again sense something abnormal from her. Jemario looked at Soarame's work of the plum tree, nodding slightly. 'Not bad. You are good at painting trees now.'

'Thank... you.' Soarame took a long breath and held it, trying to slow down his heartbeat. 'What do we paint today?'

'I don't know.' Jemario's head was still lowered. 'Maybe people? You've been painting trees for a while; it's time to change.'

'People?' Soarame was surprised. 'Didn't you say people are the hardest in painting, and should be the last thing to practise on?'

'Mind-carving is even more difficult, isn't it? Aren't you still trying to do that?' Jemario raised her head to Soarame, looking as if she's smiling, but there's something special about this smile.

'You are right,' Soarame scratched his head thoughtfully. 'So what kind of people should I paint?'

'Any kind.' Jemario lowered her head again, as if she refused to look too long at the boy. 'As long as you have a figure in mind, you could try to paint it.'

Soarame was very confused. 'Are you kidding...? How am I

supposed to be able to do that... to paint a person without a real model?' Even when Soarame painted the plum tree, he had to look at the real tree out of the window. Thinking of this, he suddenly realised something. *There's a model right here!*

Jemario didn't answer him. She kept her head low, as if she's carefully checking Soarame's work. Soarame watched her and noticed that, strangely, her ears seemed a little pink. He wanted to ask something, but lacked a good starter. Meanwhile, Jemario stayed quiet and didn't want to look at him; so the room filled with the embarrassing silence.

'Jemario, are you...' A few seconds later, Soarame tried to talk, sweat breaking out on his forehead.

'What?' Jemario finally responded. She raised her head for a peek at him.

'Are you sick?'

'...' Jemario's face changed, as if she wasn't sure she should feel amused or what. 'No, I'm fine. Are you still going to practise mind-painting?'

'Yes, I am. But...' Soarame clenched his fists. 'So I'll... I'll paint you then!'

'Me?' Jemario looked at him – again in a special way. Soarame realized the look seemed familiar – just like the time when she first offered her help on his mind-painting practise. 'I haven't agreed yet. Are you asking me for permission?'

'Err... but... but there's nobody else!' Soarame hurriedly argued, blushing. At the same time, he's once again attracted by Jemario's eyes. The beautiful eyes in front of him seemed to be superposed with her eyes in his memory, which altogether locked up his mind and made him unable to move away his gaze.

'Then just ask for permission! Silly!' Hearing Soarame's weak argument, Jemario couldn't help chuckling. 'Anyway, fine... you can paint me if you want.'

Seeing Soarame's reaction – which was actually a non-reaction – Jemario hurriedly pushed his chest. 'Hey, stop staring... wake up already! It's time to practise!'

'Ah! Yes, yes!' Soarame woke up with a blush rising to his top. He hurriedly tried to fetch the ink, but didn't realize that his body was one step behind his mind. He knocked over the ink bottle, and the ink spilled onto Jemario's lily-white skirt.

'Oh no!' Soarame's body froze. He wasn't sure what to do next.

'Are you sure you wanna paint me, not paint on me?' Seeing the boy's stricken face, Jemario didn't want to berate him, but teased him instead. But when Soarame grabbed hold of her skirt, she became anxious. 'Stop it! Let go! I'll wipe it myself!'

'Soarame, what are you doing?' Dileys' voice sounded as she came into the room. Soarame was taken aback; he's still holding Jemario's skirt in hand, looking very suspicious. He hurriedly tried to clarify, but found himself begin to stammer out of anxiousness.

'I don't... I mean...' Seeing Dileys' questioning eyes, Soarame almost wanted to cry.

'It's okay. It's late, let's finish.' Jemario also looked embarrassed. 'I need to change my skirt anyway; I'll see you guys later.'

'Wait... I...' Watching Jemario escape in a rush, Soarame was beyond anxious. 'Jemario, let me wash your skirt and return it to you...'

'What?' Dileys pushed him, chuckling. 'Which part of your brain made you think any girl would let you wash her skirt?'

'Err...' Soarame was puzzled. 'I'll pay her for the skirt then!'

'It's okay. Forget it.' Dileys had seen the spilled ink on the table and understood everything. 'Jem is much better than that, so don't worry.'

'But she seemed upset...' Soarame was anxious.

'No, she's not.' Dileys looked amused. 'Trust me, she's just going to change her skirt. Then she will join us in your dorm, for your celebration – remember?'

'The celebration is here, isn't it?' Soarame was confused. 'Are you sure she's still coming?'

'Yes she will. And sorry – we forgot to tell you that we've decided to move it back to your dorm.' Dileys couldn't help snickering as she sighed inside. *Of course we deliberately forgot to tell you about the change, so that we can let you two be together alone for once!*

But look at you... what a silly boy! Do you know how hard it's to persuade Jemario to come to see you alone, with the condition that I must watch her back? Dileys helped Soarame clean up the table, shaking her head secretly. *Do you know Vivarin and Catheray are blocking your roommates as we speak, in order to buy you time to stay with Jem?*

Of course, Soarame didn't know any of this. So he followed Dileys back to his dorm, and the first thing he saw was a fireplace in the living room – his roommates had used their chances to upgrade the dorm.

Catheray was sitting next to Kardiac, but scampered to the door upon seeing Soarame. 'There you are, Soar!' She looked beyond him out the doorway, searching. 'Where's Jem?'

'What's it about Jem? Why is she supposed to be with him?' Kardiac asked. 'Wait! I smell something odd…'

'I see!' Omifo smacked his own head. But before he could continue, he noticed Vivarin's special smile – she's leaning towards and staring at him.

'Come on in first!' Catheray had realized her carelessness. She tongued with a grimace and dragged Soarame in. Soon enough, Jemario came too – she had changed her skirt to a light green one, which looked just as good. Jemario looked completely normal, as if nothing had happened. Soarame had really wanted to apologise again, but seeing her act like that he had to swallow all his words.

Catheray sensed something from Soarame's face; she tackled Dileys to whisper to her. Soon her eyes widened, and she peeked at Soarame – her mouth did not show a sign of laughter but her eyes did.

Seeing the suspicious look on the boys' faces, Dileys clapped her hands. 'Hey, you guys need to focus! Don't forget we are here to celebrate the man of the day!'

'The man of the day…' Soarame recalled what he did back in the self-study room. He had to agree he fit the title very well.

'And we heard that he's pretty popular in our department,' Vivarin followed up, chuckling. 'Because he's good at giving weird thoughts in class.'

'Really?' Soarame was actually sick of his own catch phrase, but it slipped out anyway.

'Yes, and he keeps saying "really",' Catheray teased. 'What's your most powerful magic now? This?' A stream of water ran from the tip of Catheray's finger into a cup; she then picked up the cup and drank it.

'Hmm… you heard about that, too?' Soarame scratched his head while everyone was laughing.

'Well, this is popular nowadays,' Dileys teased Soarame. 'Some girls even use it for showering if they have enough mind power.'

'Well, glad to be of help.' Soarame had to giggle.

'What, you've helped girls shower? That's awesome!' Kardiac nudged Soarame's shoulder with his own. He's about to carry on, but got shut down by Cathcray's slap on his head.

Just then, there came a knock on the door. Soarame opened the door and was overjoyed. 'Sachastain? Long time no see! I thought you'd forgotten about me!'

'How could I do that?' Seeing Soarame, Sachastain was very happy too. 'Congratulations on your grading up!'

'Thank you!' Soarame hurriedly introduced Sachastain to his friends.

'Good to see you making so many friends,' Sachastain patted Soarame's shoulder. 'I'm here to give you a little surprise today.'

'A surprise?' Soarame was excited to hear that. Then he noticed Sachastain was holding a square-shaped ebony box, and its brownish-black wood emitted an ancient aura.

'Oh wow, this is for me?' Soarame was so happy. 'Can I open it?'

'Sure. But before that, why don't you take a guess about what's in it?'

'Well...' Soarame rolled his eyes. 'A magic wand?'

'Nearly, but not exactly,' Sachastain smiled at everyone. 'You guys can all join in this game.'

'I think it's a wizard robe!' Kardiac couldn't wait to speak.

'Kardy, you are probably the only genius who could put a robe in a box of this shape and size!' Catheray made fun of Kardiac. 'It's more likely to be a necklace or something.'

'Good guess, Catheray,' Sachastain smiled. 'Again, nearly there.'

'Earrings?' Vivarin guessed; that's her favourite gift.

'Seriously?' Omifo teased. 'Earrings as a gift to a boy?'

'Of course it can happen.' Vivarin squinted him. 'Be more fashionable, boy!'

'Not wand, necklace, or earring, but it's still gonna be a magigear of some kind, right?' Halgon was usually silent, but this time he wanted to participate. 'How about a bracelet, like a replica of *Undines' Bless*?'

Hearing Halgon's guess, Sachastain was surprised. The *Undines'* collection was a set of magigears from ancient times; not everyone knew about it – even Sachastain wasn't sure what exactly *Undines' Bless* referred to, yet Halgon had just claimed it to be a bracelet.

'Halgon, right? I must say you guys know a lot more than I expected.' Sachastain praised them. 'I was never so lucky as to see something like the Undines' collection in my life, not even a replica, but I think you will like this one better – feel free to open it.'

'A magimal egg?!' everyone screamed as Soarame opened the box – inside was an ivory-white magimal egg. This wasn't a little surprise, but a big one. The friends certainly knew some students here who had magimals, but none of them had one so far, and they had always been so jealous.

For a wizard, there were two things that were most wanted: magigears, which could enhance one's magic power; and magimals, who could be bonded with wizards and become their loyal friends. Just like wizards, magimals and magigears had the same rankings: *Novice, Adept, Expert, Master/Baron* and even *Legendary*. On top of that, a magimal egg was far more precious than a magigear of the same ranking – after all, it's a living creature!

'Yep, a magimal egg.' Hearing the happy commotion, Sachastain was satisfied. 'As to what kind of magimal, you'll find out for yourself. Now I need to go back to work; feel free to come to me if you need anything.' Sachastain was about to leave, but was suddenly pulled back by Soarame.

'No, Sachastain, I can't take it,' Soarame said anxiously. 'Thank you *so* much, but this gift is too much, I just can't!'

'What? You don't say that to me, boy!' Sachastain pretended to be upset and pushed the box into Soarame's arms. 'This gift is from me, so I decide who can take it!'

'Yes, but...' Soarame certainly wanted it – his top regret so far was that he couldn't bond with Richie. However, he felt nervous at receiving such a precious gift, especially after his master had told him that magimals were always expensive and hard to get.

'Months ago, a boy called Soarame protected the dignity of this institute and the reputation of my team,' Sachastain looked into

Soarame's eyes. 'Back then, I had already started thinking about this gift, so I've been watching you ever since. To date, everything I've seen and heard about you convinced me that you deserve it.'

'What?' Kardiac was surprised. 'Soar, what does he mean?'

'Hmm, it seems that you are not too full of yourself, Soarame.' Sachastain looked at Soarame with appreciation. 'Why don't I let you tell them your story. See you soon!'

'Thank you, Sachastain!' Soarame felt truly touched. Life was amazing sometimes; if one did good deeds at some point, (s)he would have the favour returned later at some point.

Thanks to Sachastain, it's a happy day for the friends. They were keen to see what's in the egg; everybody urged Soarame to hatch it right away.

Thanks to his repeated attempts with Richie and Scankeen's lessons, Soarame was very familiar with how to bond with a magimal, or in this case, a magimal egg. With his wand in hand, Soarame began to draw a hexagram and inject his mind power into the egg. The hexagram glowed and Soarame did a very proficient job of injecting his mind power smoothly and carefully into it for a few minutes. Everyone was amazed to see Soarame so skilful at this, and they were ready to witness the baby hatch.

However, after a while of this, there's still nothing happening to the egg.

'Come on, Soar! You can do it!' Kardiac ran out of patience first.

'Shh!' Catheray slapped Kardiac on the shoulder, even though she's quite eager herself.

Soarame kept trying for another ten minutes before he had to take a rest, and then continued for another round. But half an hour later, still nothing had happened.

'Hatching is that hard?' Soarame breathed heavily as he's exhausted. 'Has anyone ever tried it before?'

Seeing the others shaking their heads, Halgon spoke up. 'Yes, I have. It can be hard depending on the egg's ranking, so just keep trying every day. This one must be of a high rank and needs more mind power.'

'So we can't hatch it today?' Dileys was dissatisfied, so was everyone else. 'Or shall we go ask Sachastain for help?'

'No, let's not do that,' Omifo disagreed. 'We'll solve the

problem by ourselves.'

'Of course, hero.' Vivarin stared at Omifo, making him cringe. 'What now, then?'

'I'll practise mind-painting more.' Soarame was tired and he believed Halgon's claim, and he planned to try again tomorrow. 'The egg can be my model.'

'Are you sure you won't spill the ink onto the egg?' Dileys teased. This reminded Soarame of the accident; he looked towards Jemario awkwardly.

Jemario muffled a smile, face turning pink. 'Soarame, maybe we should visit the painting club tomorrow. They might have some ideas for you.'

'That's a good idea!' Soarame's eyes brightened. But before he carried on, Catheray's naughty voice sounded –

'Of course, so that you have more people to spill ink on...'

DRAGON&EMPIRES

The next day, Soarame joined Jemario for the painting club visit. The boy had been worried that the girl wouldn't want to be around him anymore, but he's soon proven wrong. Kardiac had tried to join the two out of curiosity, but Catheray pinched his ear and dragged him away.

Soarame followed Jemario for a tour around the student clubs – most of their offices were located in the same building. Along the way, Soarame sensed obvious attentions from the boys passing by – most of them were gazing at Jemario; some of them were sizing Soarame up too. Soarame pretended to be unaware of all that, but he's actually feeling good inside, for some reasons that he couldn't clearly describe.

Soarame signed up for the painting club – with a very warm welcome from the club boys due to the presence of Jemario. According to the club boys, there's no carving club because few students were capable of doing it.

Feeling disappointed, the two were about to leave, but Soarame was reminded of something – in the welcome ceremony, Dean Romboton mentioned a club named Dragon&Empires.

'Dragon&Empires?' Jemario certainly knew about it. 'It's one of the biggest clubs here. Are you interested?'

'Are you not interested?' Soarame asked back. 'If it's one of the biggest, why haven't I heard much about it in our department?'

'Because few Water students join it,' Jemario fell silent for a bit. 'Dragon&Empires is a competitive sports game. Players fight each other as if they were in a real magic battle, so…'

'I see,' Soarame said, unperturbed. 'Let's go check it out.'

Due to the presence of Jemario, the two received a warm welcome from the Dragon&Empires club too. Soon enough, Soarame learnt about the rules of this game, which was quite simple.

The game was derived from the ancient wars between mankind and dragons. There are three parties in this game: two teams of seven, representing two empires, and a third party, a player representing a dragon. Each empire consists of seven players of any lineage; the dragon is just one player, but he wears some magigears so that he's much stronger. Each party has a gem as their treasure to protect, stored in their base – a chest. Within an hour, any party that loots a gem from any other party, while keeping its own gem safe, wins the game.

The two were told that there would be a game on shortly, so they followed the student on duty at the club, Thom, to their sports ground to watch a live game.

'See that ball in the middle of the playing field? It represents a powerful magic weapon, which can be fetched only by the empires.' Thom pointed at a golden ball in the referee's hands. 'If one empire hits the other's base with it, they score. If time runs out and both gems are safe, the highest score wins.'

'What about the dragon?' Soarame asked. 'How does he score?'

'The dragon doesn't score, but only takes gems.' Thom smiled. 'I know what you are thinking – it's indeed harder for the dragon to win, because in the real history, we won. Plus, dragons don't know how to use human's magic weapons anyway.'

'The dragon is all by himself?' Soarame couldn't help asking. 'That does sound really hard.'

Jemario cut in, 'Not entirely, because he is much stronger: he wears two magigears for the game, so he usually becomes at least a tri-lineager.' She apparently knew the basics of this game. 'Therefore, the empires usually have to spend two to three people to counter him, but they may never be able to beat him.'

'That's correct.' Thom nodded. 'The catch is, if the two empires battle each other too hard, the dragon will grab their gems; if one empire fights the dragon, the other empire will seize its gem.'

'So it's all about the balance.' Soarame got the point. 'What if two empires form an alliance and fight the dragon together?'

'The dragon's cave is immune to the magic weapons and his

gem can only be snatched in two scenarios: he's out with the gem on his body, or he left the gem in the cave unguarded. If the dragon is defending his cave, the game says the dragon is invincible,' Jemario explained. 'And the dragon won't come out for a gem unless the empires are occupied at war – you got it? He can win if he does it right. Plus, the dragon can fly so he's really difficult to counter – see that *flightcloak* he's wearing?'

Soarame looked over and saw a boy in a black cloak. The flightcloak looked similar to a normal robe at first glance, but it's a magigear that allowed its wearer to fly. Usually the dragon had to be a Grade-5 student, because it costs quite some mind power to use the flightcloak.

Right now, the two teams were mostly Grade-4 students, but both captains were Grade-5; with the dragon being the third Grade-5 student. The dragon was a Fire student, and he picked the magigears of Earth and Lightness to make himself into a tri-lineage dragon. Because the players were supposed to summon real magic in the game, additional lineages always helped; in many cases they foiled each other if used properly.

Soon enough the game started, and the dragon was sitting there in its cave – a big chair with a box attached. The dragon's gem was either in his robe or in the box; no one would know unless they beat the dragon or opened the box.

'As you see, the red team has two Wind students, two for Lightness, one each for Fire, Darkness and Earth. This is known to be a good team combo, because the Wind players could speed them up with Wind spells for mobility, plus they could also attack or defend; Darkness for sneaking around and stealing the gem; Lightness for countering the rival Darkness player; Fire for intensive pushing and Earth for defence.' Thom explained as the game progressed. The green team had a similar combo, only that they had one more Darkness and one less Wind player.

So... no Water on either side? Soarame sighed and glanced at Jemario, finding her displeased to see that. *Soon enough, I will let these guys know how much Water can do!*

Firebolts and windblades were already streaking back and forth, and the Darkness players on both sides had disappeared – they both hid in the shadows of their Wind teammates, trying to approach the rival team unnoticed for sneak attacks. At the moment, the red team was pushing and the green was defending, and the red Darkness player got a chance to sneak into the shadow of the Green Earth player – which only Soarame could see, thanks to his special vision. However, at the same time a green Darkness was doing the same thing to a red Wind; and he's so good that he managed to follow the red Wind when the green team struck back and pushed the red team back to near their base.

Both teams kept putting pressure on each other back and forth, at the same time keeping an eye on the dragon. On the other hand, the dragon seemed not worried at all; he's crossing his legs and drinking juice. Soarame was amused to see the dragon student put his gem into the box and deliberately let some players see that, then secretly fetch it back and put it into his pocket.

'He's here!' The red Lightness player shouted all of a sudden. He's guarding their base, and his spell had revealed the green Darkness hiding in his Wind teammate's shadow and trying to approach. The next second, the red Wind player turned around, trying to get the green Darkness, but the sneak attacker had fled already.

This tactic went back and forth for several rounds, until both teams were more familiar with the rivals' style and became confident enough to put more force into their attacks. Right now they were having a group fight in the middle of the field, with only two members on each side defending their bases. The red team was winning the game, pushing the green team back towards their base bit by bit.

'Help, the dragon!' A red basekeeper suddenly noticed that the dragon had left his seat and was flying towards their base; he flew so fast that he's almost there already. A red Wind player dashed back from the group fight, casting windblades towards the dragon as he went. The dragon dodged the windblades easily due to his speed, at the same time using the magigear to cast *stoneballs* towards the red basekeepers. The basekeepers used the Earth shields prepared by their Earth teammate to block the attack; the three red fought the dragon until he had to leave.

Just as the red basekeepers were heaving a sigh of relief, they suddenly realised that a green Darkness player had emerged from behind their Wind teammate, and caught the ball that's passed over from the middle field; before the basekeepers could do much, he threw the ball and hit the red base.

'Green team gets one point!' The referee announced and reset the ball.

After a few more turns, the green team finally won the game thanks to their Darkness players; no team managed to get a gem. Soarame and Jemario enjoyed watching it. For part of the time Jemario was so into the game that she grabbed Soarame's arm out of stress, and Soarame certainly loved that.

After the game, Soarame went to Thom. 'Do you guys have openings on some teams? Is there any requirement for joining?'

'Yes. There are some teams looking for people, and the requirements are up to the captains of the teams,' Thom answered. 'Most competitive teams ask for Grade 4 and above, but if you just want to have fun you can form a team yourself and register with us. What's your grade and major, by the way?'

'I'm in Grade 2, Water,' Soarame answered. He noticed that the students within hearing distance all looked over, and some even sniggered on hearing him. Soarame heard them talking with each other. 'Why doesn't he go and play the card game? Water is pretty strong on the table!'

Seeing and hearing that, Jemario's face darkened. She knew what they were talking about – as she quickly explained to Soarame, there's a card game version of Dragon&Empires, and lots of students played it too. Jemario dragged Soarame's arm and signalled to him to go, but Soarame frowned at the students and approached Thom instead. 'How can I register a team, please?'

'Guys, watch your manners!' Thom yelled at the jokers; then he turned to Soarame again. 'You can register any time, it's very easy. But you need to have a team name ready, and bring at least three more people with you.' Thom patiently explained the details and helped Soarame understand the rules, until Soarame was satisfied and left with Jemario.

'Soarame, that's brave of you.' On their way back, Jemario looked at the boy beside her, eyes filling up with something special. 'No Water student has ever successfully formed a team yet.'

'Well, they didn't try hard enough,' Soarame shook his head. 'What's the big deal?'

'It's kind of a big deal to us as Waters.' Jemario noticed that she had unconsciously grabbed Soarame's arm again, so she hurriedly let go. 'It'll be so awesome to have a Water captain! The entire Water department will be crazy if you can make it...'

'I *will* make it,' Soarame interrupted Jemario all of a sudden. He stopped walking, turned around and looked into her eyes. 'Maybe it'll take some time but – I. Will. Make. It!'

Jemario was stunned for a few seconds. She didn't speak any more but lowered her head. Soarame took it as meaning that Jemario didn't believe it, but she chose not to discourage him; so he's even more determined to do it and prove it. But he didn't know that the real reason why Jemario lowered her head was that she's actually blushing, and she did not want Soarame to notice.

'Soarame is that cool?' Vivarin marvelled upon hearing this story from Jemario. 'I bet he can make it!'

'I bet he can, too!' Dileys was also excited. 'I so can't wait to see a Water captain in the real game! We finally have a hope of getting out of the cards!'

'Yes, I'll personally be a cheerleader for Soarame's team!' Catheray jumped up. 'I'm going to need some practice from now on.'

'Calm down, girl! Soarame is just in Grade 2!' Vivarin chuckled. 'He can't do it any time soon!'

'Maybe, but he seems really serious about it.' Jemario was recalling the moment when Soarame looked into her eyes and said those words, "I. Will. Make. It!" There's so much determination and courage in the boy's eyes – *It's so charming!*

Achoo! At the same time, Soarame sneezed in his dorm.

Filton once said sneezing means someone is talking about me. It must be those guys from the teams laughing at me, then. Soarame shook his head; he didn't really care about what people thought about him. During his childhood, his master had told him many times: do as you believe, and let jokers talk!

It's getting a little better! Soarame looked at his newest work – at least one could tell it's an egg now. Since he had come back from the Dragon&Empires game, he had become even more motivated to practise Water magic. Soarame was surprised to find that this new motivation was helping him much more than money did. His goal was to first master mind-painting, then move to mind-carving – by then he should have reached Grade 4 or even above; then it would be the right time to form a team for the game.

****

Time always goes fast when one is busy. A few weeks passed during which Soarame continued to practise hard at Water magic.

This day, Soarame was painting in the living room when he heard a noise by the door. There's an envelope lying on the floor; it must be the mailman who had squeezed it under the door. Soarame picked it up and realised that it's for Kardiac, but this reminded Soarame that he should have been writing to Filton, and that his uncle hadn't written to him yet.

Soarame recalled the weird dream that he had during his first night on campus, and decided to write Filton a letter right away. He took a pen and wrote a letter, addressing it to Filton's house. Although Filton might not be returning to the village, he wanted to give it a try.

Arriving at the post office, Soarame asked the officer, 'How long does it take to deliver, please?'

'To Corrugon Peninsula? Not long; a couple of days should be enough,' the officer said. 'See that fellow over there? He's fast.'

Soarame was surprised to learn that the delivery time was much shorter than he expected – the officer was pointing at a big bird of some kind. 'His name is Windy, a Wind magimal, one of the best mailmen for the school.'

'That is so cool!' Soarame marvelled. 'Where is he from?'

'I don't know, but the manager's had him since he's an egg.' The officer was obviously fond of Windy as he patted the magimal bird's back. 'So he's been our baby ever since.' If a magimal lived with mankind, it meant it had a human master; in this case it must be the manager. Soarame couldn't help thinking about his magimal egg – what kind of magimal would it be?

Windy could deliver Soarame's letter very fast, but it would take much longer for Filton to send his letter back to Soarame – if Filton could even receive the letter.

'Thanks for the letter, man,' Kardiac said to Soarame when he came back to the dorm. The girls were also there – they were used to hanging out in Soarame's dorm.

'Sure, do you know how long this letter took to reach you?' Soarame asked.

'According to the stamp, it took a month,' Kardiac sighed. 'It's too far and my parents are not wizards, so they could only use ordinary mail. What about you, bro?'

'Mine neither,' Vivarin cut in. 'Most of our parents are not, I suppose.'

'Hey, he's asking a "bro",' Omifo teased Vivarin, but seeing the girl's threatening smile, he had to quickly quiet down.

Everyone was used to seeing this, and they were amused except Soarame. Thinking about his parents, Soarame felt emotional. Just when he's trying to switch topics, there came a vague meowing sound.

'Soarame, do you have a cat in your dorm?' Jemario asked.

'What? Cat? No.' Soarame was happy to see his friends distracted.

'Then how come I heard a cat meowing?' Jemario wondered as they heard another meow. It's faint, but everyone heard it as they paused silently to listen. They were curious, wondering if there might be a cat outside. They opened the door and found it's already dark outside; with Omifo's Lightness magic they looked around the building, but found nothing.

Puzzled, the friends returned to the dorm. Soon enough, they heard another strange meow. They exhausted themselves trying to locate it, but just couldn't find the cat.

Everyone was becoming a little creeped out, especially the girls. The meow was definitely inside the dorm building, but there's definitely no cat there. The weird meow bothered the friends so much that they had to find out where the mysterious cat was.

'Halg, come help us!' Kardiac asked the only one who was lying on the couch. Before he finished speaking, another weird meow broke out.

'Soar, congratulations,' Halgon chortled, breaking the tension. 'It's your magimal egg!'

Hearing that, the friends shoved each other in the rush to Soarame's desk to surround the ivory-white egg. Halgon was right;

the meowing was indeed coming from the egg, and it's getting louder.

'Oh, dear. Soarame, Sachastain sent you a cat?' Kardiac widened his ox-like eyes in shock. 'Cats are born from eggs?'

Soarame was also puzzled. He knew that cats were not egg-born, and he had hoped there's a fierce fighting magimal inside the egg. But now it seemed very likely to be a cat of some sort – well, a magical cat, if that helped.

While Soarame was wondering, with a soft creak, a crack appeared in the "cat egg". All of a sudden, a ray of rainbow-coloured light shone through the crack in the eggshell, and the ivory-white egg started glowing. The cracks began to increase, zigzagging all over the eggshell. As this happened, a glittering and translucent aura glowed around the egg. Soarame and his friends gazed in amazement; it looked beautiful.

The intense pulse of vitality emitting from inside the egg excited the kids. With the appearance of one last light-filled crack, the whole egg exploded, its shell shattering. The little magimal body inside radiated dazzling white light; it shone so brightly that Soarame couldn't see clearly what it was. The eggshell pieces fragmented even more and became countless light dots which converged on the dazzling light cloud surrounding the egg.

This scene lasted for a little while before the lights finally faded. Soarame and his friends were so stunned that no one in the dorm had said a word. Not until the dazzling light faded did Catheray call out. 'Praise Libral! How cute this is!'

The little magimal finally revealed itself – it's a fluffy white kitten.

The girls were dazzled by the kitten's appearance; in contrast, the boys' reaction was a little different. Every one of them had been expecting something more powerful and ferocious – what could such a small cat do? Sure, it's cute, but could it beat a tiger?

'Soarame, I'm so jealous! A kitten is way better than a bizarre beast of some sort!' Dileys tugged Soarame's arm. 'Go pick it up!'

Soarame woke up from his thoughts and took the meowing kitten in his arms. Feeling the softness and warmth from the little fur ball, he suddenly melted inside and realised that he shouldn't be complaining – it's a life, and he would be its master from now on!

'Meow.' The little fluffy creature looked at Soarame with great curiosity from a pair of crystal-clear blue eyes. Surrounded by the exclamations from his friends, Soarame held the kitten up to his cheek affectionately. At the same time, he sensed that there's a mind connection established between the kitten and himself – this must be the bond that's formed through the hatching process, through all the mind-power he had put into the egg. At this time, Soarame was reminded of Richie once again – those bonding efforts had never been successful, so this kitten was Soarame's first magimal; and he finally understood the difference that having a magimal made.

The kitten also seemed to recognise Soarame as its master because of the mind connection. Its two big eyes closed into slits as it enjoyed Soarame stroking it, and it began rubbing against his face with its head.

'Soarame, can we pet it too?' The girls were entranced.

Everyone got a chance to hold this snow-white kitten. Even the boys had to admit that they actually loved it; their initial disappointment had vanished upon touching the cute little kitten.

'Should we name him... or her?' Jemario suggested. 'Is it a boy or a girl?'

'Yeah, let's find that out first,' Vivarin demanded. 'Come on man, we're all waiting.'

Soarame turned the kitten over gently and started to check closely. Everyone was watching Soarame, holding their breath and hoping to read the answer on his face. Unfortunately, time passed and Soarame was still staring at the cat.

'Come on man! Boy or girl? What are you waiting for?' Kardiac was running out of patience.

'I... I don't know?' Soarame expressed his confusion with embarrassment. 'How do you tell?'

Hearing that, everyone burst into laughter. Dileys took the cat from him and checked. 'It's a girl,' she pronounced confidently as she handed the kitten back to Soarame. She couldn't hold back her chuckle though.

'How do you know?' asked Omifo.

The girls had to laugh again. Dileys couldn't find the best way to answer this. 'You boys really should read more books!'

'Shh, I know!' Kardiac wasn't convinced. 'Look at the chest. It looks fat, so it's a girl!'

Hearing Kardiac, the girls collapsed in gales of laughter. Kardiac realised that he must have said something ridiculously wrong, so he tried again. 'I didn't mean fat like my chest, but in another way...'

'Okay, just stop, please!' Catheray was lying on the floor, her stomach aching with laughter. 'We all have kittens at home so we can tell. It's subtle, so don't worry about it!'

'It's true,' Vivarin supported her friend. 'It's hard to explain, but trust us – it's a baby girl.'

Soarame was shocked by the fact that his first ferocious battling magimal turned out to be a cute girl cat. He held the kitten in his arms and stared blankly for a while. 'Okay, at least we can name her now.'

'Let me see...' Soarame sized the white kitten up and down. 'She's as white as snow, so I'll call her – Snower!'

'I think Snower is a great name, especially for a Water magimal,' Omifo chimed in. 'But is she?'

'Magimal? Lineage?' Kardiac curled his lips disapprovingly. 'Forget that. Just take her as a pet.'

Hearing that, everyone went quiet. They had to agree with Kardiac – how powerful could a cat be, even if she could perform magic somehow?

At that moment, Snower suddenly meowed and glared at Kardiac angrily with her big azure eyes. She stretched out her little claws towards him, signalling a threat. However, Snower was so young that this movement was no deterrent whatsoever; on the contrary, it looked amusing and adorable.

Seeing how Snower seemed to be able to understand human language, everyone was surprised.

'Snower won't be that simple. She's not just a pet.' Halgon decided to speak up. 'You guys remember how splendid the hatching process was, don't you?'

Everyone was suddenly reminded. They looked at each other and nodded.

'First of all, cats don't hatch from eggs – at least I've never heard of any. Have you?' Seeing everyone shaking their heads, Halgon continued, 'So Snower definitely isn't just a cat. Besides, I once saw a high-ranking magimal egg hatching before. It's the same process but much quicker than with Snower.'

Everyone looked at each other and marvelled at Halgon's knowledge. 'What magimal do you think Snower is, then?'

'I don't know.' Halgon shrugged his shoulders. 'But I am sure that she's of a rare kind.' This time Snower looked at Halgon as if she were smiling and nodding.

'She really can understand us?' Vivarin asked in disbelief.

'I've heard of a kind of high-ranking magimal that looks like a cat. It's called a "dragcat",' Dileys exclaimed. 'Books say that they are the children of dragons and some high-ranking tiger-like magimal.'

'Not a dragcat, although they are born from eggs.' Halgon sounded very certain. 'A dragcat has a zebra print on its body and scales on its limbs.'

'How do you know all this?' Once again everyone was amazed; they threw admiring looks at Halgon. 'What's Snower, then?'

Seeing the confusion on everyone's faces, Snower held her head high and meowed, as if she's proud of her mysterious origins.

'Soarame, here's a thought.' Halgon didn't answer the question directly. 'A magimal can communicate with its master through *mind-talk*, so you can ask Snower directly what she is.'

'Oh yes!' Soarame smacked his own head. His master taught him about this long ago, but he had never had a chance to put it into practice. 'I never tried it. How do I do it?'

'It's just like performing magic, only even easier,' Halgon answered. 'Mind-talk is essentially talking using mind power. Just concentrate and sense the mind connection between you and Snower, then talk to her using the connection instead of your mouth!'

'Wow, is that real?' Everyone was excited. They urged Soarame to test it, and they couldn't wait to see what would happen next.

Soarame tried and quickly learnt the mind-talk trick. It's instinctive if one had a magimal.

{*Snower, can you hear me?*}

SNOWER'S PRESENT

{*Snower, can you hear me?*}

The beauty of mind-talk was that it's independent of the voice, and therefore the communication was always private and much faster.

{*I...I...meow!*} Snower seemed too young to communicate yet. Soarame tried several times, but it didn't work. Everyone was disappointed, but the great news was that Snower would most likely to be able to talk in the future.

'Are all magimals born with the language talent?' Kardiac protested. 'That's so unfair! I spent several years learning to speak after I was born!'

'It's not our language, nor any human language,' Halgon answered, amused. 'Mind-talk is as simple as a mind talking to another mind, passing information and thoughts regardless of any language barrier... It's an amazing way of communicating and hard to explain, until you do it yourself.'

'Wait. I'm lost.' Catheray cut in, pouting. 'So, Snower can talk to anyone, in any language, when she grows up?'

'No, she can only meow when she talks to anyone other than Soarame, so only Soarame can understand her even after she grows up,' Halgon explained. 'But as a high-ranking magimal, she can probably understand us.'

'Oh gosh, it's too complicated.' Kardiac complained, ruffling his own hair. 'How do you know all this, anyway?'

'Books. Plus, my family does some business with magimals.' Halgon hesitated a bit before continuing, 'So I know that only high-ranking magimals can mind-talk; the lower ones can "*mind-listen*", but won't be able to talk back.'

A magimal dealer family! Wow, that's impressive. Everyone

was surprised by Halgon's background. Soarame recalled that his master once told him about this, that magimal dealer families must have some very powerful wizards at their bases, because they need to battle the wild magimals and conquer them. According to his master, most magimals were enemies of humans – they invaded towns and villages and seized livestock for food; many times they did that to people too. Therefore, magimal dealers often showed up to protect people and carried out their business along the way; but sometimes they overdid it by invading magimals' territories and stealing their young.

Having learnt about Halgon's background, Soarame suspected that Halgon must have a bonded magimal himself. But Halgon never mentioned anything about it, so Soarame decided not to ask until they get more acquainted.

It's getting late, so the girls had to leave, but the investigation regarding Snower was by no means over. The next day, Soarame and his roommates went into the library, searching for books on magimals.

'Soarame, starting to explore the library already?' Rodka's voice sounded from nearby. 'Interested in magimals?'

Soarame's eyes brightened up on seeing Rodka. 'Yes, we are looking for a cat-like, high-ranking magimal. Could you help us please?'

'Oh?' Rodka's eyebrow curved up. 'You have a magimal? And it's cat-like?'

'Yes,' Kardiac chimed in. 'A strange one!'

Before anyone else had a chance to speak, Kardiac described the process of Snower's hatching. Rodka's expression changed while listening to Kardiac's description and his interest was caught. Even students that were just passing by overheard Kardiac – it wasn't easy to ignore his large voice – and threw curious looks at the friends. Rodka helped the boys search through books for the entire day, but they found nothing. At Rodka's request, the boys agreed to let him see Snower himself.

Getting to the dorm, Rodka's eyes instantly locked on the small fluffy white ball that's huddling on the couch. Soarame went over to stroke Snower. 'I've tried to mind-talk with Snower, but she's too young to do it yet.'

'Mind-talk? Really?' Rodka seemed really amazed. 'She looks just like a normal kitten! Let me continue helping you find her breed from the library. I go there all the time anyway.'

'That's brilliant, thanks so much!' Kardiac was feeling blessed. 'Any time I see all those books I get a headache!'

There's a brief knock at the door right then. 'Hey Soarame, we are here again!' Catheray called out, following Dileys, Jemario and Vivarin into Soarame's room.

'We missed Snower!' added Dileys, but she froze at the sight of the back turned to her – *He looks familiar, could it be... is it...?*

Rodka turned around to see the new arrivals, making the overjoyed Dileys' face turn pink.

...Rodka? Dileys felt a rush of happy surprise. *Why is he here?*

'Wake up girl, act natural!' Catheray whispered to Dileys and elbowed her gently. Jemario and Vivarin also chuckled knowingly. As Dileys' best friends, how could they not know about her secret crush?

'Have we met before?' Rodka asked Dileys. 'Did you help Soarame with his college application on registration day?'

'Yes! My name is Dileys,' Dileys introduced herself, looking quite nervous. Soarame had to chuckle; he had realized what's going on with her a while ago. The girls certainly knew it more clearly, and they felt so helpless for their friend – Dileys was such a confident girl, but once Rodka showed up she became almost another person.

Rodka only had time for a brief chat before leaving, which was a pity to Dileys, but she's still very happy. She couldn't help recalling Soarame's decision to gamble on Spanflow collage a few months ago. She felt really blessed that she hadn't stopped him from doing that.

Since then, Rodka started to explore libraries all over the campus. Soarame and his friends also made various efforts, but they didn't have as much patience as Rodka and pretty soon got tired of it. They didn't find anything valuable about Snower, and there wasn't much that they could do other than checking books. Meanwhile, Snower behaved pretty much like an ordinary kitten – eat, sleep, poop and meow; so Soarame and his friends lost the motivation to pursue their research. This went on for a while, until one day.

This day, the boys and girls were playing with Snower as usual, except for Dileys and Vivarin, who had gone to the library to help Rodka. Rodka was still making efforts to discover Snower's breed, which was a perfect opportunity for Dileys to get acquainted with him. But she's just too shy to go alone, so she dragged Vivarin along for company.

'Meow!' Right then, Snower was trying to mind-talk with Soarame. Although she still couldn't form words, she's able to send the rough meaning of her thoughts.

'You want to go out?' Soarame managed to catch Snower's meaning. 'Sure, let's do it.'

Jemario and Catheray joined the boys for a walk. The friends walked to the nearest lake and had fun playing and talking on the shore, until Snower started another round of mind-talk –

{There, there!}

Soarame was surprised to "hear" this. 'Hey guys, Snower just talked again.' he added, pointing towards the lake. 'She wants to go to the other side of the lake.'

The crew followed Snower's demands out of curiosity, and they walked a long way to reach the other side. However, Snower was still pointing her claw forward and meowing.

'Guys, are you sure we should still go ahead?' asked Omifo, looking uncertainly into the thickening forest. 'We don't know that area very well.'

'Hey, what are you worried about?' Catheray turned up her nose at this. 'We are on campus, it's safe!'

Most of the team agreed with Catheray, so they went on exploring. But after walking for quite a while and the trees had started to thin again, Snower was still meowing that they should keep going ahead.

'Soarame, are you sure you're not playing us?' Jemario poked Soarame's side. 'We are already at the campus boundary!'

'Snower, are you sure you're not playing us?' Soarame poked Snower's side, making everyone chuckle. 'We are already at the campus boundary!'

'Meow!' Snower was shaking her head rapidly, as if she's really anxious. *{There, there!}*

'But there's only a cliff in front of us.' Soarame looked ahead at the sharply rising cliff face above the treetops, which marked the campus' edge. 'Snower, what do you actually want?'

'Meow!' Snower suddenly jumped out of Soarame's arms and ran ahead alone. This astonished everyone; they all dashed forward to follow the kitten.

'Snower, wait!' Kardiac shouted at the top of his voice. Snower ran so fast that the crew could barely keep up with her, and they were never able to get closer.

'Praise Libral, are you sure she's just a baby?' By the time Snower finally stopped at the bottom of the cliff, everyone was breathing heavily. Soarame rushed ahead to take the kitten back into his arms, but Snower raised her claw and waved towards the cliff –

A ray of green light emitted from Snower's little paw, casting a circle of green-ish colour onto the cliff.

'Oh my, did you see that?' Jemario muffled a scream. 'What did she do?'

Everyone was taken aback. They looked at each other, with their eyes wide open.

'Guys, we should go.' Halgon suddenly spoke up. 'I have a bad feeling…' Before Halgon could finish, a blast of noise erupted out of the cliff.

JIGAGA….

The noise sounded so loud and ferocious. At the same time, they felt a big wave of suction that held them irresistibly. The next second, they felt an overwhelming dizziness that's similar to passing through the Libral Gate, but a lot stronger –

Pong, pong, pong, pong, pong, pong!

Soarame and his friends fell to the ground one after another, in a completely dark space. They got up quickly, finding themselves somehow teleported into this new strange place. Everyone was terrified.

'What the heck is this?' Kardiac cried in a shuddering voice, pulling out his wand. 'Where are we?' With that, he hurriedly chanted a short incantation and a tongue of flame emerged from the tip of his wand, providing them with some light. The crew could now see that they were standing in a cave of some kind, facing an opening – *An exit?* – not too far ahead.

'Snower, what did you do?' Soarame searched around and

finally found the little kitten huddled near a boulder, but Snower wasn't really able to properly communicate yet. She kept meowing rapidly, sounding anxious.

'What did she say?' Jemario grabbed Soarame's arm out of fear. 'Where are we?'

'I don't know. She probably doesn't know either.' Soarame stepped in between Jemario and the path to the exit. Thanks to Scankeen's training, in this abnormal situation, Soarame exhibited a calmness that's rare to see in someone of his age. 'We have to find our way out, whatever this place is.'

'Let's call Chelonad first!' Omifo suggested anxiously. 'Chelonad, we need help!'

They waited a few seconds, but Chelonad didn't respond.

'He probably can't hear us,' Halgon guessed. 'We are likely to be off campus right now.'

'Let me try.' Kardiac was about to make full use of his lungs, but Halgon stopped him by covering his mouth.

Just then, a weird noise came from somewhere ahead. *Gulala...*

'What's that?' Heads turned in fear.

Gulalalala... The noise sounded clearer than the last time, as if it's approaching. Every few seconds it started up again, each time sounding closer than the last one.

'What the heck?' The kids were creeped out hearing this. Soarame hurriedly gathered his friends together, signalling to them to be silent. He asked Kardiac to extinguish the flame, so that the cave became dark again. Snower also stopped meowing and hid in Soarame's robe; he could feel that she and Jemario were both shaking in his arms. At the same time, Soarame heard Halgon whisper to Omifo and Kardiac to take care of Catheray, then Halgon went to the front of the team.

Strangely, when they became silent, the weird noise also stopped. The kids were trying hard to keep their breathing quiet, while looking around to get a better understanding of the environment; but this place was just too dark to provide any clues. No one dared to make any noise, so they had to touch each other for signalling their communications, while breathing the tense air.

After a few minutes, the kids touched each other again to check if anyone had noticed anything new, but the answer seemed to be negative. Halgon signalled that he would start moving ahead, carefully. Catheray wanted to stop him, but Omifo dragged her back and signalled her to stay put. Halgon forged ahead for a few feet, leaving the safe contact of his friends, but still couldn't see anything because of the darkness in this place. Just as he's about to go further, a hand pressed on his shoulder, signalling him to stop.

Halgon lookcd back and could barely see Soarame holding Jemario with one hand, linking them back to the crew, and grabbing him with the other. Halgon leaned back to Soarame and Soarame whispered, 'It's down there.'

Down? Halgon turned around and looked very carefully at the ground in front of him, then gasped – Soarame was right, the cave that they were in seemed to come to an abrupt end, nothing but open-air blackness before them. Halgon was close to the exit of the cave, so if he had gone further he might have fallen. Halgon gave a thumbs-up to Soarame – hopefully he could see it – and then moved slowly towards the edge of the cave's stone floor to look out.

'No, something is down there!' Soarame's whisper stopped Halgon again. 'It's just beyond the exit, hanging on the wall down there!'

Soarame could see this because his special eyes saw the colour of magic elements – he saw a cluster of yellow, meaning Earth.

What! Halgon felt a wave of goose bumps all over his body. Halgon had no idea of what Soarame saw, but his instinct told him that Soarame was probably right. So Halgon started to fall back from the exit with Soarame, but stepped on a rock which made a small noise –

Jigaga! The next second, something jumped up from outside of the cave and landed inside, roaring. The friends were all terrified; their screams echoed back and forth in the cave. Omifo had been prepared; he quickly performed Lightness magic and lit up his wand, so that the friends could see the thing that's coming for them –

It looked like a beetle of some sort, only the size of a buffalo.

'Ahhh!' The sight of the scary-looking creature made the friends scream again. 'A monster!'

They tried to flee, but in the next second they realised that they were trapped – the cave they were in wasn't as deep as it seemed in the dark, and ahead of them the only exit's blocked by the giant beetle.

'It's a magimal, not a monster, so calm down,' Halgon took a defensive pose with his wand in hand. 'And I know that insect-like magimals usually aren't of a high rank, so we should be able to handle it if we stay together.'

'Omi, Kardy, take care of Jem and Snower,' Soarame gritted his teeth and gently pushed Jemario and Snower to his friends. With his wand also in hand, Soarame stood side by side with Halgon, confronting the giant beetle. Thanks to Scankeen's memory crystal, Soarame had seen lots of scary magimals in a very vivid way, so he wasn't panicked. But he's amazed that Halgon was as cool-headed as him.

'Do you recognize this magimal?' Soarame asked Halgon.

'Not exactly, but it is probably a Darkness one,' Halgon said, observing the giant beetle.

'It can do Earth, too,' Soarame said with confidence. 'So its scales must be tough.'

Halgon suddenly remembered what it was. 'You are right! I know what it is now. It's a beetalbull, an Adept-level magimal of Darkness and Earth. Careful; it'll charge at us and try to knock us down.'

Halgon's words reminded Soarame of the boar-like magimal he had faced when he's little, but that one was just a Novice one, according to his master – that's why it's scared off as soon as it sensed Soarame's Lightning gift. This time, the problem would not be that easy.

Gulala... The beetalbull started to make the weird noise again and moved towards the kids on its six crab-like legs. Its mouth was opening and closing in a creepy way that freaked them out. It had the serrated mandibles of an insect, but on either side of its mouth were tusk-like growths.

'Stand upright and stretch your body out!' Halgon commanded. 'Make yourself look big; or it may charge at any time!'

'Ahh!' A scream sounded from behind – Kardiac had slipped and fallen. This attracted the beetalbull's attention; it roared again and charged at the boy lying on the ground.

At the same time, Halgon jumped towards the beetalbull to save his friend. However, he's too small and light and bounced off the magimal's hard shell right away, falling over on his back several feet away. But thanks to his effort, the beetalbull's attention was diverted and it stopped too.

'Halg!' Everyone was worried, but Halgon jumped up from the ground swiftly, a shield of some kind appearing on his left arm.

'I'm okay! It can't break my stone shield,' Halgon walked forward again. 'You guys check around, see if there's another way to get out!'

Jigaga... Jigaga! Just as the crew started move together, another roar sounded from outside the cave. Everyone paled on hearing this – there's more than one beetalbull out there, and it sounded like they were coming in!

'Oh my god, we're done!' Kardiac muttered. 'No! No, no!'

'Don't say that!' Soarame yelled back at him. 'We've got each other! We'll be fine!'

'There's another one!' Omifo suddenly screamed, as they saw another giant figure climb up to the cave and squeeze through the opening.

Soarame ground his teeth hard and was determined to spell his best magic – windblades. Although he's supposed to keep his secret, at this moment he had no other choice if they wanted to survive.

'Soar, what are you doing!' Jemario screamed at Soarame, Snower clutched in her arms. She saw him walking ahead towards the two beetalbulls, alone. 'Don't be stupid! You can't fight them!'

'Trust me, guys, there's no other way,' Soarame reassured her, taking a deep breath. 'Everyone, get ready to break out with me!'

'Let me help you!' Halgon hurried forward with his stone shield in front of him, but Soarame gesticulated to him to stay back and went further ahead.

Gulala... Before anyone spoke again, the beetalbulls made their weird noise again and stepped backwards as Soarame approached. Everyone was surprised to see this, including Soarame himself. The boy hesitated for a second, then decided to try taking one step more –

Gulala! Both beetalbulls fell back immediately, looking restless for some reason. Soarame took another step forward. The beetalbulls started to roar as if they sensed a threat, and kept falling back.

'They are afraid of you!' Halgon's eyes brightened. 'But why?'

'I don't know!' Soarame was bewildered to see this sudden change. He's about to spell his windblades, but now it seemed that he didn't have to anymore. Soarame stepped forward again, and this time another beetalbull arrived at the cave entrance. It bumped into the two retreating ones and bounced up against the ceiling. The three beetalbulls were chaotically crashing against each other and making creepy noises.

'Beetalbulls don't have good eyes or ears, but they have excellent noses,' Halgon spoke up. 'There must be something on you that frightened them! What are you carrying in your robe?'

Just when everyone was wondering, Jemario suddenly screamed, 'Snower, don't!'

Snower jumped from her arms and ran towards Soarame. The next second, she climbed up under Soarame's robe and onto his chest, scratching him from inside the robe.

'Oh, you mean this?' Soarame was surprised and took something out from his robe –

A big, black feather.

'Meow!' Snower stretched out her little fluffy head from Soarame's collar, nodding rapidly.

The feather from Volsta! Soarame suddenly realised. *They can smell Volsta, and Volsta is a high-ranking magimal, so they are afraid!*

Soarame held the feather out and stretched his arm towards the beetalbulls. The three giant magimals immediately retreated several feet back, at the edge of the cave now. They looked too nervous to even roar any more.

'They fear this feather!' Soarame was certain now. He raised the black feather to his forehead and walked towards the beetalbull, making them panic and try to flee. The one in the back was the first to get squeezed out of the cave opening, screaming as it fell.

'Is this real?' Everyone marvelled at this, especially Kardiac. 'We don't have to die now?'

'Shut up!' Catheray kicked his shin. The crew started to follow Soarame and moved forwards, nervous but excited.

'Holy crap!' The team didn't take long to reach the exit of the cave, but when they looked out their blood froze. There's a gigantic cavern stretching in front of them in Omifo's light, with countless small caves – just like the one that they stood in – scattered over the walls of the cavern. The cave they were in was halfway up the wall, a hundred feet from the ground, which they could barely see. There were countless things moving between the ground below and each small cave, looking like a massive amount of ants busy at work together.

'It's a beetalbull nest!' Halgon gasped at this. 'Thank god you had the feather, Soar, otherwise…'

'Look! They are climbing up to us!' Jemario pointed downwards at a wave of dark figures. 'Dozens of them!'

'Oh no!' Soarame had goose bumps when he saw them. 'There's no way back, so we need to hold it up here!'

The beetalbulls approached the crew soon enough. They all sensed the threat from the feather but with so many of them now, they seemed to be ready to join forces and launch an attack. Right then, hundreds of beetalbulls had gathered around the exit of the small cave, hanging on the walls, encircling Soarame and his friends on all sides of the exit.

'Holy mama!' Kardiac feared he would wet his pants. 'They are going to eat us! They are ready!'

'Could you just shut up!' Catheray kicked him, tears in her eyes. Jemario had her wand in hand, peering at the still-gathering beetalbulls; she seemed to preparing herself for the forthcoming fight but she looked terrified. Omifo made a desperate attempt to shine a ray of light into a beetalbull's four glowing green eyes, but it just turned its head to avoid direct contact with the ray – no miracle happened.

'Darn it!' Halgon muttered. He took a deep breath and seemed to be determined. 'Guys, stand behind me. Let me do this.'

'What? What do you want to do?' asked Soarame.

'We may never see each other again, but I'm glad I met you guys,' Halgon cracked a wan smile. 'See you, my friends! Good luck!'

'No!!' Although Soarame wasn't sure what Halgon was about to do, he knew it wasn't going to be good. He grabbed Halgon's arm and tried to drag him back, only to find that this boy was surprisingly strong and he couldn't move him an inch. Incredibly anxious now, Soarame jumped in front of him to stop him from whatever he's about to do – 'No way!!!!'

With Soarame's roaring, a ray of green light glimmered from his necklace. The light was very dim, so no one noticed it.

'WHAT THE...?!' The next second, a large deep voice resounded all throughout the gigantic cave. 'Are you kidding me? How did you kids get in here?'

The friends recognised the voice. 'Chelonad!' they yelled back. 'Help, please!'

'Sure. Go through that whirlpool behind you,' Chelonad commanded. 'Go!'

The kids looked back and saw a whirlpool appearing on the wall. With Soarame and Halgon covering their retreat, the team quickly backed away and stepped through the whirlpool. As that happened, the gang of beetalbulls started chasing them, but Halgon managed to summon a series of stone thorns that stuck out of the wall and the ground to obstruct their way. However, a beetalbull's reaching leg still caught Halgon in the foot and tried to take him, just as Soarame was about to step into the whirlpool and leave.

'Let go, you freak!' Halgon yelled loudly, but he couldn't escape from its grasp. Soarame pounced on the beetalbull, stabbing hard at it between the eyes with the point of the feather. As the beetalbull was freaked out and sprang back, Soarame grabbed Halgon under one shoulder and dashed towards the whirlpool, half carrying him.

'Your feather!' Halgon saw the black feather had been knocked out of Soarame's hand when he leaped off the beetalbull, and had fallen on the ground between them and the beetalbull. Both boys were thinking about fetching it; however it's too risky to do that in front of a blast of beetalbulls.

Just then, a white flash emanated from Soarame's chest, grabbed the feather and returned in a blink. The boys were both awestruck and excited to see this; they threw themselves at the whirlpool without hesitation this time.

'Praise Libral, there you are!' On the lawn, the rest of the crew had been horribly anxious. They had been out here for a little while; the longer they waited, the more their fears had grown. 'Are you okay? Did you get hurt?'

'I'm fine, but Halg's leg was hurt.' Soarame was breathing heavily. 'Let's check it out now!'

'I'm fine, don't worry.' Halgon was laughing, lying on the grass. 'This is my best tour so far!'

'You are crazy, man!' Kardiac was relieved to see this. 'I thought we were dead in there!'

'Seriously, what a day!' Catheray was thumping her chest as though she's checking that her heart was still there. 'If not for Soar and Halg, we would just...'

'You kids, don't you think you owe me an explanation?' Chelonad's voice boomed. 'Why on earth were you ever in there?'

'It's...' The friends looked around at each other, not sure what to say.

'We don't know either, but it must be the black feather!' Halgon sat up. 'And we were sucked in! We didn't want to be there!'

'Show me the feather!' commanded Chelonad. 'Where did you get it?'

Soarame was hesitating about what to say, but Chelonad's voice sounded again. 'It doesn't make sense. How did you break the magic seal with a feather?'

'We broke a magic seal? How were we able to do that?' Halgon asked. 'We were just walking around and we didn't do anything. What's that horrible, scary place anyway?'

'It's an Expert trial site, for the teachers in school. It is not part of the campus and you are not allowed to be in there!' Chelonad answered. 'You could very well have died!'

The friends looked at Soarame in silence – the little troublemaking kitten was still hiding inside his robe.

'This whole thing is strange; I'll have to check it.' Chelonad sounded serious. 'Now, you are dismissed, but keep all this to yourselves and stay away from this area!'

'Sure, we will.' Soarame stood up. 'Guys, let's go.'

Inside the cave, Chelonad's voice sounded low, as if he's muttering. 'Volsta's feather, Scankeen's token... interesting,' he continued. 'Scankeen's students are all troublemakers, just like the last one... not even surprising!'

'Snower, thanks so much for the "present"! You are just unbelievable.' Back in the dorm, Soarame managed to make a joke of it all. 'How did you do that, anyway? You actually broke the seal of an Expert trial site?'

'Meow.' Snower looked embarrassed, and it seemed that she wanted to cry.

'Don't say that! She didn't mean to.' Jemario elbowed Soarame aside and took the little white kitten into her arms, cuddling her.

'Yes, we are all good, aren't we? Let it go.' Catheray couldn't bear to see Snower about to cry. 'Plus, if not for her, we wouldn't have had the chance to hear someone cry "Holy mama"!'

Kardiac blushed; that's definitely not something he felt proud of.

While the friends were still chuckling, Rodka, Dileys and Vivarin had returned from the library. 'Hey guys, guess what we found?' Seeing everyone covered in dust and dirt, they looked startled. 'Praise Libral... what did we miss?'

Kardiac was again the first one to bounce up and do the talking. Soon enough, the three had heard about the adventure; gasps sounded frequently as the story went on.

'You guys are creeping us out, but it kind of matches up!' Rodka's eyes brightened up after hearing everything. 'Snower could cast spells as a baby, and she runs fast – same as the story!'

'What story?' The adventure crew was confused.

'We might have found a clue about Snower's origin!' Rodka took out a book and handed it over to Soarame. 'It's a wizard's autobiography. Check it out for yourselves!'

A BIG ROACH?

...I finally arrived at Fallen Mountain for my trial. I've been trying to become a Master over the past few decades, but it's just so difficult and I got stuck. The only chance to break through is to engage in furious magic battles and push my limit. So, here I came.

In the first few days, it's mostly about tedious hiking to get into the deeper forest, and dealing with magimals of Novice- to Adept-level along the way. Until one day, a torrent of frightening noises passed from the inner area of the mountain, and it sounded like a magic battle. But I'm confident, or perhaps, reckless enough to have decided to go for a look.

I marched ahead with great caution, and finally arrived at the battlefield. Hiding between trees, I discovered something that astonished me completely – one party in the battle turned out to be three adult Crystal-eyed Bristled Lions. Each of those lions was supposed to be as strong as myself, if not stronger – in fact, I'm pretty sure that the biggest one was a Baron. And the even more shocking part was that their enemy turned out to be only one magimal – a small white one, of an unknown breed!

The battle was ferocious and brutal. Although I don't like to admit this, I actually panicked. But I didn't blame myself – both parties involved a Baron; I could have easily gotten killed.

I didn't know what I was thinking, but I decided to stay and keep watching. The lions were known to prefer living alone, so why would the three team up?

The unknown white magimal was so swift that I couldn't

catch a clear sight of it. And due to the ferocity of the battle, I couldn't get any closer. So the only thing I could tell was that the unknown magimal looked like a white cat, with a giant tail compared to its body size. And soon enough, I noticed that the magimal's rear legs seemed to be wounded, blood covering its fur.

As I proceeded for some distance, I found a white egg lying in the grass, with fresh blood streaks on its surface. I was certain that it's newly-laid, and there's intense aura of vitality being emitted from the egg. According to my experiences and sensibility, I could ascertain that it belonged to the unknown cat-like magimal.

But how could a "cat" lay an egg, even a magimal one? I realized I had another question before anything. Then I realised that, now that the cat was a mother, the blood on her rear legs was probably not a wound, but the remaining blood from the delivery! For heaven's sake, she had only just delivered, but then was besieged by three lions?

Suddenly, I believed that I figured out the reason behind the battle. The three bandit lions wanted to eat the mother and the egg, so that they would become more powerful. However, the mother was too strong for any one of them, so they had to unite and strike her, and at her weakest moment!

How utterly upsetting!

I just couldn't watch the horrible tragedy happen!

I know most magimals aren't friends to us but... for heaven's sake, she's a mother! She's giving her life to protect her baby! How much pain was she suffering while I stood back and watched?

No, I must help her! NOW!

So I did. I burst out to attack the lions, and injured one gravely though he had put up quite a fight, badly injuring me as well. But yes, I did it. That lion was shortly finished off – by the hysteric mother. The other two lions ran off, leaving the mother with me. She then spoke to me, in human language, verifying my speculation.

The mother urged me to take her egg and protect it. I meant to take her with me too, but she refused, knowing that I hardly had much energy left to escape alone with the egg and that the lions were likely to come back soon. Therefore, as she died of her wounds, she asked me to cut off her tail and take away her soulcore, then burn her body, so that it wouldn't be eaten by the lions. But of course, the most important thing was to take good care of her egg.

What else could I say? I had no reason to refuse a dying mother. The clock was ticking, so I had to hurriedly do as she wished. But a problem emerged when it came to burning her body – I'm not a Fire wizard and all my items had been lost in the battle. There's no time for me to burn her body, because I had sensed the lions coming back for us! What shall I do?

I don't know how I eventually got out. I do not want to recall my final choices – I had to give up on her body and escape as fast as I could. I knew this meant that her body would be eaten up by her mortal enemies, but I had no other choice if I were to save myself and her egg.

But how guilty I was feeling!

I really didn't know how I would face the mother in heaven, may her soul rest in peace.

I wish I had had a chance to ask about her breed, before she passed away. So I called her a Giantail Cat, according to her remarkably sized tail. She told me that, by eating her tail, any kind of injury could be healed. But I hadn't even managed to burn her body, how could I deserve to use her tail to get healed?

I thought it over and over, and concluded that it's a waste for me to consume her tail. I was too old anyway; even if I was healed, so what? I had not seen any hope to become a Master so far, so my life would end in a few years anyway. I thus decided to leave her tail and soulcore to my two students, one for each of them. But they didn't convince me as being Master material either, so the most precious egg itself ought to be in better hands. Therefore, I started searching for a suitable owner for the Giantail Cat egg.

However, my injuries only got worse despite my care, and I still couldn't locate a good fit. Until one day, I fortunately met a young man. He's a warrior, so he probably couldn't own the egg; but I heard that he had risked his life to assassinate a vicious wizard. After carrying out a few subtle tests of his character, I decided to trust him, and urged him to help me find the right person for the egg. Praise Libral – he agreed, even though I had told him it could put him in danger to protect this treasure against a lot of ambitious and powerful people out there who would do anything to get their hands on this egg.

I'm dying, but I still don't know how I will face the mother – if I ever meet her in the other world. I've written down the whole thing as a record, but I deliberately removed all the names throughout my autobiography. Only in this way can the precious Giantail Cat egg be best protected.

Hopefully, the baby cat will find a distinguished young wizard to bond with, and they will become best friends and take care of each other.

Only then would its mother's soul rest in peace…

The story about the Giantail Cat ended there, and the rest of the autobiography was irrelevant. Holding this thin book, a tearful Soarame felt that it's as heavy as a mountain.

Silently wiping away their tears, the group finally realised that if the Giantail Cat was really Snower's mother, Snower's origins were much more heart-rending than they had imagined. Every feature of the Giantail Cat sounded like Snower, so perhaps the egg was the very one that Snower had hatched from. However, a big difference was Snower's tail.

Everyone looked over at the little fluffy kitten, passing over her watchful blue eyes to her round little tail.

'Giantail Cat? Snower is clearly a bunny-tail cat!' Kardiac grinned.

'Yeah, it's very different,' Catheray agreed. 'Maybe that wasn't Snower's mother?'

'I think it was,' Rodka disagreed. 'High-ranking cat-like magimals are very rare, let alone egg-born ones. If Snower wasn't right here in front of us, I wouldn't even believe this story. They must be connected.'

'That makes sense,' Halgon agreed with Rodka. 'Except for the tail, they all match up. As for the tail, it can grow – all kittens have short tails, we know that.'

Everyone nodded, although there's no solid evidence

whatsoever.

'Who's the author, anyway?' Jemario's eyes were red with tears. 'He's such a great man.'

'There's not a single name in this autobiography. I've checked it thoroughly,' Rodka said heavily. 'As he said, he did this so that no one knows where the egg, tail and soulcore were, so that he can protect them.'

What a great man! Everyone had tears in their eyes. Snower widened her eyes, looking at everyone in mild confusion, meowing now and then. Looking at Snower, Soarame's heart was full of tenderness. This poor baby certainly had no idea about how hard it had been for her to get this far – if the egg in the story was really her.

'If Snower really is the baby Giantail Cat, Sachastain actually sent me a miracle!' Soarame muttered to himself. *Wait a minute... how did Sachastain get this egg?* Raising his head, Soarame found everyone looking at him in a strange way; they must have all come to the same conclusion.

'Are you guys thinking that Sachastain is the young warrior in the book?' Soarame asked, and everyone nodded.

'Go and ask him!' Jemario's voice was still thick from her sobbing. 'He's the captain of the Libral guards, which means he is a warrior!'

'He is indeed a warrior, and if that's really him, he must have assassinated a vicious wizard before...' Soarame was excited. 'I will ask him tomorrow.'

'If Sachastain really is the one, we will have all the answers!' Omifo's words cheered everyone up.

'That's a good idea. But whatever we do, we need to keep it secret from now on,' Rodka said seriously. 'This whole story about the autobiography and Snower should go no further than Sachastain.'

'But... I've already told all my friends about Snower, and they have visited us to see Snower before!' Catheray was worried. 'What shall we do now?'

'Why did you do that?' Kardiac complained. 'Can you keep any secret at all?'

'Shut up! You told even more people!' Catheray stomped on Kardiac's foot, making him cry. 'You even boasted that Snower was a Baron-level magimal! Thanks to you, now we know it's probably true!'

'Did you really, Kardy?' The friends stared at Kardiac. 'How did you even think of a Baron?'

'Enough. Everyone knows Kardy bluffs, so we should be fine. Rodka pressed a hand to his forehead for his oncoming "Kardy headache" – the girls had named it that way. 'The good thing is that they didn't know about the autobiography. So from now on, we all need to keep our mouths shut. If we spread the word, we are actually risking the safety of Snower and even Soarame.'

'Is it that bad?' Vivarin couldn't help asking. 'This is the Institute of Libral!'

'Of course it's bad. Girls talk and crap happens,' Omifo answered. 'Err... I mean people talk and... Ahh!' He's cut off by Vivarin viciously pinching his waist.

'How about the teachers and professors, then? Can we tell them?' Dileys asked, amused by Vivarin and Omifo.

Rodka pondered a bit and suggested, 'From now on, tell everyone that Snower is just a kitten. But I suppose we can tell the professors; maybe they can help us. They may even know about Snower's magimal breed already – I'll go and check with Dean Romboton tomorrow.'

Like that, the plan was set up and the crew was dismissed. Strangely, Halgon was against checking with the professors, though he didn't insist; so Rodka would talk to Dean Romboton the next day. Soarame tried to sleep, but tossed and turned all night, watching little Snower sleep with her cute, tiny snore.

I'll protect you, Snower. Soarame swore in his heart as he looked at the sleeping baby. Snower's story sounded similar to his own; both had only a vague clue about their parents. Another clue was that Snower had discovered the beetalbulls' nest from miles away and somehow threw everyone into it – how did she do that? What magic was she capable of?

Soarame couldn't get any answers just by thinking and guessing, of course. So once the sun rose, Soarame jumped right out of bed and went to see Sachastain.

Thanks to Chelonad's guidance, Soarame quickly arrived at Sachastain's house on campus. Walking towards the door, Soarame was hesitant about how to start the conversation, but before he could even knock, the door suddenly opened.

'Ahh, Soarame. It's you.' Sachastain stepped out of his house. 'Is this about the magimal egg?'

'How did you know I was coming?' Soarame was surprised.

'Well, when you grow up you will also learn these tricks,' Sachastain smiled. As a high-level warrior, he's certainly able to sense people approaching. 'The hatching is difficult, isn't it?'

'Yeah, it's pretty hard, but it finally hatched.'

'No kidding? That's quick!' Sachastain motioned Soarame into his house. 'I thought it's going to take a few more weeks.'

'Because it's a Giantail Cat?' Soarame looked at Sachastain. 'I really adore what you did, by the way!'

'What Giantail Cat? What are you talking about?' Sachastain looked confused. After hearing the story about the autobiography, he frowned. 'There's such a book in the library?'

'So, that mysterious warrior is you, right?' Although Soarame was disappointed to see that Sachastain seemed to know nothing about this story, he still gave it a try.

'No, your story sounds like an old tale!' Sachastain laughed. 'I got this magimal egg from an auction. It's sold as the egg of a piebald python, and it should have hatched into a baby python! Now, you tell me it's a cat? You ever heard of a cat hatching out of an egg?'

'But it's really a cat... even though it hatched out of an egg! Why don't you come and see her if you don't believe me?'

'No, no, that's not what I mean.' Sachastain patted Soarame's shoulder. 'I trust you, but how could a cat be born from a python's egg?'

'I don't know!' Soarame was so frustrated that Sachastain was asking exactly the same questions of his. Not willing to give up so easily, Soarame kept asking Sachastain questions and they talked for quite a while at the table. But in the end, the boy was left very disappointed; Sachastain knew nothing more than what they had already concluded.

'Why did you buy a magimal egg anyway? You are not a wizard, are you?' Soarame asked suddenly.

'No, but I wish I was, so I bought one for myself to hatch,' Sachastain answered with a laugh. 'Got you! It's meant to be a gift for a friend's son, who was supposed to be a wizard just like you, but he failed the test.'

'Oh, I'm sorry to hear that.'

'No, no, as long as you don't mind that this egg was meant for someone else originally,' Sachastain smiled. 'By the way, you are not trying to skip class, are you? As a staff member of the school, I'm obliged to report this kind of matter.'

'Oh, crap!' Soarame glanced out the nearest window and was surprised to see how much the sun had already risen. He had almost forgotten about his class today. He said a quick goodbye to Sachastain and ran out. As the only boy in the class, it would be foolish to count on the teacher not noticing his absence. Soarame called out to Chelonad while he's rushing to class, 'Chelonad, highlight the shortcut to the Water department on my emblem, please!'

'There's no shortcut, Soarame. Just the ordinary way that you go every day,' Chelonad replied. 'And don't worry, you are already late and they have already noticed your absence.'

'Thanks Chelonad, that's really helpful,' Soarame said bitterly as he dashed down the path.

'Sure, any time.' Chelonad's voice sounded suspiciously like a snigger.

Meanwhile, in Dean Romboton's office, Rodka tried his best to describe what he knew. The Dean was patient enough to wait until Rodka finished, then raised his head. 'Did you see it yourself?'

'I did see Snower, professor,' Rodka answered. 'It's right in Soarame's dorm.'

'No, I'm talking about the process of the kitten being born,' Dean Romboton waved a hand vaguely.

'That... I did not.' Rodka understood what the Dean meant. 'But they are not lying, I can tell.'

'Well, I'm not saying they were lying, but you need to be more prepared before you come to me with such a story.' Dean Romboton pointed at the pile of files on his table. 'At least you need to see with your own eyes what you have told me, or leave me to deal with my other duties, you see?'

'I'm sorry, sir,' Rodka said hurriedly. 'If I can make sure everything is as I told you, would you be interested in seeing Snower for yourself?'

'No, I'm sorry. Not interested.' Dean Romboton paused. 'By the way, when do you plan to graduate?'

'Err… Excuse me, sir?' Rodka was unprepared for this sudden change of topic.

'Well, to be honest, I don't care about a cat or a dog or whatever. I only want you to leave this trivial stuff alone and graduate as soon as possible.' Dean Romboton lifted his glass. 'The best way for a wizard to become stronger is to keep practising magic. Even if you had a powerful magimal, that's still not your intrinsic power. So I suggest you concentrate on magic, not magimals.'

'But sir, aren't magimals also a part of a wizard's power?' Rodka asked. 'I remember when I first got here, I was told that magimals are important helpers to wizards…'

'Yes and no,' Dean Romboton interrupted Rodka. 'Very importantly, that's for normal wizards, not you. You have a chance to become the most powerful wizard in the world! I don't believe a magimal kitten, however rare she may or may not be, is qualified to match you once you reach your full potential. So save your time on this and keep improving yourself, and leave the magimal thing alone.'

'This magimal is not mine, it's Soarame's…' Rodka tried to explain, but was cut off again.

'Even more reason for you to leave it. This topic is finished. You are dismissed,' Dean Romboton said impatiently. 'Don't go and bother Dean Akex either. He's busy, too.'

Watching Rodka leave, Dean Romboton shook his head. He had told Rodka before that it's crucial for a wizard to be out there and experiencing the real world, rather than staying in school for longer than he should. Although this was the Institute of Libral, it's still a small corner of the entire world out there.

That evening, everyone gathered in Soarame's dorm.

'How can it not be Sachastain? What can we do, then?' After hearing the update, everyone was confused. 'And the Dean doesn't believe us? Should we try another professor?'

'Don't bother,' Halgon cut in. 'They won't believe us either. I think we should find out who put the autobiography into the library.'

'I already asked about it, but the librarians didn't know.' Rodka was frustrated.

'I have an idea!' Vivarin spoke up suddenly. 'We take the book out!'

'Hello? We already did.' Kardiac held up the biography in hand. 'It's right here.'

'No, I mean we take it out of the campus!' Vivarin looked at him. 'There are some big magishops in Cylone City, much bigger than those on campus. The shopkeepers are usually good at identifying magigears and other items, and determining their origins. Maybe we find out about the author.'

'That's a good idea!' Rodka agreed. 'I've tried that with our magishops on campus, and they have already come up short.'

'But how do we get it out of campus in the first place?' Jemario asked. 'I heard that there's a magic seal on everything that belongs to the school. The book would be detected once it passes the Libral Gate, causing the alarm to sound.'

'Oops. That's correct.' Rodka said. 'I almost forgot about that – we have a problem here.'

'What? No!' Vivarin wrinkled her nose in disappointment. Omifo was surprised to see a different side to this brash girl, with her naughtily cute, wrinkled nose.

'Come on, guys. Be more creative,' Kardiac encouraged. 'We break the seal! Don't forget we have Snower – she broke the seal on the cliff!'

'That...' Everyone looked back and forth at each other. This solution sounded abrupt and reckless, but also... quite exciting!

'But the book was taken out under Rodka's name,' Dileys said, worried. 'Wouldn't it be a problem for him if we really break the seal?'

Rodka thought for a bit and said, 'As long as it can help protect Snower, it's worth it. But once the book returning deadline comes we will have problems. So we'd better return the book first, then break the seal and take it out again, so that we will be problem-free forever.'

'Return it, then break the seal?' Halgon frowned. 'From inside the library? That sounds really risky, and it could expose Snower.'

'We are not taking Snower there. From now on, Snower must be well hidden.' Rodka lowered his voice, 'I mean we could do it by ourselves – I'm capable of Grade 6, so if we join forces, we have a good chance...'

'You are a Grade 6 already?' Dileys exclaimed. Rodka was supposed to be a Grade 5, as everyone expected.

'Only for my Fire and Lightness, but not Wind. And I haven't gone for any exam since I improved the other two, so I still appear as a Grade 5.' Rodka certainly felt proud. He had been keeping this to himself, so that he could grade up his three lineages all together – that would definitely amaze everyone. 'So, my mind power is Grade 6, and that's all that matters to break a magic seal.'

'Great, let's do it then!' Catheray jumped up. 'We just need to inject our mind power all together into the seal to break it, right?'

'Yes, but we need to have a plan.' Rodka lowered his voice. 'Maybe we could do this...'

The next day at the library, the entire crew gathered to carry out the plan, full of excitement and nervousness. Today, they were going to break a magic seal that's of a much higher level than their powers, and no one actually knew how hard it was. And there's another problem – this library did not have a private room for studying, so they had to do everything in the public area.

It's by no means a perfect plan. However, the crew was young and brave enough to gamble on what they wanted. Everyone was nervous and sweating, but they tried to look calm and pretended to be chatting casually. According to the plan, everyone would contribute their mind power for breaking the seal, but Kardiac and Omifo would also act as lookouts for the team – they felt that they didn't do enough in the beetalbull battle and wanted to compensate. This was actually a good idea, especially as Kardiac's thundering voice would succeed in attracting people's attention and cover the team's retreat if need be.

'Rodka, what does this symbol mean?' Soarame asked Rodka, pointing at a large book, *Dictionary of Magic Arrays*, as they sat around the same table with his team. The autobiography was right beside it among many other books, appearing like there's nothing out of the ordinary to see there.

Hearing Soarame's code phrase, everyone went into action and simultaneously injected their mind power into the autobiography. Kardiac was the first to exhaust his power, so he left the team, walked to the bookshelves and carried various books back and forth, making all kinds of noise.

Omifo was the next one to exhaust his power, and went on to his next task too – he chatted up a pretty girl and deliberately led her up and down the corridor, engaging with some other students as well. A few minutes later, Omifo was able to get everyone gathered around and talking to each other.

'Rodka, how far along are we?' Soarame asked. He had been sparing no efforts and was already on the verge of draining of his mind power.

'I don't know. I was hoping this would be easier,' Rodka replied, starting to feel anxious.

'Hang on, we are almost there!' Halgon's statement surprised Rodka, but he had no time to think about how Halgon could know this. Rodka steeled his heart and allowed himself to trust Halgon blindly, gathered up all his mind power, and focused it on the seal of the autobiography.

Except Dileys, the other three girls also drained their power one after another, so they followed Omifo's lead and went to chat up boys. This really worked out well; most boys' attention was captured by the girls. Omifo led his group to join them, so that the entire library was soon involved.

Pop! With a mild noise, just like a soap bubble bursting, the seal finally broke. Dileys, Soarame, Rodka and Halgon were all exhausted, but they gazed at each other in wonderment – they'd done it!

However, this happy moment was very brief – the crystal ball at the library gate suddenly lit up with a glaring red light. Following that, all the walls in the reading room burst into a harsh buzzing sound – the alarm had been triggered.

Immediately after that, a scream sounded from beside a shelf. 'Oh, my! Roach! A big roach!' It's Kardiac; he hadn't forgotten to carry out his mission.

The four friends on the table looked at each other, eyes full of confusion. They had broken the seal, but something had gone wrong if it triggered the alarm. Now that the librarians were all alerted, they couldn't risk taking out the autobiography anymore. Dileys threw it into the corner of a shelf and hurriedly left with her friends. They split up and made their way back to Soarame's dorm, except for Kardiac and Omifo, who deliberately stayed as their cover, according to the plan.

When they got back to the dorm, the other three girls were already waiting.

'What's wrong? It failed?' they asked.

'I don't know! The seal was broken, but the alarm was triggered.' Dileys was quite upset.

'It's weird. If the seal was gone it shouldn't trigger any alarm.' Halgon was confused too.

The group was silent. For now, they had to wait for Kardiac and Omifo to return. However, ten minutes passed and the two still hadn't come back.

Half an hour passed, but there's still no sign of them.

'Give them some time. After all, the alarm was triggered; there must be some investigation and that takes time.' Jemario tried to comfort the fidgeting boys.

An hour passed, yet the two boys still hadn't shown up.

'This isn't right!' Rodka couldn't bear it anymore. He took the lead and rushed out, blaming himself for getting Kardiac and Omifo in trouble. Everyone then rushed out after Rodka, following him back towards the library.

****

An hour earlier, the librarian on duty was surveying the library following the alarm.

'What happened?' asked Dean Akex, the Vice Dean of Spanflow College, who happened to be around.

'I don't know, sir. Everything looks normal,' the librarian answered. 'I shut the library soon after the alarm went off, and I'm checking why it happened.'

Dean Akex frowned. The alarm had never been triggered before, at least not during his residency here.

Here it is. Soon enough, Dean Akex figured out the reason for the alarm – the crystal ball showed an alert message that's sent from an autobiography. Grabbing the book from the corner of a shelf, Dean Akex was confused. It seemed fine; nothing appeared to be unusual.

Oh wait... the seal on the book is gone? Dean Akex suddenly realised the strangeness of the situation. *Someone tried to steal it?* He quickly flipped through the book but soon became even more confused. *Why not just borrow it? And why this specific book? It's not even that valuable!*

This must be a trick by a troublemaker. Dean Akex took the autobiography to the crystal ball and let them cross check each other, but nothing showed up as unusual because of the broken seal. So he had to check the previous borrowing record on the book as well.

What? Rodka? Dean Akex was surprised to see Rodka's face emerge from the crystal ball. *No, it can't be true. Rodka wouldn't do this. But he seems to be the only recent borrower.* The Vice Dean tried to suppress his surprise, but just couldn't. *To break the seal, the person would have to be either a teacher or a really powerful student. Rodka... would he really?*

While Dean Akex was checking the book, Omifo was busying himself in another book, pretending to read yet peeking towards the Vice Dean now and then. Omifo didn't know how silly this action was – he wasn't aware that Dean Akex could easily sense this, being a high-level wizard.

This boy had something to do with it? Dean Akex looked calm, but inside he couldn't be more confused. *He's only a Novice, what the heck is going on here?* With so many questions in mind, Dean Akex walked toward Omifo to gauge his reaction. Omifo immediately realised there's something wrong, and his breathing quickened.

'Ouch!' Just as Dean Akex walked across the library, somebody knocked into him and made him reel a few paces to get his balance again. Dean Akex looked down and found a golden-haired student on the ground, who busied himself in apologising. 'I'm sorry, sir!'

Dean Akex made to leave, but he suddenly caught sight of this boy glimpsing at where Omifo was sitting. *An accomplice? One distracts me so that the other can escape?*

'You, come here a moment,' Dean Akex summoned a random student, pointing at Kardiac. 'When the alarm was triggered, what's he doing?'

'Him?' The student glanced in confusion at Kardiac. 'He kept yelling about a roach on the shelf.'

'Oh? Is that so?' Dean Akex looked at Kardiac and pointed at Omifo. 'Bring your friend over there and follow me, we need to talk.'

Holy crap! Hearing this, Omifo turned around to see Kardiac standing near Dean Akex. Anxious and helpless, they had no choice but to follow Dean Akex to his office.

'Let's run away!' Kardiac whispered in Omifo's ear as they were walking.

Omifo rolled his eyes. 'How?'

'I don't know, let's just run!' This was typical Kardiac style, apparently.

'It's ok, you can speak even louder.' Dean Akex had overheard their whisper clearly. As a professor in magic, he's sensitive to everything, including but not limited to sound – he could even hear the boys' heartbeats.

Reaching the office, Dean Akex didn't want to waste time. 'Tell me your reasons please, gentlemen.'

'Sorry sir, there's no reason. I tried to test my power by playing tricks on the book,' Omifo spoke up immediately.

'Praise Libral... please!' Dean Akex rolled his eyes. 'You are only in Grade 2!'

'Sorry, I was being stupid.' Omifo looked directly at Dean Akex, ignoring Kardiac's anxiousness.

'Stupid? If someone broke an Expert seal as a Grade 2, I wouldn't call him stupid,' Dean Akex teased Omifo.

Omifo and Kardiac were both stunned; they thought the mission had failed and the seal was therefore intact. 'The seal was broken?'

'A roach?' Dean Akex ignored Omifo and turned to Kardiac. Looking at the boy's awkward expression, Dean Akex couldn't help feeling amused at his comical face. 'You claimed there's a roach on the shelf?'

'Yes! A huge one!' Kardiac yelped.

'Gee, what a pair of lungs. No wonder they picked you to be the cover.' Dean Akex stroked his chin. 'But why a roach? Wouldn't a snake be better?'

'How's that possible? A snake wouldn't appear in a library,' Kardiac widened his ox-like eyes in earnest.

'Of course, you are right. But you know why?' Dean Akex

leaned back into his chair. 'Every building in the school is protected by a magic barrier, to prevent insects and wild animals from getting inside. It's supposed to be common sense, but obviously there's one student that doesn't know this; hopefully he's only one on this campus.'

'No way, everyone was scared about the roach!' Kardiac protested. 'I'm certainly not the only dumb one!'

'Well, that would be a new low, but sadly you didn't reach it.' Dean Akex laughed. 'Everyone knows it, trust me. But for some reason, there is always someone claiming to see mysterious roaches or spiders showing up here and there... usually because a boy tried to tease a girl. I've roughly counted that the frequency is about... once a week?'

'What?' Kardiac refused to believe this. 'I don't believe you!'

'That only proves that you haven't been working hard.' Dean Akex shook his head. 'If you went to the library more often, you would have known about this.' Dean Akex shook his head. 'Now, let's get back to the topic – who else were in this, and why?'

At this same moment, the rest of the crew was urgently in search of the two missing boys.

'They are not here anymore. They were taken by the Vice Dean,' Rodka explained when he came out of the library, just as the rest of the group arrived. 'I'm going to pay a visit. You guys wait in the dorm, okay?'

'I'm going too!' Soarame said at once. 'We did this for my magimal!'

'I'm not staying behind like a coward,' Vivarin spoke up. 'So I'm going too.'

'Same with us!' The rest shouted up and down, unwilling to be left behind.

'No way! You all go back...now!' Rodka thundered, but his heart was warmed.

'Snower is my magimal! You think you can leave me out of this?' Soarame stared at Rodka.

'Okay, you can go with me.' Rodka couldn't deny Soarame. 'But the rest of you must stay out of this.'

Halgon didn't buy that at all. 'In case you've forgotten, I'm the one in the same dorm with Kardy, Omi and Soar – not you. Do you want my friends to think I'm a deserter?'

'Darn it... okay, you are in too.' Rodka was impressed by their sense of brotherhood. 'But you girls don't...'

'Shut up, boy!' Vivarin cut him off. 'I say I go, so I go!'

'We did it together, so I'm not going to pretend that I wasn't a part of it.' Dileys looked determinedly into Rodka's eyes.

'I won't leave my friends,' Jemario agreed, glancing at Soarame.

'I'm just too bored, so let's go!' Catheray pushed Rodka ahead of them towards the Vice Dean's office.

'Sir, as I said, I did it.' In Dean Akex's office, Omifo wasn't going to turn in his friends. 'And there's no one else. I was just playing around and having fun.'

'Okay, boy, show me how you did it then.' Dean Akex gave Omifo a book. 'Show me how to break an Expert seal with your Grade-2 mind power.'

'Are you sure it's broken?' Omifo couldn't get over this. 'If it's broken, why would the alarm sound?'

'Ahh, this is your problem?' Dean Akex crossed his legs out in front of him, leaning back in the chair. 'Boy, it's called magic.'

Omifo was speechless; it's magic indeed.

'Okay, do me a favour please.' Watching Omifo, Dean Akex sighed. 'Why don't you call Rodka in, to save us some time? He must be looking for you two.'

'What Rodka?' Omifo was shocked, but he still tried to cover it. 'I don't know what you are talking about...'

'It's okay, Omi.' Right at this moment, Rodka's voice sounded from outside of the room. Along with the others, Rodka came into Dean Akex's office.

'Sir, we are all here!'

THE WATER PRIDE

'Her name is Snower?' After Rodka had told the entire story, Dean Akex was completely taken aback. Looking at the white kitten on the desk in front of him, he quickly cross-checked the biography. 'You think this is the Giantail Cat baby?'

'Yes, we all believe so.' Rodka took a deep breath. 'And we have to do this to protect her.'

'Hmm...' Dean Akex stood up and walked around his office, pondering. The friends watched the Vice Dean nervously until he finally spoke again. 'Okay, regardless of your being right or wrong in your belief, I understand your reasons for this. I'll let you go for this time, but this time only.'

'Really?' Everyone cheered up at the good news, but Rodka tried to say, 'Sir, about the Dean...'

'Alas. Dean Romboton has a cold face, but he has a warm heart. He meant well for you and he did have a point,' Dean Akex sighed. 'Never mind, I'll keep this little secret for you, but I can't tell if Snower is a particularly rare breed right now.'

The friends had to agree. Snower did look like a normal kitten at this point as she licked her front paw on the desk; nothing unique or special had happened since she's born. If not for the extraordinary scene during the hatching, the trouble she made with beetalbulls and the mind-talk abilities, even the friends wouldn't believe she's unusual.

'Sir, if I may...' Soarame stepped forward. 'Do you know who put this autobiography into the library?'

'I'm sorry, Soarame, I don't.' Dean Akex shook his head. 'It's probably myself, if not a random librarian. And even if you find out, that person wouldn't be helpful at all.'

'I see,' Soarame and Rodka looked at each other. 'Thank you sir, so much.'

'You are welcome. But I can't let you take the book out if I'm going to keep the secret for you. And I don't want you to make more troubles out of it.' Dean Akex lifted Snower off his desk and gave her back to Soarame. 'Good luck. You are dismissed, except for Rodka.' Dean Akex gestured the crew to leave. 'Don't worry, Rodka will be fine and he will join you soon enough.'

After the group had left, Rodka asked, 'Yes sir, what's the matter?'

'The same question as Dean Romboton's.' Dean Akex closed the door. 'When are you graduating?'

'Err... I don't know yet.' Rodka shrugged his shoulders. 'After I level up to Grade 6, why?'

'Come on, boy.' Dean Akex looked at Rodka. 'If there's a second person likely to know your real power has reached Grade 6 already, that person is me.'

'Well, I'm sorry but there's already a second person,' Rodka teased him. Dean Akex was Rodka's primary teacher and they were pretty familiar with one another – and that's how Rodka learnt about Soarame's interview details back then. So, when nobody else was around, they could have a casual conversation.

'Okay, the third person, then.' Dean Akex sat back into his chair. 'Happy now?'

'No sir, there's already a third person too.' Rodka chuckled. 'I'm sorry.'

'Okay, you give me a number!' Dean Akex was amused.

'Err... including me, there have been nine.' Rodka rubbed the back of his head. 'You've just seen them.'

'So, I'll be the tenth...' Dean Akex paused and stared at Rodka. 'What? Ten? Double digits? I'm the one that taught you everything and I'm the tenth person to know your secret?'

'Well...' Rodka was embarrassed, although he knew that Dean Akex was teasing him.

'Hmm. As a punishment, you must graduate tomorrow,' Dean Akex said with almost-false sincerity, tapping the desk with his index finger.

'I promise you, once we've learnt more about Snower, I will graduate right away,' Rodka chuckled. 'How about that, sir?'

'So be it. Let's make it formal, okay?' Dean Akex also chuckled. 'Rodka, the Dean was actually right on this – the school is just the beginning of the story. You should go and explore the outer world, the sooner the better.'

'Yes sir, I do agree,' Rodka nodded. 'I was planning to graduate soon anyway.'

'You kid...' Dean Akex was amused. 'So you actually took advantage of our deal?'

'No, I'm trying to pursue the truth and help people; not to mention that these people are my friends.' Rodka became more serious. 'As a wizard, this is more important than graduation, don't you think?'

'Yes it is. Wizards help people and protect lives.' Dean Akex certainly appreciated this. 'Ok, you are free to go, but again the biography stays with me. I'm sorry, but I'm worried that if I let you take it, things would become even worse.'

'Understood.' Rodka saluted the Vice Dean. 'And I promise you, I will graduate once we learn more about Snower.'

Back in Soarame's dorm room, the friends were chatting. 'The Vice Dean is really nice!'

'I only wish he'd let us have the book.'

'He's nice? Humph, you guys didn't see his face when only Omi and I were there!' Kardiac curled his lips. 'He can be tough, even scary!'

'The beetalbulls or the Vice Dean, you choose,' Catheray teased Kardiac as always; she found teasing this boy fun. 'Kidding. You and Omi did really great this time!'

'Only we still failed the task. Stealing is out, so what are we going to do next?' Omifo asked, glancing at Vivarin. 'Kidnapping?'

'Are you looking at me?' Vivarin jumped up from the couch and went towards Omifo.

'I suggest we take a little break for now,' Rodka was amused to see Vivarin trying to kidnap Omifo. 'What do you guys usually do for fun?'

'We watch Soarame do mind-painting for Snower,' Dileys said quickly. She always answered Rodka's questions first. 'And sometimes we watch Dragon&Empires games.'

'You guys like the game too?' Rodka was pleased. 'My team is practising today. Do you guys want to come and watch?'

'Sure.' The crew happened to have no classes today anyway. 'Soarame wants to form his own team later, right Soar?'

'Err... yes but I need to improve first,' Soarame said with a blush. He had been playing friendly games with his roommates and other students, but found that it's truly difficult to do much with Novice Water spells.

'Nice! Why don't you practise with us today?' Rodka was surprised to hear of Soarame's ambition. 'It's good to have some real hands-on experience with the Grade 4s.'

Soarame couldn't deny this invitation, so everyone went together with Rodka to their practise field. Rodka quickly introduced Soarame to his teammates, and a tall boy called Brian was nice enough to offer his position to Soarame for this practice.

'Let's have a bit of Water tasting!' The team was interested to see Soarame's performance. Soarame took out his wand and walked onto the sports grounds, to the encouraging cheers from his friends.

Right then, a boy looked over with surprise in his voice. 'Wait, the Water Boy?'

Soarame and his friends were puzzled to hear the voice. They frowned and thought hard to recall the boy's name. 'It's Robert!'

Soarame had certainly recognised Robert, the one with whom he had a duel pending. This day, the team that Robert was in happened to be practising against Rodka's.

'Stop calling him that, I warn you,' Rodka stepped forward. 'That is discriminatory. You know the rules here.'

'Come on Rodka, it's not that bad,' The captain of the other team, a lanky boy with dark brown hair falling into his eyes named Ben, came over to reconcile them. 'He's just saying hello to his old friend, right, Robert?'

'Of course.' Robert smiled obsequiously. 'How's it going, Soarame?'

'Don't worry Robert, I haven't forgotten our duel,' Soarame said coldly. 'When I grade up to Adept in Water, I'll come and find you.'

'Duel?' Most were puzzled to hear this, including Soarame's roommates, as they never heard of it. 'Fire vs. Water?'

The girls explained what had happened. Of course, everyone was mad at Robert, whose attempt at taking advantage was obvious. Rodka's teammates were also annoyed because of this; they looked at Robert with questioning eyes. But Ben's team was on the other side, and it seemed that some of them already knew about this and were supportive of Robert.

The air was thus thick with tension. If not for the strict rules of the school, they would have ended up fighting. Rodka had to quickly lead his friends away from the other team to avoid the potential conflict.

'Just ignore them, Soarame.' Rodka took a deep breath and suppressed his temper. 'Ben's team always loses to ours, so they have a problem with us in the first place. My bad – I forgot about this and shouldn't have invited you. Brian, come back in and let's teach them a lesson.'

'Hold on,' Soarame stopped Rodka. 'I never said I wanted to be out.'

'I know, but they are all in Grade 4 or above.' Rodka was starting to realize just how much strength of will Soarame had. 'This game will be aggressive, and you don't have any real experience. I don't want you to get hurt.'

'It's okay, I won't.' Soarame looked towards Robert, who was making provocative gestures at him. 'Trust me, I made it away from the beetalbulls, remember?'

That's right! Rodka's eyes brightened up. He'd almost forgotten about that, as he had not been there in person. 'Okay then, you can play, but promise me you'll call for help if anything bad happens.'

'Deal!' Soarame took a deep breath. He actually had no plan, because his previous experiences had told him that Novice Water spells were indeed weaker in practice. However, he wouldn't quit like that just because he had encountered Robert. *If I can't even deal with this small potato, how can I form a team later?*

The game started with cheering from the supporters of both sides – many of them were just passing by, and they were scattered over the field. Ever since the beginning, Robert had been sparing no effort to spell firebolts at the entire rival team, and he's especially focused on Soarame. Fortunately, Soarame was well trained so he always managed to dodge the attack and spell water arrows back from time to time – although they did almost zero damage.

'Thanks for washing my hands. How much should I tip you?' Robert laughed at Soarame, and so did his teammates. Soarame's friends were upset and yelled at Robert, but there wasn't much else they could do. Soarame was gritting his teeth hard; he's so mad at this clamouring pest and many times he almost chanted Wind incantations – yet he swallowed them all in the end.

Just then, Rodka's team got the ball and they passed it to one other, pushing their way forward. But Soarame noticed soon enough that his teammates weren't really passing it to him – either to protect him or from not believing he could help. This offered Ben's team a chance; they caught a window of opportunity and besieged the ball-holder with two players, leaving Soarame unguarded. The ball-holder realised this but he still hesitated to pass it to Soarame, and the ball was looted by his rivals soon enough.

The transition between attack and defence had been made in a blink, earning excited screams from the audience. At the same time, the dragon student was fast enough to pounce on Rodka's base as soon as the ball-holders were besieged. Rodka's team had to quickly fall back into defence, leaving Ben's team free to push forward. Strangely, the dragon wouldn't leave even after encountering Rodka's whole team at their base; instead he's engaging in a dogfight and keeping them busy. Meanwhile, Ben's team made no attempt to check the dragon's base for the gem, but spared no effort in pushing on towards Rodka's base.

'Cheats!' Kardiac roared from the side-lines. All Soarame's friends had realised that the dragon was working together with Ben's team, although they couldn't prove it.

'Darn it!' Rodka's team managed to hold their base against the dragon, but weren't able to keep it from Ben's team – the ball was easily put on top of Rodka's base chest by a Wind player; he sniggered at Rodka and walked away.

'Cheats!' Rodka's teammates were all mad. The dragon and Ben's team wouldn't accept the accusation, so they started arguing right away. Rodka had to stop his teammates, simply because they couldn't provide evidence. So the next round started, and Rodka's team managed to push steadily on to Ben's base, yet the dragon started to strike Rodka's base at a critical moment. Rodka's team was well prepared for the dragon's attack, so the invader didn't succeed; but due to this interruption, they didn't manage to score either, and the ball was again in Ben's hand.

'What now, Rodka?' Ben laughed. 'You can't blame the dragon this time, can you?' Ben's team giggled. Rodka turned around and walked away – the dragon was supposed to do what he just did, so no one could complain about it.

'I'm sorry, Rodka.' Soarame felt bad, but he didn't have a chance to do much because his teammates wouldn't pass the ball to him.

'Come on man, you did great!' Another teammate cut in. 'We stopped the dragon together just now! You even stopped their Darkness player!' This made Soarame feel a little better, but he knew that if he couldn't do something more, they still wouldn't include him in the real business.

'How could you fail like that?' At the same time, Ben wasn't happy with his Darkness player. He had deliberately sent him to sneak-attack while the dragon was distracting Rodka's defence, but that negligible Water boy had somehow managed to tackle him. Everyone was convinced this was a coincidence, but when Rodka recalled Soarame's adventure in the beetalbull nest, he suddenly realised something –

'Soarame, tell me you have a way to spot their Darkness player,' Rodka whispered in Soarame's ear. 'If so, I'll put you as a designated defence player.'

Soarame hesitated a bit but then nodded. 'Sure, I got him. Also, the dragon and Ben were collaborating, I'm sure.'

'I know.' Thankfully Rodka didn't ask how Soarame knew this, so Soarame didn't have to make up a lie about the fact that he could see Darkness elements moving so that he knew where the player was, or that he saw a beam of Darkness elements going from Ben to the dragon before their joint attack – it must be some kind of signalling method and Ben must have gifts in Darkness.

Rodka used the captain's right for a time-out. After a quick round of rearrangements, Soarame was assigned to be a designated defender, so that one of the original defenders was released to the attacking team. Half of the game time had already passed, so everyone was worried about this new assignment, but they decided to trust their captain.

The game continued, and it soon became clear that Robert was the one holding the ball most of the time, charging against Soarame. All Soarame's teammates were tackled by Robert's teammates, so that they could only watch a Grade-2 Water student getting pushed further and further back by a Grade-4 Fire.

Watching Robert keep chanting incantations one after another with ease, Soarame struggled with the impulse to cast a windblade – until a flash pierced through his mind, and an idea suddenly emerged.

'I'm sorry boy, but this is a man's game,' Robert sneered at Soarame.

With his new idea in mind, Soarame sneered back, 'But you are no man. Cut the crap and try harder, I'm sleepy.'

Everyone choked at hearing this – it seemed Robert wasn't the only troublemaker here. Soarame's friends burst into laughter; the audience on both sides also had to snigger.

'As you wish, brat!' Robert was enraged. He swung his wand and chanted once more his favourite incantation. '*Voliva...*'

At the same time, a beam of water shot into Robert's mouth. Robert was caught off guard and had to cough, and his incantation was cut off. The next second, he barely noticed a flash passing by and his hand felt light – the ball was gone.

'Attack!!' Soarame roared aloud and passed the ball to Rodka, who was already on his way. The rest of the team caught on and followed, making their hard bounce-back.

I made it! Soarame screamed in his heart with joy. *I actually made it!*

On the other side, Ben's team hurriedly dashed back into defence, and the dragon pounced at Rodka's base.

'Crap!' Ben's Darkness player fell over and showed himself on the ground, because Soarame "accidentally" kicked his shin – just like the last time. Soarame then ran to his teammates and helped defend their base against the dragon. The dragon used his magigears against the other two defenders, at the same time chanting his own incantation. '*Petra...* cough!'

Once more, a beam of water filled his throat – Soarame had been prepared for this and he's successful again!

'You... cough, cough!' The dragon hurriedly flew upwards to

get himself to a safe distance. He's surprised that the Water boy could get him right in the mouth while he's moving so fast.

Meanwhile, Rodka exhibited his superior skills and led his team to success in the attack. The game became a tie and everyone was cheering for Soarame's splendid overturning action. Rodka didn't say anything, but bumped Soarame's fist; the entire team bounded over to them, roaring with joy.

'You made it, man! It's Water!'

The girls watching from the side-lines were the most excited ones at the game. They were hugging and jumping and screaming like crazy. Even the referee of the game had to applaud, for it's the first time he had ever witnessed a Water student flipping the game over like that.

'What the heck is going on?' Ben yelled at his teammates, utterly discomfited. 'His water spray wimped you out? Wake the heck up!'

The game wasn't over though. Ben had always been a defender, as that allowed him to observe the battlefield and send signals to the dragon. But this time he decided to swap and become an attacker, because he had to teach the worthless Water boy a lesson. So, although he still used Robert to confront Soarame and push him hard, he started to watch Soarame all the time. Soon enough, Robert managed to push Soarame close to Rodka's base again; he started to chant once more –

'Cough!'

Although prepared and trying to swing his body left and right, Robert still got choked by Soarame's water arrow. The second he realised this had happened, his heart skipped a beat – *No way! How's this possible?!*

'You're welcome.' Soarame looted the ball, but he suddenly noticed a beam of black – a Darkness spell – shooting towards him, coming from Ben.

The next second, Soarame's vision went dark. Although this was unexpected, Soarame had been trained by Scankeen to be calm; instead of passing the ball out blindly, he hurriedly curled up and fell to the ground, yelling for assistance. Robert recovered from the cough and dashed to Soarame, tugging his arms for the ball. At the same time, both teams dashed towards Soarame; close combat broke out immediately.

Soarame's friends were anxiously yelling advice at him. 'Soarame, throw the ball away!' They saw a firebolt hit Soarame's back and set his robe on fire, but Soarame was fast enough to put it out with Water spells, and he held the ball tight. Fortunately, the hand-to-hand combat was soon taken over by Rodka's team.

It's a perfect time for the dragon to strike at Ben's base, but he's attacking Rodka's instead. Although there's still no evidence to prove anything, the audience was upset to see this obviously flawed action from the dragon. Everyone started booing.

'Are you okay, Soarame?' Rodka hurriedly asked for another time-out. 'What happened to you just now?'

'Ben's Darkness spell.' Soarame brushed the dirt from his body. 'I'm fine, but it cut off my vision for a few seconds.'

'That's the *nightfall* spell!' The Darkness teammate spoke up. 'But Ben can't spell Darkness, can he?'

'And he didn't chant anything back then. So it means he has a Darkness magigear!' Rodka's eyes brightened. 'This is new! Guys, I think that's his secret weapon for this year's Championship! He didn't use it on me because I can quickly use Lightness spells to neutralise it. If it wasn't for Soarame, he wouldn't have exposed his secret today!'

Nightfall? That makes sense. Soarame nodded. This spell was a perfect signalling method to the dragon, because only the target of the spell would notice it. Given the long distance, the dragon probably would see just a blink of darkness instead of a few seconds of it, which made it a perfect cheating tool.

'This guy is really clever, be careful,' Soarame warned his teammates with his speculation. The team then came back to the game, but surprisingly found that Robert was replaced by another player – this time it's a girl.

'That's Joanna?' Rodka was surprised to recognise the girl in tight-fitting cotton clothes and her hair hanging in two braids on both sides of her face. 'Soarame, she's also a Water wizard, probably Grade 4, though. It seems that you have made Water proud today!'

'But I thought this was a man's game?' Soarame pretended to be confused. 'Where's Robert?' They all laughed and looked for Robert, who was apparently nowhere to be found at this moment.

'Don't talk that way, Soarame!' Rodka hurriedly rebuked

Soarame. 'Robert was talking rubbish; there are quite a few girls who are very good at this game. You didn't see last year's championship, or you'd be impressed by the girls!'

Meanwhile, Ben had to take advantage of playing the "gentleman card". *Let Joanna take care of this Water boy, see if he's going to choke a girl!* Ben never paid attention to Water spells, so he's also hoping to test it out with Joanna. The results disappointed him soon enough – Soarame didn't target Joanna, but he water-choked everyone else, including Ben himself. One particularly skilful shot really freaked everyone out – the water beam curved around Ben's hand as he covered his mouth, and it went right into his throat. If Rodka's team hadn't been as shocked as Ben's, they could have taken the chance and scored another point.

On the other hand, Joanna couldn't manage to do the same thing as Soarame at all. Rodka's entire team was hit by her Water spells all over their bodies, but they actually loved it – it cooled them down in the burning sunshine. Therefore, the latter part of the game was no longer competitive; it felt more like a water spray party to Rodka's team.

Because of the early disadvantage for Rodka's side, time ran out before they could get another point. The game ended in a draw, but everyone knew who the MVP was. Soarame was lifted up and thrown into the air by his teammates, and the Water girls ran onto the sports ground to join them. Realising the audience on both sides were actually cheering for Soarame, Ben's team and the dragon student hurried off. They were more frustrated than they could say – the Water boy had turned out to be the hero of the game! How could this ever have happened!

The friends went back to Soarame's dorm, full of joy. This time they had no doubt that even Novice-level Water magic could achieve wonders if used skilfully – *incantation choker, what a thought!* The girls couldn't help staring at Soarame as they tried to puzzle out what's going on in his mind; this creeped Soarame out more than they thought.

On the other hand, Rodka was more surprised than anyone else, because he knew that what Soarame had done was a lot harder than people thought. First of all, this boy had figured out the advantage of Water over other lineages – water was liquid, which meant it's material in form, but transformable in shape; no other lineage had this unique ability to allow for highly flexible and manageable aiming – *windblades, stoneballs* and *firebolts* could do more damage for sure, but it's really hard to change their trajectory after casting. Second, water arrow incantation was the shortest one, which enabled Soarame to short-cut his rivals' incantations. However, this still demanded another critical skill – the incredibly accurate control of Water elements.

'How did you do that, man?' Rodka finally had to ask. 'The curve shot on Ben was just crazy!'

'It's all thanks to the mind-painting.' Soarame pointed at his table, on which there's a canvas with a small shape painted on it. Rodka walked over and could barely make out what it's supposed to be... a pig maybe?

'It's Snower,' Soarame's words struck everyone as they looked at his mind-painting. Even Snower jumped onto the table and stretched her tiny claws at Soarame, signalling her complaint.

'It's improving,' Jemario said, chuckling. 'Last time I took it to be a boar.'

'That's... understandable.' Rodka was trying very hard to suppress his laughter – poor baby Snower. Suddenly, Rodka turned to Soarame. 'You know, you should try the Fledglings Tournament. Your Water skill is impressive enough to show off there.'

'Oh yes, Soarame you should go!' Dileys clapped her hands in excitement. 'Show everyone what Water can do!'

Seeing Soarame's puzzled expression, Dileys briefly explained the Fledglings Tournament. It's an annual school tournament, for Novice students from Grades 1 to 3. The entire school always had a week off for this event, so that everyone could enjoy the funny scenes of new students trying their luck – a typical example being that two of them ran out of mind power and had to start wrestling each other. The Adept students always had fun watching the freshers trying to prove themselves as wizards.

However, Soarame had no interest in that – if there's a tournament that attracted Soarame, it would be Dragon&Empires, rather than this entry-level one. Thinking of this, Soarame felt rather depressed – Julia, the girl who welcomed him after his first

Water class, had removed their Libral Emblem connection. Soarame was convinced that it's because her maximum number of connections had been reached, so she had to clear him out. And he heard that this super talented girl would become a Grade 3 before long, which was astonishingly fast.

After Rodka and the girls left, Soarame and Kardiac kept hanging out in the dorm, but Soarame was disturbed because of Julia, and Kardiac noticed his depressed mood soon.

'What's wrong, man?' Kardiac asked. 'Haven't you just kicked Robert's butt? Why are you not happy?'

'My Water improves slowly,' Soarame sighed. 'And I can't do much about that.'

'Oh? Someone in your class giving you the cold shoulder?' Kardiac's words surprised Soarame; the usually-careless boy seemed really sensitive. So Soarame decided to tell him the truth, and this upset Kardiac at once.

'Screw that!' Kardiac barked. 'She thought she's too good? I'm grading up soon too, but I never turned my nose up!'

'You are about to be Grade 3 too?' Soarame was taken aback. 'How fast!'

'Well, Omifo is faster. Remember how you always practice mind-painting in the Water Department? I often went too, but Omifo seldom did.' Kardiac reminded Soarame. 'I was confused at first – why would he give up such good chances to see pretty girls? Then I realized he's actually studying! Can you believe that – he's a bookworm!'

'Well, we can't improve our magic power just by reading books, so I don't think "bookworm" is the right word... But I got the point.' Soarame shrugged his shoulders. 'And there's nothing wrong with what he did.'

'Come on, bro! He looks good and girls tend to like him!' Kardiac complained. 'All he needs to do is to talk to them more! But he gave up on that... what a shame!'

'Is that your real purpose to come to my mind-painting practise? To meet more Water girls?' Soarame didn't know if he should feel amused or disappointed. 'You could have just told me, and I could introduce a few!'

'Nah... It's okay. I look just as good, so it's all fine,' Kardiac said. He smoothed his hair to look cool, but didn't realise that this made his face change in appearance from chubby to turgid. 'Tell you what, I went to the Water Department because I wanna get my mind off of my lineage majors. When I got stuck in Fire or Wind practises, I went to see you painting and to talk to Water students, so that I sometimes could get inspiration from the conversations.'

'Is that so!' Soarame's eyes shone.

'Of course. If your encounter difficulties in Water, try auditing some classes in another lineage,' Kardiac nodded. 'By the way, aren't you gifted in Lightning, too? Although it's deactivated, you can go audit a class, perhaps?'

'No, don't.' Omifo came down from upstairs at that moment. 'Audit any lineage but not Lightning – it's too hard to control.'

'That makes sense.' Soarame was reminded of Scankeen's and Aertiuno's advices. 'So I'll probably try Earth then. I actually can practise Earth, but my gift is not high enough to take it as a major.'

'That's good to know. Remember – only audit a lineage you can practise, otherwise it won't help.' Omifo opened the door to leave. 'So don't believe Kardy – he went to the Water Department just to chat up girls. If Water could really help, why wouldn't I go?'

'Come on, dude! You don't have to say that!' Kardiac blushed at being caught. 'I'm just trying to look like a good student!'

'Kardy... you...' Soarame was stunned. He suddenly felt the familiar "Kardy headache" coming up again...

FLEDGLINGS TOURNAMENT

Soarame and Kardiac were still joking around as they talked about auditing classes, when Halgon came downstairs.

After hearing Soarame's plans, Halgon suggested, 'Why don't you jump over Grade 1 and audit Grade 2 Earth classes directly? I can teach you everything about Grade-1 Earth magic. Since all you want is to switch up your mind and borrow ideas, you don't need to master the spells. This way, we can be in the same class a few times, before I grade up in the near future.'

'You are grading up too?' Soarame felt rather frustrated that all his roommates were about to grade up again – Spanflow College was indeed full of geniuses.

So, a few days later, Soarame followed Halgon to the Earth Department. He had learnt some basic knowledge about Earth, and even managed to summon a little clod of dirt, although it seemed useless in real practises. As soon as Soarame walked into the classroom, he noticed a sharp contrast to Water classes. The students here were mostly boys, and they were all big and bulky, thanks to the imperceptible influence from Earth magic every day. Halgon was the bulkiest in their dorm, but he's a mere norm here.

'Today we are going to continue the build-and-defend practise,' The teacher was a bulky man, with familiar short golden hair and standing over seven feet tall. Sitting in the rear row as an auditor, Soarame was surprised to recognize him as Thomas – months ago, Casavin had challenged Sandoray in the arena, and Thomas was the other teacher on site. But Thomas didn't seem to remember Soarame – if he could see the small boy behind the big ones, first of all. 'As I said in the last class, Earth magic is known for its balance between attack and defence. We can summon a stone ball and throw it to attack, or summon a rock chunk and hide behind it.'

'So this time we are going to do the same thing: ten of you come to the stage and build a simple stone shelter, then another two come to destroy it.' Thomas pointed at a large area behind him. 'Who wants to do it – get up here already.'

The students were quite active; the quota of ten was filled up soon. As they started chanting incantations, one rock appeared after another, and stacked up to assemble a small house. Soarame watched everything with curiosity; he wanted to participate too but he couldn't as an auditor. Plus... Soarame looked at the small clod in his hand...

'The house doesn't look strong enough to me,' Soarame whispered to Halgon. 'Can it really be used as a shelter?'

'No, but it's already better than the one in the last class,' Halgon chuckled. 'But fairly speaking, construction is not easy. It takes ten people to build a stone house, but it only takes one to destroy it.'

After a while, the ten had finished the construction of the simple stone shelter. The two attackers were selected via a lottery, and started their incantations. As a wave of rocks bombarded onto the shelter, it's crushed within a minute. The two attackers looked excited and clapped a high five – obviously, most boys at this age did enjoy destroying stuff.

In contrast, the ten builders became annoyed. 'What's the point of building it then? It's not gonna last anyway, no matter who were to attack it.'

Thomas wasn't surprised to hear this. 'That's not true. It can last if you are powerful and skilful enough.' As he stretched a finger towards the ruins of the stone shelter, Soarame's eyes suddenly widened – in his special vision, a big blast of yellow dots gathered like a hurricane, and soon a small house of dark brown colour emerged from the ground beside the crushed one. The house seemed like an assembly of thick flagstone chunks, each shaped neatly and rigorously as a squared piece. But upon a closer look, there's no gaps anywhere on the house – it's an entire piece of stone itself. And the stone looked much denser than ordinary ones, which convinced Soarame that it's much tougher than them too.

'All of you, feel free to attack it till the end of the class,' Thomas said casually. 'If it collapses, I'll give each of you a magigear as a gift.'

'A magigear for each of us?' The students were excited and rushed to the stage. After a series of loud noises, dust covered the entire classroom as they attacked it with vigour. However, when everyone had exhausted themselves after a while, there wasn't even one crack on the shelter.

This is the gap between a teacher and a group of students... Soarame marvelled inside. Except for a handful of students who remained in their seats, everyone else had been trying to destroy the stone structure on the stage, till they had to sit back down with frustration.

Seeing their disappointed and frustrated faces, Thomas chuckled. 'Can we continue now?' He took the few half-hearted nods to mean that they would listen to him now. 'Remember, we are lucky to be in an era of peace nowadays. Our tasks, therefore, are more about protection than charging forward in a battlefield. As such, spells like *stone shield* and *stone armour* are not effective means to protect our people from magimal invasions; but shelters are.'

'But why not just eliminate the invaders?' asked a student.

Before Thomas could respond, another student answered, 'How? The wild magimals are endless. They multiply every day!'

Thomas nodded. 'Exactly. Plus, it's hard to predict when and where exactly they would attack, and we have limited hands. So it's hard to be there right away to save our people when an invasion happens. But we, as Earth wizards, can build shelters for them to live in. High-level Earth wizards can summon condensed stone-like materials such as you see here, which are much tougher than ordinary stones, and of bigger sizes, to construct city walls and defence lines and so on, and they help a great deal. That said, high-level magimals can damage them, so every time after an invasion ends, we fix the constructions to prepare for the next time.'

'So we are only in charge of defence?' asked the first student. 'Who's in charge of battling magimals?'

'That's usually the task of Fire and Wind wizards. If a Lightning wizard is there, that's even better,' Thomas answered. 'These three lineages are not good at defence, so that's the job for us and Water wizards. Then Water and Lightness take charge of healing; spying is Darkness's job.'

'It makes sense, but it's so tedious to only do defence.' Some boys were not happy. 'It's much cooler to attack magimals and kick the crap out of them! And it's more glorious for sure!'

Thomas frowned at the group of boys muttering their assent with the speaker. 'No. The most glorious job is to protect our people, to make sure they survive with minimum injuries. It's critical for you to understand that every wizard has his or her role! Why do we fight magimals? It's to protect our people!' Thomas said seriously, raising his voice to get through the chatter. 'As I just said, Fire and Wind wizards are not good at defence, so when they charge onto the battlefield, they are actually risking their own lives! It's not about looking cool, it's about safety! And we, as Earth wizards, must also protect our peers! In a sense, if they get injured but we don't, it's a great shame for us!'

Hearing this, more students started talking to each other. Most of them, as teenage boys, seemed to not accept that their role was to be of assistance to someone else. Sitting next to them, Soarame heard that most of them had a strong preference to be attackers, even at their own risk. Thomas watched them in silence, not surprised at all – each year, the boys behaved pretty much the same and he had seen too much of it.

Giving the boys some time to settle down, Thomas spoke up again. 'When I was your age, my master told me the following: Earth wizards should be generous and selfless, just like how the earth fosters all kinds of lives and supports their weight. Earth wizards should be caring and protective, just like how mountains block the gale and screen everything behind it.'

'If you want to learn Earth magic well, you have to comprehend this,' Thomas said deeply. 'The spirit of Earth magic is not about toughness and aggressiveness, but about philanthropy and protection. The number of invaders we defeat does not matter as much as the number of people we save.'

Hearing and seeing Thomas' teaching style, Soarame felt that this class was well worth attending, and he's occupied.

'The build-and-defend session is over for today.' Thomas had noticed that many students did not buy his point on the spirit of Earth, but he didn't want to push them. 'What I want to tell you next is that Earth magic is not only about attack and defence, but much more.'

'We all know that Water is the mother of lives. Earth has a lot to do with living too.' Thomas stretched his big hand open, showing a tender shoot growing out of the soil in his palm. 'First of all, most plants depend on the earth for their survival; second, animals feed on plants, and predators feed on animals, so they all depend on the earth for their survival too.'

'Survival...' Soarame couldn't help muttering, immersed completely in the lesson.

'Yes, "survival".' As an Expert wizard, Thomas certainly could hear Soarame. He turned to him with a smile. 'Hi there, you look unfamiliar. Is this your first time in my class?'

'Yes, sir.' Soarame stood up. 'I'm an auditor.'

'Oh?' Thomas was a little surprised. 'What's your major and grade then?'

'Water. Grade 2.'

As soon as Soarame answered, the boys started throwing odd looks at him.

'A boy, of Water?'

'Why does a Water come here?'

'A Grade-2 Water, auditing Grade-2 Earth class?'

'What's wrong with him?'

'Silence!' Thomas didn't look happy at all. 'What did I just say about the spirit of Earth? It's only been two minutes!'

The boys quieted down. Thomas still gazed at them for a moment, then had a quick chat to understand Soarame's motivation.

'Hard to improve from Grade 2 Water?' muttered a brown-haired stocky boy. 'What a genius!' His words caused a wave of snickers among the students.

Thomas pointed at the boy. 'Kyle, stand up.'

Watching Kyle stand up reluctantly, Thomas asked, 'You think he's not a match to you, is that right? How about this: you two have a duel – right here, right now. We'll see how that goes.'

'Excuse me?' Kyle looked puzzled. He looked at Soarame, whose height only reached his shoulder. 'Him?'

'Yes, him.' Halgon stood up too. 'He's my roommate, and I don't think you are a match for him.'

'How dare you insult me!' Kyle stared daggers at Halgon.

'How dare you insult me first!' Soarame countered. 'We can have a duel, as long as you agree.'

'Okay, fine!' Kyle laughed. 'How should we duel?'

'Just do it in the normal way. Your Grade-2 Earth magic versus his Grade-2 Water.' Thomas said indifferently. Having been teaching for so many years and having seen so many different types of students, Thomas was experienced enough to sense something different about Soarame. 'Any questions?'

'No,' Kyle snickered at Soarame. 'Just don't cry if it hurts!'

'Exactly. Don't cry if it hurts!' Soarame felt his temper flame.

'Good!' Thomas' eyes shone upon hearing Soarame's brave response. 'As I just said, an Earth wizard should be as caring as the earth, but also as tough as the mountains. Never yield to the challengers; very well!'

'Sir, you are a teacher in Earth, why do you keep speaking up for someone from another department?' Kyle's friends protested.

'That's a fair question, but also a naïve one.' Thomas sighed deeply, as if he's really disappointed. 'We, regardless of being wizards or not, are, first of all, human. Only after that, we have genders, skin colours, ages, nationalities, majors, careers, and even employers later on. But none of these later attributes matter as much as the fundamental one – we are human, first of all! Then, we are wizards! In order to protect the world, our moral standard, our sense of justice and fairness, has to be higher than ordinary people's!'

'I'm a teacher in the Earth Department; that's correct. But before that, I'm a wizard. Then I'm a wizard in Libral, then I'm in the Earth Department of this school.' Seeing many students start to think, Thomas carried on. 'Plus, I've just told you that the spirit of Earth is philanthropy – isn't the department bias a direct opposite to that? Look at you; we are at least in the same school, yet you are biased about departments. But philanthropy is not only about caring for all your schoolmates, it's not even about caring for only humans – it's about caring for all lives, including magimals!'

'Caring for magimals?' asked another student in surprise. Everyone was listening; this appeared to be a shared question by many students.

'Yes. For the innocent ones.' Thomas nodded seriously. 'If wild magimals invade us and attack our people, we'll certainly show our "mountain side" as Earth wizards. But if we see baby magimals, who are only just new, innocent lives in this world, are we supposed to attack them? Of course not!'

'A great point!' For some reason, Halgon looked quite excited. 'What a surprise...'

'Why does that surprise you?' Thomas glanced at him. 'Bear in mind that you are wizards! The peace and prosperity of the human world is on your shoulders! Learning magic is not to bully the weak or the small, but to keep justice and fairness!'

Silence.

Everybody was deep in thought; some nodding and some shaking their heads. Thomas watched them quietly, not trying to force them to accept anything. He gave them some time to think, and when most students appeared to have finished their thoughts, Thomas addressed Kyle and Soarame again. 'If both of you are ready, we can move to the arena down the hall for the duel.'

'Actually... it's not necessary,' said Kyle suddenly. 'I'd like to apologize to Soarame, for my rudeness. I'm an Earth wizard, so I'll be like the earth and the mountains! I'm quitting this meaningless duel.'

'Great!' Thomas was happy for the first time in this class. 'What do you say, Soarame?'

'Thank you.' Soarame was quite surprised. Thomas didn't really teach much magic in this class, but he did teach everybody an important lesson. He's reminded of Scankeen's words that he couldn't understand before: 'Education is not just to teach people knowledge and skills, but more about teaching people principles and disciplines.'

Soarame turned to see Halgon, only to find him still preoccupied. Halgon looked distracted till the end of the class, and Soarame couldn't help wondering what he's thinking. But Halgon didn't tell, and Soarame didn't pursue – he had enough to worry about on his own. All his roommates were grading up soon, so it wouldn't look good if he couldn't improve.

As Soarame kept up with the hard work and practice, another few weeks passed.

'I'm finally 14!' In the dorm, Kardiac proudly announced to his best friends – the library-action team.

'Whoa, what a flower age!' Catheray teased. 'And you do look like a flower!'

'I know.' Kardiac made a pose, trying to show his "flowering charm".

'That's a tree stump!' laughed Vivarin. 'And why didn't you invite more people? I thought you know a lot?'

'As far as I know, he did try to invite more girls,' Omifo chuckled. 'But none of them seem to have shown up.'

'Hey, at least I tried! Your birthday has passed and you didn't even hold a party!' Kardiac rounded on Omifo and turned to the girls. 'He's such a bookworm... Do you know he's in Grade 3 of Lightness already?'

'What!' Everyone was taken aback, including Rodka. He sized Omifo up, not sure what to say.

'You must be kidding us!' Vivarin gazed at Omifo, impressed. She's used to teasing the boy because she thought it's fun and he looked good, but at this moment she realized that he's more than just a cute face. 'It's only been a year, you monster!'

'I'm still in Grade 3!' pouted Catheray. 'It's hurting!'

'That's because you haven't been serious enough in your studies.' Jemario chuckled. 'It's fine, we are better than these monsters, in every other way.'

'Exactly. But Spanflow College does collect monsters.' Dileys couldn't get over it. 'Rodka is one for sure; Halgon is a living dictionary of magimals; Soarame is the incantation choker; and now, Omifo!'

'It's all thanks to Vivarin's... err... coaching?' Omifo muttered. He decided to rephrase "bullying".

'Gratitude accepted. By the way, I'm in Grade 4, so I still can "coach" you,' Vivarin said, curling her lip. 'Also, how are you gonna repay my coaching?'

'Ask her out, Omi! That's the only way,' teased Kardiac. Seeing Vivarin and Omifo both blush, everybody laughed.

'Hey hey, we have five Spanflow students here, and you praised four of them.' Kardiac decided to remind everyone of himself. 'What about the last one? What's so cool and special about him?'

'Oops. There's one more?' Vivarin stared at him and revenged herself, her face still pink. 'As I recall, his special part is... he is 14 years old and weighs 140 pounds?'

'That's not true! It's 180 pounds!' Kardiac complained. 'What else? What's so "Spanflow" about him?'

'The flowering pose?' Jemario chuckled.

'Hmm... fine. But what else?' Kardiac was anxious. 'He's got something amazing going for him too, right?'

'Guys, it's late, and we have classes tomorrow,' Catheray suppressed her amusement and faked a yawn. 'Let's go home.'

'What! Hold on! Come on...'

****

Time flew; the tournament week came around fast.

Soarame had no interest in the Fledglings Tournament, and neither did Halgon and Kardiac. Halgon seemed allergic to most public events, while Kardiac preferred to lie in the auditorium and watch games rather than play them. Omifo, however, was persuaded – well, "coached" – by the girls, especially Vivarin, to participate in the tournament..

On the day of Omifo's first game, the girls gathered that morning in Dileys' dorm, ready to go to the arena together.

'I still can't get over it,' Catheray pouted. 'Omifo is in the same grade with me now!'

'Then work harder, and grade up before he does!' Vivarin chuckled. 'Now I know why Soarame has been working so hard. He must be feeling lots of pressure living in that dorm.'

'I've been working really hard recently! I even skipped the events by the dancing club – that's my cheer leader plan for Soarame's future team!' Catheray complained. 'Also, I thought you didn't like bookworms? Why are you interested in Omifo now?'

'I'm not!' Vivarin protested. 'What are you talking about?'

'Yes, you are.' Jemario chuckled. 'You tend to bully the boy you like; we all know that.'

'No, I don't!' Vivarin looked suddenly shy and hurriedly switched topics. 'And what about you and Soar? You guys have been hanging out alone for a while. Any progress?'

'Who's been hanging out alone with him?' Jemario looked shy

too. 'Soar and I always hang out with you guys around, don't we?'

'Ahh, I see,' Dileys snickered. 'There's only that one time someone asked Soar to paint her, but instead he almost painted *on* her. Hmm… perhaps we were all around when that happened…'

Jemario pinched her arm, causing her to scream. The girls tickled and wrestled each other for a while, until Dileys pulled back and let out a sigh. 'At least Soar and his roommates are quite familiar with us. But Rodka…'

'So you need to push yourself forward!' Catheray understood her worries. 'Jem and Viv are probably just playing around with them, but you are serious about Rodka. Do something!'

'It's easy to say,' Dileys smiled bitterly. 'He's Rodka! He's commonly acknowledged as the Star of Libral!'

'But you are awesome too! You are one of the best talents in our department!' Jemario hurriedly encouraged her. 'Boys would chase you from the Libral Gate to your dorm, and line up outside waiting! Why are you so less confident in front of Rodka?'

'Because he's Rodka…' Dileys muttered. Her friends were anxious but helpless to see this. For years, they had known her as a confident and out-going girl, but when it came to Rodka…

'We need to go. The tournament is beginning,' Vivarin broke the silence. Everyone hurried off, and they met up with Soarame's group in the arena just in time.

'Omifo, the winner!' Kardiac began shouting at the top of his lungs as soon as Omifo stepped onto the stage. The audience was affected by his passion, and the atmosphere quickly heated up.

It's the first time Omifo had put himself in the centre of such a big event; he's too nervous to hear the referee when he's introducing Omifo's rival. Soon, a small, blue-eyed, blonde-haired girl came face to face with Omifo. She looked like a little princess, dressed in a cute little frilly pale pink gown and holding a little pink wand. But obviously, the girl was nervous to be standing on the stage too; she looked like she's shaking and barely dared to look at Omifo. Omifo suspected that she's a cheer leader or something, until he heard a delicately sweet voice. 'Hi there, uh… hello sir, can we start now?'

Omifo puzzled. *She is… my rival?*

How old is she? Is she even old enough to enter the school?

I'm gonna fight such a little girl?

No no no… What if I accidentally hurt her?

As Omifo was busy with his questions and worries, the girl asked again, 'Shall we begin now?'

Omifo nodded at the girl, sighing and distracted. The girl had already started chanting an incantation, but Omifo didn't really pay attention, as he's too busy worrying how to win the game in an honourable way without hurting her.

'Hey!' With a soft shout, a translucent crescent shot out from the tip of the girl's wand, heading right at Omifo.

'What!' Omifo cried out involuntarily, as did the audience. 'Windblade?'

This was certainly not as Omifo had planned. He had to leap aside to dodge the windblade. As a Grade-3 spell, a windblade could easily hurt him. Omifo gazed at the girl, mouth widened unconsciously. 'You are a… Grade-3 wizard?'

The girl didn't respond, probably due to her concentration. She's blushing, as if she were embarrassed to see her favourite spell fail to do anything. She appeared less nervous now as she clutched her magic wand and started chanting another incantation.

Whispers of 'What a genius!' and 'She looks so young! That's crazy!' floated around the audience. Meanwhile, Soarame and his friends were stunned at her capacities. Everyone's eyes were locked on the girl, including Rodka's.

At the same time, Omifo realised he had no luxury to dwell on his previous worries; he had to start chanting his incantation or else he's not sure who's going to win. However, before Omifo finished his spell, a blast of wind rose beneath his feet and whirled him into the air – it wasn't a windblade this time, but a *cyclone* spell.

Omifo's incantation was almost cut off as he's lifted into the air. He once again realised that he had underestimated this little girl; she wasn't only talented in magic, but also smart. Omifo gritted his teeth as he turned rakishly in the air and swung his wand towards his rival.

The girl suddenly felt a dazzling sensation in her eyes, and her world started spinning. It's a Grade-2 Lightness spell – *refraction*. It wasn't really a strong attack spell, but it's intended more to effectively disturb his rival. Although the girl tottered in place, she's tough enough to continue chanting for her next magic attempt. Seeing this, Omifo made an instantaneous decision and swung his wand again, casting an even less powerful spell – *reflection*. This time it's merely a Grade-1 spell that simply reflected sunlight to affect the rival's vision, but it's the best choice for Omifo at that moment.

Fortunately, it worked – dazzled by the strong light while still feeling dizzy, the girl finally fell over and broke off her incantation.

The effect of the cyclone finally vanished, and Omifo landed on the ground with a thud. Seeing that, the little girl was feeling more awkward as she stood up shakily – all her friends had told her that she would to beat all her rivals easily, but why did it not feel right? This was only her first game in the tournament!

On the other side, realising his rival was much stronger than he thought, Omifo started to chant his most powerful spell. Meanwhile, the audience were already cheering like crazy.

There were two Lightness spells that Omifo was best at: *focalization,* which caused temporary blindness; and *diffusion,* which caused temporary blackout. Both counted as half-invasive and half-restraining spells. Omifo chose to spell diffusion because he saw the girl start the next round of chanting with her eyes shut tight in order to protect herself from Omifo's spell. However, diffusion wasn't just about the light; it's more of a *mind attack* that targeted the mind ocean, and thus un-defendable by any physical means.

Distracted by her lack of vision, the girl couldn't chant as fast as she normally would have done, so for the first time, Omifo took the initiative and finished chanting his spell first. But after pondering a bit, he chose to wait for the girl to attack first.

The girl, however, didn't know any of this. She opened her eyes as soon as she finished her incantation, and closed them again as soon as she waved her wand at Omifo. This amused the audience; everyone watched her with affection.

Omifo was prepared and dodged the windblade easily. He cast the diffusion spell straight at the girl, whose eyes were shut, so there's no chance for her to dodge. Seeing the girl totter and about to fall over, Omifo hastened forward to help her sit down slowly. 'Great game. Sorry I didn't hear your name from the referee; if you don't mind?'

The girl was heavily stunned by the spell. She knew she had

lost even before Omifo held her arms. 'You won...I am Alicey.'

The audience burst into acclaim. After the referee announced Omifo's victory, Alicey's friends ran up to the stage and took her with them. Some of them peeked at Omifo, smiling – the boy did look handsome.

The friends were happy to see that Omifo had won his first game in good shape. Over the next few days, Omifo managed to win several more games; just when he's confident that he could keep winning, someone thought otherwise.

In the next game, a face familiar to Soarame stepped on stage and stalked towards Omifo. It's Kraigen, the chubby boy who had given Soarame troubles during the college application. According to the referee, Kraigen was, surprisingly, a Grade-3 in both Fire and Wind, and thus a very powerful candidate in this tournament.

The two boys didn't like each other very much. Omifo had heard about Soarame's unhappy history with Kraigen, and Kraigen simply didn't like anyone near the Water boy. So even before the battle started, the two had already been goading each other on, both getting angry. Then the battle started on the stage. Kraigen cast firebolts and Omifo beamed reflections; both were attacking and defending at the same time.

After several rounds of probing, the two had a better estimation of each other. Just then, Kraigen cast a *flamerush* at the same time as Omifo cast a *focalisation*; a beam of dazzling light struck Kraigen and a vast expanse of whiteness appeared in his eyes.

Omifo was happy that he had hit his target, although his left arm caught fire and he had to roll on the ground to put it out. Facing a rival with no vision, Omifo believed that he's at an advantage. However, he noticed that Kraigen had already finished a short incantation, and a fierce gale sprang up. The gale was so strong that Omifo had to try hard to maintain his balance and even shield his eyes from the dust. Even in the audience, some hats were blown away and it made people exclaim.

Omifo tottered in the wind and marvelled at Kraigen's tactic – *You took my vision, I take your mobility!* Omifo began to realise that although his rival had a lousy personality, he had really good skills; in fact, he's probably one of the strongest candidates in this tournament. Thinking to this, Omifo spared no effort in chanting another powerful spell – *diffusion*.

The mind attack from focalisation must have done some damage, so Omifo bet that Kraigen couldn't afford to take the diffusion. That meant that, once Omifo hit his target, he would win. With that in mind, Omifo struggled to stand against the gale and almost finished his spell when a blast of flame got him.

'Ahh!' Omifo hurriedly fell to the ground and rolled the fire out, but his incantation was cut off.

'Omi!' Vivarin shot to her feet. Soarame and the others also stood up, looking anxiously at the stage.

His firebolt got me? Omifo looked at the burning wound on his chest in disbelief. *How could this guy aim when he couldn't see?*

'Omifo, you will lose!' Although Kraigen couldn't see, he heard the painful cry and knew his firebolt had hit.

Omifo gritted his teeth to fight the sharp pain and performed a healing spell *warmth of sunshine* to treat the wound. The gale was still roaring around him, drowning out the yells from the crowd.

On the other hand, Kraigen wasn't at all affected by the gale he had summoned. He pointed his wand and shot three firebolts at Omifo.

A scattering shot? *So he can't tell where exactly I am, but he's trying to cover an area!* Omifo realized that the last hit on his chest must have just been luck. The problem was that fire could be boosted by wind and become really hard to put out, so Omifo had to make sure he dodged them this time. Fortunately, he made it; but just when he's about to fire back, the wind suddenly became stronger and he's almost blown over again.

Apparently, Kraigen wasn't stupid. Upon hearing that the last round of attacks had missed, he knew that Omifo had gotten used to the gale; so he strengthened it. Omifo cursed inside, but had to bear with it and redo his diffusion. This time, the spell hit Kraigen; but it only interrupted his incantation yet didn't knock him out. Omifo was in shock; this didn't make sense – no Grade-3 wizard could bear a focalisation plus a diffusion. Especially under the sunshine, where Lightness magic was enhanced – *Wait, where's the sunshine?*

Omifo looked up to the sky, finding a big cloud blocking the sun. At the same time, Soarame and his friends also realized that. 'Really? The Wind spells blew clouds to cover the sun, and reduced Omifo's Lightness power?'

On the stage, Omifo was anxious about this unexpected situation. *Is this planned or just a coincidence?* Kraigen would soon get his vision back, so Omifo had to do something fast, but his Lightness magic was largely jeopardised and there wasn't much he could do – unless he charged at Kraigen and wrestled him, but the wind wouldn't let Omifo get close.

Just as Omifo was at a loss for what to do, he heard a strange voice out of nowhere. {*Wind can bring the clouds, so can it take them.*}

The voice sounded so far away, yet also so near, like a whisper in his head. Omifo was startled and looked around – there's nobody beside him on the stage; where did the voice come from then?

There's no time for deep thinking. Omifo had to leave the question aside and follow the voice's directions. Biting his lips and hiding from another wave of firebolts, Omifo began to run into the blowing wind. Kraigen was nervous at hearing Omifo's footsteps and increased the wind power to reduce Omifo's mobility.

As Kraigen stopped shooting firebolts and repeatedly summoned wind, the wind blew stronger and stronger. More and more of the audience's hats flew up into the air, forming scattered dots in the sky. Facing the powerful gusts, Omifo tried all he could as he stumbled back and forth, but made no attempt to attack. This went on for several minutes, until Kraigen's eyesight finally recovered.

At the same time, the sun finally appeared as the clouds were blown away. Everyone stood up and cheered at Omifo's action. Even Sachastain chortled, standing in a corner of the stadium; he had come by to see the match and had lost his hat to the wind too.

The two players on stage were beyond tired. Kraigen's mind ocean was almost dried up; Omifo sat down on the ground, breathing heavily. However, neither wanted to quit. Seeing that, the audience were clapping, cheering and whistling in waves, to encourage the strong wills of the two competitors.

The overheated atmosphere encouraged the two boys. Both of them were struggling to prepare their last attack. The teachers on site started to worry because the two young students were getting ready to charge ahead in a battle that could lead to a life-threatening result.

'Omifo and Kraigen, you both did well,' The referee said, coming on to the stage. 'Let's call it a draw, how about that?'

'A draw?' Kraigen sneered. 'With a Water boy's roommate? No!'

'Bah! Who do you think you are?' Omifo rebuked. 'If not for the cloud, you would've lost five minutes ago!'

'Then let's see who's the loser!' Kraigen yelled back and started preparing his last strike. Seeing that, Omifo started to prepare too, unwilling to give up either.

Soarame and his friends were anxious; they yelled at Omifo, asking him to quit. Vivarin yelled herself hoarse threating Omifo in every way she could, but Omifo refused to listen.

'Omifo, here I come!' After chanting quite a while, Kraigen waved his wand, sending three windblades at Omifo – it's faster than firebolts and harder to dodge. And they were not aimlessly thrown – each of them was precisely controlled to seal all possible angles that Omifo might escape from.

'Watch out, Omi!' Vivarin screamed.

'Ahhh!' Before Vivarin's voice faded, Omifo shouted in pain and Kraigen dropped to the ground. Seeing no way to escape, Omifo gave up dodging and was hit by two windblades. At the same time, he managed to shoot out a concentrated stream of diffusion. As a result, Kraigen was knocked out right away. Omifo was also seriously hurt – one of the blades had cut deeply into his leg, and another had gone through his rib, cut through the bone.

Everyone was scared by the scene. Vivarin dashed to the stage to check on Omifo. Teachers and nurses also charged forward, some going to heal Omifo while others checked on Kraigen. The result of the match was clear: Kraigen had lost, and Omifo had won, though at great cost.

'The windblades missed the main arteries. He got lucky; his injuries are not life threatening.' Teachers and nurses were examining and treating Omifo together. Thanks to the healing spells, Omifo's surface wounds were quickly healed and the broken bone was also reconnected. Omifo's friends had gathered around him; Vivarin watched Omifo with worried eyes, until he struggled to get up and gave her a weak smile. Vivarin stared at him, turned her head, and walked away without a word. With a bitter smile, Omifo hurriedly got up and stumbled after her.

The teachers were smiling as they watched it, but suddenly there came a shout from near Kraigen.

'Come quick, this boy is not going to make it!'

THE CURE

In Soarame's dorm, the friends were worried. They had heard the teachers' words about Kraigen's condition, but then Kraigen was taken away and they were dismissed; so they didn't have a chance to know more.

'What? Did they say Kraigen might die?' Omifo asked anxiously. He had returned later together with Vivarin, and no one knew what had happened between them – at this point, no one cared either.

'I thought he just passed out?' Vivarin also wondered.

'No. It's worse than it looked,' Soarame sighed. 'Kraigen was attacked when he's exhausted, so he had no mind power to defend himself from the mind-attack...' he tailed off.

'Omi, don't blame yourself. The whole thing got out of control, and the one in hospital could easily have been you,' Kardiac comforted Omifo while the rest nodded. 'Rodka may come back soon with updates.'

'Omi is in Grade 3; his spell shouldn't cause death,' Halgon said, trying to calm his friends. 'But Kraigen could be hurt badly, and it will take a long time for him to recover. At worst, the damage could be permanent and he might lose the ability to practise magic.'

Halgon's words shocked everyone. The friends shifted around nervously in their seats, talking about how terrible it would be to lose their powers, when the door suddenly opened.

'Kraigen is fine!' Rodka announced as he walked in.

'Fine?' Everyone cheered with relief.

'Yes, he's out of danger, but he may lose his wizard

qualification,' Rodka added soberly.

'That's... exactly what Halgon predicted.' Everyone turned towards Halgon. 'How did you know that? And tell us if you also know how to solve the problem, please!'

'I'm sorry, I don't,' Halgon sighed. 'But there might be something we can try, if Soarame agrees...'

Kraigen was lying in a private room of the campus hospital. He felt woozy and his entire body ached. The news about the accident had spread all over the campus and alerted many professors. Dean O'heven – Kraigen's Dean – had personally come to visit Kraigen, along with many other teachers. Even the referee of their match was accused of dereliction of duty, and was put under investigation. But all this didn't make a difference for Kraigen's injuries; his mind ocean was badly injured, and the professors were convinced that there's little chance to heal him. Cures for mind ocean injuries were very rare and Libral had none in storage.

'Why did this happen to me?' He kept repeating to himself, crying. He'd been devastated after the teachers had told him that he might lose his magic powers forever. Kraigen couldn't tell them how much he regretted this, and blamed himself over and over again. He had risked his life for a stupid tournament that nobody actually cared about at the end of the day. Plus, he had not even won.

From the window in the door, Omifo watched in silence as Kraigen wept. He blamed himself for causing Kraigen's condition, but was also aware that it could easily have been him lying there. The hair rose on the back of his neck when he thought about it, and he shivered.

Omifo took a deep breath and cautiously opened the door, followed by all of his friends. Kraigen became upset once he saw Omifo, but he couldn't do anything about it.

'I am sorry, Kraigen...' said Omifo, head down.

'So what?' Kraigen cried faintly. 'How about I beat you to a pulp then say "sorry"?'

'Hey, Omi didn't mean this. You didn't attack any less seriously than him; you broke his ribs! The windblade could have gone through his heart!' exclaimed Kardiac.

Kraigen kept quiet for a moment, realising that he's no more innocent than Omifo, and then started to cry again.

'It's okay, Kraigen. We have come to cure you,' Soarame said hurriedly. 'You'll get better.'

'All the bad things happened because of you! What can you do to cure me?' Kraigen accused through his tears. 'Even the Dean said that I am handicapped. Now, a Water Boy is telling me he can cure me?'

'Kraigen, you are so rude.' Dileys frowned. 'Soarame didn't get you injured, and he doesn't have to help you. Grow up and think about it!'

Kraigen choked. He stayed silent for a while.

'We've brought you medicine.' Soarame smiled at Dileys and pulled out a bottle. 'Take this and you should be cured.'

'Nonsense! All the doctors and professors have said there's no cure!' Kraigen started sobbing again. 'My injuries are in my mind ocean; there's no such cure!'

'Kraigen, I know what you are thinking. I had the same thought at the beginning,' said Kardiac. 'But this can cure you, trust me!'

'Why should I trust you?' Kraigen squinted him. 'I don't even know you!'

'It doesn't matter.' Kardiac smoothed his golden hair in imitation of Kraigen's hair style. 'See? We have a similar figure, similar hair style, similar face, and even similar thoughts! So you can trust me.'

'What kind of logic is that?' Kraigen wasn't sure if he should feel upset or amused. 'Who has a similar face to yours? I look great!'

'That's right! Me too! That's called "similar", ok?' Kardiac shot back, then softened his tone, 'Now, listen – I'm telling you this as a friend: we are taking a great risk to treat you! You must sign a non-disclosure magic pact about this – you can never tell anyone we were once here to help you, and never ask us anything about the medicine! No matter how amazing this medicine functions!'

The friends watched Kardiac, speechless. They were not convinced that the two boys looked that similar – besides their chubbiness and their similarly-coloured gold hair, their only other similarity was that they both had poor taste in jokes.

Kraigen silently regarded Kardiac. He didn't know why, but he decided to believe him, for the odd logic that he refused to buy only seconds ago. So Kraigen signed the magic pact and opened the bottle. 'What's this? It smells!'

'You want to be cured or not? Just drink it!' barked Kardiac.

'Come and smell it yourself!' Kraigen barked back. 'I'm not taking this weird drug!'

'Do you want your wizard ability back, or do you want to lose it?' Jemario urged. 'The medicine can cure your mind ocean injury, but it needs to be taken as soon as possible because it decays, so stop wasting time like this!'

'How do I know this can cure me? I don't believe you anymore!' Kraigen changed his mind due to the overwhelming smell, and moved to throw the bottle away.

'Hold him, plan B!' Vivarin shouted to Halgon while grabbing the bottle out of Kraigen's hand. 'Let's hope it's still fresh!'

Halgon hadn't said a word since he came into the room. There's only one reason why he's here – he moved at the speed of lightning and grasped the struggling Kraigen tight.

'What the hell? How dare you!' Kraigen was freaked out by Halgon's overwhelming strength. 'Nurse! Somebody help!'

Everyone was disappointed by Kraigen's reaction, but they were well prepared. Catheray and Jemario went to guard the door, while the others helped Halgon to restrain Kraigen. Rodka had even created a magic seal to silence any noise from the room.

'Halg, you bull!' Soarame was astonished to witness Halgon's strength. Kardiac forced open Kraigen's mouth by pinching his nose. 'Shut up and drink it!'

Kraigen resisted and held his mouth shut, but he could only hold his breath for so long. When he finally had to open his mouth to breathe, Vivarin darted in, grabbed his chin firmly, and poured the entire contents of the bottle down his throat.

I will kill you all! Kraigen glared at this pushy crew as he's forced to swallow it, despite the strong smell. Grinding his teeth and breathing heavily, Kraigen stared at Soarame's crew, coughing. 'Soarame, you'd better kill me right now, or you will regret it!'

'Shut up man! How do you feel now?' Kardiac asked. 'I told you we are here to help, believe it or not!'

'Well, I'll "help" you back very soon!' Kraigen yelled at Kardiac. 'I thought you said we were friends!'

'We are, darn it!' Kardiac yelled back. 'Just check your mind ocean!'

'Humph!' An angry Kraigen unwittingly followed Kardiac's words, visualising his own mind ocean once again.

In his head somewhere, a dried-up mind ocean revealed the ocean bed, with a number of remarkable cracks caused by Omifo's mind attacks. It's these cracks that wouldn't allow his mind ocean to refill; and this was why Kraigen had lost his magic powers – if there's a big hole in the bottom of the tank, how could one refill it?

This had happened because Kraigen's mind ocean was already dried up when he's hit, so Omifo's mind attack had hit the "ocean bed" without any buffering from the "ocean water". Luckily, Omifo was merely a Grade-3 wizard; otherwise it would have killed him.

This was a vivid example of the possible severities of mind attacks. There's no joking with mind attacks, and this was the reason that enriching one's mind ocean was always treated as the top priority of every wizard. Soarame recalled how a year ago he had tried to push his limit to spell the fortieth windblades, and that upset his master. At this moment, he fully appreciated his master's wisdom, and was grateful to the old man.

While Kraigen was checking his mind ocean this time, he didn't hold out any hope. However, he soon discovered something completely stunning – the cracks in his ocean bed were diminishing slowly, with some small ones even about to vanish. This hadn't happened despite all the best attempts of highly skilled doctors and professors, because it's impossible to treat ocean bed cracks in ordinary ways – especially the biggest one in the centre. Nonetheless, that horrible big crack had obviously shrunk!

'This is...' Kraigen couldn't help raising his voice. 'This is unbelievable!'

'Now do you believe us?' Seeing the unwritten word "success" in Kraigen's face, Omifo drew a breath. 'We are going to let go of you, so promise me you won't do anything stupid!'

'I... I promise,' Kraigen stuttered, still trying to recover from his shock. Halgon stepped away from Kraigen and Kraigen looked towards Halgon with new respect – only after experiencing it himself could he believe how incredibly strong this boy was. Being grasped by him was like being seized by a beast, which really didn't feel good. But more than that surprise… his wounded mind ocean had almost healed, just like that?

'Remember you've signed a magic pact!' Vivarin reminded him. 'Don't violate it, or you know the consequences!'

'Somebody is coming!' Jemario suddenly alerted them. 'It's Dean O'heven!'

'Let's go!' Rodka breathed out in relief and opened the door. 'Greetings, Dean O'heven!'

'Rodka.' The Dean nodded at him but didn't say more; he walked directly to Kraigen. 'How are you feeling?'

'Err… I'm feeling good.' Kraigen was still basking in joy. Kardiac hurriedly blinked to signal him, asking him to act normal.

Dean O'heven glanced at the friends, and puzzled a bit upon seeing Soarame. But he wasn't in the mood to think about anything else; he's feeling very sad about losing a student with good potential. Witnessing his sincere grief and care, Soarame couldn't help sighing inside. He realized that he didn't really know this dean – Dean O'heven had given him troubles during his interview, but that didn't mean he's a bad person.

'To be honest, I still can't believe it really worked.' Back in the dorm, the girls looked at Halgon with amazement. 'How did you come up with this gross idea anyway?'

'I was just giving it a desperate try. There's no other solution anyway.' Halgon chuckled. 'I was hoping there's a store of *dragonblood* in the school, but there's not.'

Dragonblood was well known as a top-ranking cure for almost every type of injury in a human, including mind-ocean injuries. But it's almost impossible to extract blood from a dragon nowadays, so it's vanishingly rare.

Rodka wasn't satisfied with Halgon's answer. 'Yes, but why did you think Snower's pee could compete with dragonblood?' he pushed. 'Why don't the professors know about this, but you do?'

'What if I say I'm just guessing?' Halgon shrugged his shoulders. 'I've seen lots of magimals during the hatching process, and none were even close to Snower's. During her hatching process, the entire room was filled up with Life Energy; and the reason that dragonblood can work wonders is because it contains abundant Life Energy.'

'I see... but that doesn't guarantee the pee will work as a cure,' Omifo pointed out.

'If the pee doesn't work, we'll have to try her blood and it will work,' Halgon said confidently. 'But Snower is too young, so I'm trying to avoid drawing blood from a baby.'

'But if it hadn't worked, Kraigen would have taken it for nothing.' Kardiac giggled. 'Halg, you are bad! Poor Kraigen, he's signed a magic pact so he couldn't even ask anything.'

'Don't you think that's better for him?' Vivarin said, and everyone chuckled.

'Snower, what are you anyway?' Soarame held Snower in his arms and checked her up and down; she still looked like a normal kitten.

'I think she wants to know the answer too.' Rodka looked into Snower's innocent eyes. 'We should try searching for the answer again. I just can't stop wondering.'

'I agree! The library accident shouldn't stop us.' Dileys was the first one to second Rodka, and she's soon followed by everyone.

'If so, let's carry on with our old plan.' Rodka was happy to see everyone re-energised. 'We can go off-campus and try to find clues.' Rodka recalled the Dean's words – the campus was indeed going to be no more than a short story for them, and they had to get off it sooner or later.

Saturday morning came around soon. Soarame had cancelled his ice-carving appointment with Dafinol, and joined with his friends for the off-campus tour this day.

'Finally, I'm out!' Kardiac yelled once they got through the Libral Gate. 'We should have done this long ago!'

'Shh... there are people watching you!' Catheray pointed at a big crowd in front of the Gate. 'We are wizards, watch your manners!'

'Look, wizards!'

'Young wizards!'

'Oh my god, a team of them!'

'We got lucky today!'

'Wow!'

There's a large group of people standing in the distance cheering at the friends. Most of them were tourists, just like

Soarame and Filton when they first arrived. Every day, people from all over the world came to visit the Libral Gate, yet very few of them had the luck of seeing student wizards coming out.

As the group walked by, the cheering from the crowd became louder and louder. That said, the people were cool and smart enough to control their passion and keep their distance from the young wizards, out of respect.

'Your Honour, good morning!'

'Your Honour, may I shake your hand, please?'

'Please, your Honour!'

Soarame had seen people show respect to Scankeen along the way when they travelled here, but he didn't expect them to treat young wizards like themselves in such a special way too. Thinking of that, he's also wondering how Filton was doing now – he still hadn't replied to Soarame's letter.

'Praise Libral, this feels great!' Kardiac lowered his voice, which was very unusual for him. 'They treat us like heroes!'

'We *are* heroes!' Vivarin raised her head, tall and proud. 'We are the honoured wizards and we'll protect the world!'

'Your Honour, could you please let me take a quick photo of you? Please!' An old lady called out, waking Soarame from his memories. The lady was holding a mamera – basically a magic-driven camera that allowed normal people to use it even if they had no ability to perform magic. A Libral guard was blocking her, waiting for Soarame's permission.

'Yeah, sure, go ahead,' Soarame answered casually.

'Sir, this is usually not a good idea,' a guard reminded him, hearing Soarame's off-hand reply. 'Usually wizards don't like their photos to be taken.'

'Oh is that so?' Soarame was about to change his mind, but seeing the old lady's begging face, he softened. 'Can I let her take just one?'

'Yes, if you really want.' The guards let the woman come close to Soarame. A thin crystal chip popped out of her mamera – inside of which there's now a picture of Soarame.

'Your Honour, may I take a photo too?'

'Your Honour...'

Seeing that the old lady had succeeded, the rest of the crowd was encouraged and everyone wanted to do it. This scared

Soarame; he hurriedly left, with his friends surrounding him and the Libral guards stopping the crowd from following.

'Ha ha, Soar, how do you feel?' The girls were chuckling along the way. 'You were like a star back there!'

'Well... wow.' Soarame took a long breath. 'That's unbelievable.'

'It's actually more unbelievable than you think,' Halgon cut in. 'In case you didn't notice, your photo just got sold.'

'My... what?' Soarame choked on his words. 'Sold? How?'

'How what?' Catheray teased. 'How much?'

'It can't be a low price,' Rodka chuckled. 'Young wizards' photos are rare. I've only seen one so far.'

'Which is mine?' Soarame scratched his head. 'How could she just sell it right behind my back? She shot me just to make a sale?'

'No, she must be a poor woman, as her mamera was pretty old. She must be in need of money, although she probably didn't plan to sell it,' Jemario said. The friends had noticed that she always tended to be detail-oriented. 'There were a lot of people bidding for that photo just then, and someone seemed to get it in the end.'

'Relax, Soar, it's not that bad,' Vivarin chuckled. 'If you really are that worried, we can go back and grab it.'

'No, Soar permitted it. It belongs to the woman now,' Omifo disagreed. 'So she has the right to keep it, dump it, or sell it.'

'So what?' Vivarin didn't seem to care. 'We are wizards, we do what we want and they will obey.'

'Wow, careful, lady!' For some reason, Halgon was unhappy all of a sudden. He rounded on Vivarin and commanded, 'You take that back!'

'Hey, what's going on?' The friends got between Halgon and Vivarin. 'Halg, what happened?'

'Yeah, calm down!' Kardiac also sensed something very odd. 'She's just joking, right Viv?'

'Yeah... yes.' Vivarin was scared. She felt a burning anger from Halgon. 'I didn't really mean that.'

'I'm sorry,' Halgon regretted his loss of control. 'I don't know why I did that, I just...'

'It's okay, my bad,' Vivarin apologised, as she did feel bad for what she had said. For the first time, this aggressive girl showed a soft side that the boys didn't expect, which really surprised them all.

Everyone started to talk about other things, trying to forget about the incident. But Rodka was still wondering why Halgon had overreacted, because he had always been such a cool and calm person. And Halgon was a wizard himself, but his burst of anger just now basically showed that he didn't appreciate wizards' privileges at all – why?

'Look! A magishop.' Catheray point at a direction to distract her friends. They soon entered the shop and saw quite a few magigears of different kinds – wands and robes were the most common ones, along with parchments, potions and more. Besides those, there were crystal balls and crystal cubes – the latter were a common energy source, which was used in many magic devices such as Scankeen's magic carriage and the old lady's mamera.

Unfortunately, this shop didn't have anything to do with magimals. But this was normal, as magimals were not common.

Rodka wasn't worried about this. 'One of the biggest magishops in the city is called MagiMax. It should have magimals there.'

Hearing that, the crew rushed to MagiMax's, full of bright hope. This attracted attention from passers-by along the way, and soon enough people started to recognise the famous Libral Emblem on the crew's clothes and another wave of cheering began to build. The crew wasn't in a mood for this; they ran all the way to MagiMax's, followed by a large group of people who just wanted to see the young wizards. Eventually, the followers had to stop at the tall iron gate of MagiMax, because this magishop had a well-known policy: only wizards were allowed in.

When the crew stepped into the MagiMax shop, a wooden robot the size of a man showed up. 'Hello there, how lovely you all look!'

'Wow, what's this?' Kardiac was startled by the robot's greeting.

'You've never seen one before?' Rodka asked. Obviously he had been here a few times before, so he even knew the robot's name. 'Hi Blamer, long time no see.'

'Indeed, your Honour.' The robot bowed to Rodka. 'How can I help you this time?'

'The robot sounds like a real man!' Omifo couldn't help marvelling.

'Because it's controlled by its owner via a magic chip inside its body,' Halgon answered. 'The controller must be in this building somewhere.'

'How smart you are, my boy!' The robot turned to Halgon. 'I'm indeed in this building. Oh, as a robot I should say, my master is indeed in this building.'

'Hope to see you one day, Max.' Rodka knew the controller was named Max, the owner of the magishop. Max seemed not to like meeting people, so Rodka had never had a chance to see him. But this wasn't completely abnormal for wizards; many high-level wizards tended to avoid social interactions and preferred to spend their time to doing their own thing.

'Why is the robot named Blamer?' Omifo asked.

'It's just a nickname for all the robots,' Blamer responded. 'If I make mistakes in person I have to blame myself, but if I use a robot to do so, it is the one to blame.'

'That's so cool – I wish I had a Blamer when my mom blamed me.' Kardiac sighed. 'How many Blamers do you have?'

'Oh, look around you,' the robot said, waving an arm at their surroundings. The friends realised there were quite a few robots spread around the place.

'That's impressive.' Rodka took a step forward. 'Max, where are your magimals? I saw them last time, but they are gone now?'

'They are downstairs now.' The robot said. 'You wanna see them?'

'Yes. And we are especially interested in those born out of eggs.' Rodka urged.

'Egg-born?' The robot led them downstairs. 'This way then.'

As Everyone followed the robot downstairs, they were astonished to see hundreds of eggs in different colours and sizes. 'Praise Libral... look at this!' The eggs were sealed in big crystal showcases, sitting on a number of giant tables.

'Holy...' Even Halgon, a member of a magimal dealer family, had to marvel. 'What rankings are these magimals when they are fully grown?'

'These are relatively low,' the robot answered. 'All of them are Novices or Adepts.'

'Okay, I think we are looking for one on the higher end.' Rodka managed to say, shocked too. 'Do you have any?'

'I can get you Baron-level eggs, but can you afford it?' The robot turned around and looked at Rodka.

'No, but can we just look?' Jemario asked. The friends looked at each other – there actually were Baron-level eggs! How unbelievably exciting!

'No, I'm sorry,' the robot denied. 'You do know what you are asking, don't you? Barons can't just be seen whenever people want to; not even for young geniuses like you. I'm very sorry.'

'Do you mind showing us some live magimals, then?' asked Omifo. 'Like those that you feed?'

'Of course.' The robot seemed to attempt a smile. 'This way please.'

The friends followed the robot around to the back of the stairs, where a door led to a hidden room. In this room, filled with straw and feed troughs and water fountains, the crew saw a number of magimal babies playing around. There were baby wolves, foxes, bears and more, ranging from several weeks to several years old.

The baby magimals were so cute that they quickly melted everyone's heart. They stayed longer than they planned, and Blamer begun tapping his wooden foot, reminding them that he expected them to purchase one of these magimals or they should be leaving. Catheray was desperate to stay a little longer though; she's still holding a six-week-old baby bear, reluctant to let go.

'Alright guys, what do you say?' Rodka asked the group after they had left MagiMax. 'This Blamer – Max – can we trust him?'

'You mean, should we try to get his help for Snower?' Soarame asked. 'How? Do we just bring Snower to him?'

Halgon pondered for a while then said, 'Of course not. We need to know first if he has sufficient knowledge to help us. Even the best assessors from my family couldn't give me a clue after I sent them images of Snower.' Halgon paused briefly before continuing, 'But the good thing is that I've asked them to send me a rare type of magimal egg which they have assessed. We can use this egg to test Max, see if he's able to tell what's in it.'

'Oh dear!'

'You actually did that?'

The friends were excited to hear this.

Halgon lowered his voice. 'Yes, I'll leave you guys here and go get the egg now. It's pretty high-end, so keep it to yourselves.'

'Don't tell us you have a Baron egg,' The friends stared at Halgon.

'People, it's a Baron, not bacon. You think a Baron can be found everywhere?' Halgon rolled his eyes. 'Of course not. It's an Expert rank, Level 8.'

Everyone was amused. No one ever expected a higher rank than that. For a group of Novices and Adepts, a Level-8 magimal egg already sounded like a dream.

'Halg, you can't do this,' Soarame spoke up. 'Risking your magimal for mine? That's not what I would want you to do.'

'Don't say that,' Halgon pat Soarame's shoulder. 'It's not as risky as when you saved me from the beetalbulls.'

'Well...' Soarame felt touched by this show of brotherhood. 'But...'

'But what? You don't take me as a friend, or you don't want to help Snower anymore?' Halgon looked at him. 'It's the best way I can think of. If Max can tell what it is in the egg, we can then ask about Snower.'

'You know what's in your egg?' asked Catheray.

'Yes, it's a special kind and you will love it,' Halgon smiled. 'It's a duckbear – a mix between a bear and a duckbill, so it'll look almost like your favourite baby bear.'

'Praise Libral, that's so cute!' Catheray cheered. 'Your family people are amazing!' She actually didn't know what a duckbill looked like; all that she cared about was that the mix looked like a baby bear.

'So, if Max can tell correctly what it is, then we move on to Snower.' Halgon said, seeming unwilling to talk about his family.

'What if he can't?' Catheray asked. 'May I have the baby duckbear?'

'Err...' choked out Halgon. He wasn't expecting this.

'Gotcha!' Catheray laughed. 'Just kidding!'

'Well, I was just about to say yes, but now that you're just kidding...'

'Wait, no!'

MAGIMAX

The next day, the crew reunited for MagiMax again. The robot was surprised to see the crew coming back with a wooden box. 'What's this about?'

'We want to know what magimal this is,' Rodka spoke for the group. 'Could you help us, please?'

'Oh, that's the real deal?' The robot's wooden eyebrows lifted. 'I can, but there's a fee for that. A hundred gold coins if it turns out to be a high level magimal, thirty if not.'

Rodka was prepared for this. 'Okay, we can pay you, but how quickly can you do it? We don't want to leave the egg here.'

'Of course. It won't take long.' The robot took the egg out, rolled it in his hands, and noticed that there were some letters on the surface that he couldn't recognise. The next second, the robot shook and staggered, as if it's going to fall over.

'Wow, easy, man!' Rodka hurried forward to support the robot. 'You don't want to drop the egg!'

'My apologies! I guess that's why I'm called Blamer.' The robot found its balance and started to check the egg again. After a while, the robot gave the egg back to the friends. 'This egg looks strange. I'll need to do a thorough check with devices, if you don't mind?'

The friends followed the robot to a room labelled "Identification Room", where another robot was working as an assessor. The two robots looked almost identical, but the assessor was wearing a heavy burgundy robe which concealed his body. The assessor took the egg and walked to the table, where several crystal balls were placed in a circle. With a slight whirring, the assessor's robe flapped while he's turning; the assessor then put the egg into the centre of the circle.

'These crystal balls are here to identify the egg. Each of them has memorised the features of different eggs,' the assessor explained to the friends while the crystal balls started functioning. Soon enough, some words and figures emerged from two of them, and the assessor drew a conclusion accordingly. 'As you can see, two crystal balls responded; one says boa and the other says falcon. That means it's a wingedsnake, a Level-7 magimal!'

'Really?' Everyone glanced at Halgon, whose face showed no reaction to the assessor's verdict. 'It's a wingedsnake?'

'Yes, congratulations!' The assessor let the friends check the egg and the crystal balls. 'Whose is it, anyway?'

'It's mine, thank you,' Soarame took the egg for Halgon, who still looked expressionless. Before they had come, Halgon had asked Soarame to pretend to be the owner of the egg, because he wanted to keep a low profile, as always. Just when Soarame was about to ask the assessor to confirm it again, Halgon tugged his arm and instead he said, 'That's great to know. Let's go!'

'Wait, you guys forgot something.' The assessor emitted a coughing. 'The payment.'

'Oh, there you go,' Rodka said, taking out a bag of gold coins. 'A hundred, you can count it.'

'That won't be necessary. I trust you.' The assessor sounded like he's smiling. 'See you soon.'

'Halgon, the egg is a wingedsnake? I thought...' Catheray couldn't help asking as soon as they walked out of the shop.

'Shh!' Halgon stopped Catheray. 'Let's go first.'

'Halgon, what's wrong?' The crew followed Halgon all the way to the Libral Gate, walking past the cheering visitors as fast as they could.

Back in the dorm, Halgon looked really upset. 'Believe it or not, the egg was replaced! My bad... I didn't expect this guy to be a professional thief! He swapped my duckbear egg with a wingedsnake egg!'

'What are you talking about?' Vivarin didn't buy this. 'That's the biggest magishop in Cylone, and we all watched everything. You must be paranoid!'

'Vivarin, calm down,' Rodka cut in. Although he had doubts about Halgon's words too, he knew this boy wouldn't make things up. 'Halg, how can you prove that?'

'The letters changed,' Halgon pointed to the letters on the egg. 'These are faked.'

'They don't look fake to me.' Rodka took out his emblem, casting the hologram of the original egg into the air. Everyone had to agree that they looked the same.

'You can't check it like this – the letters are a special kind of magical code in my family; only I can tell the difference,' Halgon shook his head. 'Did you guys pay any attention to the robe on the assessor? Why would a wooden robot need a robe?'

'Because it looks better?' Catheray shrugged her shoulders. 'I don't think it could hide the egg under its robe; it's too big and we would have noticed that.'

'Of course not inside the robe, but inside a space-ring!' Halgon's words confused everyone. 'That assessor had a space-ring on its hand. The robe was just a cover to make the ring inconspicuous!'

A space-ring! Soarame was startled to hear this. He immediately recalled what his master told him about a space-ring – it looked like a normal ring but had a storage space in it, and it's very rare. Moreover, there's a bad guy who had used a space-ring to steal an important item from the druids; his master had gone after that guy until Volsta got badly injured!

'What "space-ring"?' Most of the crew never heard of this before; but luckily Rodka had, so he quickly explained. The friends looked at each other in bewilderment, not sure what to say.

'I believe Halgon!' Soarame had never been this serious before. 'I did see a ring on the assessor's hand, but I didn't think about it.'

'Even if that's really a space-ring, the egg was always in his hands,' Dileys said slowly, trying to recall the scene. 'If the robot swapped it we would have noticed, right?'

'Unless it turned around, and the egg was behind its body for a moment – remember the slight whirring when it turned?' Halgon said seriously. 'The swap only took a blink of time with a space-ring!'

'Halg, all this makes sense but it's still a guess.' Rodka took a deep breath. 'Is there any more evidence you can show us?'

'Yes. The letters on the genuine egg won't come off however hard one tries to wipe it, because they are actually a magic seal that my Dad put on – it is to prevent the egg from hatching.' Halgon explained, wetting a towel and using it to wipe the letters on the egg. 'However, look at this one.'

The friends drew together to see that the letters did become lighter; this would never happen to a true magic seal. 'Halgon, why didn't you say this back there?'

'Do you really think we can fight him?' Halgon countered. 'We needed to get out first to be safe.'

'Wait, you really think we'll get hurt in downtown Cylone?' Vivarin didn't buy this. 'I'm not scared of him! I'll go back there and ask for the egg now!'

'No we can't,' Omifo interrupted Vivarin. 'You really think a fraud would admit what he had done?'

'Then let's report it to the school!' Dileys suggested. 'Or maybe the Cylone City council!'

'It won't work.' Halgon shook his head. 'We can't prove it, so no one will believe us because we are just kids.'

'But we can't just let this happen and do nothing!' Catheray was really angry. 'You do realize that today is Sunday, and if we don't do something today, we'll have to wait until next weekend – that will be too late!'

'There will be other ways, and I'll ask my family to help,' Halgon said to calm the others down. Although Halgon was upset too, he wasn't as anxious as the others. 'Remember the seal on the egg? Max won't be able to hatch the egg anyway. And if he sells it to another person he will have more troubles, because the buyer will come back for sure when the egg won't hatch!'

The friends didn't sleep well that night. Everyone was indignant that they had been swindled. Halgon got up in the middle of the night for the restroom, but noticed that Soarame's bedroom was open and empty. Hearing noises in the living room, he went downstairs and saw Soarame at the table, with a canvas stretched out before him.

'Painting at midnight?' Halgon smiled and walked over to Soarame, but froze halfway – he's sensitive enough to notice that Soarame was different from normal. The boy was mind-painting but with his eyes closed. Halgon said hello to Soarame, only to find himself being completely ignored.

Sleep walking? Halgon was startled to reach this conclusion after carefully observing Soarame, and couldn't help being amused. Like any "good roommate" would do, he started recording him using his emblem. *When you wake up I'll show you this funny story!* However, after looking at the canvas, Halgon suddenly became serious – the painting was so clear, detailed and delicate, in sharp contrast to Soarame's last work of a pig-like Snower. If Halgon hadn't been watching Soarame paint in real time, he wouldn't have believed that this was his mind-painting work.

What's going on here! Halgon was shocked to see this unbelievable scene right in front of him. Looking at the painting again, Halgon recognised that it's the assessor in MagiMax; the wooden robot was wearing a robe and holding an egg with letters on its surface. Halgon looked carefully at the letters, and was surprised to see that they looked exactly the same as the real ones.

Halgon was no longer in the mood to sleep. He stood aside quietly and watched his best friend painting, until he had painted the assessor's other hand – there's a ring on its finger. After painting some letters on the ring, Soarame finished the work and started to fall over.

'Soar!' Halgon rushed to grab him before he banged his head on the floor. 'Are you ok?'

Soarame was silent. Halgon hurriedly checked his breath and heartbeat, only to find that Soarame was in a deep sleep. Astounded, Halgon carried Soarame back to his bedroom.

Soarame didn't wake up until dinner time the next day, to find that everyone had gathered around his bed. He didn't believe what they told him at first but was finally convinced – after seeing his delicate painting work and Halgon's recorded scene of him. Soarame didn't know why he would be dream-painting, but the most likely reason would be his overwhelming concern of the space-ring.

'Soarame, this is unbelievable!' The friends marvelled at the high quality of the work – it looked just like it had been taken by a mamera, only without colours. However, when Soarame tried to do another mind-painting of Snower, she's still in the piggy style that amused everyone so much. It seemed that making a dream-painting didn't mean he had mastered the art when he's awake. Snower kept looking into the mirror to verify that she didn't have a snout, and wasn't really as fat as a pig.

Holding his necklace in his hand, Soarame suddenly started to doubt if this was due to his master's token; and he's wondering if there's a way to contact his master, but the token seemed not to have a communication function and Soarame still didn't know what exactly it could do. On the other hand, Halgon seemed very confident about his father's seal on the duckbear egg; he urged everyone to keep it quiet and leave it to him, despite the fact that he chose to let Sachastain know about it when the man visited them again a few days later.

'MagiMax? Space-ring?' After hearing the story, Sachastain was startled too, and he didn't have good advices for the kids. But after hearing about the seal, he's a bit relieved. 'So Max will have it in his hands, but won't be able to hatch it or sell it. I wonder what that feels like?'

****

'Look at you!' A few days later, Kardiac was holding the campus newspaper and pointing at Kraigen's photo on top. 'You made the headlines!'

'Yeah, because I look good.' Kraigen was proud of this – his recovery had amazed everyone and he had soon become famous. Seeing Kraigen never asking about the medicine, everyone chuckled. The Fledglings Tournament had ended; because of Kraigen's accident, Omifo had no interest in competing anymore and had withdrawn.

Because Kraigen had been healed, the problem between him and Omifo vanished. Surprisingly, Kraigen had changed a lot after this incident – he came to visit Soarame and his roommates every day, and soon became a close friend to them. Another surprise to Soarame's crew was that Alicey came along and hung out with them; she even brought her friends. The friend-zone therefore kept growing bigger and bigger.

Interestingly, Alicey even had a magimal – a baby girl *windwolf* named Niuniu. An adult windwolf was ranked Level 9, and it's born with Wind and Darkness gifts. When the friends first met Niuniu, they were so amazed by her high ranking; for that reason, Halgon decided to reveal that he actually had a magimal too – how could a magimal dealer family member not have a magimal? This afternoon, Halgon had brought his bonded magimal to the dorm and introduced him to his best friends on campus.

'How adorable!'

In the dorm, the girls screamed in delight. Halgon's magimal was a male *firntiger*, named Icer. Icer's birthday was shortly after Snower's, and he stayed with his mother over the past few months. So once Icer came to join the family on campus, he already had two big sisters – Niuniu and Snower.

Grrr... Icer was making his naïve roaring sound towards his new friends, looking excited.

As the king species on the icefield, Icer was born captivating and strong. Unlike Snower, who looked like a cute little cat, Icer looked quite tough and ferocious even though he's only a few months old. Adult firntigers were ranked at Level 9 too, but some of them could level up to Baron once they were fully grown. So before long, Icer could be stronger than his big sister Niuniu – even though he failed when he tried to challenge her right now, and she tackled him and trapped him under her.

'He's really playful and naughty, huh.' The girls watched Icer in amusement. 'Why didn't he fight Snower? He could probably win easily.'

'No he wouldn't,' Halgon stroked Icer to calm him down. 'He recognises that Snower is special, so he won't even try.'

'Really?' Soarame was surprised. 'Not because they have similar names?'

Halgon laughed. 'By the way, his name was actually inspired by you. They are both pure white; you chose Snower, so I decided to choose Icer.'

'Hey guys, what did I miss?' Rodka's voice piped up. 'We've got new family members?'

'Yep, and they are getting along pretty well,' Alicey cheered, watching Niuniu strut around. 'Rodka, have you ever wanted a magimal for yourself?'

'Hmm, good question.' Rodka smiled. 'Two years ago, I won a tournament of the school and got a chance to choose an award. The best options were a magimal egg, a magic wand, and a defensive cloak, all of Expert level.'

'So you chose the wand?' The friends got it. They had seen Rodka's high-ranking magic wand that he carried with him all the time.

'Yes, it took me days of struggle to make my decision,' Rodka recalled. 'Sometimes you just don't know which option is the best, but you still have to choose.'

'I feel for you,' Kardiac cut in. 'Take naps or take snacks, it's always hard to choose but you still have to.'

'Hard? You always chose both!' Omifo chuckled and turned to Rodka. 'I feel for you too – as wizards we need to prioritise our own power over anything else. At least, our Dean claims so all the time.'

'Yeah, it's actually the Dean's words that led me to this decision. Otherwise, I probably would have chosen the magimal egg.' Rodka sighed. Then he sat up suddenly. 'By the way, I just heard something about MagiMax.'

'What's MagiMax?' Alicey asked. She didn't know about the duckbear story yet.

Halgon quickly explained to Alicey and turned to Rodka, 'What was it about?'

'There will be a big sale this weekend. Everything will be half price for students with Libral Emblems.' Rodka looked around at his friends. 'I really don't like that shop, but I do need to buy some expensive magigears while they are on sale.'

'Sure, let's all go,' Halgon agreed. He knew what Rodka was thinking – Rodka didn't want Halgon to be unhappy.

'Oh no! Why didn't you tell us earlier!' Dileys' crew was complaining. 'We already made plans with other friends...It's such a shame! But Alicey, you should go; hopefully it won't be too crowded to get in.'

'Cool, I want to go!' Alicey said excitedly.

'Alicey, it's really not that much fun...' Soarame tried to discourage Alicey from going for her protection, but lacked a good reason.

'You don't want to take me?' Alicey was disappointed to hear this. She looked at Soarame in surprise and embarrassment.

'Whoa! I didn't mean that!' Soarame claimed hurriedly.

'Don't mind him, just go with them,' Jemario said with a glare at Soarame then a smile for Alicey. 'He always does weird things. Let me tell you a secret about him...'

'What secret?' Soarame butted in, seeing Jemario whispering with Alicey. 'The sleep walking was just an accident!'

'You sleepwalk?' Alicey muffled a scream.

Great! Soarame rolled his eyes and decided to zip his mouth. Jemario chuckled and whispered again to Alicey; Alicey burst into laughter, and the girls hurried out of the boys' dorm with quick goodbyes.

'Wait, what's that whispering about?' Soarame shouted at Jemario's back.

'The point of a whisper is that I can hear it but you can't!' Alicey chuckled as she ran away. 'See you guys tomorrow!'

Just as Soarame was about to shout back, Omifo suddenly dragged him. 'Hey guys, Alicey reminded me of something!'

'What's it?' The friends asked.

'During the Fledglings Tournament, when I competed against Kraigen, I heard someone whisper to me. It actually helped me beat Kraigen!' Omifo looked around at his friends. 'It's very weird – the voice sounded like a whisper, but there's no one beside me. And now as I recall it, it felt like it's coming from inside my mind.'

'Really? What did he say?' Halgon seemed very alerted. 'You should have told us about this earlier; it's very abnormal!'

'How so?' Omifo was surprised to see Halgon's reaction, so he tried his best to describe all the details.

'That's a mind-talk! That's the only way it could sound as you described.' Halgon looked serious. 'Someone communicated with you directly through his mind power – just like what Soarame does to Snower – only that you are not his magimal.'

Soarame nodded in silence. His master could do mind-talk, so he knew mind-talk could happen between people too. After he had Snower, Soarame had realised that mind-talk from his master felt exactly the same as talking to Snower using the mind connection.

'Could it be Chelonad?' guessed Kardiac. 'But Chelonad's voice can be heard by everyone, not just you.'

'Plus the voice wasn't Chelonad's,' Omifo confirmed.

'How about the Principal Gazbell Raymend?' Rodka asked. 'I

heard only Masters can do mind-talk, and our Principal is the only Master-level wizard on campus.'

'No, it wasn't him. I've heard him giving speeches before,' Omifo shook his head. 'But I've never heard this voice before.'

Soarame suddenly thought of a possibility that he did not dare hope for. 'Guys, don't panic. It could be my master!'

THE MOST POWERFUL MAGIC

'What?' Halgon looked at Soarame. 'You have a master?'

'Yes, before I came here I learnt magic from my master.' Soarame got excited. 'He can do mind-talk!'

'What's his name?' Halgon asked right away.

'Mr Swanflew,' answered Soarame.

'Swine flu?' muttered Kardiac. 'What a... unique name!'

'Let's hope you are right.' Halgon looked thoughtful. 'And hopefully whoever helped Omifo is also a friend to us.'

Master! Soarame was screaming inside. *It must be him! Master is hiding and watching me!*

'Soarame, if it's truly your master, could you ask him to help us get the duckbear egg back?' Omifo asked.

'Well, I can't get in touch with my master, unfortunately,' Soarame said, shrugging his shoulders. 'I guess he's here observing me even though he won't show up. But if he does, sure!'

'It's okay,' Halgon said quickly. 'My family can handle the duckbear egg.' For some reason, Halgon seemed reluctant to accept external help for that. 'This time we are only going to MagiMax for shopping. No one makes trouble about that, okay?'

The weekend came soon enough, and the boys went to MagiMax together with Alicey. The small girl was really excited about going out with the older students; the boys had just learnt that morning that she's only nine.

What a genius! They were amazed at her talent. A nine-year-old was actually a Grade-3 wizard!

'Hey guys, what's that about?' Alicey was the first to see a large crowd in front of MagiMax.

The friends soon reached the crowd, and people began to cheer.
'Hey, another group of Libral wizards!'

'Morning, your Honour!'

'No wonder there's few people by the Libral Gate this morning.' The crew walked through the crowd and noticed that the city force was here too to keep order. A large amount of people in the city had gathered to see the line of Libral students in front of MagiMax. The mayor and all the government officers were worried and had sent out their security forces, in case an accident happened.

'Praise Libral, we thought we were early?' moaned Kardiac. Seeing the long line outside MagiMax, everyone was dumbfounded. There were *so* many students queuing up to enter MagiMax, and each of them was holding a Libral Emblem, forming a spectacle that's rarely seen.

'Oh dear, "half-price" has such power?' Alicey goggled at the scene.

'Oh yeah, that's the most powerful magic in the world,' Rodka said, a bitter smile on his face. 'So, what do we do now?'

'Don't know.' Soarame looked around and all he could see were Libral students one after another. 'I didn't even know that our school had this many students.'

The friends stood in line outside MagiMax until noon, chatting, but the line was still so long that they finally lost patience. 'Let's go, we won't even get there before it closes,' Halgon tried to persuade his friends to leave.

'Yeah, he's probably right.' Rodka had to agree, although he's really disappointed that he would not be able to get the magigears he wanted. 'We should have listened to the girls; they knew it would be super crowded so they didn't even bother to change plans.'

'That's because it's not a shoe store, man,' Kardiac said. 'Otherwise we'd have a chance to witness their real power...'

Right then, a voice was broadcasted from the building. 'Ladies and gentlemen, your attention please!' Soarame and his friends stopped talking to listen to the announcement. 'First of all, thank you so much for your passion and support for MagiMax. I really appreciate it.'

'However, due to the high volume of purchases this morning,

half of my stock has already been bought up. I hope you all had a good time robbing me,' the voice continued, and everyone knew that it must be Max. 'To be honest, I really wish I was on the other side of the counter buying things with you.'

'This Max is pretty funny, isn't he?' Kardiac was chuckling like everyone else. 'If not for the crap last time, I would really like this guy.'

'Yeah, I heard he's got a good reputation out here,' Omifo said, shaking his head. 'He should pursue an acting career.'

'However, if this goes on I'll go bankrupt, so I have to update the policy.' Max's voice attracted everyone's attention. 'For those of you who have done business with MagiMax before, you can still come in and try to bankrupt me. But for the rest of you... sorry; MagiMax welcomes you next time. My deep apologies!'

'Oh nooooo!'

'What the heck? That's ridiculous!'

'Talk about wasting our entire morning!'

Hearing this, many students started yelling and complaining. However, a bunch of robots were already blocking the gate and checking purchase histories, causing most of the students to be turned away. On the other hand, Soarame's crew was overjoyed; they proceeded into the store very quickly with Rodka, and the robot was nice enough to let Alicey in too.

'This robe looks so nice!' Alicey dashed to a dress stand and picked up a bright pink robe dotted with embroidered shimmering blue stars. 'Blamer, how much is it?'

'Blamer, how much is this wand?'

'How about this necklace?'

The students were competing with each other to choose their purchases; none of them had ever seen a half-price deal in MagiMax. Soon enough, most of the students there couldn't afford to buy any more and had to leave, until there were only a few students left.

'Guys, everybody is leaving, we should be going too.' Halgon checked the light outside; it's getting dark. 'If you want, we can come back tomorrow.'

'I'm sorry, but we will no longer offer the deal tomorrow,' a nearby robot answered.

Halgon frowned upon hearing that. With a glance at the robot, he turned to his friends right away. 'Guys, we need to go. Can you really afford any more anyway?'

'Okay, I'm done,' Kardiac said as he came over, arms full of bulging shopping bags. 'From now on, Kardiac is a poor guy. I'll have to rely on you guys for my next meal!'

'Same here.' Rodka had also finished his shopping. 'I got some good stuff, but I'm poor as hell now, ha-ha.'

'I'm ready too!' Alicey came over, bouncing and vivacious with a bag on each arm.

'Soar, you didn't buy anything?' Kardiac asked, seeing Soarame's empty hands.

'Well... yeah, I don't really need any of these,' Soarame waved vaguely towards the nearly empty shelves, a little shy about admitting this.

'Oh no, my bad.' Kardiac smacked his own head as he remembered that Soarame wasn't from a rich family, so he couldn't afford to buy stuff here, even though it's on sale. Thinking of this, he rummaged around in one of his bags and handed over a ring. 'I almost forgot, I bought this for you!'

'Kardy, your finger is as big as Soarame's thumb!' Omifo teased and put a wand into Soarame's hand. 'Soar, I got you this. Really, this is for you, I swear. Your wand was old; it's time for a new one.'

'Thanks!' Soarame was a little overwhelmed by the generosity of his friends.

'Your name is Soarame, right?' The robot nearby spoke up. 'Since your friends have bought so much today, I'd like to offer you 70% off one item, of no more than two thousand gold coins in value. How about that?'

'Wow, really!' Alicey's eyes widened with excitement. 'Soar, let's go and choose something!'

'Guys...' Halgon immediately sensed something odd – ever since the Blamers let Alicey in as an exception, he had already been suspicious. Max was by no means a good man; why would he do this? Looking around, Halgon suddenly realised that they were almost the last customers. There's only one group of students other than them and they were checking out.

'Hey guys, how's it going?' Halgon called out to the other students.

'Not bad, yourself?' A dark-skinned boy gave Halgon a big smile As he held up a big case.

'Sir, we are closing, please.' The robot beside them hurried them along.

'Hey, guess what? The shop is giving us a 70%-off special offer!' Halgon waved at the other group of students to come back. 'What do you think we should buy?'

'Sir, you can't do this!' The robot beside Halgon was suddenly anxious.

Something is wrong! Seeing all of this, Rodka was the second to become suspicious. Although he's really excited himself, he had not forgotten what had happened last time. *Halgon is giving us a signal!*

'It's okay Blamer, we just want some advice,' Omifo became aware of the situation too and stepped back from the robot.

'No, you can't do this. Otherwise you will have to give up the special offer,' the robot insisted. Several other robots began to move towards Soarame's crew.

'Hey, it's okay. We won't interrupt then. Good luck, you guys!' The other group of students also sensed something weird and tried to leave. Halgon was so anxious that he tried to think of a way to signal them to run for help when they got out. However, somewhere in the building, a man was observing all the details from a crystal ball; it's too late.

'Smart kids, you can all stay now,' Max's voice echoed in the store as all of the robots suddenly dashed over, and the gate of MagiMax closed by itself!

'What do you want, Max?'

Seeing the sudden change, Rodka hurriedly pulled out his magic wand and motioned his friends behind him. Inside he felt so frustrated and stupid; how could he have been such an idiot as to ignore Halgon's repeated signals until it's too late?

Max didn't answer, but the robots used their actions to respond to Rodka's question – the other group of students was tackled by a group of robots. The robots were much stronger than the kids, so there's hardly any resistance before the kids were captured and taken away somewhere.

'Smart move…' Meanwhile, one of the robots looked at where Halgon was standing, a bit surprised about the boy's fast reaction –

Halgon had kicked down a robot and hid himself in the shadows by using a shadowcape spell.

'What's going on?' Alicey was terrified by the menacing robots. She's holding Rodka's robe and hiding behind him, shivering.

'Soarame, you take care of Alicey, okay?' Rodka commanded. 'No offence but your Water spells won't help much here, so leave the fight to us. But promise me you will stay with Alicey and look after her!'

'I will,' Soarame nodded curtly. Although he's a bit nervous too, he had been well trained by Scankeen to stay calm and judge the situation.

'It's okay, I don't mean to hurt you,' said a robot in answer to Rodka. 'I only wanted to talk, and then you will be free to go.'

'Talk about what?' Kardiac asked. Nobody understood what's happening here, but everyone suspected that it's about the duckbear egg. Strangely, the robot didn't answer him.

'How come it's so hard to perform magic here?' Rodka had been trying to prepare his spells, but he suddenly realised that he could no longer summon magic elements. 'Something is wrong! This place is weird!'

'The emblem is not working either!' Omifo had been trying to send out messages, but the Libral Emblem stopped functioning.

'Of course,' a man sniggered in the darkness on the other side of a crystal ball – Max. He had spent lots of time and effort in setting up a magic seal around the building to isolate everything from the outside world. This meant that the magic elements outside couldn't be summoned, and therefore very little magic could be performed by using only the magic elements inside the building. Halgon had been lucky enough to summon just enough Darkness elements to hide himself in the shadows. Without magic power, the kids could be taken down easily by the wooden robots. More importantly, the magic seal disabled the Libral Emblems, so that the kids wouldn't be able to call for help.

'Now if I were you, I would sit down and try to answer questions, so you can walk out of here in one piece,' Max's voice sounded from a robot.

Crack!

Before he finished speaking, a robot fell to the floor and broke apart. The robots next to it rushed over, only to find that the crystal chips inside the fallen robot had been broken by some kind of sharp weapon.

'Halgon, you've surprised me yet again!' Max's voice boomed throughout the building. 'You are not only a wizard, but also a warrior at the same time?'

Crack!

What answered Max was the noise of another robot falling down and breaking apart. Everyone was surprised by Halgon's sneak attacks; Rodka clenched his fists tightly, ready for a physical fight too.

'Stop! Or I will have to hurt your friends!' Max yelled anxiously, but it's an empty threat – another three cracks sounded simultaneously, and three of the robots surrounding the friends fell over and shattered. At the same time, a shadow dashed over to the friends and pushed a dagger into each person's hand. 'Spells won't work here, just use these and fight your way to the gate!'

'You are not going anywhere!' The robots yelled as one at the shadow, but the shadow appeared briefly again and kicked over another robot.

'You heard him! Wake up and fight!' Rodka roared to his friends and pushed his dagger into a robot's wooden chest. After a similar cracking noise, the robot fell to the floor.

'Go, go, go!' Kardiac was the next one to get a robot. Although he's frightened, he's able to use his body weight to his advantage as he lunged at a robot, knocking it over. Soarame and Omifo also broke out of the circle of robots, dragging a screaming Alicey with them.

'Screw you!' Max hadn't expected the kids to have such fast reactions. He had lost ten robots in a few seconds; that's just careless. With growing anger, Max controlled all the remaining robots and made them dash towards the friends, with a few of them heading towards the gate to guard it.

'Get the heck away from me!' Kardiac was screaming. He tried to knock another robot over but found himself grasped in the robot's hard wooden hands and lifted into the air.

'Kardy!' Omifo rushed over to help Kardiac, but halfway there he's tackled by another robot and dropped his dagger in the struggle. The robot holding Omifo was pushing into him, but suddenly it fell over with a *crack*.

'Help Soar protect Alicey and follow Rodka! I'll take care of Kardy!' Halgon's voice sounded out of the shadow floating over Omifo towards Kardiac. Omifo bit his lips and jumped up, fetched his dagger to help Soarame take down another robot, then together they dragged the frightened Alicey towards the gate.

Soarame heard some crunching noises from behind him but when he turned to see it, Halgon already had Kardiac on his back and was rushing towards the friends. Kardiac wasn't sure how it had happened; he had only seen a shadow pass in front of him, and the next second he's released from the robot's arms and was sitting on the shadow's back.

'Halg, you bull!' Feeling himself moving like wind on the shadow's back, Kardiac couldn't help his excitement. 'You'll have to teach me all these martial arts!'

'Only if we can get out of here!' Halgon didn't even sound tired after the intense fighting he had done so far. 'Here's your knife back, but be more careful this time!'

'Screw these kids, screw that Halgon!' In the secret room, a mad Max was roaring aloud. He expected the kids to be taken down by his robots easily, but Halgon's incredible fighting abilities made Max less sure about his seemingly perfect plan.

It had to be plan B, then. Max looked at the twenty expensive robots that were destroyed, and he almost wanted to cry.

Due to the large number of robots, the kids' attempts to break out of the building didn't work out, unfortunately. They were cornered against the locked doors, and this time they couldn't manage to do much anymore. They were in one big group, weapons in hands, facing the robots, in a stalemate. Max didn't want to lose more robots, so the robots stayed in a circle and didn't approach.

'You kids have really upset me!' A robot stepped forward to face the kids. 'As I said, I only wanted to have a talk and set you free after that, but now you have made such a mess! You will pay for this!'

'Ha-ha, of course we should trust you,' Halgon mocked with a bitter laugh. 'Like when you stole my duckbear egg!'

'You knew about that?' Max was shocked. 'You knew and you played the fool?'

'I was just wondering how you are gonna clear up the mess here,' Halgon sneered. 'You tried to kidnap us for whatever reason, but you think that's the end of it? Everybody saw us here at your shop, and you think you will be just fine after this?'

'That's not for you to worry about,' Max sneered back. A big secret skill of his was hypnosis, and it could solve a lot of problems – he had just hypnotized the other group of kids, making them forget about what happened and send them away. When those kids get back, all that they would remember was that they enjoyed the half-price shopping at MagiMax. In fact, Max had used this hypnosis trick to settle a few previous incidents, so that no one had been able to discover his secret activities so far. However, he needed to capture the kids first before performing hypnosis, and his plan was encountering some serious problems right now.

All because of this Halgon! Max's eyes flared with rage as he stared at Halgon in the crystal ball. 'So, it's actually your egg? I thought it's Soarame's.'

'It doesn't matter now. Whosoever it is...' Halgon was a little sorry for having let his secret slip, but he didn't care anymore. Just then, he suddenly smelled something strange which made him nervous. 'Watch out, it's poison gas! Guys, hold your breath!'

'Ha-ha, you are really impressive, boy!' Max laughed through the robot. 'I am really curious about who you are now – even Rodka doesn't understand things the way you do! But it's too late, have a nice sleep!'

Soon enough, the kids fell over, one by one. The robots came and tied them up, then carried them to a display of various types of wands. The robots stopped at the display and waited it for a few seconds to flip around, revealing a staircase behind it. The robots went in – downstairs to the basement – and entered one of the secret rooms, then tied the kids to chairs in front of the waiting Max. He's fully covered in a voluminous black robe, with his face hidden under a hood and veil, only leaving his eyes visible.

'Finally, there you are,' he said, glee barely contained in his voice.

A few days ago, after Max got the duckbear egg, he had performed a thorough check on it and realised the magic seal. He then spent days and nights trying to break the seal, only to determine that he couldn't do it. In the end, he had to take a break while he tried to sort out what had happened since he first got the egg.

~~~~

'Interesting.' That day, in a dark room, Max was looking at a crystal ball through a thick pair of glasses. The crystal ball was showing the robot's vision, and Soarame and his friends were handing over an egg. Seeing the unrecognisable letters on the egg, Max stood up quickly, a pen in hand. But he's rather fat, and his belly almost knocked the table over.

'Darn it!' Max was worried that the shaking of the crystal ball might have caused the robot to fall over and crack the egg, but luckily that didn't happen.

'Wow, easy, man!' By the robot's side, Rodka hurried forward to help. 'You don't want to drop the egg!'

'My apologies!' Max breathed in relief. 'I guess that's why I'm called Blamer.'

After that, Max went over to a shelf and fetched an egg that looked identical to the kids' egg, and wrote the same letters on the egg. Although he didn't know what language they were in, as a skilled old hand at forgery, he could still capture all the details of the letters and copy it.

Max was satisfied with his work. He then opened the door and let in a robot. Max took off a ring from his own hand and put it on the robot. After pondering a bit, he fetched a robe and put it on the robot too.

Due to a fortunate incident years ago, Max had gotten the space-ring that he's wearing, and had been able to do the swapping trick ever since. He had always been lucky so far – half of the magimal eggs he owned were gained by the same trick – one of a lower level for one of higher level, with the value difference usually being a factor of ten or sometimes even more.

But this time, Max found himself running into a brick wall – the duckbear egg turned out to have a seal on it, and therefore its value almost equalled to zero. This had occupied and exhausted him for days and nights, until one day, a voice passed through the crystal ball –

'Blamer! Are you in?'

Max looked at the crystal ball and saw a yellow-haired boy, tall and thin, talking to a robot in his shop.

'Yes Casavin, how can I help you this time?' By the front gate of MagiMax, the robot bowed to Casavin and the boys surrounding him.

'This wooden robot really knows your name!' Casavin's friends were surprised.

'Of course, I'm a VIP client here,' Casavin said proudly and walked into the building. 'Blamer, have you got anything new?'

'Sure I do.' On the other side of the crystal ball, Max sighed. Libral students are out there; that meant a week had passed.

'Some new robes, wards, crystal chips, and an... that's about it.' The word "egg" almost slipped out but Max swallowed it in time.

'That's it?' Casavin curled his lips in a sneer. 'I thought you sold magimal eggs too? You do or you don't?'

Hearing the word "egg", the robot's voice sounded unhappy. 'Why are you guys suddenly all interested in magimal eggs anyway?'

'"All" interested in?' Casavin was surprised. 'Who else asked about magimal eggs?'

'Some students from the same school as you, but you probably don't know them anyway.'

'Try me! There's hardly anyone that I don't know,' he said, puffing up his chest.

'Okay... Soarame, as I recall.'

'Soarame?' Casavin and his friends all knew this name for sure. 'He came to buy magimal eggs? Did he not have one already?'

'Yes, he had one. He came to check the species of his egg.'

'Well, that must be a cat... Wait, what? It's an egg? Another one?' Casavin had heard rumours about a cat-like magimal belonging to Soarame – probably thanks to Kardiac blundering around.

'Another one?' Max was also surprised. 'That kid has more than one?'

'Well, he had a high-ranking, cat-like magimal that hatched from an egg a while ago.' Casavin was jealous. 'What's the egg this time?'

'It's a duck... no, a wingedsnake.' Max's surprise was beyond words – this little boy, with such low magic power, capable of nothing, how the hell could he have so many high-ranking magimal eggs?

'Crap, this kid is too lucky!' Casavin barked, making a sour face along with his friends. 'How does he deserve that?'

Max put on a careless tone as he replied, 'It's not a big deal, it's just two eggs.'

'Yeah, just two eggs, one of them is a Level-7 and the other one may just be a Baron!' one of Casavin's friends complained in a weird tone – that "Baron claim" must be from Kardiac.

'A WHAT?!' This time Max could no longer pretend to be calm. His eyes were seeing red from what he had just heard. 'A BARON?!'

'He can dream about it!' Casavin yelled back. 'Just because he couldn't figure out what species it is, it must be a Baron... ha ha, of course!'

Max got the message now. Although Soarame's cat-like magimal had not been identified as a Baron, it must still be a rare kind. Wait... if it's cat-like and hatched from an egg, it must be a really rare kind!

Max sat back down into his chair and took a deep breath, trying to slow down his speeding heartbeat. He propped his chin on his hand, deep in thought.

~~~~~

Getting back from his memories, Max stared at the kids, who were sitting comatose in the chairs. It had been years since he's so angry – almost half of his robots had been destroyed, and he had lost so much of his profits to the bogus half-price sale. Thinking to this, Max was at his breaking point and ready to explode.

The sale was a trap in the first place, and the only purpose was to lure Soarame's team to MagiMax. In the past few weeks, he had been trying to contact Rodka in different ways, telling him that he had new magimals in the store and hoping the kids would come visit, but they all ignored him. Now, Max finally understood why.

Thinking of this, Max couldn't help feeling a headache come on. He still needed to perform careful hypnosis and question these kids about the cat magimal and the duckbear egg, but he didn't know whether he could get what he wanted in the end. This gamble was supposed to be easy, but it had turned out way too costly.

Max began to regret his reckless actions, but after so many years of hiding inside a tedious store, he wasn't really enjoying his life anymore. Nothing in this world seemed attractive to him, except for money – and even more money – and some barely attainable magical treasures. If he could get a potential Baron magimal, plus understand the mysterious magic seal on the magimal egg, it could add so much more colour to his drab and furtive life!

Thinking to this, Max didn't want to delay any longer. Max held a small potion in front of each of the kids and let the disgusting smell work its evil way up their unsuspecting noses, and they all woke up soon.

'Ahhhgg! Where are we?'

Everyone was startled and afraid for the first few seconds, but soon enough they calmed down as trained wizards. Even Alicey seemed to have adapted herself to the situation; she didn't cry anymore, although she still seemed terrified and kept her head down and her eyes closed.

'Alicey, are you ok?' Soarame was worried. Alicey didn't speak but just nodded. Because her head was bowed, Soarame could barely see the frown on her face and how she seemed to be really concentrating on something.

'Max?' Finding everyone was safe for now, Rodka turned his attention to take a long hard look at the obscurely dressed, pot-bellied man.

'Answer my questions and you will be free to go,' Max didn't want to waste any time now. 'First question is to Halgon: how do I break the seal on the duckbear egg?'

'What seal?' Halgon looked really confused. 'I don't know what you are talking about.'

'Darn it!' Max looked into Halgon's eyes and was convinced that the boy didn't seem to be lying. So he turned to Soarame instead. 'Second question to you: what does your magimal look like?'

'What magimal?' Soarame was acting the same as Halgon. 'I don't know what you are talking about.'

'Crap!' This wasn't doing anything good for Max's rapidly

rising blood pressure. 'You really take me for a complete idiot, don't you?'

'Soarame, I think he's talking about the wild cat you just adopted,' Rodka cut in. 'I just can't believe everyone thinks it's a magimal – how could anyone really believe that? Where did you hear about all this anyway, Max?'

'You don't ask me questions! I ask questions and you answer them!' Max could feel his heart pumping in irregular and probably dangerous ways – after all, the information about Soarame's magimal was purely from Casavin. Max had done some investigating and obtained some hints that confirmed Casavin's words, but he couldn't get onto the Libral campus for more information.

Thinking of this, Max lost the few shreds of patience remaining to him. He took out a few odd-looking crystal balls from a nearby cabinet, getting ready to perform his special hypnosis. This wasn't hypnosis in the normal sense like he had done to the other group of kids; it didn't just hypnotise people, but also cast their memory into the crystal ball, allowing others to view it. In that way, everything that Max wanted to see would be crystal clear. Max hadn't planned to use it originally because it came at a much greater cost, but now he realised he's forced to.

'What are you doing?' Soarame instantly felt nervous. Whatever Max was doing, he's sure it would not be good for them.

'Don't worry, it doesn't hurt.' Max put one crystal ball in front of each kid. 'When you wake up again, you will be back home already.'

'NO! STOP!' Halgon was truly panicked for the first time, as he recognized the crystal hypnosis instruments. He couldn't afford to have his memory visualized, because it would be a disaster for everyone, and especially for his family.

'That's enough, Max!'

Just when Halgon was determined to do something, a cold voice sounded from behind Max, and the keen blade of a sword appeared against Max's neck.

'WHAT THE HELL?' Max almost wet his pants – a man was holding a sword behind him? How could this be possible? How had he gotten into his secret room, and how long had he been there?

'Sachastain!' Soarame was the first to recognise the mysterious man half-concealed in darkness. 'How come you are here?'

'Sorry to keep you waiting, guys.' Sachastain gave the kids a big smile, pressing the sword against Max's neck. 'And you too, Max,'

'Who the hell are you?' It's now Max's turn to panic. 'How did you get in here?'

'Don't worry about that,' Sachastain said coolly, throwing one dagger towards each kid to cut their ropes. 'All you need to do is to lead us out and turn yourself in.'

'Sachastain, it's really great to see you!' Halgon was overjoyed. Sachastain had saved his life; if he'd showed up one second later, who knew what nightmares might have occurred? Unlike his friends, who could probably walk away after being hypnotised, Halgon would be put in extreme danger if his memories were revealed.

'Alright, let's get the hell out of here,' Sachastain said as the kids stood up. 'Open the door, Max. Or do I have to say "please"?'

'Not until you tell me how you got in here,' despite his terror, Max was persistent about this. 'There's no way that you could have snuck into my secret room, no way!'

'Emm... Max, he's right behind you!' Kardiac laughed.

'It's called magic,' Sachastain winked at the kids. 'I don't think you are in a position for bargaining, Max. So, open the door before my hand slips and accidentally slits your throat.'

'Humph, you do it if you can, you sneaky rat,' Max turned his head to look at Sachastain. 'Remember, *you* killed these poor kids here!'

Sachastain instantly sensed danger. 'Watch out! Fall back!' he yelled to the kids. He tried to move his sword, but found that it's stuck to Max's shoulder for some unknown reason. But Sachastain didn't have time to figure out why; all that he could do in the next second was to let go of the sword and throw himself onto the kids, covering them as much as he could using his own body.

BOOMMMM!

An explosion ripped through the secret room, and the walls were blown to pieces. The walls and roof collapsed, covering everyone in ashes and debris. Max was the first to step out of the ashes, uninjured. Sachastain, on the other hand, spat out a great stream of blood as he sat up – he had been badly injured for his protection to the kids. Thanks to him, the kids had only suffered a few cuts and bruises.

'Sachastain!' Soarame rushed to support Sachastain with his shoulder.

'A pre-set bomb!' Sachastain coughed in sharp pain. 'You are not a simple shopkeeper! Only a lifetime criminal would do something like this!'

'It's too late to talk about all this right now, isn't it?' Max stepped towards Sachastain. 'You miserable, sneaky rat! I offer you one last chance: tell me how you got in here and I'll spare the kids' lives.' Max's vague threat made the kids pale.

'You really expect me to believe you?' Sachastain was breathing heavily. Max wasn't entirely unaffected by the explosion – his hood and veil had been blown off, so his face was finally exposed to the light. It's a big, pear-shaped face with a huge, heavy jaw and a thin forehead. He's clean-shaven, but his cheeks were pockmarked from acne.

Everyone was staring at Max. Beside the ugly face, he had some stringy grey hair on both sides, but he's completely bald on top. But all these details didn't matter; what did matter was that the kids saw his face. As an experienced warrior and assassin, Sachastain clearly knew that the likelihood of kidnapping victims getting out alive dropped significantly if they had seen the kidnapper's face.

And now they do see it – thanks to me! Sachastain wished he could tell how bad he felt. This was the worst possible scenario, but most of the group did not realise this – not even Rodka.

'Believe me or not, you think I care?' Max sneered. 'Tell me, and I will give you a quick, merciful death. Otherwise…'

'Ouch!' Before Max had finished speaking, a shadow threw itself into him in a flash. Max was caught off guard and almost went down, but the shadow stopped abruptly when it got close to Max and froze there. A dagger appeared; its tip was a mere inch away from his fleshy nose.

A DRAGON?

Halgon stopped sharply, feeling as if he had crashed into an invisible wall in front of Max. Halgon had been waiting for his chance to pull off a snap shot and he would have succeeded; however, due to the invisible wall he had hurt himself instead.

'He must have a defensive magigear!' Sachastain said to Halgon. 'That's why I couldn't manage to put him down in the first place.' Sachastain was amazed by Halgon's snap attack; it seemed that this kid knew about kidnapper's rules, so he had made this desperate attempt to save them.

'What defensive magigear can do this?' Halgon was pale due to the pain. The blockage function of the magigear was very unusual, and he's unprepared for it. Everyone looked over Max's body, and soon noticed a diamond-shaped crystal plate on his chest; it's of a good size and could be partially seen through his torn clothes.

'That plate must be it. And it must be of really high rank, although I don't know what exactly it is,' Sachastain said, coughing out another spray of blood. 'You guys go now, I'll take him!'

'How dare you!' Max was shocked by Halgon's sudden assault; sweat was dripping from his forehead. At the same time, Max suddenly realised something – perhaps because of Halgon's assault – and pointed at Sachastain. 'I see! Shadowcape! You can perform Darkness magic too? That would be the only way to sneak in!'

Max had got it right this time. Sachastain had heard of the MagiMax sale and felt it abnormal, plus he knew about the duckbear egg from the kids. So once he saw Soarame and his friends leave campus, he decided to follow them secretly. Thank god he had come; there's really a big problem here.

Sachastain had actually gotten into MagiMax quite a while ago, during the busiest time in the morning, while Soarame's crew was waiting outside. While people knew that Sachastain was a highly trained warrior, he'd been keeping the fact secret that he's also capable of Darkness magic; so getting into a big busy building using the shadowcape spell with no one specifically looking for him was as easy as strolling in the park. Then he hid in the darkness and waited to see what would happen. Because Darkness elements are black in colour, they blend perfectly in shadows and even Soarame's special eyes didn't spot the trick. Thanks to Sachastain's patience, he's still there when Max closed the gate and trapped the kids.

Sachastain didn't hurry to rescue the kids because Max hadn't shown himself yet, and there's almost no way to find him in a strange building full of traps and secret rooms. Sachastain kept watching and waiting and was ready to fight if the kids were really in danger, but what Halgon was capable of had really amazed him. He didn't have to do anything to help until the kids were put to sleep. After that, Sachastain took his chances and followed the robots into Max's secret room. Max might have had a chance to detect Sachastain in normal circumstances, but he's too angry and distracted.

'You will be sorry, you two pathetic rats!' Figuring out what must have happened, Max really blew his top. If it hadn't been for the defensive magigear being one of the best in the world, he would have been put down. Max knew he wasn't able to physically fight a professional warrior, even if the warrior was injured; and then there's Halgon, who wasn't bad at all either. There's nothing else for it; before the kids realised what's happening, a series of chittering noises echoed through the corridor and the broken room.

Alicey suddenly raised her head and screamed. 'Rats! Thousands of rats are coming!' She's right, but it didn't mean the friends had much time to prepare; they were under attack by the teeming horde of rats in the next second. A cacophony of chittering, scratching, yelling and screaming filled the air.

'You call us rats?' Soarame howled at Max, holding Alicey in his arms. 'You are the biggest rat of all!' Soarame appeared to be the only one who wasn't at all affected by the wave of rats – for some reason the rats were encircling him but not attacking him.

'Go away!' Soarame didn't spend much time wondering why. He took out Volsta's black feather and waved it around, trying to cover his friends and gather them together. 'How can he control so many rats? Are they all his bond magimals?'

'These are just ordinary rats, not magimals!' Halgon shouted back. 'He must have bonded himself to a magimal rat king, so the king commanded his soldiers to attack us! We need to find the rat king!'

'Darn it, I really wish Snower was here!' Kardiac shivered behind Soarame. 'She should be good at handling rats, right?'

'What the heck is that mangy feather thing?' Astonished by Soarame's actions, Max made the snap decision to withdraw the magic seal from the building, so that he could perform magic and put an end to this chaos.

How could he perform magic? Soarame was the first to notice that Max had started summoning magic elements, thanks to his special eyes. 'Guys... things have changed! He's performing magic, watch out!'

'We can perform magic now, too!' Rodka hurriedly shot a firebolt towards Max, but it's blocked by the transparent wall too. 'Crap! Let's run!'

'Go! Don't look back!' Sachastain herded the kids out of the broken room, but once they were gone the ferocious rat wave focused all its attention on him. Sachastain knew he couldn't really hurt Max because of that mysterious defensive magigear, but his intention was to win some time for the kids to escape.

Hearing Max starting to chant a long and obscure incantation, Soarame turned back around and swung his wand, purely by instinct, and sprayed a beam of water at Max's mouth. However, the invincible incantation choker didn't work this time, as it's blocked by the invisible wall too. Max gave Soarame a sneering glance; he could see that the boy was a Grade-2 Water wizard, according to his emblem. *How pathetically weak!* he sneered inwardly.

'Soarame, get the heck out of here!' Sachastain barked at Soarame. Soarame clenched his fists and hesitated for another second, but then he had to run after his friends.

However, after getting out of the broken room, the kids were stunned to see the things in front of them – there were countless twisted corridors intersecting each other.

'Bloody hell!'

'It's a maze?!'

'No! What shall we do now?' They were all flustered. 'We are so doomed this time!'

Calm down, calm down! Knowing that Sachastain was unlikely to survive the terrible rat wave, Soarame couldn't help yelling at himself inside. *There has to be a way to survive this, I just need to figure it out!*

'This way... follow me!' Just when everyone was on the point of desperation, a small shaking voice sounded through the dust and chaos. Although it sounded weak and tremulous, they all swore that this was the most beautiful voice they'd ever heard, with the best news they had ever wanted to hear.

'Alicey?' Soarame was surprised to recognise that the voice came from the little girl who they thought they were trying to protect.

'Sachastain, come with us!' Alicey darted past the boys and into a debris-filled corridor. The boys dashed back to Sachastain and together they dragged him out, following Alicey. Although no one knew how or why Alicey could figure out the maze, they had to blindly trust her and run as fast as they could. They were pleading in their hearts as they rushed blindly along, hoping for Alicey the genius girl wizard to lead them to the right way out as the rats chased them.

However, a few seconds later, the friends made yet another turn and found themselves face to face with –

'What!' Their hearts sank. There's a blank wall in front of them.

'Alicey?' Soarame looked at her anxiously.

'Break it! The shortest way out is behind the wall!' Alicey was already preparing her spells, which Soarame recognized to be windblades.

'*Lepida-tou-anemou*!!'

'*Petra-bala*!!'

'*Bouloni-fotia*!!'

Right away, everyone started chanting their best attacking spells; windblades, firebolts and rockchunks knocked into the wall. Just when Soarame was ready to give up his secret and cast windblades, his necklace suddenly lit up with a dim green glow.

Instantly, a beam of refreshing coolness flowed into his frantic mind – *I must stay calm and hold out, it's not the last moment yet!*

While Soarame was breathing heavily to restrain his eagerness, the rest of the crew had cracked the wall open –

Gee!

Aww!

'What the …??'

The friends jumped through the hole in the wall but were suddenly transfixed – they were in a spacious magimal room. A large number of baby magimals seemed to have been resting and sleeping in the room, but now they were showing every sign of alarm at the uninvited guests.

'I'm sorry, I'm so sorry!' Alicey screamed to the poor babies, who were shaking and hiding, terrified to see them breaking in. 'We're just passing through – but come to think of it, you guys might want to run with us too!'

Alicey was right – the rat wave wasn't going to just let them run away like that. They had followed them all way down there, still trying to attack them. However, an unexpected scene happened in the next second – although the magimal babies were scared of the bunch of humans, they seemed to be pretty excited to see the countless small creatures coming to their dinner table. After all, they were magimals, and there were a lot of them, too!

Meowowow!!

Wuaaa!!

Awwwoo!!

The baby magimals burst into action and instinctively lined up to fight the rats. The cat-like magimals especially – although they were mostly of Novice level, they were born to be the natural enemies of rats; this unexpected live hunting treat was something that they had seldom had a chance to enjoy before.

'Stop staring, run!' Alicey was still really afraid of the rats. She opened the door of the magimal room and dashed out and up the stairs, followed by the entire crew.

'Damn you all!' A raging howl issued from behind them like an unholy gale – Max was approaching too!

The crew had come out into the main hall, only to find that they couldn't get out of the building – it's protected by a magic barrier that they couldn't break. However, the situation was much better than back in the secret rooms, because here they had a much bigger space to dodge and all that.

With a series of whining noises, a disorderly flock of terrified baby magimals followed the friends to the main hall, trying to escape and hide too. They could no longer enjoy hunting the rats and had to flee – right behind them, a big belly stepped out from the shadow.

'Where are you going?' With a wave of Max's wand, a number of snake-headed whips of flame burst out, roaring and rolling, coming towards the kids.

'Holy mama… *firesnakes*?!' Seeing the spell, Kardiac cried out in terror. He finally saw his dream Fire spell performed by a real Fire Expert, except that this wasn't an ideal situation to witness it.

Firesnakes? Everyone was trying to take this in. The worst case had happened – the firesnake spell indicated that Max was a professor-level wizard. There were dozens of firesnakes, roaring and blowing flames with scarily high temperatures, coming towards their targets. Sachastain tried to block one of the firesnakes with his sword, but with just a single touch, the sword melted. Luckily, he's swift enough to roll over and dodge the snake. Rodka was also making different attempts to fight against the firesnakes, but he failed miserably.

'We are so dead.' Kardiac was hiding behind the counter, surrounded by two firesnakes. The high temperature from the flames was going to bake him dry, but luckily the firesnakes didn't jump on him – it seemed that Max was trying to avoid accidentally burning the building down.

Right then, everyone found themselves surrounded by several firesnakes each. 'It would be a shame if I killed you so easily without getting what I want,' Max sneered at Soarame. 'I will keep you as a hostage, and let you watch your friends get burned alive – starting with the little girl here, how about that?'

'Ahhh!!' Seeing a firesnake moving towards her, Alicey burst out into high-pitched screaming.

'Shame on you!' Soarame was nauseated by the outrageous threat; he jumped in front of the tearful Alicey, spreading his arms wide to protect her. 'If you hurt her or any of us, you will never get Snower!'

'Snower?' Max was puzzled for a second, and then his eyes lit up. 'That rare magimal of yours?'

'Yes, she's a real top-rank,' Soarame answered. 'If you let my friends go, I will give her to you.'

'Ha-ha-ha, you think I'm some sucker kid like you?' Max laughed aloud. 'You sign a magic pact and go get it for me, and then I'll let your friends go after they sign it, too!'

'No way! Let them go now, or you won't get her, ever!'

'Really? We will see about that!' Max was angry enough to do more or less anything. With Soarame protecting Alicey, the firesnakes couldn't get to her, so Max switched to his next target – the firesnakes waiting around Halgon suddenly pounced on the boy. Max had put six firesnakes around Halgon, so that he had no opening to dodge the siege.

'Nooo!!' Seeing this, everyone knew that Halgon would get burned up entirely. But the group was too far away from Halgon to do anything – except for Kardiac, who was surrounded by two firesnakes himself.

'HALG!' Kardiac didn't think about it; he just leaped towards Halgon. Although Kardiac was terrified, he just couldn't watch his friend die. Kardiac couldn't forget what had happened in the beetalbull nest – he had wimped out and Halgon had saved him.

At that moment, the firesnakes were inches away from Kardiac and he could feel the burning temperature. He closed his eyes and hoped that his friends would avenge him for his sacrifice. The next second, Kardiac was knocked flat by a huge force and lost consciousness.

HOAWWW! Out of nowhere, a sonorous dragon roar filled the vast room. A giant figure flashed by, putting itself between Kardiac and the firesnakes. This happened amid bolts of lightning and the sparks of firestone, and left everyone awestruck –

A dragon?

It's a dragon!

A dragon had emerged from somewhere, and blocked the firesnakes to protect Kardiac and Halgon!

A dragon, with scales glimmering all over its body and a pair of huge wings on its back, was roaring in front of everyone!

They were dumbfounded, jaws hanging slack. Max had stopped his attack, and he's rubbing his eyes in astonishment. He kept rubbing them, as if to make sure the live dragon in front of him wasn't some kind of illusion.

Yes, it's indeed a real live dragon, and it's gasping heavily from the pain of the massive burns caused by the firesnakes. Its wings were covering the larger part of its body that suffered the most from the firesnakes; they also protected the unconscious Kardiac behind it.

But this is impossible! After the Grand Migration of dragons, how could there still be any in the human world? Masses of thoughts flashed through everyone's mind, especially Max – he found himself completely lost. *It's part of the irresistible power of a magic pact that no dragon survived in the human world after the Grand Migration!*

The heavy breath of the dragon woke Max from his wondering; now wasn't the moment to ponder it all. While the others were still in shock, Max ordered the remaining firesnakes to gather, roaring, ready to launch another strike.

Hoawwww! The dragon roar sounded again, with its unique ability to coerce and deter its enemy. It's the legendary innate talent of dragons, the *Dragon Awe*. An adult dragon could overawe an enemy of Max's level into submission with just a single Dragon Awe. However, this one didn't seem powerful enough to do that to Max; it only made Max anxious and afraid but didn't make him yield. That said, it did awe Omifo and Alicey into unconsciousness at the same instant that the dragon showed up; so only Soarame, Rodka, Sachastain and Max witnessed what happened.

Judging from its physical size, the dragon was small compared to the descriptions in the books, so Max believed that this dragon wasn't an adult yet. This gave Max a golden chance to defeat the young dragon, and Max couldn't help feeling lucky – although the whole thing was uncanny.

'Halg?' Soarame barely understood what had just happened, and he couldn't believe what he saw – one moment Kardiac was running to save Halgon, and the next, Halgon disappeared and a dragon appeared instead.

So... Halgon was... a dragon? This was a bit too much for tired, frightened brains to cope with. It wasn't a good time to think anyway, because Max was about to launch his next attack.

Hoaaww! Halgon fought with all his strength. Facing the next round of firesnakes, Halgon only had time to summon an *icearmour* to the surface of his body, but he's already at his limit and probably wouldn't survive the next attack.

'Go to hell!' With a savage laugh, Max was about to finish off the unknown dragon with his firesnakes.

'Aawwh!' At this critical moment, Max suddenly shrieked, looking at his right arm in horror – his right hand had suddenly broken apart from his body and dropped to the floor!

Max was stupefied. He stared at where his missing hand should have been. His wand had been in that hand and, because of that, his next attack was cut off and Halgon got a short break.

Looking around, astonished, Max saw a mad Soarame, his newly purchased wand in hand. His friends being in danger had roused Soarame to craziness – his hair was standing on end, his wand was drawing something too fast for the naked eyes to see, and the incantation he's chanting went so fast that even Rodka couldn't follow.

Windblade! It's Soarame's best spell, windblade, which had caught Max off guard!

Halgon collapsed to the ground, bruised and battered and burned. But seeing Soarame injure Max, Halgon revealed a hint of a smile in the corners of his dragon eyes.

Meanwhile, Soarame was surprised too – he hadn't expected his windblade to work, because he saw that Max's magigear had easily blocked Sachastain and Halgon's attack. Why had his attack worked?

Max was still in painful shock. According to Soarame's Libral Emblem, the boy was a Grade-2 Water! How was he casting windblades?

A dozen of windblades of every size whistled toward Max. This time Max saw it clearly – those were indeed windblade spells. Not only that, those windblades were at least of Adept level!

A Water student? Grade 2? That's the funniest joke ever!

The transparent wall around Max was functioning again this time, and it blocked all the windblades. With that, Max quickly picked up his wand with his left hand. The excruciating pain he felt told him that everything was real, but glancing at his missing hand, Max still felt that this was a horrible nightmare.

With one hand gone, Max knew that his plan was completely ruined. Even if he got what he wanted, it wouldn't make up for all his loss. This gamble today had turned out to be a miserable failure. And he wouldn't even be able to cover it up anymore; he'd have to flee soon.

'Damn brat, you will die! You must die!' As Max barked, several firesnakes rushed towards Soarame, trying to engulf him. So far, Soarame was the only one that had injured Max – not Rodka, not Halgon, not even Sachastain! *How does this kid hurt me and deserve to stay alive!*

'Soarame!' Sachastain and Rodka were frantic, but none of them could really help. The firesnakes were so fast and they had caught up with Soarame already.

BOOM! The firesnakes ran into Soarame and a blast ensued. The flames burned down the wall in just a few seconds and this broke the sound isolation seal that Max had set up on the building. Now, for the first time, people in the city heard the noise and noticed the building on fire.

'SOARAME!!!' Sachastain and Rodka – the only two who were still awake – were devastated.

'I'm okay!' Just as the two tried to make a desperate strike, Soarame's voice sounded from above.

'Soarame?'

'You… can… fly?'

A moment ago, the desperate Soarame had roared, seeing the firesnakes coming toward his face. His eyes went black as the roasting of the fiery heat surrounded him. He seemed to see his soul breaking away from his body, rising up to the sky.

No, I'm not dying like this… I haven't seen Dad and Mom yet! Soarame wasn't resigned at all to death coming for him. The next moment, he heard his friends crying, and became aware that it wasn't his soul that's rising up; it's actually his body.

'You. Must. Be. Kidding. Me…' Max was also staring up, stupefied. As far as he knew, the *flying* spell was of Expert level; even the graduating students from Libral couldn't fly. Soarame himself didn't understand this either – he's just an Adept; how had he managed to fly without even learning it?

But this is real! I can fly! Soarame roused himself from his confusion and moved his body around as he floated in the air, getting the feel for flying. *Wait, what's this?*

Soarame suddenly noticed a dim ray of green from his chest – it's the token from his master.

Master's token! It saved me? Soarame had a strange feeling that the green light was somehow shining into his mind ocean, so that he's feeling unprecedentedly refreshed and robust. The next second, he dodged the attack from a firesnake – Max had already started attacking again. Although Soarame didn't know how he learnt to fly, all that he needed to know was that he no longer had to die.

'Resurgence!' Sachastain muttered, his voice was shaking due to the over-joyous scenario. 'That's what it is – Soarame has just *resurged!'*

Relying on his instincts, Soarame soared to the ceiling of the building, where he had more space to dodge the firesnakes away from his friends. The firesnakes went in hot pursuit of Soarame, but his small figure and nimble moves allowed him to dodge them all. Soon enough, the firesnakes burned through the roof in trying to strike him, so Soarame could finally get out of the building from the top.

'Look! What's that?' Some people had already noticed the fire at MagiMax, and they had tried to get help from the city. Now more people observed Soarame flying out of the building, with smoke trailing from all over his body.

'That's a kid!'

'He's flying! He's a wizard!'

'With moving flames chasing him!'

'What the heck is going on?'

The longer the fight lasted, the braver Soarame became and the more skilfully he flew. Max's breathing became heavier and heavier from exertion. Watching Soarame soaring in the clouds, Max finally admitted his total failure. He had been tired already from controlling the robots for the sale, even before the battle started; now he finally couldn't take it anymore. Summoning and controlling the firesnakes was costing him mind power every single second. If he didn't try to flee soon, he would be in deep trouble once the city force arrived.

'Screw you all! Go to hell together!' With a desperate laugh, Max called back the firesnakes and directed them to make one last attack – to kill everyone on the floor.

'NO! STOP!!!' Soarame was puzzled for a second before he realised Max's intentions.

Clang! Right then, the wall of MagiMax was broken from the outside and something freezing plowed through it.

'What!' Max found that everything had disappeared in a huge wave of steam and vapour. In the next blink, a big shining chunk of ice in the shape of a dragon came out of the vapour and dashed towards Max, bringing with it freezing temperatures.

An ice dragon spell? Max panicked – The kids' helper has arrived! Max hurriedly commanded all the remaining firesnakes to tackle the ice dragon, creating a huge cloud of vapour which covered the entire building.

'Who's that?' Inside the vapour, Sachastain yelled. 'Help the kids, please!'

'Max, the owner of the shop, attacked us! He is a criminal!' Rodka yelled too. 'Catch him before he runs away!'

Hearing no response, Sachastain yelled again. 'Hello? Anyone there?' Sachastain struggled to stand up and moved carefully in the mass of vapour. All he could hear was Soarame, from above, asking if everyone was safe.

After a while, the vapour gradually dissipated. Soarame quickly landed to check on his friends. The good news was that everyone was alive, including a naked Halgon.

'What's going on?' Rodka asked, pulling out a robe to cover Halgon's body. 'Who was that and why did he ignore us?'

'I don't know. Whoever it was, he saved our lives... and perhaps he went after Max!' Sachastain took a deep breath. 'At least we survived, didn't we?'

'We were blessed!' Soarame looked out and saw a group of people in uniforms running towards them. Meanwhile, Max was nowhere to be found, so they were finally safe.

'City force! What happened?' The uniformed group arrived soon. Sachastain went up to answer them, while Rodka hurried to dress Halgon in the robe.

'Soar, you were insane!' Seeing that the situation was under control, Rodka punched Soarame in the shoulder. 'That's awesome! How did you do that?'

'I don't know!' Soarame was also full of joy.

'It's called Resurgence.' Sachastain quickly offered an

explanation. To a wizard or a warrior, resurgence means that someone has a breakthrough and levels up in an act of extremely strong will – usually in a situation where he is about to die or lose the most valuable thing to him. Sachastain knew this because he had experienced a resurgence himself and learnt the shadowcape spell, with which he had survived back then. It's a grey and painful night when Sachastain resurged, and he never wanted to recall that time.

During resurgence, a person could sometimes learn a new skill with which (s)he could survive. But resurgence rarely happened; most of the time people failed. In Soarame's case, he's really lucky to get help from Scankeen's token during the resurgence and learnt the flying spell. If he learnt a different spell, he wouldn't have been able to rely on it to survive.

'That's amazing!' Rodka marvelled, but he knew it wasn't quite the time to celebrate yet.

'It's mainly you guys and Halgon's work, though.' Soarame was still breathing heavily. 'How's Halg?'

Sachastain wasn't sure what to say about Halgon other than, 'He's badly burnt, but he won't die, so don't worry.'

Soarame was right; if not for Halgon, they would not have made it so far. Thinking to this, everyone was at a loss for words. No wonder Halgon was always cautious about everything and always preferred not to be known by the public. His secret was really big and scary.

Sachastain was the most grievously injured person. He had taken a direct hit from a bomb to save the kids. If he had not been injured he might have had a chance to challenge Max one-on-one, or he could have escaped for sure; but then all of the kids would have died. Soarame and Rodka were so grateful to Sachastain for his heroic action and asked the city force to take him to hospital immediately.

Just when they started to tell the story to the city force, a few dots appeared in the sky. Soon enough, Principal Gazbell Raymend and some other teachers from Libral showed up in the air. Gazbell landed right by Soarame and Rodka, while the teachers started to check on the rest of the kids.

'What! Max did this?' Gazbell was shocked after hearing the story – Soarame intentionally hid Halgon's role in it. Gazbell blamed himself for not paying enough attention to Soarame – even though Scankccn had told him not to treat Soarame in any special way, it didn't mean that he should ignore him so completely. However, how could Gazbell know all this? From the campus of Libral, there's no way for Gazbell to see the firesnakes in the sky over the Cylone City.

'Wait a second,' Gazbell said suddenly, noticing something, and went further into the broken building. There's some special kind of energy moving around, which was invisible unless one was highly sensitive.

'What's this?' Gazbell closed his eyes and focused on feeling the energy that remained from the battle. 'Does Max have some special magigear?'

'He had a really high-ranking defensive magigear,' Rodka answered. 'It blocked the attacks from Sachastain and Hal... uh, me.'

'What does it look like?' Gazbell seemed to be coming to a realisation.

'It's some kind of crystal plate, but we are not sure. When it worked, it made some kind of transparent shield that blocked everything and rebounded attacks.' Rodka tried to recount all the details. 'It made Sachastain's sword stuck, my dagger stuck, and my body bounced off it. Only Soarame's windblades got through it.'

'Windblades could get through it?' Gazbell had looked really excited in the beginning, but he frowned at this part.

'I think it's because Max didn't expect it, so he didn't trigger the gear,' Soarame cut in. 'When I shot more windblades later, they all got blocked.'

'That makes sense!' Gazbell's eyes shone. 'He's saving energy for that magigear because he's not powerful enough to use it continuously. I'm almost sure that's what happened, but it's a shame that I couldn't see it with my own eyes to confirm it.'

'Sir, I can try painting the magigear out for you to see,' Soarame spoke up. 'I feel I can do it right now.'

'You can? Now?' Rodka knew what Soarame meant – the mind-painting, so he immediately asked for some ink and canvas from the city force. Although Soarame had only succeeded once so far and it's during his dream-painting, thanks to his master's token, he had a strong hunch that he could do it awake right then.

Soon enough, Gazbell marvelled as he witnessed Soarame's unique mind-painting. 'This is impressive! I didn't know you were so talented!' He became even more excited when he saw the diamond-shaped crystal plate hanging on the chest of a half-bald man –

Indeed, that's it! That's it! Gazbell's breath came faster as he checked the details of the crystal plate on the canvas. 'Thank you so much, Soarame! And all of you! You did a great job! The teachers will send you back to school, and I will visit you later.'

Seeing Soarame and his friends off, Gazbell breathed a long sigh of relief. 'Unbelievable...' Soarame's accident did make him feel guilty and worried; but now that the kids were safe, Gazbell's attention was caught by Soarame's painting of Max's defensive magigear. He really regretted that he had not been aware of this whole thing until now; otherwise he could easily have protected Soarame, thrown Max into prison, and dealt with the even bigger matter of that magigear –

'It's indeed the *Mercy of the Demiurge...* Unbelievable!' Gazbell took a long and deep gasp. 'That Max person had it? But how is this possible?'

MERCY OF THE DEMIURGE

The battle was over and the friends were brought back to campus safely. Everyone had bruises and burns all over, but fortunately there were no life-threatening injuries, and that included Halgon. Dean Romboton and Dean Akex almost lost their jobs because of this. They went to the hospital and tried to take good care of the kids – they did have some responsibilities for this entire episode, after ignoring the students' requests in the first place. The good thing was that the whole mess seemed to be over – at least for now.

The next morning, Soarame and Rodka woke up in the hospital and found that they were surrounded by their friends. It's a big crowd; everyone was there, including their classmates, Dileys' entire crew, and many more that they knew. Omifo, Kardiac and Alicey had woken up before them, so the only one who was still unconscious was Halgon – he's in a separate inner room.

'Soarame, you are up!' Seeing Soarame was awake, the crowd burst into cheers. 'You guys are heroes now!'

'Emm… What?' Soarame didn't get it, still clouded from sleep.

'Yes, especially you, Soarame!' Kardiac boomed. 'Mr Principal told me everything about the battle. He's putting us on the front page of the campus newspaper!'

'You were there, why did you have to hear everything from the Principal?' one student asked, confused.

'Hmmm, good question.' Kardiac puffed up his chest. 'I got hit by six firesnakes, so I must have lost part of my memory.'

Catheray couldn't help laughing out loud. Everyone was chuckling and nobody bothered to pursue the matter further.

'What are you laughing for?' Kardiac wasn't happy. 'You don't believe me?'

'Kardy, you were not even burnt!' A girl just had to point out.

'You call this not burnt?' Kardiac pointed at his hair – half of it was gone, thanks to the firesnakes.

'He did try to save Halgon using his own body,' Soarame spoke for Kardiac. Omifo and Alicey also nodded hurriedly, backing up Soarame's claim.

'See?' Kardiac was proud of himself, even though he also began to wonder why he wasn't injured, but Halgon had been so badly burned...

'Soarame, I heard you actually flew in the end?' Alicey had waited so long to ask this question. She's furious that she had been knocked out and missed so much. 'You are a Water student, aren't you?'

'Ya! How come you can fly? Can you show us?' Everyone was very confused and at the same time eager. 'People saw you flying and they are putting it in the *Cylone Times* – that's hundreds of times bigger than our campus newsletter!'

'Guys, give him a break,' Rodka cut in, seeing Soarame at a loss of words. He's really in a good mood – everyone had survived the crisis; what could be better than that?

'Oh, Sachastain just came over, and he said he will visit again later,' Omifo said. 'He seems to be fine, and he's already out of the hospital.'

'That's great! Sachastain is the real hero here!' Soarame explained hurriedly. 'If not for him, we wouldn't be able to sit here and talk to you guys now!'

'Really! It's that bad?' The crowd was astonished. 'Tell us more!'

The students had a long talk about everything. When the sun was about to set, the big crowd finally headed off to dinner, leaving only Soarame's closest friends.

Looking at Alicey, Kardiac hesitated but finally had to ask, 'So Alicey, can I try your earring? I really want to see how it works.'

During their previous conversations, the friends had learnt that Alicey had been able to lead the way out of the maze because her earring was actually an Epic magigear; it provided a bird view of the maze to her brain. Magigears with special functions like Scankeen's token and Alicey's earring were usually of Epic level and hence very rare, compared to those that cast spells, such as Saja's and Casavin's magigears. From this, the friends could hazard a guess that Alicey must be from a significant wizard family – that sort of explained why she's in Grade 3 but only nine!

'It's an Epic magigear, so only she can use it!' Catheray teased Kardiac. 'Plus, you really want to wear a girl's earring?'

'But how come an earring provides vision?' Seeing Alicey chuckle, Kardiac scratched his head, but accidentally touched the burnt part. 'Ouch!'

'Because it's called magic.' Halgon walked out from his special-care room. 'You guys finally finished with the crowd?'

'You mean you were faking the coma?' Everyone was overjoyed. 'It worried us!'

'I'm sorry, guys,' Halgon shrugged his shoulders. 'Thank you for saving me,' he said to Soarame with a complicit wink. His transformation into a dragon was his final secret ace card; he had almost used this in the beetalbull nest, but luckily Soarame had saved him from doing so. That's why he's always grateful and had been taking so many risks helping him since then.

'Sure, you're welcome,' Soarame returned the wink. 'Thank you for saving us too.'

The rest of the crew was puzzled. Jemario was sensitive enough to catch it. 'What's that wink about?'

'Ya, what's going on?' Others also wondered.

'Let's just go back to the dorm first,' Rodka laughed and grabbed Soarame and Halgon by the shoulders. Just then, Halgon whispered in an extremely low voice to the two of them. 'I know you've all been wondering about me, but I can only say that my mom is a human wizard, but my dad is not. Keep it to yourselves, ok?'

What! So his dad is a... dragon? Soarame and Rodka were both stunned. They looked at each other in silence. *But this is bizarre!*

Although they tried hard to act normal, they were thrilled – it sounded as though Halgon's father wasn't restrained by the Grand Migration Pact for some unknown reasons, just like Halgon himself. If this was true, it would be the most explosive news in the world and could easily terrify every single human being, especially those in the Sunrise Alliance!

If one thought deeper about it, Halgon's parents had actually committed a grave crime – humans and dragons were mortal enemies! Thinking about this, they finally understood why Halgon always tried to stay low key and had little trust in the public of human; if he hadn't tried to help Snower and repay Soarame's rescue in the beetalbull nest, Halgon would never have gambled like this.

And the duckbear egg – no wonder Halgon could spot the swindle right away – the seal that his father had put on was probably some kind of dragon seal! So Halgon could tell the fake one at a glance, whereas no one else could. And that must be why Halgon had never worried that Max might break the dragon seal!

Oh yes, Halgon comes from "half-dragon"! Thinking through everything in a flash, Soarame nodded in silence. *Just like Filton named me after the "soaring flame" he saw when he found me... I should have thought of that!*

Wait, aren't dragons supposed to be dangerous? Soarame and Rodka looked at each other again. *Crap! Halgon is our brother, whatsoever!* After a moment, the two boys reached the same conclusion. After the deadly fight shoulder-to-shoulder against Max, they had witnessed Halgon's willingness to sacrifice for them. There's no reason to doubt their sworn friend.

'Hey, you boys, we are not done yet.' Vivarin crossed her arms over her chest, the typical "Vivarin smile" on her face. 'Omi, you want to say something? Why were they winking like that? What do we not know?'

'Errr... I don't know either!' Omifo shrugged his shoulders. 'They fell in love with each other?'

The three suddenly choked while the others were laughing.

'Guys, I'm sorry that bad things happened, but I'm glad to see that you are fine.' On the way back to Soarame's dorm, Chelonad's voice sounded all of a sudden. 'I can't go out of campus, so I didn't know what's happening.'

'Oh hey, Chelonad! Thanks for scaring us.' The friends teased him. 'Chelonad, we are always curious – where are you? You are not doing mind-talk right now, are you?'

'No, I'm much more special than that,' Chelonad sounded proud. 'And I'm always beside you, everywhere on campus.'

'But can we see you face-to-face?' Alicey asked.

'No. If you do see me one day, it means something really bad has happened. So you had better hope that day never comes! Later, guys, good luck.' Chelonad's voice was gone just as quickly as it had arrived.

The friends scratched their heads, trying to understand Chelonad's words. Chelonad refused to respond after that, so all they could do was to keep guessing.

Back in the dorm, Halgon went directly up to his bedroom. 'Guys, I'm actually not fully recovered yet. I still need to sleep for a while, but I just don't wanna stay in the hospital anymore.'

'Okay.' Rodka remembered reading that dragons could heal themselves by hibernation, so he could guess what Halgon was going to do. Plus, it seemed that Halgon was facing a really big headache as to how to explain things to his friends. He certainly needed some time to sort it out alone.

'Take care, and have a good rest.' Soarame had heard the same hibernation story from his master, so he wasn't surprised either. But everyone else was worried about Halgon, so he had to promise them that he would talk to them after he felt better, and everyone promised not to interrupt his rest.

'So, what now?' Kardiac asked. 'We are all set? No more fun?'

'You mean fun that knocks you out, or burns you dry?' Catheray said. 'I can do it if you need help on that.'

'No, no, not now.' Kardiac waved her away hurriedly. 'But maybe we can upgrade this house a bit more? I still have two chances saved up, so with you guys we can do a major upgrade! Shall we try making this building triangular?'

'Yeah sure, so that you can go live with Rodka, because there are only three corners in a triangle,' Soarame teased. 'How did you get such a genius idea?'

'No, I mean Halgon can live in the middle and we surround him to protect... Wait, what's that?' Kardiac stopped and pointed at the dinner table. 'There's a crystal ball there. Since when?'

'No kidding, we never had such a thing.' Omifo frowned. 'It had better not be Max! He had so many just like this in his room!'

'Darn it, let's move!' Soarame grabbed his friends and tried to run. Suddenly, the crystal ball began to light up, and the hologram of a figure was cast into the air.

'Watch out!' Rodka dashed forward to shield the others.

'Soarame, I already know what happened.' A voice came out from the figure.

Hearing the voice, Soarame couldn't believe his ears. 'Master!'

'That's your master?' Everyone was surprised, but relieved. 'Mr Swineflu?'

'Yes!' Soarame quickly introduced them. 'Master, these are my friends, Kardiac, Omifo, Rodka…'

'I'm sorry that I couldn't be there in person to help.' Scankeen continued without responding to Soarame's words. 'But I know that you and your friends did an amazing job, and now you should be all safe.'

'This is a recorded hologram.' Rodka was the first to realise it. 'It's not a real-time communication.'

'My boy, do you remember Volsta's story? You were almost there. I know you were probably wondering who saved you, and I can only wish that it had been me.' Scankeen looked thoughtful while he's talking, and only Soarame could understand the meaning behind the words. 'It's a great shame that I couldn't be there, but fortunately, someone offered his help to you and delivered this message for me. However, he also made me promise him that I wouldn't say who he is.'

'One thing I can say, though, is that you may try asking him about your parents, if he decides to meet you one day.' Scankeen's words kindled something in Soarame. 'Besides that, you should stick to the plan and improve all your three lineages to Expert level. Then you can report to the Sunrise Alliance; there you will get to know a lot more about everything. I have faith in you! Goodbye, my boy!'

'Master!' Seeing Scankeen's hologram disappear, Soarame ran over to fetch the crystal ball. However, the crystal ball also disappeared into thin air.

The friends watched Soarame in silence. Everyone was wondering what the message really meant, as there's quite a lot of information that they didn't have any context for. However, they knew it wasn't the best time to pursue it.

'Soarame, why does your master look familiar?' Rodka asked after a while. He thought this might be a proper question to ask.

'His Honour ought to be someone in the Sunrise Alliance,' Dileys reminded Rodka. 'So you might have seen his picture somewhere before.'

'Praise Libral, no way!' Rodka seemed to remember something. 'Is it really him?'

****

The next morning, the crew rushed to a specific library that Rodka chose. Along the way, many students looked at them and whispered with excitement –

'Look, that's Soarame!'

'And Rodka! They were on the front page!'

'*Cylone Times*, man! That's crazy!'

'See? I told you we are heroes now,' Kardiac said, waving at the students as he whispered to Soarame.

'We? Are you included?' Catheray enjoyed teasing Kardiac as always. 'Why did I only hear two names?'

The friends spent time among the library books, and they finally found Scankeen's picture. With a myriad of exclamations of 'wow', Soarame, for the first time, learnt his master's true identity –

'Master Scankeen Hollen, Legendary Master, Board Member of Sunrise Alliance. Note: Master Scankeen Hollen is the last student of Master Spanflow Libral.'

'Are you kidding me? Student of the Great Libral?!' Soarame felt like he's living in a dream. 'He never told me this, I swear!'

'And his Honour is titled *Legendary*!' Rodka's eyeballs almost popped out. 'That means he's one of the most powerful beings in the entire world, among all human Masters and magimal Barons!'

'Soarame, how could you ever get his name wrong? Swineflu? It doesn't even sound right!' The girls kept blaming Soarame.

'It's really not my fault...' Soarame was trying to clarify, but no one seemed to believe him – he had had a reputation for having difficulties with names ever since he met the crowd of Water girls.

'Okay. Soar, Omi, Kardy and Alicey, it's time to go. The Principal is waiting for us,' Rodka cleared his mind from the shock. 'We'll kidnap Soar and question him later.'

The friends who were there in MagiMax had received a

message from Gazbell this morning, summoning them to his office for a private meeting. The meeting was to officially reward Soarame and his friends for their bravery in countering evil and revealing MagiMax's true face. The most important reason, however, was that they had coincidentally found a clue to the Mercy of the Demiurge. This was kept strictly confidential, so Soarame and his friends didn't know the truth.

What they didn't know either was that, the day before, after Gazbell returned to campus from MagiMax, he had hastily summoned all the professors for an emergency meeting, to announce the matter of Max's escape and the clue about the Mercy of the Demiurge.

~~~~

'What! It's Max? That clown?' The Deans were shocked. 'How was he capable of escaping from the druids?'

'Mr Principal, are you sure it's the Mercy of the Demiurge?' Dean Romboton couldn't help asking.

'Take a look yourselves.' Gazbell showed them Soarame's two mind-paintings – one was of Max and the other was the dream-painting. Seeing that the delicate paintings amazed everyone, Gazbell pointed at the canvas. 'See the letters on the robot's space-ring? It's indeed Naclad's space-ring, but god knows why Max was wearing it.'

'Maybe he hid it at Max's place?' Dean O'heven came up with a thought. 'Remember, years ago, Scankeen did say that he couldn't find Naclad's space-ring after the bloody battle? So he had to let him walk away due to lack of evidence.'

'No way, it's Mercy of the Demiurge, the legendary defensive *Godmade*!' Another professor said, trembling. 'Naclad stole it at the risk of his own life, and then left it with Max for all these years? If he had started the war between druids, elves and mankind, he would have at least made it worthwhile for himself!'

'Agreed. Druids and elves wouldn't believe this either,' Dean Harries added.

A *Godmade* referred to a superior magigear that's made by someone of the next level above *Master* – according to some ancient books, it's called *Halfgod*. Even Scankeen, titled *Legendary Master*, wasn't a Halfgod yet. But there used to be a number of Halfgods throughout history, according to those ancient books. However, that's top secret even among the Sunrise Alliance, so very few people knew about it. What they did know was that, thanks to the existence of those Halfgods, there were some Godmades left in this world. The Mercy of the Demiurge was one of them.

'We'll find out the truth after we get the Godmade back. The good thing is that Aertiuno is here, so he can help explain it to the elves and druids.' Gazbell looked at the green-cloaked blond-haired man with long, pointed ears, who nodded back at him. 'The priority now is to release a "Wanted" notice everywhere. We need to recapture this important property for the Sunrise Alliance at all costs!'

'Notify the Sunrise Alliance immediately! Send out holograms, images, and voice recordings of Max to every corner of the human world!' There's a flame in Gazbell's eyes and in everybody else's. 'I want this fraud to be known by every single person on the four continents! I want his true face to be revealed to the entire world, and I want to make sure he has no place to hide, no matter where he flees!'

~~~~~

A knock on the door aroused Gazbell from his thoughts – Soarame had arrived with Rodka, Kardiac, Omifo and Alicey.

'Soarame, come on in!' Gazbell gave them a big smile as he waved the kids into his office. 'Thanks to all of you for everything that you've done, at the risk of your own lives.'

'It's a pleasure, sir,' Soarame answered. 'And to be honest, we didn't know things would turn out to be that bad and hadn't planned on risking our lives.'

'Well, fate is always unpredictable,' laughed Gazbell, appreciating Soarame's honesty. 'I'm summoning you all because I want to reward you for what you've done, and that includes Halgon and Sachastain after they fully recover.'

He looked each student in turn in the eye as he said seriously, 'First of all, I'd like to say I'm very proud of you all.' He looked at Soarame last. 'Especially Soarame, you surprised all of us! How do you feel having had to keep your Wind secret for so long?'

'Err…' Soarame was a bit shy. 'It feels hard.'

'Ha-ha, the hard feeling paid off with your survival, though,' Gazbell was amused. 'From now on, you are registered to be a Wind student too, although we need to give you a test to see if you are a Grade-5, or a Grade-6 already.'

'What!' Kardiac's eyes widened. 'Soarame could be a Grade-6? Like Rodka?'

'No, I'm still far from Rodka; he's a Grade 6 in three lineages!' Soarame made a dismissive gesture. 'I still have a long way to go for my Water and Lightning.'

'Oh dear, we all forgot you are a Lightning wizard too!' Kardiac smacked his forehead. 'You are a monster, Soar! What are you made of?'

'Kardiac, I heard that you tried to protect Halgon with your own life, and I'm very proud of you,' Gazbell interrupted Kardiac to change topic. 'And for that, he has asked me to deliver a gift to you, besides the reward from the school.'

'Halgon sent me a gift?' Kardiac was puzzled. 'He didn't mention that yesterday!'

'His family people came to pick him up overnight because they preferred to take care of Halgon themselves.' Gazbell smiled at the students. 'Halgon didn't want to wake you, so he left the gift with me.'

'He's off campus now?' Soarame was surprised. The friends hadn't wanted to bother Halgon when they came here, so they hadn't checked in on him and weren't aware of his absence. Soarame and Rodka glanced at each other; both seemed to understand something. After all, keeping Halgon's identity secret wasn't going to be an easy matter.

'Yes, but don't worry, he will be back soon,' Gazbell said, and Soarame was convinced that that the principal didn't know Halgon's secret at all. 'The reward from the institute is that each of you can have a magigear of Expert level, of your own choice. It can be anything in this booklet.'

'Wow, Expert level?' Everyone's eyes lit up in excitement. 'That's awesome!'

'Enjoy your gold-mining,' Gazbell was happy to see their overjoyed reactions. The friends flipped through the booklet and saw a lot of options to choose from, covering all kinds of magigears and even some magimals.

'There are magimals too?' Omifo marvelled. 'I'll definitely pick a magimal, then!'

'Take your time.' Gazbell smiled knowingly and handed over a box to Kardiac. 'This is the gift from Halgon. He said you would like it.'

'Cool!' Kardiac opened the box and found a magimal egg with a familiar mark on it. 'The lost duckbear egg? We got it back from MagiMax?'

'More than that. Thanks to you all, MagiMax's property was taken over by the city and the institute,' Gazbell said happily. 'We knew that this was Halgon's property, so we got it back for him; but Halgon wanted you to have it, Kardiac.'

'WOW!' Kardiac jumped and thrust his fist in the air in victory. 'We got it back! We got it back!!'

'Congratulations!' Soarame was very happy for Kardiac. 'What about you, Rodka? You said you wanted a magimal too, right?'

'Yes, but not this time,' Rodka said thoughtfully as he went through the booklet. 'I've decided to go for a defensive magigear. The one that Max was wearing was way too useful.'

'Me too!' Alicey agreed with Rodka; she had Niuniu already. 'I'll get one too!'

'Smart move, you two. Soon you will find you need the defensive gear a lot,' Gazbell nodded. 'Especially Rodka, since you are approaching Expert level yourself. Once you become an Expert you will need to go for your Expert trial; there you will find the defensive gears more useful than anything else.'

'Exactly. That's my plan,' Rodka said, nodding. 'And I am graduating and leaving soon, so it would be inconvenient to take a baby magimal with me...'

'You are leaving? When?'

Back in Soarame's dorm, Dileys was pale.

'Maybe by the end of this month. I promised the Deans.' Rodka saw Dileys' eyes watering, and this time he realised something. 'But don't worry, I will come back to visit you guys.'

'You guys?' Dileys had a bitter and sour smile on her face. She sat back down and lowered her head. *After all this time, I'm still just a part of "you guys"?*

The girls stared at Rodka with discontent. Rodka finally

278

understood what's going on. He had noticed that Dileys seemed to have feelings for him, but he hadn't thought about it because he's so focused on his magic practise. Now that he's leaving, he believed that he probably should do something instead of just saying goodbye.

So, for the rest of his time at the Institute of Libral, Rodka began to hang out with Dileys in private. Rodka was surprised to find that he actually liked Dileys more than he thought he would. However, he's still going to graduate and still wanted to experience the outer world. During the fight with Max, Rodka found himself no better than Halgon or Soarame in a real battle, and that's a source of great shame to him. People took him as the star of Libral as a Grade-6 tri-lineager, yet he hadn't made much of a contribution when it really counted. Instead, he had relied mostly on Sachastain, Halgon, and Soarame. Other than that he hadn't passed out, he had done little more than Kardiac, Omifo and Alicey!

I have to go! I must become stronger! Rodka clenched his fists. *Sorry, Dileys...*

DO YOU LIKE ME?

Finally, the day came for Rodka to graduate and leave Libral.

This early morning, with dawn barely breaking, the friends – Soarame, Catheray, Vivarin, Omifo, Kardiac, Alicey, Kraigen and Jemario came out to the silent Libral Gate to give their good wishes to Rodka.

'Rodka, take care!'

'We will miss you!'

'Same here!' Rodka looked around at his friends, searching their faces. 'Where's Dileys?'

'She said she already said goodbye to you last night,' Catheray answered. 'She doesn't want to see you off and cry here, you know?'

'I... I see.' Rodka sighed. 'Please tell her I said goodbye then.'

'Don't worry, we'll look after her,' Vivarin said. 'Don't forget to visit us sometime!'

'For sure! Good luck, my friends!' Rodka walked away. He turned to wave back several times until he disappeared from the friends' sight.

'I thought he would fly away instead of walking?' Kardiac tried to amuse everyone, but nobody cared to take the joke.

'Soarame, how hard is flying?' asked Jemario. 'Even Rodka is not able to fly.'

'Well, I got that purely by luck,' Soarame admitted, scratching his head. 'Flying seems to be really hard if one practises in a normal way.'

'That's why there are only two people who can fly here!' Kardiac hurriedly cut in. 'Guess who they are?'

'Soarame and... you! Of course.' How could Catheray miss this chance to tease Kardiac?

'I didn't know you were a smart girl!' Kardiac teased back, but got a slap on the head for his troubles. 'What? That's not true?'

'It's true I'm smart, but prove that you can fly too!' Catheray curved her lips.

'Bingo, watch carefully!' Kardiac was just waiting for this. The next second, a blast of air came out of nowhere, and Kardiac rose up into the sky.

'What!' The girls were all dumbfounded; but the boys knew the secret already, so they were all chuckling.

'Kardy can fly too?! How is this ever possible?' Catheray squealed.

'Hey! What does that mean!' Kardiac complained from the sky. The next second, he started screaming, 'Guys, help! I've lost control!'

Thud! With a nice landing curve, Kardiac fell on his bottom.

'I told you not to do this until you're proficient,' Soarame laughed. 'But you are lucky that you lost control so fast, otherwise if you fly up high…'

'What's this?' The girls came to check Kardiac's cloak. 'Don't tell me it's the famous flightcloak!'

'Where did you get it?' Catheray questioned Kardiac. 'It's an Expert-level gear!'

'That's why Kardy picked it as the Principal's award,' Omifo said. 'But you already saw what happens if you are not powerful enough, though.'

'You guys stop laughing at me!' Kardiac got up. 'At least I can fly!'

'Okay, okay, you can fly,' Catheray chuckled. 'But you know what the best part of the cloak is? It has a hood to cover your half-bald head.' With that, Catheray pulled the hood over Kardiac's head.

The friends couldn't know that right at this moment, a man was floating in the cloud above them, watching.

'Thanks for doing me such a big favour, Soarame,' the vague figure inside the cloud muttered with a sneer. 'Mercy of the Demiurge, finally… Don't worry Max, I'll find you soon – through our little friend!'

The figure was holding a photo of Soarame on an old, out-dated crystal chip. If the friends could see it, they would find that the crystal chip look very familiar.

Right then, a breeze came and blew the cloud away, so a beam of sunshine fell on the man's face. If Soarame could see it, he would be surprised to recognise this face – although it looked like a man in his forties, it looked uncannily like the young Wind wizard from Scankeen's memory crystal ball, when Scankeen showed his battle against a magimal to teach Soarame as the first lesson.

Crack! The man crushed the crystal chip into pieces with his fingers. 'I hate sunshine!'

Thanks to Kardiac's flight show, the sadness at seeing Rodka off was diluted somewhat. The friends went back to Soarame's dorm and suddenly realised that this dorm building had been a gathering point for a year already. Since Soarame joined the school, he had been fortunate in meeting all these friends, and in sharing fun and tears with them. Now that Rodka was gone, it's time to say "goodbye" to the past and "hello" to the future.

Speaking of the future, Soarame certainly couldn't forget that Snower's true identity was still a mystery. Gazbell had performed an identification check for Snower in person, yet the crystal ball showed no match at all. This had bewildered everyone, because it hadn't happened for centuries. Considering that the "cure" provided by Snower was comparable to dragonblood, there's an almost unimaginable possibility that Snower might be even more powerful than a dragon once she's fully grown!

Besides that, Scankeen's legendary stories were appealing to the friends, although everyone had promised to keep his name secret. Then there's the mystery about Chelonad – Soarame had asked Gazbell, but he refused to talk about it. Therefore, it seemed that Aertiuno would be Soarame's only hope because they seemed to know each other well; however, this persuasive-whisperer himself was just as mysterious. Furthermore, Soarame began to doubt Sachastain's words – this man couldn't be as simple as he claimed; his skills were so similar to those of the young warrior in the biography. There must be something he wasn't telling!

Soarame still cared about the Dragon&Empires team that he wanted to form. It seemed that this plan could be carried out sooner than he had expected – he had seen a real dragon and he's now able to fly. Soarame really wanted to see Dafinol's face after the man came to hear that his assistant had realised his dragon dream; but Soarame firmly knew that the dragon's presence was a top-class secret and could never be leaked.

Although capable of flying, Soarame still wanted to be recognised as a Water captain for Dragon&Empires, and to bring glory for all his friends in Water. Therefore, Soarame went on with his mind-painting and ice carving; hopefully he would make it to the auction hall before long. Oh yes, Soarame hadn't forgotten his duel with Robert, but ever since his Wind gift was revealed, that boy seemed to be missing everywhere.

'Guys, check it out!' Omifo went to his bedroom and came out with a little creature in his arms.

Everyone was agog.

'What! What's that?'

'Don't tell us that's your magimal?'

'Mr Principal helped me bond with him. His name is Pipi,' Omifo said, stroking the little brown and black baby monkey he carried. 'The Principal suggested him because a teacher just discovered him during his trial and adopted him as an orphan.'

'Peepee?' Vivarin stared at Omifo. 'You are really good at giving names.'

'No, not that Peepee!' Omifo quickly spelt the name.

'Thank god. Hey, Pipi, nice to meet you!' Vivarin shook hands with the baby monkey. 'From now on we are a family!'

Snower went over and sized up Pipi, full of curiosity. Icer and Niuniu followed her everywhere so they came too. Halgon had left campus, but he deliberately left Icer with the crew so that the baby firntiger could play with the family.

Pipi looked very shy, but at the same time he's curious about his new friends; he looked back at them, scratching his head and touching the others gently. Soon enough, the baby magimals began to play together as if they had known each other all their lives. Snower was already holding Pipi in her paws and licking his head, while Icer and Niuniu were wrestling again – with Niuniu winning again.

'Pipi is so funny, isn't he?' Catheray said, watching the baby monkey. 'Especially when he's scratching his head, it looks exactly like Kardy.'

'Shut up Catheray, unless you don't want the gift that I got for you!' Kardiac felt really emotional when he thought about the events of the past year, and he decided to speed up his plan – it's a plan that he'd only just conceived of, but now he no longer wanted to wait because this seemed to be a perfect time already.

'What?' Catheray was overjoyed to hear this. 'I like gifts!'

'It's this.' Kardiac ran quickly to his room, and came back to hand over the duckbear egg from Halgon.

'WHAT?'

'WHAT?!'

'ARE YOU JOKING?!'

'ARE YOU SERIOUS, DUDE?!'

'AH!'

'AHH!!'

'AHHHH!!! ——'

Everyone was stunned, and Catheray was beyond herself. 'Really?! But no, you can't! This is Halgon's gift to you!'

'Not exactly. Halgon left it to my charge, so it's up to me what to do with it.' Kardiac was so grateful for his brother's consideration. 'And the seal has been removed, so it can be hatched any time – Catheray, it's yours now.'

'Praise Libral!' Jemario, Vivarin and Alicey all looked crazily jealous at Catheray as she reached towards the egg in disbelief. 'How unbelievably awesome this is!'

'If I can have a full head of hair back, that'd be even more awesome.' Kardiac handed the egg over to Catheray, and deliberately asked in a casual tone, 'Do you like me?'

'Yes! Yes! Of course!' Catheray responded without hesitation; she's too excited to notice that he said "me" instead of "it".

'I like you too!' Kardiac followed up right away, looking as serious as he ever did, and stared into Catheray's eyes.

'What?' Catheray just realised that Kardiac had played a trick on her. She tapped him on the head. 'You bad boy!'

'Wow, Kardy!' Soarame marvelled. 'How did you come up with that?' He felt that he had learnt something real. Surreptitiously, Soarame glanced at Jemario, finding her not looking back at him, but looking straight ahead, somewhere else. Jemario seemed focused, as if there's something really interesting, which reminded Soarame of his own odd behaviours when he saw magic elements as a little boy.

However, Jemario didn't have special eyes, so she's probably staring blankly; and for some reason, there's a blush on her face when Soarame looked again and caught her looking quickly away from him.

'It's called magic,' Kardiac said with a wink at Soarame. 'Plus, I can fly!'

(To be continued)

If you like this series, please introduce it to your friends and spend one minute to write a short review on amazon/goodreads. Reviews give me reasons to release the future books – if I see you care to write just one line to demand a 300-page book.

Follow this series on:

book website: www.codeofrainbow.com

Amazon: https://www.amazon.com/Weiqi-Wang/e/B01MY7ZML1
Facebook: https://www.facebook.com/codeofrainbow
Instagram: https://www.instagram.com/codeofrainbow
Twitter: https://twitter.com/CodeofRainbow
Goodreads: https://www.goodreads.com/author/show/16128074.Weiqi_Wang

Weiqi Wang

ABOUT THE AUTHOR

Dr. Weiqi Wang is a scientist who travelled the world. He went to University of Oxford and obtained his PhD degree. During that period, he travelled Europe and started writing the Code of Rainbow Series. Then he went to the east coast of the US and spent one year in Rhode Island as a postdoctoral researcher. Next, he drove across the country for Stanford University, where he worked as a data scientist and his responsibilities included multiple projects with NIH (national institute of health).

Thanks to his scientific background and passion in magic fantasy, Weiqi has a theory that science and magic could be connected in a certain way. Therefore, he took advantage of his knowledge in science and put his theory into the Code of Rainbow, a teen fantasy book series that nurtures the bloom of MAGIC in the soil of SCIENCE.

After all, philosophy is intended to explain the world; some choose to use scientific languages, others do it through writing about magic also.

Book website: www.codeofrainbow.com
Amazon: https://www.amazon.com/Weiqi-Wang/e/B01MY7ZML1
Facebook: https://www.facebook.com/codeofrainbow
Instagram: https://www.instagram.com/codeofrainbow
Twitter: https://twitter.com/CodeofRainbow
Goodreads: https://www.goodreads.com/author/show/16128074.Weiqi_Wang

COLOUR NOMENCLATURES

Red – Fire
Blue – Water
Grey – Wind
Yellow – Earth
White – Lightness
Black – Darkness
Purple – Lightning
Green – Life
Brown – ??
Gold – ??
Silver – ??

ACKNOWLEDGEMENTS

This book was written in the UK when I was studying at Oxford, but I only wish self-publishing services was available back then. I'd like to thank Prof. Rene Banares-Alcantara and Prof. Zhanfeng Cui, who were my D.Phil. supervisors, for supporting me on this book.

I must give enormous thanks to Bonnie Karrin, my main editor, for her splendid work. I'd also like to especially thank Mingming Li and Stephanie Kuersten for editing/proof reading the book. All of them have been amazing in different ways, and all of them have greatly helped me on polishing this book.

I also want to thank Mark Lucas-Taylor, Donamarie Goldsmith, Shelly Steward, Brian Busby, Margaret Bentley for the ARC feedbacks, and all "Coders" (short for "Code of Rainbow readers") for your long-time support!

There could be more than one type of philosophy to explain the world

One of them is called science

Another one is spelt M-A-G-I-C

Made in the USA
Las Vegas, NV
09 March 2023

68807476R00173